If Crows Could Talk

If Crows Could Talk

Debz Hobbs-Wyatt

To claire -
Happy reading!
Debz Hobbs-Wyatt
2024

Walela Books

British Library Cataloguing in Publication Data

A Record of this Publication is available from the British Library

ISBN 978-1-914199-74-5

This edition published 2024 by Walela Books
Manchester, England

Cover illustration © Justin Wyatt – www.justindoodler.com

Dedicated to family, no matter the race or color and to my wonderful parents for teaching me that love is what matters most. They believed in me when I didn't and taught me never to give up on my dreams.

Let no man be judged by his color

ALL LIVES MATTER

Contents

Prologue

Wednesday April 10th, 2019

It's the day every path led back to.

April holds the coffee cup with both hands; fingertips pressed lightly to the paper folds. Her reflected face ghosts against the rush of passing trees and gray office buildings. Her neat red bob is caught in the *flickedy-flick* of the changing landscape. It was still dark when she left the apartment, still dark when she fumbled with the email saying where they were to meet. Only she always knew where they would meet. Still dark when the Amtrak left South Carolina.

And there it is again – *the feeling.*

She should have told him. What if he never understands?

The world *clickedy-clacks* its way past. People fumble with luggage and make their drunken-like stumbles to the bathroom, reapply lipstick and slap tired faces awake with cold water. Seven hours on a train – but April is sick of driving, sick of flying, sick of the lies.

She pictures Joe back in Lexington, folded into the lilac duvet, a Post-it stuck to the refrigerator. Not the note he wanted. She was planning on talking to him; she didn't mean it to turn into a fight. *There's something I have to do.* And there she was, fingers teasing open the blinds, looking out onto the street, listening for the cab, hoping he didn't stir, because if he did how could she explain?

What would she say? That she isn't who he thinks she is?

Chapter 1

I

March 12th, 1953, Jacksonville, Florida

"George!"

Momma's boom cuts the air. George takes gaping strides; counts 'em one by one, three from the bedroom to the bathroom. He likes the *slap-tap* rhythm. As he pees, he thinks. George is a day dreamer. Everyone says it.

"George, honey!"

Already the heat is pressing down heavy, sweat glaze like his skin has melted into thick black oil. Hot for this time of year, feels more like the summer. The heat will be unbearable in that classroom.

"George, where you at?"

This time it's Grandmomma Josie's voice. They're both in the kitchen waiting on him. He already told 'em, yesterday, and the day before that, how he wanted to stay home. He could help Momma with the chores. *Why does he have to go to school on his birthday?* He's almost a man now. Pap was already working on the plantation by the time he was fifteen.

George counts four strides to the kitchen. Momma's deep in conversation. She looks bright today, all pinks and reds – first thing George sees. First thing he smells is last night's chicken stew; hits like a slap. Onions. George hates the smell of onions. He looks out through the screen door, no breeze. In fancy houses they have air conditioning. Not in LaVille, not in Clayton – maybe one day. Abe always says *things are changin' for the colored folk.*

"Well there you are," Momma says. "About time."

George pulls out a chair and sits, stares into his bowl; how many times does he have to say he hates grits? He hates grits more than he hates the smell of onions. He digs in a spoon and lets the grits cling. Momma is still talking to Grandmomma, both with one eye on him. What did he think? Momma would give him something different, something special just because he's fifteen now? He shovels it in anyhow, head hung over the bowl, listens to his momma saying something about the Harrisons, how that second boy o' theirs is thinking 'bout joining the war, so now there'll have two sons to worry about not coming home.

"Jacob?" He looks up mid-scoop. "You mean Jacob?"

They'll know what he's thinking; they'll be thinking the same thing. Jacob's not exactly the brightest kid, not that George is smart but he's way smarter than Jacob Harrison. He wouldn't know which end of a gun was which. Everyone knows he's a retard.

A line of sweat makes its way along George's back; he feels it like an itch under his shirt. Abe went to Korea on his eighteenth birthday, made up his mind, weren't no one gonna stop him. Made a plan with Isaac Harrison and with Benjamin Morris the summer they all turned seventeen, got it all figured out. Only they never said a thing until it was too late to stop 'em. In the army President Truman said all coloreds are treated equal. That's what Abe said, right here in this kitchen. Momma was stirring black-eyed peas and rice in a pot on the stove when Abe said it; he watched her slow right down, look at Grandmomma.

Pap was at the table with his head over a glass of Old Crow. He looked up for a second, like he was about to say *he believe that when he see it.* He'd heard him say it enough times but he never said a word, folded his fingers round his glass, grabbed that whiskey by its neck and pushed back the chair so it scraped the wood. George stood in the kitchen, watched Pap on the stoop, listened to the squeak of that old rocking chair, watched the way that line of menthol Kool twisted in the air. He was still watching when Abe went out, sat with him, on the step, and they shared smokes and liquor. Pap never shared smokes and liquor. They talked long after Momma told George to get to bed. They must've drunk the rest of that bottle. George would say that was the day Pap accepted Abe as a man. Next day, Momma said how Pap was proud his oldest boy would be fighting for his country. She never said she was. "But what if he gets his-self killed?" George said. She never answered but he knows she felt the same because on the day he left, she sat in her bedroom for three days: no food, no conversation, no nothin'. Till on the fourth day Pap lost his temper, said she ought to be proud of her son. Bills didn't pay themselves; rent was due and folks' houses didn't clean themselves neither. So that was that; she got up. Only it wasn't what Pap'd said. It was George. He went to the bedroom after Pap left, taking his temper with him. He climbed onto that bed, wasn't supposed to, and he told her straight – made her a promise he weren't never gonna fight in no wars. She had her head pressed to the pillow, tears running sideways across her face. Just staring. Never spoke – not when he said it, not when he slid off the bed and not when he closed the door to the bedroom. But five minutes later there she was – dressed ready to clean houses.

Now she waits – for news, for Abe to have his leave, for the other thing; the thing she won't say out loud. But she doesn't have to worry about George. At least George is going nowhere. Besides, George is gonna be a poet, maybe even a teacher.

The three boys that went away to fight, they did everything together, from the first grade, so no one should've been surprised they decided to join the army together. All Momma said was, "And now they gon' get themselves killed together too."

"Don't talk that way," Pap said. "They come home heroes either way. Men to be proud of."

Either way?

He learned what either way meant when they heard Benjamin Morris was not coming home. It was on a Thursday. Six weeks ago today. Grandmomma said bad things always happen on a Thursday. She only says that because Grandpap Zeb died on a Thursday, way before George was born. She says *life can feel perfect one second and the next everythin' can turn on a dime – jus' like that.* He is not exactly sure what turnin' on a dime feels like, although he knows how he felt when Abe left. Now Grandmomma thinks every Thursday the men from the army will show up, like they did on Mrs. Morris's doorstep. Not today, not his birthday, nothin' gonna turn on a dime today. Pap says, "Abe gon' come back a hero."

George only hopes not a dead hero. Benjamin Morris will get a medal for his bravery but what good is a medal? He is sure Mrs. Morris would rather have her son than a medal.

"George, you daydreamin' again? Finish your grits; don't want be late for the bus."

"But, Momma, I was hopin' I could stay home…" he catches the smile on Grandmomma's face. Well, a boy's gotta keep tryin', ain't he.

"George, I already told you. You learnin' to read and write makes us proud. You a clever boy, George, so you keep up your lessons. We have a surprise for you when you get home."

"What surprise?" They know George hates surprises. And she surely doesn't mean Grandmomma's lemon cake. Not baked that since Abe went away to fight.

"Get your things together, you find out. Now be a good boy. It's a good surprise, George."

She stands and looks at him, hands on her hips, he looks again at the dress: bright colors make him think she must be in a happy mood. Since Abe left, she never seems happy; maybe the surprise is Abe, maybe he got his leave for George's birthday. That would be a good surprise. He asked God for that these past weeks, same as he asked for Chloe to notice him. Maybe he listened. He'll think about Abe getting leave until he comes home. He hated it more than his momma did when Abe left, he promised to take care of George, that's what older brothers are supposed do and then he went away. Two years is a long time. But maybe today he's coming home and maybe this time he's done with the fighting. He doesn't want to think about what happened to Benjamin Morris. George ain't never gonna fight for his country to make no one proud, least of all his pap.

"George, you don't want miss that bus."

"No, Momma."

Bag heavy on his shoulder from the poetry books he borrowed from the colored library, he turns at the door, Momma and Grandmomma looking at him. "You got so tall," Grandmomma says. She always says that, like he grew two inches every night. Everyone knows he's tall like his pap. But he's not like his pap, not got a temper like his pap. Momma blames the liquor. Abe – he's the one like Pap. Never seen either of them reading poetry.

As he turns to leave, he hears his momma say, "And happy birthday, George."

———————————

George watches the second bus pull away; starts the ten-minute walk to the colored school. He passes three white schools on the two buses it takes to get from Duval Street to Williams Ave and one in the time it takes to walk to Eastfield High School. Usually the back of the bus is full, but not today. It's the influenza, keeping them away, but everyone knows the kids don't like to go to school. Abe says *white schools got better teachers, real teachers.* Mr. Lewis is a real teacher he told him. *And they got better books.* He told him they had books, only not so many. *And better classrooms, better facilities.* Nothin' wrong with the classrooms. He wonders how many will show up today. His *best* friend – if he still is his *best* friend after the fight – wasn't even in school yesterday. He wonders if Chloe will be there. But Abe is wrong about Mr. Lewis; he's a good teacher. He's the one who told George to go to the colored library; they had plenty of books there. Told him look for Langston Hughes. He said it was a good place to start, with the Negro writers, especially the poets. Last night George copied the first part of that poem into his notebook.

I dream a world where man
No other man will scorn...

George scrapes his feet on the sidewalk, counting the thirty-seven strides from where the bus stopped on Williams Ave to the corner, slap-tap-slap-tap where he cuts across the park. It's fifty-seven less strides if he takes the shortcut. He only goes the long way when he wants to be late, like when he's got words in his head and poems he's writing inside of himself. Words flow when he counts the beat. Even Mr. Lewis says he writes good. He calls him a day dreamer but when he says it, it's like it's a good thing, not like when Pap says it.

He feels the sweat seep into his white cotton shirt. At least there's a breeze now but still not enough. The air smells of the orange blossoms, sweet in a sickly way, soft, citrusy – he wrote a poem about that. The state flower. Not as good as Langston Hughes or that other poet Gwendolyn Elizabeth Brooks – Mr. Lewis said she was the first Negro to win the Pulitzer Prize for poetry… biggest prize there is and Mr. Lewis says that's really somethin'. By the time he heard of Gwendolyn Elizabeth Brooks, Abe was already fighting in Korea but he's decided to tell him about it. He's the one who said big changes comin', how one day everyone go to the same school, sit in the same classroom, next to white folks. Abe might not like poetry but he'll be impressed to know Gwendolyn Elizabeth Brooks won the Pulitzer Prize for poetry. Being a Negro an' all.

George loses count of his strides as he crosses the park. The school is a box with windows, red brick and mostly wood – nothing to write poetry about.

At the school gate he stops and counts crows. There are a lot of 'em today, huddled together like they're gossipin'. He should write a poem. A poem about crows. He thinks how he'll write it down at recess or during math. No one cares as long as it looks like you're doing something.

George counts seventeen strides from the gate to the door of the school. He thinks how there's more crows than kids today. Should've been one less kid too. Maybe it's not too late. He could turn around right now, walk back across the park, all thirty-seven strides to the bus stop, maybe even walk home. Not like anyone will miss him, not like Chloe will even notice—

"George Tucker!"

Mr. Brown the school principal is standing in the school yard; looks like he's watching the crows too. George can see some of the kids already inside the school.

Principal Brown is tall and thin, peppery gray hair. He dresses smart, brown suit, shiny shoes and he dips his head in George's direction. "Don't be late, George Tucker."

He thinks how he should have started walking the other way from the bus stop, but now it's too late. At least he has a surprise after school. He thinks about what he'll say to Abe. He'll hug him first, if that's still allowed now he's fifteen. His momma wore bright colors; it must mean something.

Inside the school George counts thirty more strides to Mr. Lewis's classroom. Shoes make a different sound on the wood floor, more a shuffle-squeak. The school always smells like soap. He doesn't look too closely, includin' him he thinks there are five of them in the class today – no Chloe – only her twin sister. Mr. Lewis might not be able to tell them apart but to George, Chloe's way prettier. There are two empty seats at the front. No sign of Mr. Lewis. George is two minutes late – which means Mr. Lewis is late and Mr. Lewis is never late.

George sits down next to the empty seat at the back, where his best friend is meant to sit. It was a bad fight. It was over Chloe. But now neither of them is in school. George decides he doesn't need a best friend – he's got Abe. And tonight, he'll be home. George stretches out his long legs under the desk. No one says happy birthday but they probably don't know. So, he looks out into the yard, at the crows, thinks about how to start his poem when he thinks he sees something, movement along the trees – bigger than a crow? But must be a trick of the light, because when he looks again all he sees is Principal Brown in the school yard looking up at the sky. A minute later he sees Mr. Lewis in his gray suit, that battered leather bag of his under his arm. Next thing he's talking to Principal Brown, now they're both looking up. Maybe there are crows on the roof? The clock at the front of the classroom says they're five minutes late.

George hears giggles in front of him. He thinks about saying how it's his birthday but he thinks better of it. No Chloe, so now he doesn't feel so sociable. Maybe one day he'll write a poem for Chloe but now he thinks he needs to not think about that, he needs to think about the new poem. George reaches into his bag, places his notebook and his pencil on the desk. He'll show Abe his poem when he tells him about Gwendolyn Elizabeth Brooks. Abe will be the best birthday surprise and now he's thought about it so much, no other surprise will do.

Next thing he hears the scrape of the chair next to him. "Seems like I ain't the only one late today." So he did make it. He still has signs of a black eye. Are they still best friends? Before George can respond, Mr. Lewis appears in the doorway. He looks flustered, says sorry, mumbles something about his pregnant wife making him late. As he takes the register, he seems distracted, keeps on looking out into the yard. Next thing he says he forgot something. Says he'll be right back. He leaves his brown leather briefcase on the table.

George wonders what he forgot. He thinks maybe he should say something: about the fight, his black eye, about Chloe, but instead he opens his notebook.

I dream a world where man
No other man will scorn...

Langston Hughes is a fine poet.

Maybe one day George'll be a fine poet.

He writes the title of his new poem, ponders on the first line. He needs to write it so he can show his brother.

But tonight, it won't be Abe standing on his doorstep. Seems Grandmomma was right about that dime. It will be two men wearing uniforms and George will never finish his poem or know what his birthday surprise was meant to be.

II

March 12ᵗʰ, 2003, Jacksonville, Florida

A kid's voice calls out. No one will answer. It's not real – you can always tell. First thing Grams does in the morning is turn on the TV.

Other sounds drift up: the clink of a spoon, the stack of a dish, the gush of a tap.

Now the low slow clearing of a throat.

"April!"

She already told them she's not going.

She perches herself on the edge of the unmade bed. Showered, dressed: jeans, T-shirt, nothing fancy. Even a spray of perfume for Jesse. *Sweet Roses*. The one he said he likes. But no school. Not today. She promised.

She looks at her mud-caked sneakers. So, she likes to short cut across the park. They tell them not to, kids get abducted, nowhere's safe. She knows. She fingers the edge of her backpack, thinks about Mrs. Johnston. Mrs. Johnston who Jesse says is different to the others. Took to the ninth grade to meet someone like her. *You can trust this one, April.* She'll be pissed when she sees April is not in school. She tells April she mustn't be influenced, be her own person. But today she is influenced.

"April, you ready?"

Pops's voice drifts up with the smell of French vanilla beans. TV gets louder; someone fires a gun. She pictures Grams standing in front of it with the controller. Hands pressed to her ears until Pops turns it off. Pops says it's because she's old. She gets confused. April tells him not everyone gets to get old; some don't even get to grow up. She wrote a poem about that once, when she was young. Made her second-grade teacher cry. Pops didn't say if he liked it or not, later she heard him tell Grams: *Something's off with April again. She shouldn't be writing stuff like that. Not at seven years old. What are you letting her watch?*

They will have been talking about her. Downstairs, while

Grams tries to make Pops's coffee, otherwise she forgets how much to scoop in. "Hell, Helen, you could stand a spoon up in this."

They think she doesn't hear when they talk about her. They're always talking about her. April Jefferson is a topic. But not just about April, about her friends too. Mrs. Johnston says April is talented; a gifted student. She just needs to apply herself. Not be led by others. The disruptive behavior needs to stop.

They said it would be hot. For her birthday. *Unseasonably* hot. Lifting her hair, she slides her fingers along the nape of her neck. She should fix her hair, wear it up for a change. She got these frizzy curls from her mom. She knows because she saw the photograph. Same crazy red bangs. Strawberry blonde her grams says. Same crazy green eyes. Same crazy thoughts – that's what they all think. It was her mom called her April. She was supposed to be an April baby, came early but they'd gotten so used to the name by then they kept it. March baby called April. She has always been different.

"April!"

They'll be wondering how to make her go to school. They won't want another fight. Not on her birthday.

More smells drift up. Bacon. Pancakes. Lemons.

"April!"

She told them no breakfast. Grams likes to dust the pancakes in icing sugar, just the way she did when April's mom was a little girl. How many times has she heard that story? Birthday pancakes. A Jefferson tradition. Like balloons for every occasion, like trips to the beach every other weekend in the summer, like the rule that says there are some things you're not supposed to talk about. Rose says all families have secrets. Today the birthday pancakes will be wrapped in tin foil *to go* and by the time April throws them away, the icing will have melted. She hates pancakes. Grams never remembers and Pops never says how it was her mom who loved the pancakes.

Footsteps cross the hall, the soft *tap-tap-tap* of Pops's brogues on wood, hesitation before he calls her name again. He likes to walk her to the bus. He waits for her to get on it. Make sure she goes. If she misses it, he drives her but she hates it when he drives. He loses his temper too easy.

The front door opens and clicks shut and now April moves to the window. The palm out-front usually sways like a Hawaiian dancer but today there's no wind. Lotus Drive is a leafy neighborhood with nice houses, people with *some* money but not *too* rich, not like over in Arlington. *Stuck-up bitches.* Some even have maids. When she said that to Pops, he went crazy, saying she had no right to talk that way, they had friends in Arlington. When he grew up they all had maids. And who even talks that way? Those friends of yours? She learned to keep her mouth shut after that. She was only repeating something Owen told her. But some things are best kept secret. Like why April lives with her grandparents. Like that Pops keeps a gun in the house.

Blue skies overhead: no cloud. She sees the back of Pops's head, sleek gray hair pushed back. He's lean and walks with a stoop. Never used to. She sees the light blue of his polo shirt. Last night she told him she can't go to school because of the influenza.

"You need a fever for that."

"Ain't going no school."

"Don't talk like that. We raised you better than to talk like that. What kind of English is that? And you have to go, April. You can't keep doing this."

"It's the influenza."

"Does your throat hurt?"

"Nope."

"Do you have aches?"

"Nope."

"Then it's not flu."

That's when she felt it, worse than any fever, closed her eyes, grasping her hands tightly together. She knows she was mumbling because next thing she heard him say, "Not this again, April, I thought you were doing better."

"Jesse says—"

"Jesse this, Jesse that…"

He puts on his nervous smile. The one he always uses when she talks about her friends. She tries to see him for what he is – a kind old man who has no idea what a crazy world it really is – only he knows, of course he does. Look what happened to April's momma. They won't even talk about that.

They think she will end up just like her.

"No more nonsense, okay. You'll go to school."

"April!"

This time Grams's voice cuts through the daydream. She never even heard her on the stairs. April is one to daydream. They all say it. *That girl spends too much time inside her own head.*

When she turns, Grams in standing in April's room in her white toweling dressing gown with her hair wrapped in a towel.

The gifts and cards are still lined up on the dresser where Pops put them. Not opened yet. A silver foil balloon with the number 15 in purple sparkles on the side. Grans doesn't seem to notice. Has she forgotten the day already? What she wants aren't gifts or balloons or a party, she hopes to God, Pops hasn't arranged a party at the bowling alley like last year. Doesn't he get it? Not like anyone from school will come. Her friends hate bowling. Forget gifts. Forget parties. What she wants is *not* to go to school today. Besides, she has her own plans with her friends later.

"April, Pops is waiting for you."

"I'm not going, Grams."

"Oh but, Catherine, you have to go to school."

"It's April, Grams, not Catherine."

Grams edges closer, shuffling in her slippers.

"Good girl, now you go to school. And when you come home, Catherine, honey, we'll have a nice surprise for your birthday."

April can't fight her, not today.

"You know what happens when you don't go to school, Catherine."

She's thinking about the letters, the visits to the school. *We might have a problem with April.* Grams holds out the foil-wrapped pancake. April takes it, puts into her backpack, then pushes the bag onto her shoulder, walks to the door. April will get the bus but doesn't mean she has to go in.

———————————

There's no breeze. April had watched Pops as the bus pulled away and then planned to get off at the next stop but she missed her chance when more kids got on, crowded deep inside so she was pushed right to the back. Anyway, where would she go? The library? Plan B: get off the stop before the school. It's what she does with Jesse sometimes, and with Rose and Grace. It's only her today. They made a promise.

It's a six-minute walk to the school. But April won't go in.

April watches the time change on her watch; it's gone 8.40.

They'll be settled in class now. Mrs. Johnston will have taken the register. What will she think when she sees April's not there? None of her friends are there. She fiddles with the charm on her backpack; it's an angel. A gift from her dad. She wonders what he's doing right now, if he even remembered it's her birthday. They won the angel. A visit upstate, at a fairground. Pops says it's cheap tat, but he says that about anything her dad gives her. Just as well he doesn't give her much. She sits on the grass, lowers her head, presses her fingers together. A moment later she feels it; looks up. They lift from the bough of one of the oaks and she feels the uprush cool her skin as they pass overhead. It's the first time she's seen crows in the park. April closes her eyes.

I dream a world where man
No other man will scorn...

The soft *rap-tap* of feet on grass, a hand on her shoulder, her name whispered.

"April?"

"Martha?"

"No, sugar, not Martha."

She opens her eyes. "Mrs. Johnston! What are you doing out here? I thought you'd be in class..."

"I ought to be asking you the same question."

"I can't go, please don't make me, please, I—"

"Stand up, April."

Her cheeks are wet, lips got the mumbles.

"I can't go in."

She can't catch the air. Mrs. Johnston tells her *breathe.* "It's okay, April." She presses a Kleenex into her trembling hand.

"I had to cut class."

"Like you had to all the other times? Because your friends told you to again?"

She looks down at her muddy sneakers.

"I want you to tell me whose idea it was this time."

"All of them. We agreed together."

"You can't keep blamin'—"

"Don't make me go to school."

"Come with me."

April watches her walk to a bench under one of the oak trees. She pats the spot next to her. April shuffles closer. "April, sugar. Sit."

Mrs. Johnston is about the same height as April. Today she's wearing a white blouse and that pink skirt she's seen her in before. April has always been fascinated by the way her thick black hair is like all twisted-out, sits on her shoulders. Her skin is the color of Hershey's Kisses and Mrs. Johnston is sweet with it, only the look on her face right now is not so sweet.

April lowers herself onto the bench. "Am I in trouble, Mrs. Johnston?"

Mrs. Johnston looks right at April, cups her big hands over hers. "No, sugar, nothing we can't fix. But you and me, April, we need to talk 'bout these imaginary friends of yours."

Chapter 2

I

March 28th, 1958, Jacksonville, Florida

Wind whips through.

It jingles the wind chimes. After Pap died, George's momma hung them on the stoop. She thinks every time she hears that *jingle-jangle*, it's him paying them a visit. Like he's sat right there, rocking in his chair. Sometimes she says she smells his Kool. But in truth it's been six months since any of them caught a menthol breeze or since anyone rocked in that chair. But one time she even said she could see it, a plume of cigarette smoke hovering over the front yard. *See it, George.* It was easier to say he did when he didn't. Now the chair's gone and he hopes she won't pack the wind chimes.

A clairvoyant called Devine Borrowspell told Momma Pap is still in the house. George thought it was as nonsense as her name. House isn't haunted. Devine Borrowspell said a place could hold on to the energy, especially if the spirit died with unfinished business. Momma had a strange look on her face when she told him that. And though he thinks Devine Borrowspell didn't know what she was talking about, sometimes he convinces himself he can still feel Pap's anger tearing through the house like that wind. The wind is so strong this morning it whips right through. Slams the door at the back near off its hinges. So loud George cowers like a fool, for a second, thinking his own heart will give out. Just the same way Pap's did. Of course, they all know that is only part of the story. Now his hands are trembling. Trash bags he's holding doing a shimmy.

His momma is standing at the window. He doesn't know if she saw him cower like that or catches the shake in his hands. Or the way he's been staring up the street for the past ten minutes. Same way she is. Maybe they're both waiting on a miracle that will never happen.

Momma does a lot of staring out. Must be a family trait. Only now George is staring in. The house looks different all packed up.

Grandmomma says *it's gon' be someone else's house now*. She says it like she welcomes it, even though she spent more than half her life in Jacksonville. But she says she spent the better part of it growing up in Georgia. Only moved because she fell in love, but Grandpap Zeb is long gone. She says she wants to die where she started. Momma tells her to stop – there's been too much talk of death and she gives George the look, the gaze. She has it on her face now as she stares out of the bedroom window for the last time.

Momma says the move will be good for them all. She thinks Atlanta will make everything okay. But you can't bring people back. Can't undo a ghost. When he was younger, he might even have written a poem about that. But George hasn't written a poem in five years. As for the house being someone's else's now – that's not quite true either.

Momma always said she would never leave Jacksonville, never leave Clayton, never leave this old wooden house, even though the whole place pretty much needs tearing down. Mr. Derwent, the landlord, made promises all the time; he would do this, do that, fix this, fix that. Never did. And now probably never will. George heard the whole neighborhood will be torn down, so they can build fancy houses. All part of *The Rejuvenation*. LaVille, Duval, right up to Arlington. Jacksonville is the place *to be*. But they *won't be*. Momma says a change of scenery will be a good thing. She never sounds like she believes her own words. George thinks maybe she doesn't want to leave Pap's ghost.

Or Abe's.

As for a change of scenery? That's another illusion like Pap's ghost. He remembers when his momma said the exact same thing right after George's fifteenth birthday – when they sent him away. Every time something bad happens, it seems like Atlanta is the end of their rainbow. But one thing George learned – a long time ago – is there are no pots of gold. And ghosts don't stay inside houses – they go with you.

The wind picks up again. George is standing in the yard, face lifted into the smell of Momma's white roses, he wonders if someone will rip *them* out too, or maybe she plans on digging them up and taking them with her. Of course, he knows she won't. They can't take a rose bush in Cousin Thomas's car. He thinks he's something having a car, but he told them, one suitcase each, maybe room for six boxes in the trunk. That's it. Never said nothin' about rose bushes. Their whole lives packed into the trunk of a station wagon.

He drops the last of the trash bags on the side walk, stares some more into the street. He pictures Abe. In his army uniform. Walking with that familiar swagger. Like he expects him to turn the corner, come wave them all off. He wipes a tear away with his finger and turns back to the house.

This house is the only house George remembers. Abe remembered the one before it, even the one before that. He thinks how just about all his memories are inside this old single-story wooden house. When George was born, his momma said they would move, there weren't enough rooms, but in the end, this was all they could afford. Just as well they didn't have any more babies. Momma said it *jus' never happened*. After Abe it took six years to fall for George. After George – nothing. By the time George came along Abe was already in school, but he and Grandmomma had plenty to keep them busy and when she had her stroke and couldn't do so much, he made his own fun, the whole time waiting on the brother or sister his momma promised, and for Abe to come home from school. George learned to make up poems with Grandmomma Josie. She liked the rhyming ones. But that's not all he made up. He told Momma once he liked to play best with the friends *he made up inside his head*. Grandmomma gave Momma a stare and said, "He'll grow out of that soon as he go to school."

In the end George gave up waiting on a brother or sister. And not like he didn't make friends at school – eventually. All George really wanted was his brother – never trusted no one more than Abe.

One time, George heard Momma and Grandmomma talking, saying she was afraid of Pap's temper around a new baby. She meant now he was drinking so much, said he was never like that when they were babies. Only she said she made him angrier because she wouldn't let him touch her. George knows nothing about women or relations. His momma says once they get to Atlanta, and his cousin finds him a decent job, even though he never finished school, but he can read and write good, he'll meet a nice young lady, settle down, *put all of this behind you, George.* But they both know life's not all roses.

He still thinks about Chloe Johnson.

As they grew, the bedroom George shared with his brother got smaller, but some of George's best memories are of lying in bed, poster of Jackie Robinson on the wall, you can still see the marks where it was tacked. He was Abe's hero – first Negro to play Major League baseball, even if he did play for the Brooklyn Dodgers – although Abe said they did their spring training in Daytona, Florida. Abe said it was just the start. They were living in a different world now. *Changes a-coming. The life of the Negro is gonna change forever. No more colored bathrooms, no more separate drinking fountains.*

Jackie Robinson was born in Georgia.

As he straightens up, he sees Mrs. Harrison in that pale green cotton dress of hers. She looks even bigger than the last time he saw her, like that dress is pinching good and tight. She is standing on the sidewalk, with something in her hands. A letter?

"Hey, George. Your momma inside?"

He dips his head.

"Alright if I go on in? Just wan' give her this before y'all go." As she lifts it up, he sees it's a photograph. He knows exactly which one. She must've made a copy of the one at her house. Taken the summer Abe, Isaac and Benjamin turned seventeen. He remembers them talking in whispers while he sat on the porch drinking the sweetest lemonade he ever tasted. Jacob gawping at him like he was fixing to catch flies. Jacob never did go to Korea. George thought maybe they didn't take retards, but the real reason is the war ended a couple of months later.

But the world changed that day, all it took was a moment. While George sipped that sweet lemonade on Mrs. Harrison's porch, Abe and his friends made their plan. A plan that would turn them all into ghosts. And leave a fifteen-year-old George standing in his momma's kitchen mumbling to friends that weren't even there; Grandmomma saying *somethin' needs to be done.*

Two weeks later he was on the bus to Georgia.

His momma has a different photograph. It's in a wooden frame. It was in her bedroom but it's probably in one of the boxes now. The three of them – three new soldiers – the day they left for the war. It was the last one of all of them together.

He watches Mrs. Harrison as she nudges the door open, shifts herself sideways as she goes inside.

When the boys left, when Abe moved out of the bedroom, George would look at that old poster every night and pray for his safe return. All his stuff right there waiting for him. Like his baseball glove. Like all the stuff he was waiting to tell him. And all the stuff he wanted to ask, especially about girls – he never saw Chloe after he stopped going to school, passed her on the street once.

George never went back to school.

Abe and George would never share that bedroom again.

And the poster of Jackie Robinson is rolled up in the trash bag.

It was Cousin Thomas who said maybe they ought to move to Atlanta. Probably his idea to send George there a few weeks after his fifteenth birthday. Stay with his four cousins. They thought it would do him good, make some *real* friends. Only all George remembers of that time was a house full of strangers, barely knew any of his cousins. That was when he decided to stop speaking. All it ever did was get him into trouble, get him sent away. He never spoke a word. Only inside his head, only place anyone would listen. Cried himself to sleep every night. Six weeks later they sent him home – *maybe he was better off in Jacksonville after all.* But didn't matter where he was, George Tucker never spoke a single word for a whole year. He read someplace that grief is madness. Seems a lot of madness visited this old house.

George looks past Momma's rose bush, across the street at the

Browns and the Robinsons and the Clarkes... soon all of them will be gone. Maybe it's easier to leave a place when it won't be there to go back to. Only it will always be there – just like all his memories – even the ones he locks away. Especially the ones he locks away.

Mrs. Harrison left ten minutes ago, George watched her and Momma whispering; standing at the window then a long hug like they were never seeing one another again. Won't be long before Cousin Thomas gets here. Already George has stacked the suitcases and boxes outside the house. People have already said their goodbyes. He hates it when he sees pity, like it's piled up in the lines around their eyes, like they think they're all leaving because they did something wrong and not to start a new life. Even if it doesn't feel like a new life when all the bad stuff just climbs right inside those boxes and those suitcases and rides along with you.

Grandmomma is sat at the kitchen table. Last night she said goodbye to the house by walking 'round every room, stopping outside George's bedroom for the longest, like she was thinking about something she couldn't say out loud. Eventually she said, "Well, that's that then." Her boxes were ready to go and to George it didn't seem a whole lot to show for seventy-some years. But she says everything you need is inside of you. Unless you forget. She must've been thinking about Grandpap Zeb, didn't even know who she was when he passed. Was only sixty. She says some people lose all their memories like that. Luckily, after her stroke hers all came back. Sometimes George thinks that might not always be a good thing.

Cousin Thomas's car must be twenty years old. It arrives all *clitter-clatter*, exhaust hanging halfway off. It makes George wonder if it will even make it to Atlanta. Cousin Thomas takes no nonsense from anyone. Staring eyes, big hair, sunglasses, fuzz of what looks like it's supposed to be a beard. After he's taken a drink and used the bathroom, he sees the boxes and the suitcases, rolls his eyes.

There are eight boxes, five suitcases but with George's help, a little manipulation, they manage to get them all in. All this while Momma stands on the sidewalk gazing into the street. George is glad there's no breeze because he doesn't want her to remember the wind chimes. He follows her gaze to the end of the street, wonders if she's thinking the same thing he is, or maybe they're waiting on different miracles. *Pap used to be a good man.* That's what she says.

Momma and Grandmomma are arranging themselves inside the car, squeezing themselves onto the back seat. George says he needs the bathroom. Momma stops mid-fidget and looks at him. She probably knows he already went to the bathroom.

George stands in his room. Imagines a time when everything was the way it was supposed to be. Abe hadn't made any crazy plans to join the army; made promises he was never able to keep. It was the day Jackie Robinson was selected to play for the Brooklyn Dodgers and it didn't matter about the color of his skin. It was the summer of 1947; Abe was fifteen. The six years between them didn't seem so big. Just happy kids playing, Abe saying he would get a poster, put it right there on the wall. He moves to the window and stares out. Hears Cousin Thomas working that car horn. Momma and Grandmomma are on the back seat, Momma with boxes piled so high it's a wonder she can see out. George doesn't move. He stands, stares out some more. As he turns, a chill rucks his flesh. Is that menthol? Next thing he's turning around, shoes *slap-tapping* across the wood. Past Grandmomma's old table, the sink where he's seen Momma standing staring out, waiting on Pap to come home from the plantation and later the factory. Waiting on George to come home from school. Waiting on Abe to come home from the war.

Outside the house he hears the horn again. His fingers fumble behind for the door as the wind picks up snatching it clean away, slamming it shut. This time George doesn't cower from the ghosts. He straightens up, brushes himself off, makes a decision: he has to be the man now. He walks across the front yard, wind whipping up around him like Pap's fury. When he gets to the car, he looks one last time up to the end of Denzel Street, where it crosses Duval Street, the place where he used to catch the bus to school. He thinks even a mirage would do. But no mirage and no miracle.

From the front seat, arm rested on the lip of the open window, he looks one last time at the house, at Momma's white roses dancing there next to the empty stoop. The sound of the *jingle-jangle* floats in the air, like it's saying goodbye. Only as the car pulls away, he realizes the wind chimes are gone.

II

March 28th, 2003, Jacksonville, Florida

Imaginary friends are common in all children and are a part of normal development and play. They reflect a healthy imagination – Smith, Anthony. "Exploring Imaginary Friends". **US Journal of Psychology, vol 6, 1966, pp. 203-219.**

Ruby-May Johnston keeps a quiet classroom.

She likes her students to be fully engaged. Not too much talking because what she's learned is the more leniency you give, the more they jabber. They get to talking: about last night's ball game, what party they went to on the weekend, what they plan to do over the Easter vacation, even what happened in some TV show that's on *way* past their bedtime.

But not April Jefferson. April Jefferson is a whole other story.

April sits apart from the others. April always sits apart. Pages softly rustle as they turn. Wall clock tick-ticks around to home time. Five minutes till the bell. Sunshine forces its way through the blinds, an arc of light picking out the photos on the wall, bright colors like candy wrappers. Favorite book covers – it's a thing she has everyone do at the start of the semester. No one likes a dull classroom. And if they're not tacked down right, the edges flap like butterflies in the air con.

April sits in the front. There are empty seats either side. She has her hands pressed tightly together – head bent over. She's praying. Might be more appropriate in a religious ed. class, which this is not. She's been like that for ten minutes. And she's got *the mumblings*. April is prone to *the mumblings*. April is prone to a whole lot more. At least today it's only *the mumblings*, and at least she stayed in school till the end of the day. Only words she catches are: *The Lord will be revealed.* She says it over and over.

When April first walked into Ruby-May's classroom last Fall, she saw it. Sure, she looked sweet – petite, strawberry blonde curls falling halfway down her back, nice little figure coming too, but wasn't hard to see the worry. Maybe it was the way she held her expression: a stoic concentration, sometimes vacant, sometimes defiant – but always there – it's there now as she prays. It's a look that says *April always has something on her mind.* And that blush of gray sat right there under her eyes says *this girl had not slept good in a long time.* Of course, Ruby-May already knew about April. Reports said she had a troubled time in middle school, even in elementary there were signs, of course it all seemed "so normal" at that age. Ruby-May takes her for English and April was to report to her at the start of every day and after lunch. Counsel her as needed. There is a lot of *as needed.* Ruby-May has met a few troubled children in her twenty-three years of teaching. Troubles come in many forms. Everyone hoped April would grow out of hers in high school.

Imaginary friends are a healthy part of a child's social development. As a matter of fact, children who have them usually do better – have an above-average IQ. She has said that enough times. Some say they "invent companions" to fulfil a need. April *is* an only-child. Others say they invent them because they are *super-creative*; before they get real friends, they create their own. And it's all completely normal. She has said that enough times too. Thought it. Said it. Wrote it. Sometimes she wonders if she's just trying to convince herself.

> *Rodrigez, Henry. "Defining Friendship: Case Studies on the role of ICs (Imaginary Companions) in Personal Development". Imaginary friends usually disappear by the age of nine –* **American Psychiatric, 2001, pp 45-49.**

April is fifteen and no sign of those imaginary friends leaving any time soon. And that's the part that keeps Ruby-May from *her* sleep. But *usually* is not the same as *always.* Recent evidence suggests children who still have imaginary friends into teenage years *usually* turn out fine.

Except in the seven months she has known her, there's one thing Ruby-May knows for sure: there is "no usually" about April

Jefferson. Her grandparents say the same five *friends* have been with her since she was three years old.

Ruby-May has gone too easy on her. But today she has to do something she doesn't want to do. *Really* doesn't want to do. She finished the report last night. Her recommendations are long overdue.

Husband Randolph says she's gotten too close, too involved. *Ain't healthy, sugar* he says. But then Randolph always says that. And she always tells him the same thing: she can't do her job if she doesn't. He tells her *you can still care, honey... just be careful.* Of course, he's thinking about what happened last time.

But this is not the same as what happened last time. *Is it?*

April always chooses to sit away from everyone else – she has no other friends and God knows Ruby-May has tried. Those imaginary friends should have their own files, have their names on the darn register. When Ruby-May moves students around April always finds a way to sit apart. Sometimes she says she is saving the seats for her *friends*. Won't let anyone sit there, or even come close. And sometimes she speaks to them in class. Ruby-May usually ends that pretty quick with *the look*; they have made some progress at least – the *we have talked about this* look and most times she hushes. But not always. Some days she gets louder, shouting, crying. One time she even started throwing things: her pencil case, then her books. Saying all kinds of jabber nonsense. That's when the first letter went home to her folks. *April has some behavioral issues.* That's when Libby asked if she needed her to step in. "I got this," Ruby-May said.

But maybe she doesn't *got* anything.

Ruby-May glances at the file sticking out from her bag that's hanging off the back of the seat. She feels the sweat on her palms making greasy marks on her class notes. She looks back across at April, red curls falling across that pretty white face of hers.

No matter what Ruby-May does to encourage April to work "together" April always does something to offend. Last time, April got into a fight. A *hair-pulling, leg kicking, terrible language* kind of fight. All she said was Rose told her to do it.

April was back in Principle Hugh's office and another letter went home to the Jeffersons.

Ruby-May must've held April back after school most nights since, told her this disruption has to stop. Had meetings with her grandfather; the grandmother has Alzheimer's. That can't help. She tells April she needs to stop "blaming" her *friends*. After last month's outburst Ruby-May knows what she's got to do. And that's the reason for the sweaty finger marks on her class notes. Why she called Libby Gerard last night – Libby said she'd come to her classroom at the end of school, after the bell.

> *There are differentials when assigning cause to disruptive behavior and overt anxiety in children. Those who invent imaginary companions often blame them for their own misdemeanors. The problem comes when defining "normals" While blaming an imaginary friend for bad behavior is normal for some, for others children claim a voice tells them to do it. When this becomes compulsive, disruptive and stressful for the child a clinical problem cannot be ruled out – Bowlings, Peter, M.D. "Children with Imaginary Friends". **Armond Press, 1997, p17.***

Ruby-May watches the students, heads pored over *Of Mice and Men*. They've been taking it in turns to read out, some mumble, some whisper, some shout. April doesn't even look up from her praying. So, she has asked them to read inside their heads until class finishes. Four minutes until the bell.

> *Signs of anxiety in children include disruptive behavior, failure to concentrate and difficulty making friends. The children frequently have lower than average class attendance – Joshua K Washington. "Personality Disorders in Minors." **Child Psychiatry, vol 14, 2001, pp. 101-109.***

April's attendance record is the worst it's ever been. It's a small mercy she even made it to class today. Libby is the best educational psychologist she knows. And she's a good friend. She told her *she had it all in hand, no need to worry yet, give her time to settle in.* She'll be mad she waited, but she'll know why; sometimes they do turn those corners all on their own. But now she realizes no amount of praying or waiting will make that happen. Right now, as she watches April with *the mumblings,* she knows she's doing the right thing, but the *right thing* doesn't always feel like the *right thing.*

Three minutes until the bell.

Mr. Jefferson knew April wouldn't come into school on her birthday a couple of weeks back. That's why he called. Ruby-May was in early grading papers. The secretary came with the message scribbled on a sticky note. He'd seen April on to the bus, but did not believe she'd arrive. Ruby-May knew what that meant. So, she had Mrs. Walker take care of registration while she took a chance. She had seen April skip school to hang out in the park before – though she had never seen her like *that* before. That poor child was on her hands and knees, not just praying she was sobbing up a storm. No child acts like that – not unless something is really wrong. "Talk to me," she said. "How can I help you, April, if you won't tell me what's happening?"

She learned a long time ago about *breakthrough* moments. And in that moment, she really hoped it had come, right then – in the park – on April's fifteenth birthday. She needed something, because Principal Hughes was already talking about getting her assessed.

"April, sugar. If something's wrong, you know you can trust me."

"I know, Mrs. Johnston. Jesse told me."

Ruby-May lifts her head and looks along the row of desks, and out at the school yard. She senses the bell in the expectant shuffle of papers, the clink of pens and the zip of pencil cases. But they know in her class you wait. Wait for the bell and then wait for the instruction.

As April mumbles, her hands grip tighter. It sounds like she's quoting scriptures again. But that's not what she was quoting in the park. It was the line from an old poem. She had to look it up when she got home, just to be sure.

She looks at the file nudging its way out of her bag. She looks back at the class. At April. At the way the others just accept her odd behavior now.

Two minutes until the bell.

It was the way April grabbed a hold of her that day that sits uneasy. The way one second, they were sat on that bench, and April said something about the crows but Ruby-May was sure she was mistaken as she never saw any crows. All she saw were trees, wind rustling the leaves.

> *A hallucination is a false auditory, visual, gustatory, tactile, or olfactory perception. It is not the same as illusions (misperception), fantasies, imaginary friends, and eidetic images (visual images in the memory). Children as young as the age of five have reported hallucinations – – – Sullivan, Edward. "Exploring the Imagination."* **Psychiatry World, vol 17, no.3, 2001, pp. 55-61.**

The studious ones still have their heads buried in the world of George Milton and Lennie Small, others stare out at the yard. Eager for home. April is never eager for home.

One minute until the bell.

"We need to talk about your imaginary friends," Ruby-May had said, that day at the park.

"They're not imaginary, Mrs. Johnston."

April had shuffled along the bench, like she was making space between them.

"April, sugar, how do you know that?"

"Just do."

"Okay, then tell me about them. Can you describe them?"

"They're not here now."

"But you can still tell me about them, right?"

"Oh. Maybe. I—"

April's eyes had shifted to the left, like she was thinking hard on that. Then she said, "Not really."

Next thing April was scrambling to her feet saying she would go to school. That it was safe now and she'd grabbed a hold of Ruby-May's hand, held it so tight it pinched.

"It wasn't safe before?"

"Nowhere's safe, Mrs. Johnston."

"But it is now?"

"I think so."

"Why wasn't it safe before?"

And she'd said it, the thing she had to look up later.

"My soul has grown deep like the rivers."

"Pardon me?"

"My soul has grown deep like the rivers."

She was sure she knew that line.

April was tugging at her hand, coercing her to stand. "Come on, it's okay now; let's get to class."

"April? What you said…"

She pulled again until Ruby-May was on her feet and April was leading her towards the path. "Come on, Mrs. Johnston… we're already late."

And that was that.

She found the poem later.

It's a Langston Hughes poem. It's called *The Negro Speaks of Rivers.*

The bell is followed by a clattering of backpacks on desks. Ruby-May waves her hands to restore the peace before she dismisses them, telling them to make sure they'd written down the homework. Raised voices and scraping chairs on wood precedes the stampede. Hands raise. "See you, Mrs. Johnston" and soon the noise has left.

But not April Jefferson.

She still has her head bent in prayer.

Ruby-May pulls her file from the bag and places it on the desk, glances at the time. "April, sugar?"

She opens her eyes, hands still together. "Yes, Mrs. Johnston?"

"You okay?"

"Sure."

She lowers her hands and pushes her book into her bag. To look at her now it was like nothing was wrong, except for the worried face.

"I wanted to ask you about that poem."

"The homework?"

"No, the one you quoted me a line from, remember, in the park on your birthday."

"No."

"You don't remember?"

"No."

"Can I ask you something?"

"Yes."

"Will you to do something for me? Would that be okay?"

"Depends."

"I asked you to describe your friends to me, remember?"

"Yeah."

"And you said *not really*. Do you think you could write it down, like we do when we write about the characters in the books we read in class? A few lines about each of them."

"Why?"

"I'm just curious. You can tell a lot about a person by the friends they keep."

A smile creeps into her eyes. "Okay, let me think about it."

She slowly puts her backpack onto her shoulder, pushes back her seat, makes her way to the door. As the classroom door clatters shut, she sees Libby Gerard waiting outside.

Chapter 3

I

April 10ᵗʰ, 1961, Atlanta, Georgia

Working in BB's grocery store, not even serving because you *ain't so good talkin' to folk*, is not exactly the kind of job George had imagined for himself. Filling shelves and cleaning floors. It's temporary. But at least he has dimes in his pocket.

BB's is a family-run grocery store that Cousin Thomas's pap – Brayton Brown – started in East Point back in the 1940s, out of his home; now it's got its own small building. Place is nothing to look at. *Run by the Negroes for the Negroes* Thomas always says. Maybe he should write that over the door: *Coloreds only.* You enter by the front door. Only looks like even BB's will be gone soon.

George needed a job; his cousin called in a favor. George said yes to please his momma. Too much of a daydreamer everyone says. No way he wanted to work in a factory. He always said he would never end up like Pap.

He runs his finger along the flap of the box, flips it open. Erma has the radio on out back. There's a new number one: Ernie K-Doe.

Grandmomma Josie says everything's changed since she grew up on East Washington Street. She said they only had two rooms for the whole family, right next door to another family. She said if he thought their house was bad in Jacksonville, he should've seen where they lived when she was growing up. When *her* pap worked in the oil mill. A shanty town. Houses like shoe boxes – and falling down. Leaning into one another like dominoes. In the beginning her family worked on the Connally Plantation. They all came from slaves: her parents, their parents and theirs before that. After they got their freedom, some of them didn't know what to do with it. Her parents were sharecroppers working the land for rent but they were never treated fair; after that lots of them worked at the mills and the factories; still slaves she said, in one form or another. Built the houses right alongside the factories – so you got to work on time. *No white folk would live like we did* she said. She said Grandpap Zeb came along and rescued her. His brother had made a better life in Jacksonville and so would they.

But in the end, she said, turns out white folk hate you the same everywhere.

George did not like staying with his cousins in those first few months, all crammed inside like corn on a cob. Same place he had been sent when he was fifteen.

The place they moved into is not much better than that one in Jacksonville only now it seems *The Rejuvenation*, they say moved all the colored folks out of Clayton, is coming to East Point. They call it the *urban renewal*. It had already started when they came, but it didn't affect them back then – it's hard to ignore it now. He heard the government had grants to do the place up. He doesn't know what will happen but it won't be long his momma says. That man she's been seeing, John Langton, he says it's more like *white invasion*. Bulldozing everything they'd built in the community. *Won't be none of it left* he says. What George likes most about the East Washington community, is it's like they got their little part of the world, hiding away from Jim Crow. Like George lives in his own special bubble. They always said George did that. They were talking about *his friends*. The ones he used to talk to in his sleep, or mumble to when he thought no one was listening. But even he knows no one can live inside a bubble. Whatever it is you're hiding from – will find you in the end.

And the world – is still a long way from the world Abe said it would be. Outside of his bubble, he still has to line up and use the side entrance in stores, although since Rosa Parks, he doesn't have to sit at the back of the bus.

The new president says he will make things better for the

Negroes but best not to believe anything until you see it. Though Abe was right about some things changing.

This afternoon George will register to vote.

George places cans of black beans onto a shelf, wipes a line of sweat from his cheek. All the fans do is throw the stuffy air back in your face. Even with the door wide open the air doesn't move. Place always smells musty, floorboards always creak. Time always drags. He looks at the wall clock. Ten minutes.

It took some coercing to get George to agree to register. In the end, it was Grandmomma's words that persuaded him. The kitchen was filled up with the smell of sweet potato pie cooking – his favorite. Momma was out with John Langton again. While he was waiting for supper, his grandmomma told him how Grandpap Zeb had lined up every few years to register to vote, at the Baptist church on Mission Street. They even gave lessons to people like him, taught him to read and write. He wasn't much good, but he said it didn't matter if he was the best reader in Florida – no way he was passing that literacy test. But he kept on trying. And then there was the poll tax, the character test, the civic test, being quizzed on the Constitution. They made it a lot harder for *them* than they did the white folk – but people were fighting back she said. It was the *Grandfather Clause* that really got into his bones. He always said that was dumb ass. What was the point of letting a man vote just because his grandfather did, if every Negro he knew came from the plantations – all of their grandfathers were slaves.

"That's why they did it," Grandmomma told him. "They don't want no Negro havin' a say." She said Grandpap promised himself *things were gon' change*; one day he would get that vote. It was his right, said it right there in the fifteenth amendment, only the white supreme had other ideas, changed the law to suit their own needs. Grandpap was a clever man. Lined up even though he knew they would never say yes. He did it on principle she said. Make sure they saw him.

"Saw him?"

"Grandpap Zeb always said *not everyone can be rich and famous or even a hero, but don't matter, long as you get seen.*"

George has thought about that a lot. He thinks he spent most of his life doing the exact opposite.

"Zeb was a proud man," she said. "Proud till he forgot who he was."

Something about that and the way she looked at him or maybe it was just the smell of that sweet potato pie wafting, but George knew he would say yes even before Grandmomma said *if he weren't gon' do it for his-self, he sure ought to do it for Grandpap Zeb.*

So, the next day, he told Pattie Holmes, okay he would ride the bus with her; and it was free after all. They'd go register to vote. She said they've changed things and there were lots of people standing up in court these days to prove the rules for the coloreds are not the same as the whites. Winning too she said. It's easier to register and that's why everyone's doing it. Cousin Thomas has been asking him to *do it* since he arrived in East Point – he is on a crusade to get people to vote, says it's the only way for things to change. George knows about Thomas and his secret meetings with the NAACP – that's the National Association for the Advancement of Colored People. George always said no before. They seem to think now he's been visiting the library; he will fly through that literacy test. He's clever; they need people like him to vote. But the smile on Grandmomma's face when he said he would go was the real reward.

Pattie Holmes started coming into the store six months back. Sweet enough, on the plump side, which he doesn't mind, but something about her has stopped him going sweet on her the way she is sweet on him. It was Cousin Erma who said it. She said Pattie Holmes was *smitten.* She used that very word. *Look how many times she comes into the store, buys one thing at a time just to see you, George, but you got your head buried so deep inside that book o' poems you wouldn't notice if John F Kennedy himself walked in.*

He told her she *might be needin' to get her eyes fixed.* Until a month later Pattie asked him out for lemonade at Dixie's. He said he was busy. That was before she even said when. George likes a person to be forward, because George is not good with *the sociable*, everyone knows it, but when she said she would just keep on asking him, he wasn't so sure he liked that kind of forward. Erma says there is nothing wrong with women being forward, she says there has been enough suppression, women have rights too. But there's forward and there's *pushy.*

He's not so sure Pattie is the right one for him. He's not so sure any woman is the right one for him. When he was fifteen, he would've said it was Chloe Johnson. Was even planning on writing a poem about her. But that was like a whole lifetime ago. He might have found Langston Hughes again and some new poets too, not *all* Negro poets – but he has never written a poem in all these years.

Last week Pattie asked George again, only not to Dixie's for lemonade or even to the Squeeze In, as she said she liked to dance, this time she said she was going to register to vote. Her uncle was the one who drove the free bus into Atlanta. There was room for one more.

"We should do it," she said. "Everyone should register, my daddy says. And I know you can read good, George, ever' time I come in here you hidin' up at the end there with your head buried inside one book or other. Too good for a grocery store clerk."

He'd looked at her over the boxes of Kellogg's Cornflakes. She was wearing jeans, a yellow blouse, probably too tight but they did show off her curves. Hair pulled back off her face. Skin blacker than his, real dark so the whites of her eyes shone out. "Well?" she said.

"Maybe."

"Well it's better than no or I'm too busy," she said. "Told you I'd wear you down in the end, George. You let me know 'fore I offer that place to someone else, 'cause you know I will."

He took some time to think on that before he said yes – about the registering to vote. He is still not so sure about her. She does have nice curves, maybe a sweet smile but there is no *flutter-flutter* the way the poems tell you it should be. Not like E.E. Cummings says; library had a book with his poems in and his words are the kind that stick.

I carry your heart…

George knows about carrying hearts, some so heavy they squeeze his lips tight shut, and mess up all his thoughts. That's not the way the poem means it, it's about *romantic* love. Maybe George never will know about that, but he knows he does not carry Pattie Holmes's heart.

He places a can on the shelf. Elvis is on the radio, singing about being lonesome. He knows about that too. Cousin Thomas tries to persuade George to go to the pool hall, seems lots of stuff happens there, not just shooting pool. Doesn't interest George. Thomas says, "No girls inside but there sure is a lot of 'em waitin' outside, George. I've seen that Pattie Holmes there." He winked when he said that. Seems like Erma had been talking; she never could hold her words, not like George.

He always tells Thomas he's too busy, which everyone knows is an excuse. Especially if Pattie is one of the girls. Maybe that's part of why he's not sweet on her. His grandmomma warned him about the type of girls who hang out at pool halls.

He places the last of the tins of black beans on the shelf as the door rattles, bell *jingle-jangles* and Mrs. Wood comes in. If she gets any wider, she won't fit through that door. Calls out to Erma and stands with her grocery list in her hand. George pretends not to see her as he moves on to the next box. Momma says he should say yes to Pattie, walk out with her. She says at twenty-three she was married to Pap and pregnant with George. Only she was married long before then. Grandmomma is the one who told him how his momma *had* to get married – and he'd worked out when he was only young that it meant she must've been pregnant at seventeen. Momma says Pattie is educated, says he could do a lot worse.

44

"He could do a lot better, Olivia," Grandmomma says.

"Not like he got 'em lining up. Nothing wrong with Pattie. Be good for someone like George. What he needs. Confident."

She means *pushy*.

They always talk like he's not standing right there.

Whenever Momma talks that way, Grandmomma gets her mood face on. "Leave the boy alone, Olivia," she says. "Something not quite right about that girl."

She doesn't have to say it but he knows what Momma thinks when she says that: that there's something not quite right about George either, not making any new friends.

"I smell trouble," Grandmomma says. "Knows her own head too much. What you need is someone sweet-natured, jus' like you. When the right ones come along you know it. George, honey, you wait for her. You'll know first time you see her, the one you gon' marry. Way it was for me and Zeb."

Momma's eyes like to roll when she says that. That's because she knows what's coming next. Most of their conversations go round on a loop of repeats, like a vinyl that got stuck in the groove.

"If you had waited, not settled, you could have done a whole lot better."

She used to mean Pap, but George is sure that includes John Langton now. He's got an anger on him like Pap; only he doesn't use his fists. At least not yet.

It seems it's not only their conversation that likes to repeat. History has a way of doing it too.

George keeps his eye on the clock. He said he would meet Pattie at the bus but she said she would come to the store; like maybe she thinks he won't show. So, he told her to be here at 1.50. Erma says he can leave ten minutes early as long as he makes up the time. Bus leaves at 2. He does not want to be late.

He must decide what to do about Pattie. Erma says he can't keep stringing her along. She needs to know. Erma has finally appeared, looking flushed – maybe Samuel has paid her a visit. She needs to be careful she doesn't get herself a reputation like the girls who hang outside the pool hall. Erma attends to Mrs. Wood's grocery list while George finishes up. Five minutes until Pattie gets there.

But of course, Pattie is early.

It looks like she got dressed up for him. Red dress that hugs all the right places. Short too, pulls his eye in to her legs. He catches himself gawping and looks away. She even did something different with her hair. Maybe Momma was right. Maybe love is for the poets, and in real life it comes more slowly. Takes time to carry someone's heart. She waltzes up to him, stands close. She's wearing that perfume again: sickly sweet and powdery. She says it's jasmine.

She says she will wait. He nods.

Maybe love does grow on you, like the scent of jasmine.

Bus heaves and sighs and finally stops on the corner of Auburn Avenue across from Yates and Milton. It's a drug store. It's the place where you register to vote. Pattie had her leg pressed against his the whole of the bus ride; all George did was gaze out of the windows as the streets got busier. He was thinking about the day he arrived, in his cousin's beat-up station wagon. He's got a newer one now. Always seems first time you see a place it looks different from when you've been there a few weeks. It's like that on East Washington. He doesn't come into Atlanta much so it still looks new. That made him think about Clayton. He heard everything's changed; wouldn't recognize the place now. He thinks about Momma's white roses – long gone, pictures the house, the stoop. Momma couldn't find a place to hang Pap's wind chimes – just as well. He does not miss that stoop, or remembering the *clunk-thud* when Pap fell down dead. After the fight.

He was not sad to leave Clayton, but George does know one day he *will* go back. He knows there are too many bad memories, but it's the only place he can feel close to Abe. No one talks about him. Never got medals, never even got called a hero.

"You ready?"

She doesn't wait for an answer. Pattie pushes her hand into his and next thing they are crossing the street going into the drug store to register, just like Grandpap Zeb never could.

April 10th, 1961 is a date George will remember. Not because it's the day he registered to vote. Although he will always remember he did – standing in line in that busy drug store – part of a chain, bigger than any of the white-owned ones (Pattie told him that) thinking they wouldn't let him, like it was for Grandpap Zeb. But seems all the protests and all the sit-ins that were on the front pages of the *Atlanta Daily Record,* the colored newspaper, and the court cases must've done something. No one asked him if his grandpap was allowed to vote, maybe they should've – but George wasn't like him, didn't like to make a fuss. All he knows is in the end they let him register. No clerk turned him away, not like Grandpap Zeb all those times.

But that's not what George will remember the most about April 10th, 1961. In fact, while he was waiting in line, he had other things on his mind. He was *seen.* Oh, he was definitely *seen.* Just not in the way you'd think.

George sits in front of the TV. He is not as fascinated by it as Grandmomma Josie. She has an eye for the Westerns, she has two favorites: *Cheyenne* and *Bronco.* He never sees her face so fixed in concentration as when she watching Wild Bill Hickok. TV belongs to Cousin Thomas. He and Grandmomma come over to his house every Monday night while his momma is *entertaining.* It's the night she has John Langton over for supper.

George watches, but tonight, more than usual, his head is in a whole other place. Thomas and that pretty wife of his, Nettie, keep on talking about the sit-ins, asking him if he saw the newspaper about the freedom riders being in Atlanta, fighting for the rights of the Negro, and to make sure he uses *that* vote. But George is somewhere else entirely. He never was one for the politics. Heard enough of that talk from Abe and… George does not want to think about that. George has other things to think about. As he watches, he expects there to be a newsflash right there on that TV. *George Tucker has a date on Saturday.*

It was a long line. People talking, some fanning their faces. Him looking at Pattie. She was standing close. The sickly scent of jasmine in the air. Momma's voice in his head saying Pattie will be good for him. What *he needs.* Made him look at her extra close in that line. That was until. Until the best part. Until he was *seen.* He also had lots of poets in his head too. Some say love takes time to grow, say it *has to watered* like corn to grow so high. Not everyone has love at first sight.

Except that might be exactly what happened right there in that line in the Yates and Milton drug store.

George Tucker has a date on Saturday.

And it's not with Pattie Holmes.

Something tells George Pattie Holmes might not be coming in to buy groceries one item at a time, not anymore. She swapped seats on the bus ride home and by the time they got back to East Point she was already pressing her knee and making the eyes at Walt Robbins. She probably has a date with him on Saturday. His grandmomma was right about her.

He first saw her when he was waiting in line to register; she was done and waiting. He didn't know for what or who. Could have been her boyfriend for all her knew. He expected by the time he was done getting registered, she'd be gone. Pattie must've seen him look at her because next thing she was reaching for his hand. He pulled it away.

She was slimmer than Pattie, but she had the curves. All in the right places. Wearing a cotton dress, cornflower blue and straight down, not too short. Respectable. Hair was up but curls hung around the edges of her face. It was the smile. Best smile George had ever seen. Not just on the lips, whole face radiant, eyes shining. If Langston Hughes and been there to see it he would have called it *enchantment.*

He kept his eye on her but every time she looked at him, he found something to look at on his shoe. No way he could talk to her. *Could he?* He told himself he needed *to man-up* but why would she be interested in George? So, he shuffled in line, avoiding Pattie's gaze; she had the warning look his Momma used to use on him when he was mumbling to his friends.

Shuffle – wait – shuffle – wait. He had run out of things to say to Pattie. Not that he ever had a whole lot to say.

Atlanta is busier than East Point. The drug store was the busiest drug store he'd ever been in. Never seen so much stuff all lined up neatly on the shelves. George liked East Washington, his little bubble away from the troubles. Atlanta is a big place. Grandmomma said Atlanta would be the making of George. That the *change of scenery* would *help with the healin'* – that's how she said it. He needs to learn to be more *sociable* is how Momma said it. She thinks he still speaks to *his friends*. The ones inside his head. She catches him mumblin'. Calls it his *problem*. But her head is so full of John Langton she doesn't know anything. Maybe she fell in love with him at first sight. He doubts it. He doesn't see John Langton look at his momma the way he knows he was looking at her… today in line to register.

After Pap died, he heard Momma say maybe they should take George to the doctor, that it ought to have grown out of *his problem. His mumblings.* She said he wasn't coping. Grandmomma looked at Momma and she said all he needed was *a reason to shine.* They've been in Atlanta three years and today George found his reason to shine.

So, there he was. *Shuffle – wait – shuffle – wait.* Every time he looked up; she was looking at him. Still waiting on whatever it was she was waiting on. He made a bargain with himself, if she was still waiting when he was done registering, he would walk right over to her and ask her name.

It didn't quite work out like that, that's just the way he sets it down in his head. But she was still there waiting by the door of Yates and Milton smiling away in her blue cotton. She spoke to *him* first. She asked him if he had the time. Said it quiet so he had to go over, ask her to repeat. Left Pattie talking to the others while he edged closer.

"I thought you were never gonna talk to me," she told him.

Three minutes later, after she told him how she was waiting for her pap, only she called him Daddy, she said he was a preacher, he asked her if he could take her out for coffee on Saturday afternoon. Of course, he expected her to say no.

That's when Pattie called over using her loud voice to tell George the bus was waiting. Now Pattie did not look too happy. She had a big ol' scowl on her face like she did not want him to be talking to the girl in the cornflower dress, the girl with the *enchanting smile*. And Pattie must've seen when she handed him the note. She had scribbled down her address on some paper she'd found in her purse, had pressed it right there into his hands. But George weren't worried what Pattie thought about that. He was more worried that all the sweat on his palms would wipe the words clean away. But it hasn't. He has it in his pocket; every time he goes to the bathroom, he checks he can still read it. Only he doesn't need to now, because he has it memorized – by heart. He told her he didn't know where it was but he would be sure to find it.

"Three o'clock," she said. "Don't be late."

George used to be late for everything, on account of his daydreaming. But he won't be late for her. He will be early.

Then right as he was leaving the store, she said, "Is there something you forgot, George?"

A kiss? But even he knows that's too forward.

"You told me *your* name; you don't want to know mine?"

Her name. Before he could tell her how is not so good with *the sociable*, she said it. She said, "It's Molly Ann Collins."

Words rolled out of her like a melody.

And they were dancing inside his head as he left that drug store and headed to where the bus was waiting on him on Auburn Avenue. Pattie was already sitting next to Walt Robbins.

George planned to tell Momma and Grandmomma soon as they got home from Cousin Thomas's. No way he was saying anything in front of Thomas – but it seems Momma and John Langdon are otherwise engaged. The bedroom door is shut, radio turned up loud. The Shirelles: *Will you still love me tomorrow?* He is not sure what he sees on Grandmomma's face. She does not approve of John Langdon, just as she did not approve of Pap. She said the only good thing that came out of that marriage was him.

"And Abe," he said, but she never answered.

While the milk boils on the stove for her hot chocolate, he tells her. He watches her the whole time. It looks like a light turns on, lights up her entire face. She even claps her hands. Almost lets the milk boil right over the sides of the pan. He tells her Molly Ann Collins's family is originally from Dallas. That's the only part he remembers about her family, apart from that her daddy is a Baptist preacher somewhere in Atlanta but he doesn't recall the district. He can't remember the last time he saw Grandmomma smile like that.

He's not sure his momma will react the same way as Grandmomma, that she'll still think he should've made a date with Pattie. But she will have to wait. She has other things on her mind.

"I only registered to vote for Grandpap Zeb," he says.

Grandmomma takes his hand in hers. Big warm hands that close over his. "And there she was, your Molly waiting for you. Like God put her right there."

Your Molly. He likes the sound of that.

He never says he has not believed in God since he was fifteen; she already knows that.

"And it's a good thing you registered, George. Thing's changin'."

She sounds just like Abe.

"You were right what you said."

"I am always right, George. About what in particular?" She still has a hold of his hand.

"'bout waitin'. 'bout Pattie Holmes. Ain't fair on her, she deserves someone who *sees* her the right way." Maybe someone like Walt Robbins, only he never says that part. Maybe he'll like that jasmine perfume. Now all George knows is every time he smells jasmine, he'll think of *almosts.* Or maybe it ought to be *things that jus' weren't meant to be.*

Grandmomma squeezes harder. "That girl's gon' be fine."

"I knew it soon as I saw her. *My Molly*."

"You'll marry that girl," she says.

"Ain't even been on one date yet!" He can't help grinning all the same.

"When you know, George, you know. Just a pity I won't be there to see it."

"To see what?"

"You gettin' wed."

"Why not?"

"Look at me, George. My time's almost done."

"Then I won't wait. I'll ask her tomorrow!"

She laughs. "Now you found her, you wan' scare her off 'fore you get started?"

He feels the squeeze her hand long after she lets go.

George will not sleep tonight.

Maybe he'll write a poem, call it *Molly's Smile*.

Won't be as good as Langston Hughes.

Or maybe he'll call it *April 10th, 1961*.

It is the date George did what Grandpap Zeb never could.

It's the date George did something *he* never could – he got *seen*.

And it's the date he knows what E.E. Cummings meant in his poem. Because April 10th, 1961 is the date George started carrying the heart of Molly Ann Collins.

II

April 10th, 2003, Jacksonville, Florida

Ruby-May has lost her spring. Usually with the birds tweeting and the sun shining it's sat right there in her step. Especially today: April 10th, but not this April 10th.

Today is the day April's grandparents will have her first meeting with Libby Gerard.

Libby had the letter sent home to the Jeffersons a week after they talked; she wanted to meet before the Easter break. It said to come to the school after class. Ruby-May did not choose the date.

She looks at the yard, at the roses on their second flush: cotton-white blooms along the hickory fence, air pricked with their sweet scents. She senses Randolph at the window. Since the cancer, he cut right down on his hours, works mostly for Clayton's free community newspaper now where even roses having a second flush might be a story. But sometimes they ask him to cover something for the *Jacksonville Daily*. That's where he worked for best part of thirty years. When she met him, he was the guy who wrote the obituaries, *the intern*. She wasn't sure what to make of that but her momma said everyone has to start somewhere. That newspaper served him well. Not many work the same job in the same place for all them years. Still sees some of the old reporter guys, even meets up with Charlie Wilkes once a month for a Bud, not a reporter; he's a cop at Clayton Police Station, planning on retiring soon. Helped him out a few times over the years on stories.

Randolph'll be watching her now as she stands still like the sweet acacia tree along the front fence, breeze so light it has the softness of a sleeping baby. Randolph will be watching her as she walks to the gate, onto the street all the way until she waves back from the corner. Most of her friends would kill for a man like Randolph. That man has loved her through the worst and best of times.

"Well, what did you expect?" he says. "I married you for better and for worse and for everything in between."

And he had.

And she had loved him right back the same way; had loved his PSA score down all the way to zero. Love alone is the cure he told her. She is pretty sure the op helped. And the fact it hadn't spread anywhere else. Of course, love can't hurt.

But even though it's April 10th and they made a promise, he'll be worrying. She should never have spoiled today, *especially* today – it's a special number. She should never have told him about the meeting.

"That mean you'll be late?"

"Not too late."

"I'll do supper for seven, give you two hours."

"It won't be two hours."

"You won't be talkin' with Libs after?"

But she never answered. She wasn't so sure how this would go. Libby might be her friend, might even have been the one she talked to, like when Libby's marriage failed – but something like this – this was different – there were protocols. Once April was in the system, being assessed it was a whole lot more serious, this wasn't a nice chit-chat in Starbucks after work. As Libs herself put it last week, "Ruby – it could be clinical." She means back off, don't get too involved, you've done enough. But it's never that simple. She knows; she has been here before.

Ruby-May lets the scent of the roses wash over her face; only it seems nothing is shaking her mood.

She has been keeping a journal for Libby about April's behavior – in class, outside of class, at recess, in the cafeteria. Who she talks to, interacts with (that's easy) what triggers her *outbursts*. The book with her scribblings sits in her bag – feels like the weight of those words has just gotten a whole lot heavier. She straightens up, looks down at her cotton dress, blue with white dots (half off in the J C Penney sale), takes another step to the gate; their little silver Golf is parked up on the street. It's twenty years old but reliable. Even though Randolph doesn't need it so much now, she still likes to walk.

Last night she read her notes again while Randolph cooked

black bean stew. Sometimes you know something is there, you've seen it enough times, but when you see it written down like that, count up how many times April's behavior disrupted the class or how many times she was mumbling to her friends, refusing to take part in her lessons – it's hard to deny what's right in front of you and that's when she knows she's doing the right thing – even when if it feels like she's not.

She lifts her bag up onto her shoulder and nudges open the wooden gate. She wonders if April will even be in class today.

Last night as she read over the notes, she'd felt the jab of Randolph's stare but this time he never said a word. The same stare that follows her now, that followed her across the kitchen this morning as he set down her toast, even made her coffee. No fuss. She told him, no fuss.

"I'll cook your favorite for supper."

She knows what he thinks but they're done with fighting on this. The past does not have to repeat. April is a bright kid, so her point average is on the decline, that happens when you choose to cut school, but she is the brightest kid in her class. As she steps onto Tabebuia Drive, she looks down. The neighbor's little black cat is weaving itself around her ankles near tripping her. "Shoo now."

When she couldn't sleep last night, she was making lists in her head all the things that could be wrong with April: *it could be clinical.* A is for ADHD. D is for Disruptive Behavior Disorders. P is for Personality Disorder. S is for Stop. *This is not helping. Let the experts do their job.* That's what Randolph has said enough times. But there she was: tangled in a loop of words, same words she had scribbled in another notebook many years ago.

There are lots of reasons why a fifteen-year-old could still have imaginary friends. It doesn't have to be clinical.

Does it?

As she walks along Tabebuia, Ruby-May sees Randolph at the window and she can still see that black cat on the path. She thinks about what people say about black cats and not for the first time this morning she pinches her fingers together and hopes that black cat is a good omen. Only the last thing she sees, when she turns at the corner to wave at Randolph, is that black cat spraying its pee all up her white roses.

The day doesn't just drag, it digs its heels in good and tight, just like Ruby-May knew it would. Always does when you want something to be over with. April Jefferson was in class. That's something. She was there in the way she is there but not there. Ruby-May had watched her at registration and later in English class. Alone, mumbling, worried face. At least the praying phase seems to have ended. Libby was the one who said, "Having imaginary friends in ninth grade is not normal." Only what she actually said was, "… is unusual." And something about accepted *normal* criteria.

Normal. Unusual. Clinical.

You say tomatoes.

They'd find out soon enough.

She looks at the empty classroom. The meeting will be in the office. She has five minutes to prepare. She hates that word. When Randolph was being tested for the cancer that's what the doctors said. "You have to prepare." All she said to that doctor was, "How exactly do you suppose we do that?"

That's how she feels now as she thumbs through her notebook.

The window is open and a sudden gust whips up papers from her desk and flaps the photographs on the wall of the favorite book covers. April Jefferson's is the one at the top right-hand corner. Now most of the children choose classics, some contemporary favorites – some changes over the years but a lot of the favorites remain: *Fahrenheit 451, Animal Farm, The Great Gatsby… Winnie the Pooh…* more recently *Harry Potter*. But not April Jefferson. Ruby-May had seen most covers of most editions of most books. Sure, there were the odd surprises in there. One year someone chose an obscure little book of plays she had never heard of, and every now and then someone puts the bible up there.

But not many poetry books. Only there it is, a simple cover with a little blue bird on the front.

She looks at the little blue bird. Looks like its flapping its wings right there in the classroom. She pictures April when she left, does she even know her grandparents are in today?

Libby wants to lead the discussion, then they could talk about what's been happening in class. As she thinks that, Ruby-May's cell vibrates on the desk and she glances at the name. He'll be calling to wish her luck. Randolph always does that. When she doesn't answer he'll leave her a voicemail. She glances across. When April first showed her that book cover, she'd asked her, "So, you like poems, April?"

"Not me."

"But this is a poetry book."

She'd shrugged.

"It's not your favorite? Only that was what I asked you all to bring."

"Yeah. Kind of. Well not *my* favorite."

"Oh."

But it's what she said next that Ruby-May thinks about now. She said, "Do you carry a heart, Mrs. Johnston?"

That's when she sees movement outside in the corridor. The Jeffersons are already here. It's time.

―――――――――――――――

Libby Gerard's office is airy. There are windows, a brightness in its pale-yellow walls and blue carpet tiles. Even the scent is light, floral, a vase on the table, little pink flowers. Everything about this space says *it's safe here. You can talk here*. When the Jeffersons have been invited to the school before it's been in the classroom, one time Principal Hughes's office which is stuffy, bookish and serious. This meeting is anything but light and airy, but everything about the room says it is.

The Jeffersons are already seated across from Libby, there is no desk between them; she prefers an open circle. Ruby-May sits down, drops her bag at her feet. Mrs. Jefferson has a mop of silver hair that looks in need of a cut, wears a simple green dress, something that looks like toothpaste on the front. Open shoes, toe nails polished red, chipped. Mr. Jefferson in that gray suit she has seen him in before. Smart shoes, shiny as mirrors. He's a small man: lean, still has a decent head of hair, not as silver as his wife's. Small round glasses that prop. She nods when she sees her, wears the face he always does – like a bad smell just walked in; he does not like her, never has. Mrs. Jefferson smiles, like today she remembers who Ruby-May is. When he replied he'd said he would bring her if it's *one of her better days*. She guesses it must be. That might be about to change.

The Jeffersons don't say a whole lot. Ruby-May watches them as Libby Gerard outlines the things that worry them most about April's behavior. She tells them how April always sits alone in class and in the cafeteria, how her sudden outbursts disrupt lessons and how all of that impacts on her learning.

"But we want to help her," Libby says, leaning in, looking right at Mr. Jefferson. "We need to ensure April gets the best education. If there's a problem, then it's our job to find out what that is."

Mr. Jefferson nods, doesn't speak.

"April will be assessed, based on what Mrs. Johnston here has flagged."

Hard to tell what that look means but there's a definite hardness in Mr. Jefferson's stare when Libby says that. As for Mrs. Jefferson – she is smiling; glancing around the office.

Libby says they have some real concerns. April is way above average, a clever girl but her behavior is getting worse, her attendance is a problem and she has no friends in school. Of course, they all know when she says that, it isn't quite true. Not real flesh and blood ones. They have *tried, encouraged, coerced,* but April prefers her own company. They all know this.

"Has she *any* friends outside of school?"

Mr. Jefferson shakes his head.

"None? No after-school classes, sports, clubs?"

He shakes his head again. "We tried. It never works out." Only he looks at Libby as he speaks – like he can't even look at Ruby-May. He clearly blames her – for all of this. She ought to have done more – has she wasted seven months?

"We always thought it was healthy," he says, again looking at Libby. "The *friends*. She always caught on fast, learned to speak, walk, all of the milestones ahead of schedule, and imaginary friends they said were common – especially for an only-child, a bright one. Shows she has a great imagination, right?"

Libby leans forward. She's in her *I-mean-business* black suit. Blonde hair tied neatly back off her face. "You're right, Mr. Jefferson."

"Ted, please. Ted."

That's new, he never asked Ruby-May to call him Ted.

"You're right, Ted."

Libby glances at Mrs. Jefferson. "Helen," Ted mouths. Libby nods. "You are quite right, but April is fifteen now, and as you know her outbursts in class are quite disruptive. She gets very anxious."

"We… we do our best."

"I know you do. This is not about blame. If there's a problem somewhere, then we need to identify it. So that's why we want to do the formal assessment."

"What does that involve?"

"We do a series of psychological tests, questions. It's a multimethod assessment."

"By a doctor?"

"No. It's a psychological assessment at first to look at what's stopping her learning as she should. Once we've interpreted the results then our aim is to look at what we can do to help her." She adds, "*All* of us."

"Then you'll send her to a doctor?"

Ruby-May watches Helen Jefferson, her eyes fixed on the window.

"One step at a time. If the assessment suggests there might be a *medical* problem, then we can refer her for further evaluation, but let's see not get ahead of ourselves."

"You mean send her to a shrink?"

His voice breaks as he says that and for a moment he glances at his wife.

"Let's do the assessment first. This meeting is to formalize what we plan to do and to reassure you that this is about April; she is our priority, it's her interests we have at heart in determining what the problem is. We'll look at how it started, why it's still there, what else might be going on."

"It started when she was three," Helen Jefferson says and now all heads turn in her direction.

Libby nods, Ted stares at her. "They know that, Helen."

"Imaginary friends usually come around that age, some later, but if she was an early talker…"

Helen nods. She looks down, rolling her wedding band around her finger. "Same five friends all this time."

"They know, Helen, that's why we're here."

"I'm going to give you a questionnaire to take home with you. Perhaps you would be so kind to fill it in." Libby leans forward, teases some sheets from the pocket of her laptop bag.

"What kind of questions? You know I have been writing things down, like Mrs. Johnston here asked me to." He says her name like she's a bad taste in his mouth. Oh, he blames her.

"These are more formal questions that will help assess April's educational issues: about her memory, her behavior, even right back when it all started."

"What about when it started?"

Libby sits the papers on her lap. "Anything you can tell us will help. Anything you remember. Sometimes, there's a trigger. It can be the birth of a sibling. I know that is not the case here, but something changes, maybe this has something to do with her parents splitting up?"

They will not like that. You can feel the air change, the tension prick.

Ted shuffles his feet on the carpet tiles and his face is blushed pinker than those little flowers.

"I think we need to get you home, Helen."

"I know this is painful but anything you can remember from that time: her dad leaving, her mom's—"

They both glare at her.

"…death. I heard she died when April was young. It could be a trigger."

"Come on, we need to get you home."

Ted is now on his feet, his hand clamping his wife's arm, but she is making no effort to stand. "Helen, come on."

"Take this with you," Libby says now holding out the questionnaire.

At first Ruby-May thinks he's not going to take it, but then he holds out his hand, she can see he's trembling.

"I know they're personal questions, but we all want the same thing."

The blush in his cheeks, the way he fumbles, nudges his wife, says he does not believe that.

Now Libby is also on her feet.

Helen is also standing, her arm looped with his.

"Please, fill it in and send it back to me. We'll make the arrangements for the assessment."

"It's not our fault!" It's Helen who speaks.

Ted tugs at her sleeve. "Shh now."

"Everyone always thinks it is, but it's not. It never was. It was never our fault what happened."

"She gets confused," Ted says ushering her towards the door. "Helen, enough now."

"Nobody is blaming anyone," Ruby-May says.

He shoots her a stare. "They always blame us."

Ruby-May stands. "No, I—"

Libby lifts her hand; she knows what it means – *don't speak. I'll handle this.*

But the Jeffersons are already at the door. The meeting is over sooner than planned. She watches as he shakes Libby's hand awkwardly. He refuses to shake hers.

They watch them as they walk into the hallway. That's when

Helen Jefferson speaks again, even louder, her words clattering into the empty corridor. "Ted – don't let it happen again."

━━━━━━━━━━━━━━━━━━

Libby left quickly, promised to call, arrange the assessment. She was tired, needed to get home for the girls. It was clear she did not want a discussion. She did not want to talk about what they heard Helen Jefferson say. She even forgot Ruby-May's notebook. And now Ruby-May has been in her classroom for fifteen minutes. The janitor came with his whizzing 'n' whirring machine, wanting to buffer the floors. When she finally noticed him standing there in the doorway, she waved him in, but he must've seen something in her expression (the rolled-up Kleenexes might have also been a clue) because he said he'd come back.

She knows she should leave, the walk usually helps, although something tells her not even that twenty-minute walk will help today. Her cell rings again. Randolph. *Sweet* Randolph. The meeting had to be today, didn't it? There had been a lot of different April 10th s. Some good, some not so good. April 10th was the day they made a promise. They would always remember it as a good day. And twenty years ago, it was the best.

It was a Sunday.

She looks down at the cell, she has let it ring three times. This time she answers.

"I'm right outside," he says.

"You are?"

"I know it must've been a tough day, sugar. And I thought, being it's a special number an' all, maybe you wanted to swing by the special place."

That man *always knows.*

"Sure."

"I bought candles."

"Okay."

"Don't be long."

No fuss. No tears. Only celebration. That is what today is supposed to be. Because twenty years ago Ruby-May was dancing around that room in their first little house with her arms out, as happy as the day she married Randolph. It had taken them seven years for it to finally happen – a couple of months after her twenty-seventh birthday, a month after Randolph was promoted to Chief Editor at the *Jacksonville Daily*. Like all their prayers were answered at once. And April 10th was when they found out about the baby.

Slowly she stands.

Before she leaves, she is sure she sees that little blue bird in the corner flap its wings, even though the window is closed. She thinks back to what April said in the classroom that day about that E.E. Cummings's book called *Selected Poems*.

She never answered her question then. She had only known April a week and not many children surprised her – but April Jefferson was never like other children. And soon that will be official. No way to stop it now. She tugs her bag onto her shoulder; her feet make a quiet clop on the classroom floor. The janitor is whizzing 'n' whirring in the classroom next door and her sweet wonderful Randolph is waiting outside, because he knows. He *always knows* what she needs, even before she does. They don't always go to the special place, but today is a special number and he *always knows*.

Just like he knows how they felt that day. They never knew joy could be so pure.

As she turns out the light and closes the classroom door with a soft click, Ruby-May thinks about that feeling, that flutter. It was gone three weeks later. It never came again.

April 10th is a day to celebrate life – even life that was – and then wasn't.

April 10th was a day twenty years ago when everything was as perfect as it would ever be: untainted, unbroken, expectant. That's the feeling they try to hold on to.

April 10th, 1983 was the day Ruby-May found out she carried another heart inside her. But not for long enough to know who he or she was *supposed* to be.

So today they will light a candle in a little corner of Clayton Memorial Park; not pink or blue, just white, like the jasmine that grows there.

And not in a cemetery – in the remembrance garden – because sometimes there is nothing to bury.

Jasmine, Ruby-May told Randolph is a shy little flower.

"How can a flower be shy?"

She had looked him right in the eye. "Because it only blooms at night, yet this tiny flower has enough scent to sweeten every day."

Chapter 4

I

May 2nd, 1964, Jacksonville, Florida

A wedding takes a whole lot of preparation. Molly says it's all in *the preparation.* But even with the best preparation, George did not expect to be in Jacksonville. Not the day he is *supposed* to wed Molly Ann Collins.

The cemetery is on the corner of Williams and Duval. George has been standing at the gate since the bus set him down. The morning sun is still beating down hard. The wind is whipping up the scent of the wildflowers. Sweet, musky. He doesn't know their names. Grandmomma was always good with that. Her voice's been in his head the whole fifteen minutes he's been standing here. But it's not the only voice. While he sat on that bus yesterday, the nearer he got to Jacksonville, the louder the *chitter-chatter.* Although he's pretty sure it was Grandmomma saying *what you doin', George? You got cold feet?* And as he pressed his head to the glass, listened to the *judder-judder,* he had a whole lot of time for thinking. Only this is not cold feet.

Everyone knows George Tucker is not good enough for Molly Ann Collins.

George never told anyone he was coming. It's not like it was planned.

Yesterday he was having breakfast with Molly at their favorite place. It was supposed to be the very last time they went to Lane's as single folks, before Molly Ann Collins became Molly Ann *Tucker*.

And now she won't.

Next thing George was running.

Molly was crying, calling out his name, but George just kept on running – let the words fly right past. Ran all the way back to

Momma's house. Paced up and down his room, counting the paces, all he could think about was the way she looked at him; like she didn't know him. His momma was working at the laundromat. Before he had time to think, he was on his way to the bus station. Didn't even leave a note. Just enough money in his pocket for the bus fare.

In his head, words were getting all mixed up. He'd done the one thing he promised he never would. George Tucker broke Molly Collins's heart. And then he ran. *George is a coward. A big fat coward.* Just like everyone said.

So that's how George came to be in Jacksonville on what is supposed to be his wedding day. In truth George's been thinking about this trip since the day he left Clayton. He just hadn't figured on it being today.

On that bus he thought about the day he left. A lot's happened since. Molly is the best part. And now he feels the ache click his throat. But Molly could do a whole lot better than George. He heard them say it. Heard his very own step-pap say it to Momma three days ago. He wasn't meant to hear it but he did and now he can't *unhear* it. He said George needs to hold down a job – or how else is he supposed to support a wife? Grandmomma would've come to his defense, say *he can't help it if he ain't the sociable type.* Only his grandmomma is gone and this time his step-pap is right. He wonders what Grandmomma would say now. *George Tucker has messed everythin' up again.*

It was supposed to be a small wedding. Just like Molly said. But with her daddy being a preacher that was never gonna happen. George has been keeping his mouth shut his whole life – why'd he have to say something now? But if there's one thing George is, is honest. How could he stand up in a church, in front of all them people, when he doesn't believe in God? And how can he believe in God after what happened on his fifteenth birthday?

Clayton might be the past, but Clayton is where Abe is. And now, so is George.

What George wouldn't give right now to sit and talk with his big brother. Abe would put him straight, *unmess* his head. When they were kids, they made each other a promise. That's what was in his head when he got on that bus yesterday morning. A promise made when George was ten, though he wasn't thinking about girls then; it was way before Chloe Johnson took his eye, and Molly Collins took his heart. Right there in front of that poster of Jackie Robinson. *I'll be your best man, if you be mine*; spat on their palms and shook on it.

Now Abe is gone and Cousin Thomas will be wondering what to do with that speech.

On those buses, a whole day of *hoppedy-hopping*, George had a lot of time for thinking. He thought of all the things in life you can't undo. You can get off a bus but you can't *uncatch* it. You can cancel a wedding but you can't unmake the cake or unwrite a speech. Of course, Molly was the one who got busy with all *the preparation*. He wonders if you *unprepare* once you get prepared. Those preparations kept Molly and her momma busy these past few months. Especially *that* dress. It's the *hush-whisper* dress. He wasn't allowed to see it. All he knows is Marcie Collins has made it from the best lace. *Too fancy*, Molly says. But nothing is too fancy for Molly.

He wonders what will happen to the *hush-whisper* dress now. Now it's made, you can't unmake it.

Clayton Cemetery was one of the first Negro cemeteries in Jacksonville. A lot of things changed in ten years since they began the *desegregation* but he doubts any white folk would want to be buried next to a Negro. Or any Negroes want to be buried next to a white man for that matter.

Folks talk a lot about the changes. Seems to George like everything is exactly the same. He still uses the colored library. A couple of months back, four students in St. Helena, in Greensburg, Louisiana, were shot at for wanting to use the public library. George did vote; everyone said that democratic president was on the side of the Negroes. He's not so sure soldiers all get treated the same; now they're fighting in Vietnam. Makes him think about Langston Hughes saying *I, too, am America*. He looks on through the gate, thinks about all the soldiers buried inside. He thinks about Abe, the last time he saw him.

He's never talked to Molly about what happened. He never even told her he had a brother. He's not talked to Molly about a lot of things. Like the voices in his head. Or about the fight the night his pap dropped down dead. That was the last time George threw a punch. First time was his best friend in school, but that was different.

Everyone knows George doesn't have God, he has the devil inside him. Another reason why he can't marry Molly.

Yesterday at Lane's was not first time he and Molly have gotten into a fight; except the other times they were more differences of opinion. Last time was when Molly was talking about enrolling in nursing school, her dream, but what if she wasn't any good; maybe she'd wait until after they were wed and George saying what was the point in waiting, Molly would be a great nurse. It was not like the *differences of opinion* that Pap or even his step-pap had with his momma. Those were more than differences of opinion. Seems like his momma chose another man who liked to use his fists to make a point. But with Molly it wasn't like that. And George would never use his fists again.

All George wanted was a simple ceremony – at City Hall. Like Momma did with John Langton – only that's probably not the best example. They never told no one. George only knew because when they were fighting, he said how *she was a lousy wife – should never had gotten wed*. That's how he said it. *Was a drunken mistake.* Couldn't *unhear* that either, or Momma's sobs or the making up afterwards.

Only he always knew they would not get wed in City Hall – he was marrying the daughter of a preacher. But he was okay with that part; he had been to that little Baptist chapel in Acacia Hills, only the one time, found excuses the other times, but it wasn't so bad.

He even smiled like he believed. But this was different – how could he make vows – in front of all them people? Vows is serious business, like *cross-your-heart* promises.

Molly deserves better. That's what he told her.

What George has learned about weddings, since Thanksgiving at the Collins's house, is pretty soon they take on a whole life of their own. It started out as ten – *immediate* family only – at that chapel, George could do that. But now there's seventy-five.

Seventy-five people.

George did not think he knew seventy-five people, but that's how many'll be packing out that chapel in Acacia Hills, Atlanta, at 3 pm this very afternoon. All come to see for themselves the man the preacher's daughter said yes to last Fall.

Or at least that's what was meant to happen.

He tried to say something but that was before everyone got too excited with their bellies full of turkey, and mud pie, and Mr. Collins's Jamaican rum. They'd only been engaged a week. *Saying no point in waiting too long. Get wed, start a family.* He tried to say it then, *nothing too fancy and nothing too big neither.* George never was good at speaking his mind. And even when he did, he learned a long time ago, no one listened. Besides, how could he tell *his Molly* with that smile, how he only wanted a small wedding. It sounded like he didn't want to show her off. And if there's one thing George *always* wanted – it was to show off Molly Ann Collins.

You can't get wed to a preacher's daughter when you don't believe in God. That's what he said and now he can't unsee *the look* Molly gave him in Lane's. Like she doesn't know him at all. And maybe she doesn't. He told her he was not good enough for her, she deserved someone better. Someone with a decent job who could take care of her; not someone who couldn't even hold down a job without getting his-self fired. Parking lot attendant, lasted a week, gas station two weeks, local hardware store a month (better), even tried working elevators in the black hotel, only you need to be sociable for that. George is *different. George ain't sociable.* George's face never fits. And once George started with the *jibber-*

jabber, all the words he'd been storing up, gushed right out along with his tears. He didn't wait for her to answer. Because after that all there was to do was run. And now he's here.

Can't undo the past, George. Can't uncry the tears. And now he thinks he can't *unsay* the words.

Now George is all *blubber-blubber,* looking in through the gates of a cemetery and Molly won't get to wear the *hush-whisper* dress.

There's a tissue crumpled to mulch between George's fingers. He made a promise last Fall, in a park in downtown Dallas, only now it's undone. That trip *was* planned; that trip was more planned that any trip George had ever taken in his life. Not that he has taken many trips. Nettie is good with the planning. Seems she and Molly are good friends now – which probably means Nettie'll hate him too.

It was long weekend that started on a Thursday, staying with Molly's family: Aunt Nina, her pap's sister, and her husband, Uncle Louis. They also got to visit with her aunt Daphne and Uncle Benjamin. George is not so good with families. But it was hard not to like her cousin Lydia, just turned sixteen. She has a baby brother too. Turns out *their* pap – Uncle Benjamin – is a preacher just like his brother.

It was all planned out: the picnic, the park and the ring. He must've checked his grandmomma's engagement ring was still in his pocket so many times Molly told him to *quit with the fidgetin'.* She must've wondered why he barely touched that pie Aunt Nina made specially. And then when Molly was done eating, she must've thought he'd tripped on his laces, wouldn't be the first time, he does get clumsy when he's nervous, she was telling him *get up, George,* until she realized the real reason he was on one knee. She said yes even before he got all the words out.

George would say that was the best day of his life. Apart from the day they met. Today was *meant to be* the best of all. Just like Abe was *meant to be* the best man. Only some things don't get to be.

Lots of folks will remember that day when Molly said yes in a park in downtown Dallas. They'll remember exactly where they were and what they were doing because of what was happening at another park in downtown Dallas. It probably happened while George was still fumbling to put his grandmomma's engagement ring on Molly's finger. They were so caught up with themselves they didn't know it until they got back to her aunt's house. It was Cousin Lydia who said it. She was already waiting for them, said she'd come to invite Molly shopping, there was a special dress shop, *real cheap, real close*. Lydia told them the news; said she heard it official from a friend. Though she said she knew it would happen even before it did.

Just six months later George has broken his promise to Molly. But if he knows one thing: Molly will learn to *unlove* him, learn to love someone else. Just like Pattie Holmes, she even went and married Walt Robbins. Some people just seem to breeze through life, some don't. Molly is a *breezer*. And one day she'll marry the man she's supposed to, find the man who believes in God, who knows how to take care of her. Because George is not a *breezer*. George is broken. And sometimes things get so broken they can never be fixed. Like a president.

———————————————

George does not go into Clayton Cemetery. Came all this way, even slept in a park, if you can call it sleeping. Then he turns right around and heads back to the bus stop. It was a voice that told him to come, like all those other times. He'd been watching the sun come up as he sat there waking up with the birds thinking how it was meant to be his wedding day; and he knew he just had to. Next thing he as catching the bus to Clayton Cemetery. He even spent his sixteenth birthday right here. That was until Momma and Pap dragged him home. They said it was not healthy for a boy of sixteen to spend so much time at a graveside. Even Grandmomma said he needed to stop; made him do a *cross-your-heart* promise in exchange for extra birthday cake. Lemon of course. She said he had to say it out loud. It was that *cross-your-heart* promise that got

George talking again for the first time in a year. *Got to look forward, not back* Grandmomma said. President Kennedy said something similar, only he said something like you *got to know where you'd been, to know where you're heading.* Maybe that's why George came back.

George doesn't go in because he's still keeping that promise to Grandmomma.

Everyone knows you can't break a *cross-your-heart* promise. Maybe that's the kind he should have made when he promised to marry Molly. Only Grandmomma's promise wasn't about extra cake, even if it was lemon; it was hearing his momma say that first time, when they were dragging him home on his sixteenth birthday, how *maybe George needed to see someone. That it wasn't normal.* She meant it too, he could see it in her face. *It weren't normal: all them hours at the cemetery, him not talking to no one.* That was before she knew about the voices.

And today, after he's stood there looking in, smelled the wildflowers, he leaves. Besides, what would he say if he did go in: he's still sorry? Sorry he gets to carry on living? He doesn't go back to the bus station, not yet. There's something he needs to do first.

Go back and find your girl. That's what Grandmomma would tell him he needs to do first.

But it's too late for that. With so many secrets, George will never be good enough. Period.

George rides a bus that *chug-chugs* itself up Williams, right past the place where his school used to be. He hears someone say it had burned down a few months back. He doesn't know if they mean burned the way the Klan burned down all those buildings. This whole area, right down to where he used to live is nothing like it was; same as what happened on East Washington. Whole place has been bulldozed and rebuilt. The bus goes all the way up to Duval – even that's changed – don't need two buses to get there. George tells the driver he wants to get off. He has thought about this for a long time. Though nothing is the way you think it.

Though George knew the place had changed, you don't really see it, until you *see it*. The house where we grew up's long gone. It's a whole new neighborhood: new houses, new streets and even new street names. No Denzel Street; now names sound like trees.

The street is gone.

The house is gone.

The stoop is gone.

But not the memories.

Not Momma's roses. He thinks he still sees them but he probably doesn't. Just like he thinks he hears the voices inside his head.

George walks the whole of Denzel Street. To him, that's what it will always be, not a fancy new name like Tabebuia Drive. As he walks, he shoos memories out of every corner. And at every corner, he thinks, right before he turns, he'll see his brother. Stood right there waiting on him. George saying how he better have a fancy suit if he's to be his best man.

But there will be no wedding. Just as there is no Abe.

Jacksonville is a city of ghosts.

———————————

There's an orange tree in Hemming Park. Snuggled right on the corner, away from everything else. George has been sat under that tree for long enough that if he had got wed today, they'd be cutting that cake about now. He ran out of tissues, then out of tears. He has just enough money for the bus ride home. He stood in that bus station looking at all the names on the front of the buses. George does not belong any place, not here, not Atlanta. He thought about jumping on the next bus out, wherever it was heading; but once he got there, he wouldn't get far with nickels and dimes. For a moment, stood there, just like he did at the cemetery, he wondered if he's been standing on the outside for his whole life. That's when he turned around and came to Hemming Park, oldest park in Jacksonville.

When it got to three o'clock this is where he was sat, thinking about the seventy-five people waiting at the chapel or if maybe someone told them not to come. He wishes he had more tissues.

What happened, George?

It's only when the voice comes for a second and then a third time, even louder, that he realizes it's not inside his head. But one thing George does not expect when he opens his eyes is Molly.

Molly in yellow, all *shimmer-shimmer* like the sunshine.

She bought that dress in Dallas. It was the day after Mr. Kennedy was shot.

George thinks he might be dreaming it. Or maybe Molly's a mirage in the late afternoon sunshine. But Molly is anything but a mirage. Molly is standing right there in front of him as real as this orange tree. And beside her are Cousin Thomas and his wife Nettie. Cousin Thomas is dressed up smart in a blue suit like he still planned on going to a wedding and Nettie in a short purple dress, she is as tall and thin as a cotton plant. They look mad. Molly ought to look mad but all he sees on *his Molly's* beautiful face is relief. And she is beautiful – most beautiful thing he ever saw in that dress. First time she's worn it. But she's not *his,* not anymore. And today there's no smile. She says the same words for a fourth time, like he didn't hear right all the other times.

"What happened, George?"

It was Cousin Thomas who worked out there was only one place George would go. And since he was not at Momma's or at the library or at the park reading, then he was probably in Clayton, Jacksonville. It's a long way to come if they'd been wrong and it's just as well Cousin Thomas got himself a fancy new car (this time not a station wagon), because it took them best part of seven hours with the weekend traffic. No wonder they looked mad. Then they had to find him. They didn't know he would be in Hemming Park of course, but when they'd figured since he wasn't in their old neighborhood, then he probably wasn't too far from the bus station. It was Molly who spotted him first. She said he knew he would be away from everyone else; that's George.

Molly has been standing in front of George for a couple of

minutes. She steps towards him. He braces himself, ready for the angry words. Only they don't come. Instead, she throws her arms around him in a grandmomma bear-hug, pulls him so tight she's wrinkling the *shimmer-shimmer*. Now they're clinging onto one another like they're drowning, hard to tell who's rescuing who. Next thing they're both blubbering. There are no angry words – just one word – the same word over and over.

Sorry.

But it's not George who says it first.

Only it don't matter, don't change a thing. Everyone knows it's too late.

Cousin Thomas and Nettie have gone to find a payphone, to call his momma. Nettie says they can all stay with her sister over in Picketville tonight; says it'll be a squeeze, cozy, but no one wants to be driving all the way back tonight.

"George," Molly says. "I told you, I'm the one who should be sorry."

"You need someone a whole lot better. Look at me."

"I am looking at you, George. You the only one I want to look at. Don't tell me what I need."

George shakes his head. Looks across towards the fountain.

"It don't matter what you say, George."

"But I got a past, somethin' happened."

And he wants to say it, to tell her. But he can't. How can he?

"Who doesn't got a past, George?"

She stands back so he can see her face, eyes all shining like the *shimmer-shimmer*. She's got them yellow shoes on too Cousin Lydia gave her.

"George, I knew you didn't want all of this, it's Daddy, invitin' all them folk. I should've stopped them – this is our wedding. We should've kept to the way we planned it."

Her hand pushes into his, light glinting off Grandmomma's engagement ring like she's right here winking at him. "And what you said, George. I know how you feel about God. I always knew that."

Before he can speak, she says, "I know an excuse *not to go to church* when I hear it, George, don't matter to me. Can't we jus' start over?"

He catches sight of Cousin Thomas walking towards them, Nettie, walking with attitude. He looks back at Molly. "Everyone knows a preacher's daughter gotta marry a man who believe in—"

She presses her fingers to his lips. "Love. Love is all your gotta believe in. Anyway, when did we care 'bout what everyone thinks?"

"But, everyone—"

"Hush now, George. You and me are different, we make our own rules."

"But Molly, I ain't who you think I am."

"Well then, we got a whole lifetime to find out who you really are, George, don't we?" She pinches his hand. "I'll take my chances."

"But Molly—"

"I don't care, George. 'bout nothin' else. When I told your grandmomma how much I loved you, that very last time we saw her in the hospital, I made her a promise."

"What kind of promise?"

"There are kinds? A dying-wish kind, that's all I know."

"Did she make you cross your heart?"

"I believe she did."

George feels a tear roll itself right along his cheek.

"Do you love me, George Tucker?"

"I always loved you, since that first time I saw you waitin' at the drugstore."

"Then let's do it our way, me and you and Thomas and Nettie can be our witnesses. Marry me, George Tucker. Marry me right here and now in Jacksonville, at City Hall, if that's what you want. We got witnesses. I got this dress." She sways her hips, sashays for him, then looks at Cousin Thomas and Nettie. "That's if you'll still have me."

And right there in that little corner of Hemming Park, about the time George and Molly were meant to be having their first dance,

Molly leaned in for a kiss and just like that, it seems that *some* things can be undone, a mistake can be *unmade*.

And turns out, all you need is a kiss.

II

May 2ⁿᵈ, 2003, Jacksonville, Florida

They mustn't see, mustn't know the secrets. Some things have to stay tucked in tight.

That's what April knows – tucked inside the way a cat sleeps, tucked around itself. The letter came last week. Mrs. Johnston said April has to meet with the school's educational psychologist. That's *not* what Pops calls her. She'd heard him mumbling to Grams, saying that *no shrink could help Catherine*. All April knows is she has to do well, say the right things, be prepared, like studying for a test – she is always good at tests. She knows what happened to her mom, it's the thing no one talks about. And she mustn't tell. Especially Miss Gerard.

At lunch, April makes an effort to sit with Hannah – Hannah with the big flicky blonde hair, only Hannah doesn't just flick her hair, she flicks her finger and in a *pathetic* voice says these seats are taken – the way April has done to her so many times she's lost count. But with her, the seats *were* taken. She is ready to say something back when she sees Mrs. Johnston is still standing the other side of the cafeteria. *Best behavior, April Jefferson.* She picks up her tray, moves to the next table, where goof-ball Simon Morgan is with his bunch of nerdy friends. It's the freak table. He offers her his apple. Is he for real? She shakes her head, gets out her book. It's a book she borrowed from Clayton Library. She feels the bite of Mrs. Johnston's stare the whole time she eats her chicken sandwich, head pored over Louis Simpson's *At The End of the Open Road.* All she has to do today is act *normal.* Maybe she should've said yes to the apple. How hard can it be to act normal?

Normal is relative. April's normal is just another kind. What's so wrong about that?

April has made it to afternoon recess. Mrs. Johnston has told her she does not need to go to Mr. Burke's math class. She is excused. That way her appointment with Miss Gerard does not have to be in her own time.

Miss Gerard's office is close to reception. She asks April to sit down opposite her. Room smells sweet, like someone's been eating cinnamon buns. Miss Gerard has blonde hair; it's pulled off her face which makes her look stern. She's tall, but not slim – white blouse and black pants pinching. Maybe she likes cream pie like Martha. She knows the kinds of kids they send to see Miss Gerard. But she is not like any of *those kids.*

The conversation is all sweetness and polite-talk. She tells herself: *talk the talk, April.* How does she like her classes? "Great." How does she like her teachers? "Great." How do you like you classmates? "Great." Everything is just great. *Nothing wrong with April Jefferson.*

Miss Gerard has a *pondering* face, like she's planning on her next move while April studies her hands, threads her fingers together then stops. They watch your body language. *Give nothing away, April.*

It's like ping-pong. Polite question. Polite answer. Keep your hands still. April says she does not have a favorite class because she loves them all. They're all *great.* Miss Gerard leans in closer, a notebook on her lap but she doesn't write anything. She says, "Then why do you cut class so much?"

She's good.

April shrugs. She ought to come up with a smart answer; she was here four and a half days last week, what more do they want? But all she's got is *her friends need her more.* And they do, they really do. But Miss Gerard won't like that. A shrug is the safer bet. She plays out the rules in her head as she straightens up on the seat. *Don't say too much. Don't tell them about your mom. Don't let them think you're crazy.*

"Where do you go when you cut school?"

She can't say she's with her friends, can't get them into trouble. "Library mostly."

"Okay, that's good, April. But we need to understand *why* you cut class; if it's something happening in school, we can help."

"You mean like… bullying?"

That gets her interest. But April's not playing silly games. She wants this over; she needs to get home. She has plans.

"Is someone bullying you?"

She shakes her head. Okay, so Owen used to bully her but that was when she was small and not in a long time.

"So, is it something *about* the classes?"

April's eyes are drawn to the window where the blinds are open enough to see into the yard.

"Do you find classes *too*—"

"Boring?"

"I was going to say *easy*, but okay, you find the classes *boring*?"

"Maybe."

"Because they're too easy?"

"Maybe."

"Do you cut class because you're not learning anything new? Is that it?"

"Maybe."

April finally looks back at Miss Gerard.

"If it is, we can help with that. We can give you extra work, things that you'll find less *boring*. More of a challenge."

"Great." Just what she needs, a challenge. She has enough to deal with with her friends and their troubles.

Miss Gerard writes something down. Did she pass?

"Okay, now let's talk about your friends. Start with their names?"

Like she doesn't know? Come on.

Tell them what they already know, April. It's not a trick.

April says the five names, reels them off straight while Miss Gerard just carries on staring. Miss Gerard already knows this. Miss Gerard is playing *the game*. But April's not dumb, not a *retard* like the other kids she sees.

Mistake number one. April did not mean to mumble or to say that out loud. Now Miss Gerard is giving her the stare. It's the one Mrs. Johnston uses when April's acting up in class. "Retard is not polite, nor is the right word," she says. "You know better than that, April."

"It's not my word."

"Then whose is it?"

She shrugs. *Keep it zipped, April.*

There are trees in the school yard, the window is open just enough for the smells of spring to skip right in. Wind chimes make a soft tinkly-ding, soft as a whisper. They're in the tree that's right outside Mr. Burke's classroom; she often listens to them during class. It's where she is supposed to be now, learning algebra. She's not sure which is worse.

"April? Are you listening? I said tell me about these friends."

She turns back to meet Miss Gerard's curious but not so friendly stare. "What d'you want to know?"

"Anything you want to tell me."

She shrugs. Waits. *Don't tell 'em anything they don't ask.*

"How about you start with the first time you met them. Tell me about that. I heard you were, like, three years old?"

"Maybe."

"You're not sure?"

"Do you remember when you were three years old?"

"Good point. So, how about kindergarten?"

"Yeah, of course."

"Okay."

"You remember the first time you spoke to them?"

"No."

"Are they here now?"

April rolls her eyes. She does not like the falseness of the smile she sees right now on Miss Gerard's face. Makes her look butt-ugly. Jesse thinks so too. *More hush, less mumble, April.*

Too late. Mistake number two: best not call the educational psychologist "butt-ugly", even if you were supposed to keep the thought tucked in tight. But April is not answering that dumb-ass question. Sure they're here. They're *always* here. Most of the time anyway.

Libby Gerard does not tell her off for calling her butt-ugly, all she says is, "April, do you know what imaginary friends are?"

Jesus. She does think she's a fucking retard now? Is she for real?

"Do you think Jesse, Owen, Grace, Rose and Martha are imaginary friends?"

That's it. She drags her backpack up from where it sits at her feet. Rests it on her knee. The shiny angel on the zipper makes a rainbow on the blue carpet. She lifts her finger lightly tracing its arc in mid-air.

"April – I asked you a question."

"Nope. They are not, and you can quit with the fuckin' questions."

Mistake number three. Not good to use the fuck word when you're trying to prove to the educational psychologist you are *normal*. Except using the fuck word is pretty normal – her dad uses it all the time. Or he did; she assumes he still does.

"I'm going to let that go for now, but don't you ever tell me—"

"Sorry." *Act normal, April.* "Sorry I didn't mean that."

Miss Gerard nods. "Okay. Let's just move on. Why don't you tell me about your other friends?"

"What other friends?"

"You don't have other friends?"

She shrugs.

"These are your only friends?"

"Isn't five enough?"

"Okay, okay. Then tell me, do your friends ever tell you do things, April?"

"Like what?"

"Cut school, talk back to the teacher, disrupt lessons?"

She's had enough. Miss Gerard knows all of this. She shuffles on the seat; turns so she does not have to look right at Miss Gerard.

"What's going on, April?"

"Nothing. Everything's great."

"Only that's not true is it?"

"It's all fucking great."

Uh-oh. Might that be mistake number four but does it still count? She already used the fuck word. Same bad.

"Less of the colorful language. April, I have to tell you we're all worried about you. Sometimes Mrs. Johnston says you get so agitated in class, she can't console you. She says you shout and you scream and… she's worried, okay. We all are."

Snitch. No one likes a snitch. No one likes a coward…

She looks at the window. She needs to leave.

"What's it like living with your grandparents?"

April looks back, what is she up to now? Changing tack? Is it a trick?

"Great."

"And your parents?"

"I don't live with my parents."

Another trick? April is on to her.

"Tell me something about that."

No way.

"It can't be easy losing your mom so young."

"If you say so."

"Do you think about her?"

"I don't remember her."

"It doesn't say here how she died. Was she sick?"

Say nothing. There's a good April, do it for Pops.

"I don't remember."

"What about your dad?"

"Sure… I remember him. I have a camping trip with him next weekend."

Miss Gerard nods. "So, you get on well with your dad?"

"Kind of."

"And how often do you see him? I heard he wasn't around."

April turns the angel between her fingers. He's promised her a road trip, maybe down to Sugar Loaf. She feels the burn of Miss Gerard's stare.

"Yes, *he is* around. You think I'm making this up? An imaginary dad?"

Is that a smile?

"He's taken you camping before?"

"Sure."

She doesn't tell her about all the times she was all packed up ready when he didn't show. But he will this time. He forgot her fifteenth birthday but this time he'll show. He promised: *cross my heart.*

83

"You like hanging out with him?"

"Most of the time."

"Not all of the time?"

Will she quit?

"He has his problems."

Oh, so now she's interested again? This whole thing sucks. At least they're not taking about her mom.

"What kind of problems?"

"Just stuff."

"How do your grandparents get on with him?"

"They hate him."

"Now I'm sure that can't be—"

"Miss Gerard, they hate him. He isn't allowed in the house."

"Do you know why?"

"Isn't hating him enough?"

"But why do they hate him?"

Keep it zipped, April. Pay attention.

She glances at the clock. Seems like it's almost time for the bell.

Miss Gerard lifts a sheet of paper from her lap.

"I ask everyone to fill this in; it's about what you like and don't like in school and what we can do to make you like classes more. What you struggle the most to learn, that kind of thing."

"I already told you."

"I know, but I want you write it down. It's easy to forget when we're sitting here like this. So which classes in particular do you find *boring,* for example? Bring it next week; I'd like us to meet again, okay?"

Does it make any difference if it's not?

April nods.

"This is like homework?"

"If you want to think of it that way. We're just trying to figure things out; we're on your side. You need to know that."

"I didn't know there *were* sides."

She slides the questionnaire into the front pocket of her pack. "Miss Gerard?"

"Yes, April."

"What you said, about *imaginary friends*?"

"Yes."

"I want you to know I'm not crazy."

"No one thinks you're—"

"My friends, all of them, are real."

"Okay."

She has to pass, doesn't want to see a shrink. She straightens herself in the chair, takes a deep breath. "They're not bad, you should know that too. They just… they… they're like my dad, okay."

"In what way like your dad?"

"Troubled."

"In what way?"

"Guilty of wrongful deeds."

"What do you mean, April?

She has her hands pressed to her ears, feels the soft rock of her body. *Straighten up. Act normal.*

"Wrongful deeds must no longer go unpunished."

"What wrongful deeds, April? You know this, here," Miss Gerard opens her hands out, "is a safe place. In this room you can tell me anything, April. You can trust me. Is this about your dad?"

"Can't trust no one."

She doesn't even realize she's mumbling or crying until Miss Gerard holds out a box of Kleenex. She's said too much – but nothing about her mom. She never told.

"Can I go now?"

"Who can't you trust?"

"No one!" This time she knows she's shouting, now she's standing, fingers tightly clasping the handle of her pack.

"Let me ask you one more question, April, then you can go, okay?"

She nods. If it will get her out of here sooner.

"Do you feel like you're in any kind of danger?"

"All the time."

"At home?"

She turns back to the window. "Nowhere's safe."

"April, does it help having your friends around you, when you're worried or sad or feeling unsafe? Like you just need someone?"

"Miss Gerard, you do know what friends are, don't you? Of course it does!"

"So how do they help? They talk to you?"

She said one more question. Why do they always have to lie? All teachers lie. So do educational psychologists.

"Last one," Miss Gerard says, like she's reading her mind, "I promise." April knows this time she had her lips glued good and tight.

"What was the question?"

"I said do your friends talk to you? You hear their voices?"

What kind of dumb question is that? She's not deaf.

"Of course, I hear their voices. They're always talking to me."

She is not sure what she sees on Miss Gerard's face as she slings her bag onto her shoulder.

She snaps the door shut behind her. April is pretty sure she must've passed because she never said what happened to her mom. No one has to know about that. Or the bad thing her dad did.

———————

Ruby-May wraps her fingers around her *Great Gatsby* coffee cup and asks Libby to repeat. They're the only ones left. It's been an hour since school was done for the week. The janitor is using his whizzing 'n' whirring machine in the hallways. The staffroom was empty. She'd been planning on leaving when she saw Libby. Usually she has to go before now. She says the girls are with their dad.

Libby is not saying a whole lot. Ruby-May knows *that* look. She's seen it before; Ruby-May should never have told her what happened last time. It was way before Libby came to work at Clayton High School. And now she'll think she's doing it again – getting too close. But this is different. April is not like Billy. This does not have to be clinical.

She unhooks from Libby's pokey gaze, stares into her coffee cup.

"I said have your ever thought something's happening at home?"

"That's what I thought you'd said. And the answer's no."

"She won't talk about her mom."

"I know."

"And the dad?"

"What about him?"

"She says her grandparents won't let him into the house. So, I just looked at the school records, thought maybe we need to talk to him but there's a note on the file."

Ruby-May lowers the cup. "What kind of note?"

"Says if the dad contacts the school or comes to collect her, they're not to let her go with him and to call the Jeffersons right away."

"Dangerous you mean?"

"It doesn't say that."

"Not unusual for there to be notes, you know how families are. If he was dangerous, it would say that, right? It would say call the cops."

"He doesn't have custody of her, Ruby, do we know why?"

"No. But his wife died; he was on his own? Maybe he couldn't cope."

"Maybe. April says she's taking a camping trip with him next weekend."

"Doesn't sound like he's dangerous, sounds like they don't like him."

"That's what April says."

"There you go. They don't like their son-in-law; it's hardly front-page news. It happens."

"You believe everything April says?"

There's a question. April says a lot of things.

"She has some fanciful notions, but I'd say she's honest. Wouldn't you?"

Libby cuts her with a stare so sharp, Ruby-May can almost feel the skin nick. It means *you think I don't know how to do my job?* Ruby-May hadn't planned on catching Libby or asking her how the assessment went but there she was. Libby didn't seem too pleased, but they're friends, surely that counts, so she said she could spare the time it takes to drink a coffee. Besides, she said she had something to ask her. Ruby-May was not expecting it to be *that* question. Sure, April's folks weren't always easy, but a problem? A dead mom and AWOL dad didn't help, but they're decent folks from a decent enough neighborhood.

"But her dad? You think there might be something there?"

"You're serious? Like what... abuse?"

"I'm not saying that. But she said something; I wrote it down, about wrongful deeds that go unpunished. That nowhere's safe. You heard her say anything like that before?"

She stares into her reflection in the coffee cup. Has she? April says a lot of things that don't make sense. A lot of things that sound way beyond something a fifteen-year-old would say.

"Ruby, it sounds to me like April's imaginary friends are a way of covering something up."

Now Libby is all itching and fidgeting like she's said too much and needs to leave. Ruby-May's gaze follows her over to the sink where she swills her cup. She didn't even drink that coffee. She looks like she's done, ready to go but Ruby-May's not done. How can she leave it hanging like that? Oh, she is so not done.

"Dead mom, semi-absent dad, no siblings, grandmother with Alzheimer's, awkward grandfather... that's a lot of stuff. She finds it hard to socialize, so she invents friends. It figures."

But even she knows that doesn't account for all the outbursts, the upsets... the things she says.

Libby still has her cup under the sink, rinsing, back turned away from her. She doesn't respond.

"So, you really think the dad has something to do with this? But 'wrongful deeds'? April quotes poems, it's probably somethin' like that."

Libby shakes her head. "All I'm saying is it's possible."

"Lots of things are possible."

Libby is watching her when she looks back. She hooks the handle of her purse over her wrist. "I really have to go, Ruby."

Suddenly the coffee's lost its appeal. Libby is heading for the doorway.

Maybe she is getting too close. She needs to get home. Randolph says he'll order take-out, hire a movie. Or maybe go out to eat.

At the door, Libby turns. "Have a good weekend. Try not to worry."

Ruby-May walks over to tip her coffee; watches it swirl around the sink and thinks *if only it was that simple.*

Chapter 5

I

May 15th, 1971, Atlanta, Georgia

George clutches on tight to freshly picked blooms. The stamens leave yellow marks on the front of his white shirt. He steps over the clutter of boxes. It's not the best time to be moving; but then Molly wasn't supposed to be in the hospital. That wasn't supposed to happen for at least another month.

His key is looped over his finger, all *jangle-jangle*, as he clumsily tugs at the front door. It's gotten stuck like that ever since they took over the lease, a month after they wed. He catches the scent of White Angel lilac from Molly's pots on the front step. It's one fragrance he does know; always reminds him of his grandmomma.

He juggles with the *jangle-jangle*, manages to get the car door open and sets Molly's blooms down on the passenger seat; they're half-wrapped in old newspaper. He pulls the car door shut with a *slam-clunk*. This rusty old four-door saloon has lasted them well. It was already old when they were given it but not so rusty. It was a belated wedding gift from Mr. Collins, like a whole year belated, which is the time it took him to get over him marrying Molly in Jacksonville in City Hall and not in front of God. Although Molly was quick to remind him God was everywhere, just like he told her. He didn't know what to say to that but even Henry Collins came around in the end.

That car sat out on that street a good few months before George found the pluck to take lessons off Cousin Thomas. George does not like cars; he did not like taking lessons off Cousin Thomas, and George does not like driving. But like Molly said, "If we're gonna start a fam'ly, George, then we're gonna need a ve-hicle."

George was not so sure anyone would give him a driver's license. Seems everything is harder for folk like them, just like registering to vote, borrowing books from the public library and buying a house. Especially buying a house.

No way George ever thought he'd be buying a house.

If only his grandpap was alive to see it. First a voter, now a home-owner – not that he voted for President Nixon – he is not on the side of the Negro, not like Mr. Johnson. But his grandpap would've whooped liked a coyote when that mortgage was finally approved, *from slave to landowner.* He can almost hear him now. The banks are not so keen; that big deposit off Mr. Collins helped a whole lot, of course. "Inheritance early," he said. "Get you started." They changed the law: it was supposed to be easier for Negroes to buy houses, only nothing ever is. Seemed there were an awful lot of *the complications.* Like maybe they forgot about the Fair Housing Act… Cousin Thomas says they don't want Negroes moving into neighborhoods where white folk live, he says it's like they all form a wall. Only Molly had her heart set on that street, on that little house. 131 Peaches Avenue. Nice neighborhood in Grant Park.

They *finally* get the keys next week.

But if it hadn't been for *the complications,* if it had gone like it was meant to, they'd already be in that new house with that baby nursery already waiting.

One good thing: turns out getting a driver's license was a whole lot easier than buying a house, even if George did have to take that test three times. He'd been about ready to give up. But on days like today, he's glad he never. How else will he bring his son home? On the bus?

The old brown sedan still runs well in spite of the rust and the dents. George was not so good at the driving at first but he soon learned to be careful especially when he had Josie-Ann in the car, went so slow that first time when he brought her home from the hospital Molly said it would've been quicker to walk. *Precious cargo,* he told her. *Nothin' ever gonna hurt our daughter.* And today he gets to meet his son.

Last night the nurses told George go home. He'd been there all day. They said they'd call. He wanted to stay; baby was early, what if there were problems? Then she's in the right place they said. *Baby's coming but no point in you bein' here, it won't bring it any faster, Mr. Tucker.* Told him get some sleep. He'll be needing it soon as that baby comes. But he did not get some sleep; not without Molly there. This morning they called.

They still haven't decided on a name. Josie-Ann was named after his grandmomma Josie, and Molly's grandmomma Ann. They still hadn't decided on any names for the new one, whether it was a boy or a girl. They planned to by the time he or she was ready to come; they just hadn't figured on it coming early. Maybe name him after their grandpapas. Follow the pattern. *But Zeb-Zachary?*

George feels the poke of the envelope in the pocket of his pants. Today is most certainly a day for news. Only he's not so sure what Molly will think about this.

The Gradies is a twenty-minute drive. Traffic is quiet, not too many folks out on a Sunday. Josie-Ann is still with Grandmomma Marcie; they like to take her to church, which he is not so keen on, only Molly says at four years old, what harm can it do? Maybe she's right; his own grandmomma did the same thing with him. As he pulls onto the street, he thinks about the first time he held his little girl in his arms. He was so awkward he was sure Molly and his momma were gonna take her right off him; tell him he was not cut out to raise a baby if he couldn't even hold one. Only Molly told Momma leave him be, wait. And she was right – he soon got the hang of it. Molly said the baby just needed to feel safe in his arms. *Support her head, she knows no different, she'll find her way to fit with you.* And she did – a perfect fit. That little girl knows who her daddy is. Molly says she's a daddy's girl. Just like she is. Of course, he never planned on blubbering like a fool first time he saw her when that nurse called him into the hospital room. Never knew he could feel that way about anything, except for Molly. George has written a lot of poems about love, about Molly, but this was different. Sometimes love can feel an awful lot like an ache. Like you're so afraid of something bad happening to them, you forget to enjoy the moments. Grandmomma always used to say you can't live your whole life scared. *Soon as you open your heart to love, you can lose, but what you gon', do? Never love nothin' 'case you lose it?* She used to say it when he was in his dark place, thinking about Abe, about Jacksonville. He misses his grandmomma, that's one ache that sits right there on his chest every day. But he is quite sure she would do her *skippedy-hop* happy dance right across the kitchen, like she used to at that house in Clayton, knowing she was a great grandmomma again. As he pulls away from the sidewalk and drives all the way across town, he is sure he can still smell that White Angel lilac.

The whole drive and later as he parks up, George's mind is full of baby, he also thinks about that envelope. About Molly. She has been telling him for weeks to quit the house painting – he is not a good house painter, to take the job here at The Gradies, they can travel to work together. Just as well her momma is happy to take care of the babies so she can still take some shifts. Times are changing. She says they both need job security, especially with a mortgage to pay. But one thing George knows is he not cut out for cleaning. Soon as he mentioned it, said there was a janitor's job George said no. No. Definitely no and everyone knows George is never that forceful. George has done a lot of jobs. They always say the same thing – *George ain't exactly friendly to folk – George is too much of a daydreamer.* But at thirty-three, now with *two* children – George needs a job that pays good. The one he's been offered will do – *eventually* – but now he has to figure out how to tell Molly he will be working for free. That to start with he'll be an intern. But one thing George knows for sure – this is the one job that does suit.

Picking up the blooms, George heads across the hospital parking lot. Right now, he has to think about his son and later he'll collect Josie-Ann who doesn't even know she has a baby brother yet. And now he has two little people to worry about. Nurses said the new baby might've come early and they had a few problems (what problems?) but he's gonna be just fine. Once he heard *just fine* he forgot to ask: what problems?

George has this. He can do this. He always dreamed about having a son. Being the kind of daddy Pap never was to him. A son to play baseball with, teach him all about Jackie Robinson. Hasn't told Molly yet but the next one, or maybe the one after that, will be baby brother for him. Maybe even a whole baseball team.

Molly is beat; but then she has just had a baby. She keeps on telling him he worries too much; everything is just fine. Only she doesn't look *just fine*. She looks beat.

The baby is too small; but then he is a whole month early. Molly says some babies are smaller than that full-term. She says he is *just fine*. Only he doesn't look *just fine*. He looks fragile.

Josie-Ann was a week late and eight pounds six ounces of noise.

This baby hasn't made a sound, only he's not sleeping, his eyes are wide open. George is afraid to touch him. Of course, he felt the same way first time they put Josie-Ann into his arms. But he looks so *breakable*. Five pounds three ounces of *breakable*.

Everyone keeps on saying how everything is just fine, nothing to worry about but there is *always* something to worry about.

Like why his wife looks so beat and his baby boy so breakable.

"Mr. Tucker, you want to hold him?" the nurse says, taking the flowers from his *quiver-tremble* hands.

George edges closer.

"Why don't you take a seat, I'll be right back when I've put these in a vase and I'll hand him to you."

George nods. He pulls up the chair, gently sits, eyes still on his son, close enough to see his little face clearly. He looks like Josie-Ann only smaller. Same broad nose, same lips. He feels the pull on his heart and the pull of Molly's stare and looks back at her – but her eyes are closed. George can do this. Everyone says it's all fine, then it is. Except what he knows is when they say *everything is fine* so many times, like they're trying to convince themselves, everything is not so fine. *You can't trust no one.*

George has been staring into his son's wrinkled face for the past ten minutes. He feels so light in his arms it's like he just has a hold of the blue blanket they handed him over in. Josie-Ann with her big lungs had been all kicks and fidgets; but this baby is like a doll, just lies still, stares into George's face. He's never seen a baby so placid. "I'm your daddy," he says. He decided on Daddy, not Pap when Josie-Ann was born. George is Daddy, plain and simple, like Molly calls hers. Mr. Collins knows how to be a real father. No way George wanted his children calling him Pap, making him think about the man who made Momma's life miserable for all those years. He doesn't regret what he did – just wishes he did it sooner.

As for his step-pap, he is long gone and good riddance. His momma sorted that one out all on her own. He guesses even she'd had enough of the fighting in the end. Now it's like she found her brave; reinvents herself at least once a week. Last week she said she was gonna enroll on a college course, week before that she was gonna be a singer for Motown, like Diana Ross, even started to grow her hair big. Now she's joined the peace movement.

Molly still has her eyes closed; he lets her sleep. If she was awake, they'd be picking out a name, but Molly needs her rest. Three different nurses already been in to check on her. Now they're waiting on a doctor. They know Molly is a nurse in this very hospital, only she works with the elderly patients, not the babies. She told him once *it's like a revolvin' door: one checks in, one checks out.* George did not find that funny. She said it was not meant to be funny; it's just the way life works.

The door opens again. He expects it to be the doctor.

It's not the doctor.

Or maybe his momma?

It's not his momma either.

Besides, she's supposed to be at a peace rally against the war in Vietnam. Of course, she didn't know this little boy would come early.

It's not Grandmomma Marcie either.

She'll be at church.

Nope, it's someone he does not expect to see.

It's Molly's cousin.

Lydia is standing right there like a vision in a bright pink top and blue jeans. Smiling all wide and white teeth. "George," she says.

95

"Thank God, I been all over this hospital tryin' to find you. Not too late, am I?" She looks at Molly then back at him.

"Too late? You mean for the birth; he was born last—"

Her stare shocks his words right off course; she seems to be looking right at him, he thought Molly had some looks, he's never seen *that* look, like she was looking without seeing. Then like she snaps out of it, she steps closer. "And how's that beautiful little boy? I told her she was having a boy, told her soon as she said she was pregnant."

He takes a good look at Lydia; she's filled out some since he last saw her. She's younger than Molly of course; he does the math, she must be twenty-four. Molly said her momma, Daphne, died whilst cleaning houses, dropped down. That was last month, only what with the pregnancy and all they couldn't go to Dallas.Of course, Marcie and Henry went.

"Why—"

"Am I here?"

George nods.

"We came for a visit with Aunt Ismene – she doesn't live far – invited us at Momma's funeral. But seems lots of things happening in Atlanta, and Marcie, well she said the baby had come early, so here I am. Jimmy is staying on at Aunt Ismene's. Papa has business back home – at the church. He's keeping his-self busy."

Lydia smells sweet, like cookies, as she steps closer to him and softly flicks the edges of the blanket away so she can see his face better. "Sweet," she says. "Like my brother Jimmy was once, not so sweet now."

She straightens up and looks over at Molly.

"She's tired," George says.

Lydia nods, acts like she's about to say something when the door opens again and this time it's the doctor.

Dr. James is white. He's tall, thin, gray-haired, small half-moon glasses. He looks at George and nods before he says something to the nurses. Why do they always talk in whispers? He catches the expression on Lydia's face. He's not so sure he likes it. And what

96

did she mean *is she too late?* He heard about her *intuitions.* Maybe there's something wrong with the baby? Is that what she meant? He looks down, he so small, so… still.

It happens so fast; one second George is holding his son, the next the nurse is taking the baby from him, setting him back down in the crib, asking him and Lydia to please step outside while the doctor examines Molly. Her eyes are closed and now one of the nurses has a hold of her wrist and is slapping out her name. What's happening? Why won't she open her eyes?

"Come along, you can wait outside," the nurse says. The other nurse pulls back the blankets that were covering Molly's legs, that's when he sees what he wishes he didn't – all the blood. It's thick like Jello blood and now his legs are all a-wobble. He feels a hand on his arm. When he turns, it's Lydia.

"Molly!"

The nurse ushers them towards the door. "Let the doctor work."

"What's happening?"

The doctor is now standing in front of her bed.

George is shooed out of that room so fast he doesn't even get to turn around, see her one more time. The nurse is telling them to take a seat in the waiting area. It's the bad-news area; every hospital department has one. He remembers when they told him and Momma Grandmomma was dying. What's happening to Molly? She can't be dying. Not *his Molly.* His legs are trembling, all he wants to do is go back in the room. "Molly…"

"I got you," Lydia says. "Come on, we need to sit."

"Is she dying?"

He looks into Lydia's dark eyes, doesn't know what he sees.

"Is she? Is she dying?" Lydia leads him over to the seats. And now they've got to wait. Just like they did when Grandmomma had that second stroke.

"Lydia, tell me she's not dying. You see all that blood? You asked if you were too late? You knew?"

But all Lydia does is take a hold of his hand, big warm hands just like Molly's and she squeezes. What he needs to hear now is how that is not what she meant, that Molly is gonna be just fine.

And so is that baby boy. Didn't even cry the whole time he's been here and everyone knows babies are supposed to cry. "Is that why you came, you knew somethin' was wrong?"

But Cousin Lydia doesn't say another word.

Hospitals smell. George hates the way they smell, catches in your throat. George hates the noises, machines that go *bleep-bleep*, telephones that ring out. Nurses with their pity faces. He hates it all. He has been waiting fifteen minutes, every time he wants to stand up, stretch out those long legs of his, maybe go ask one of the nurses what's happening. Lydia squeezes on tighter. But she still doesn't speak. Molly says Lydia knows things, but he doesn't want her to know something bad about Molly, or that quiet little baby he hasn't even heard cry yet or given a name to.

Every time he closes his eyes, hoping it will make the time go faster, he sees the blood – all that blood and then he needs to walk and Lydia squeezes on tighter.

Must be another five minutes before he hears his name. Dr. James. There's no expression to read, is this his good-news or his bad-news face? George finally teases his hand from Lydia's grasp as he stands. *Let it be good news. It has to be good news.*

"Mr. Tucker?"

George nods. Lydia now stands at his side.

"Your wife had some bleeding. We've controlled it best we can but we need to take her into theater." It's just as well Lydia is standing right next to him; he feels her hands on his arm, holding him steady.

"It's a known complication, happens to some women. A postpartum bleed, we need to get it stopped…"

"Or she'll die?"

Dr. James has blue eyes, soft blue eyes and George is sure he sees bad news in them now. "We just need to control the bleeding, Mr. Tucker."

The rest could have been another language; next thing Molly's in an OR. Lydia must've heard something he said because she kept on saying how if they could stop the bleeding, she would be fine.

98

So, all they can do now is wait some more.

But what about his baby? Who is looking after the baby?

Lydia says the nurses got it; don't fret. But it's way too late to not fret.

Something's wrong. They've been waiting close to two hours. George walks the halls, counts his steps, goes out into the lot, counts some more. Nurses say soon as there's news someone will come. Lydia fetches coffee. Lots of coffee. All he's got in his head is the bad news. Once you see that blood, with all those clots, you can't unsee it.

If he believed in God then now is when he'd be praying, only one thing he is not doing is praying. All he sees over and over in his head is Dr. James, saying how they did all they could. It's what they say. Lydia has been visiting the payphone, says she can't get hold of Aunt Marcie or Uncle Henry, as they're probably still in the church. She says she'll keep on trying.

George is back in the waiting area counting out coins into Lydia's hand for more coffee when Dr. James appears. As George steps away he hears the *clinkedy-clink* as a coin rolls onto the shiny floor. "Mr. Tucker, your wife lost a lot of blood and there was a complication."

A complication? Seems his whole life is a complication. He feels the pinch of Lydia's fingers on his arm. "The only way to stop the bleeding was to… I'm sorry…"

Sorry? No… no more bad news.

"… perform a hysterectomy." He looks into George's eyes, adds, "We had to take away her womb."

The words don't settle, not until he says, "She'll be fine, Mr. Tucker, but it's a long recovery. We'll let you see her soon."

And the sound that follows is one big puff of relief as he sinks onto the chair. He knows what a hysterectomy is; but all he thinks is she will be fine. She has to be. She can live without a womb. They have two children. Before the doctor turns to leave George says, "My son? Is my son okay?"

"Your son is just fine."

"He seems awful *quiet*?"

"He's fine, Mr. Tucker. Why don't you go right on through and be with him."

He watches him leave, feels Lydia's eyes on his. "I'll stay for a while, in Atlanta, help with the move and the baby," she whispers. "Molly's gonna need time to recover."

As she shifts against the hardness of the seat he thinks about the envelope, the job offer from the public library; he can't be an intern if Molly is too sick to work.

"It's gonna be okay, George."

But it's the way her voice cracks, like she doesn't believe her own words, that sets his heart all jumping. Surely the worse is over – baby's fine, Molly will be fine. Only something's wrong; he sees it in Lydia's face. Now she won't look at him.

"What is it?"

There's that stare again, is she crying?

"Lydia?"

"Molly and that baby gonna be just fine."

"Then what is it?"

She lifts her face to look at him. Big brown eyes all wet with tears.

"It's Uncle Henry."

"Molly's dad?"

"Somethin's happened, George."

"To Henry?"

"I'm so sorry."

"What happened?"

"His heart." She holds her hand to her chest. "This morning, at the church, he... it was quick. Went the same way as my momma."

"That's the real reason you came? You came to tell Molly?"

"No, it hadn't happened then, George."

"And it has now? You spoke to Marcie?"

"No."

"You only think it has; you don't know for sure?"

"I do know, George."

"But, not Henry... Josie-Ann is there."

100

"Come on," Lydia says. "Your son needs you now."

Henry's heart? But he's not dead; she doesn't mean that, right? Only when he looks back at her he knows she does. That's exactly what she means.

All she says is, "We'll need to be strong for Molly."

And for a second, he is sure he smells White Angel lilac. And right there, on that shiny floor is a dime, glinting where the light catches.

II

May 15th, 2003, Jacksonville, Florida

April hates school trips. Especially school trips to museums. And *especially* school trips to *military* museums.

April should've stayed home.

The Museum of Southern History is on Herschel and Lexington, only a short bus ride from Clayton. Pops loves the military museums, probably visited every one. Even tried to take her once, said it might help with her studies. That's when she told him she hated war and she *really* hated guns. She remembers the way he looked at her. She knew it would hurt him. She's seen his old uniform. She knows he was a soldier.

He thinks she doesn't know what happened. He thinks she never saw what her dad did.

Pops keeps his gun locked in the basement.

It's a small museum and it's open just for them – two small classes. It's for a history assignment and Mrs. Johnston also wants them to use it for research, for something creative – a short story or a poem. April likes the sound of a poem, not so much the history.

She sat at the back of the bus; tuned to her Discman on the ride over – it's the Discman Grams bought her for her tenth birthday, the one she thought she'd lost. Of course, most people listen to MP3 players now. She likes her Discman. The CD's still playing as she shuffles in line to the museum, none of the modern stuff, she prefers "Brown Sugar" to "Lady Marmalade". It's her dad's CD. She stole it from his trailer.

The Museum of Southern History is not much to look at – a pokey white box-like building: burgundy door, flag outside flapping its salute in the afternoon sunshine.

Mr. Franklyn, the history teacher, is ticking off names as they enter. Mrs. Johnston is here someplace too. She saw her on the ride over. All she's done all week, since April's camping trip (or *supposed-to-be* camping trip) is ask her a ton of questions.

She pretends like she just wants to know what she did on the weekend at Sugar Loaf – April told her they never made it as far as Sugar Loaf. Of course, then she wanted to know why she never made it as far as Sugar Loaf. April told her the trip was cut short. So, then she wanted to know why it was cut short. All April did was shrug; said they had a fight. She did not want to tell her what really happened. Maybe she should have kept her mouth shut just like Jesse told her. He said people always poke in, ask too many questions. She knows what Mrs. Johnston's doing, same thing Miss Gerard's doing – pretending they actually care when all they want to do is prove she's crazy. Well she's not.

At the door, Mr. Franklyn tells April to turn it off.

"Huh?"

He points to the earphones.

"What?"

She knows exactly what he wants, so she turns the volume higher, shrugs as she steps inside, walking in time to the poppy upbeat of the Rolling Stones singing about a slaver whipping women at midnight.

They're directed to a room full of glass cases, flags and black and white framed photographs. The room is all red, white and blue and the walls are like crazily busy. Mrs. Johnston is standing in front of the blue flag with the red stripes and white stripes, her head against the circle of stars. April feels sick, why'd she come? It's all bullshit. When Mrs. Johnston sees April, she smiles but April digs deeper into the sounds. The words have a groove of their own as the Stones sing about brown sugar tasting so good.

April knows it's too loud, knows it even before Mrs. Johnston gives her the look and mouths her to turn it off. Now *she's* pointing at the earphones. Next thing someone she doesn't know, an old guy with white hair, she guesses someone who must work at the museum, is tapping her on the shoulder and telling her the same thing. This time she reluctantly drags the plugs from her ears and pushes them into the gap in her bag where the Discman sits, presses it off. The whole time under Mrs. Johnston's beady stare.

But she's already told herself – if it gets too boring she's turning it right back on.

She's already had it confiscated three times this week.

Not her fault the classes suck.

And that's exactly what she wrote on that questionnaire Miss Gerard gave her. All over it – in red pen, she wrote about every class: it sucks. She handed it to her last Friday, but in a scaled envelope. She didn't open it right away. Miss Gerard was full of questions too but April knows how this goes and she knows what not to say. Oh, she asked, asked about her dad, about how she got on with her pops (she didn't like those questions), nothing about her mom this time. She wanted to know more about her friends. Mrs. Johnston asked her to write down about them once; she still hasn't. She didn't say a whole lot last week because that was the day her dad was coming over, after school. He'd not taken her on a road trip in a long time and all she could think about was that clock ticking round to home time. Of course, she asked about that too. She told her straight how her pops was not happy about her spending a whole weekend with him. But he's never happy when she sees her dad. He did not want her to go overnight, but she's fifteen now, not five. It's allowed now. She never said that part, or how it was the judge's fault they weren't allowed sleepovers when she was younger. Miss Gerard won't understand. Her dad loves her; doesn't matter what a judge or her grandparents or an educational psychologist thinks about that. Everyone can see it. Daddy loves Peach. He just has some problems. And sometimes he calls her Pumpkin. That's what he used to call her mom.

He wasn't always bad.

He didn't mean to do it.

April sits, looks at the room and waits. This sucks – when does she get to write her poem? She knows they have to work in pairs for the assignment and has already been put with Kevin Spall. At least Kevin is not one of the nerds but Kevin is Mr. Popular, Grade A student and football player. April's already seen the way Hannah looked at her when Mrs. Johnston read out their names. This could be fun. Only Hannah's not the only one who's jealous. Owen is not too happy either. He gets jealous of Jesse too sometimes.

The room is stuffy; smells musty and there's not enough air. April switched off a while back while Kevin, who's sat two rows in front, was frantically scribbling notes. It's all Civil War and Native Americans. She listened at first; now she's wondering why Mrs. Johnston keeps glancing in her direction. The guy at the front, the one with the gray hair who's doing most of the talking, has one of those soporific voices.

Finally, it seems the talk part is done and now it's time for their project. She has the questions someplace and the essay she's supposed to write. Kevin is now making his way towards her. But all she wants is to write a poem. The best poets write about war. She has a book of William Childress poems she borrowed from the public library.

Owen is pissed at April; says she's been too flirtatious with Kevin which *so* isn't true. All she was doing was *being nice,* talking, and only because Mrs. Johnston was watching. She's already reminded her *to be on her best behavior.* Kevin is tall, a mop of dark hair, always looks like it needs a cut, chiseled face, hazel eyes, handsome but everyone knows he's going steady with Hannah. All April wants is for this afternoon to be over. She follows Kevin while he looks at the display cases and reads the notes. Lots of people who work there as volunteers telling them what things mean. She thinks about plugging back into "Brown Sugar". The history assignment is on the Civil War, the Southern Confederacy, not that she knows a whole lot about that, should have paid more attention in class, though Owen says he knows. Well he would, wouldn't he? He's into history. She follows Kevin through into one of the other rooms, more flags on the walls – more display cases – same fetid smell, like flowers that have been in a vase too long. Mr. Popular now holds up his notebook and says, "We need to write how the Confederacy was formed in

1861, which seven states were involved from the start and to…" He flicks the sheet of paper, looks at April. "…discuss the reason behind it, *why* it opposed Lincoln's government…"

"White supremacy," April mumbles and Kevin looks up.

"Huh?"

"That's the reason. White supremacy."

"Yeah, I know."

"Based upon the great truth that the Negro is not equal to the white man; that slavery, subordination to the superior race, is his natural and normal condition."

Until now, she's been acting like she's not been listening, which is true, but that's not the reason for the look on Kevin's face. She's not exactly being quiet, so now one of the volunteers is looking in her direction. Of course, they think she memorized that; they have done this in class, in Junior High too, or she read it off one of the displays but it's Owen whose telling her.

Kevin watches her, then reads some more from the assignment sheet. "Discuss its role and impact in the American Civil War until the thirteenth amendment outlawed slavery."

April stands still. Her eyes drawn to the display case in the corner. Kevin's voice drifts into her mumbles, because she is mumbling now. She can't help herself. See, she told Mrs. Johnston she wanted to work with Owen. All Ruby-May said was Mr. Franklyn had already picked. Owen is now tugging at her hand. "Show you somethin'."

"You okay?" Kevin is now standing next to her.

Behind Kevin she sees Hannah who is talking to Mr. Franklyn, probably saying and that's why no one works with April Jefferson. She's like a total freak. Which she's not. All April is doing is saying what Owen told her.

April wanders away from the Civil War stuff until she's standing in front of the display case in the corner. Kevin says that's not the Civil War Confederacy stuff. She knows that. Does he think she's dumb?

It's a different war. Same one her pops was a soldier in.

But April does not like guns, so why is Owen showing her the guns?

But she knows.

It's a boy thing. Pops likes guns. Her dad likes guns.

It was an accident.

Kevin is now standing behind her. He says again, "You okay? Like seriously, what's up with you?"

April stares in at the collection of... what are these? Muskets?

Nope. Owen tells her to read the label.

Korean War Guns, 1950–1953.

April presses her fingertips to the glass, lightly as if she's reading Braille until she sees. It's the gun labelled Browning Auto-5: Self-loading Shotgun, that's the one. She has seen one of these before. The sign says the distinctive high rear end gives it the nickname "Humpback".

Next thing: tears are dripping, Owen is saying something she doesn't hear, Kevin is gawping at her like now he knows it's true what they say about her. She turns, her blue sneakers squeaking on the shiny museum floor. Which way's out? No time to think. She's running.

"What the fuck?" Kevin's voice bounces off the red, white and blue.

"I need the restroom!" she shouts. One of the volunteers points.

And April keeps on running.

"And she hasn't come back?"

Ruby-May is standing at the bus counting students on, and it comes as no surprise that no one has seen April Jefferson. Kevin Spall says she had one of her *freak-outs* and said she wanted the restroom, but no one has seen her since.

Ruby-May glances at Larry Franklyn. "Go check the restrooms," he says. "I'll carry on with this."

She nods, looks inside the bus where most of the students are now seated, all full of Friday chatter. "Okay, I'll be right back."

Ruby-May nudges the door and steps into the restroom. There's a soapy smell, fruity, like bubble-gum. A soft drip sound coming from one of the taps. Looks like the stalls are empty. Then she sees the last one. Under the door she can see blue sneakers, feet crisscrossed.

"April?"

The name echoes.

"April, sugar, you okay? We're ready to leave now."

When April doesn't answer Ruby-May steps closer.

"I said you okay, April?"

There's a sound. Low, like a soft groan coming from the stall.

"Did somethin' happen?"

Sound gets louder, now she recognizes the April mumbles.

"Can you open the door, sugar?"

"It's not safe."

"Only me here, April. It's quite safe."

"Jesse said hide."

"Well maybe so, but no need to hide now. Bus is waitin' on us."

"Need to get to the closet."

"Closet?"

Now nothing, just eerie quiet and the drip of that tap.

"April, honey. We need to get goin'."

But April has other ideas because now it seems she's sobbing. She wonders if she should tell Larry to leave without her, call April's grandfather. He was meant to meeting with Libby this lunchtime; she wants to get something in place before the summer vacation. They'll be done by now. Or maybe she could get Randolph to swing by and give them a ride home. Only she knows what he'll think about that: she's getting too close. Just like last time. But when April gets like this it can take a while. Only soon as she thinks that, there's a soft click and the door squeals slowly open.

April is sitting on the toilet seat, head bent forward, curls falling over her face, gently rocking. Her pencil case is on her lap and she has what looks like paper crumpled in her hand. Or maybe it's tissue.

"Look at me, April."

She shakes her head.

"April Jefferson, I said look at me."

This time she slowly raises her head; cheeks all pinched pink, eyes all red.

"Oh, sweetie, what happened?"

"Nothing."

"Well, it does not look like nothin'. Kevin says you got upset. Did he say somethin' to you?"

She looks back down. Clenches her fingers over the ball of paper.

"April, did Kevin upset you?"

"Jesse said hide, it's not safe, Mrs. Johnston."

The words come out broken.

She tells her, "Breathe. That's it." She should've noticed she was missing. It's her job to notice. Last time she saw April she'd been with Kevin and looked like she was actually taking an interest, talking to him all sweet, some might even call it flirting and she has never seen April that way. She took her eye off her and now April is crying in the restroom.

"He did a terrible thing, Mrs. Johnston."

"Kevin? What did he do?"

"Not Kevin."

"Then who, April? Who did a terrible thing?"

Ruby-May is seriously thinking she needs to call Mr. Jefferson when April lifts her head and looks right at her. "Discontent will not pass."

"Excuse me?"

"Until justice is served."

"What happened, April. You can tell me."

"No."

"Who did a terrible thing? Is this about… *your dad?*"

April's stare is like a dagger. "Mustn't tell."

"You can tell me. I can help you."

"Mrs. Johnston…" Aprils looks right at her with those pretty green eyes, she knows that look; she has seen it before and not just

April. "I want to make it stop now." Then just like that, she puts her pencil case in her bag, stands up, hands Ruby-May what she's crunched tight into a ball and brushes right past her. "Come on, Mrs. Johnston, we can't miss that bus."

The bus has left; she watched it pull away from the school gates. All the children have been collected. Mr. Jefferson came for April. As Ruby-May watched her walk to his car, she had those damn earphones in again, walking to the beat like she didn't have a care in the world, like she was a whole different person to the one crying in the restrooms an hour ago. No sign of Libby; her office is already locked up.

She peers out of the classroom window, thinks about Randolph, says he'll come by, pick her up, she told him she needed fifteen. Her bag sits ready packed up with her marking. There's the piece of paper April gave her now folded flat on the desk. Seems she has already written a poem. Best not to think about that. She needs to think about something nice; Randolph. Well, it's almost the weekend and it's date night. He says he's booked that seafood place she loves. *Thoughtful sweet Randolph.* She fumbles with her cell phone, hesitates over L, L for Libby, but it might be too late for something nice. She dials the number.

Ruby-May is not sure Libby'll pick up. She's been kind of distant, like this is hers to deal with now. But they both know in a school, when you care about a kid, it's never that easy. Can't just walk away now, can you?

She reads the first verse of the poem while she waits.

> *I saw the soldier clutch his head*
> *To hold his ears in place.*
> *I saw the soldier fall to knees*
> *He cannot pray; no lips on face.*

She won't leave a message; she needs to talk to her. She is all ready to hang up waiting for that message to come on, when Libby answers. She sounds flustered. Three girls under five'll do that.

"Libby?"

110

"Bad time."

"It's important."

She hates awkward silence but that's what she gets. She looks down at something on the floor, something the janitor missed? He came by early, caught the back of him with his whizzing 'n' whirring machine.

"Ruby, if this is to ask about today, about the meeting with the Jeffersons, you know I can't—"

"I changed my mind."

"About what?"

"April Jefferson."

"Changed it how?"

"Something happened today. On the museum trip."

"Okay."

"I think maybe you're right. About something happening at home. She said she mustn't tell, that *he* did a *terrible* thing. And she said she wants it to stop now."

"Did she say who, what?"

"No. But somethin' happened on her trip with her dad last weekend; they had to cut it short, a fight."

"Ruby, look I—"

"I think maybe you're right, about the dad."

It takes all the effort she's got left to keep her voice from wobbling and those words from breaking clean apart. She reaches in the flap of her bag for a Kleenex. Then she looks down at April's poem. Thinks about Randolph. He knows it's getting to her. She's barely slept this week.

"I learned something. Today. In my meeting," Libby says.

"About the dad?"

"Ruby, what can you tell me about April's grandfather? You got to know him, right? You've spoken to him a few times, got a sense of him."

"Ted Jefferson. Yeah, I got a sense of him. He loves April if that's what you mean."

"He's good with her?"

"He brings her to school, calls the office to check she's in class.

So, yeah, he's good with her. I asked him to keep a diary so we could chart her *outbursts*. He did – seems compliant. He hates the dad though. I do know that much."

"You trust him?"

"The dad?"

"Ted Jefferson."

"In what way? You mean what he says?"

"Did you know he was in the military?"

"No."

"We were talking about rules; you know bed time, homework, discipline. He said he handled all of that, he was in the US Army, he knows about following rules."

"He said that?"

"Yeah. He fought in the Korean War."

"Oh."

"Said they had always been firm, about the rules. Said his wife was the one April could always get around. I asked him about rules for having friends over…"

"But she doesn't have any *other* friends."

"So, she says. That's why I asked, and about *boys*…"

"Boys?"

"He said right away there were no boys. And no friends over. He seemed pretty adamant about that, said she is fifteen, plenty of time for all that later. He said she knows because it's in the *rule book*."

"There's a rule book?"

She pictures Ted Jefferson. She can see that about him: army, neat, regimental. He's always offhand with her, but that's not unusual.

"You think he doesn't let her have *normal* friends?"

"Ruby, I'm sorry. I have to go. We can't do this now."

"Libby, she's scared of someone. But you sure it's not the dad? They were supposed to go camping, something happened…"

A muffled *wait up. I'll be right there.*

"He drinks, Ruby."

"The grandfather?"

112

"The dad."

"Oh, I—"

"Ninety days sober *this time*… only… he had a drink; that's why April cut her trip short."

"*She* cut it short?"

"She took the train home."

"Well, that's sensible."

"The Jeffersons have good reason not to trust him. He makes her all kinds of promises he can't keep, and he falls off that wagon every time he seems to be getting somewhere. Mr. Jefferson said April was really upset. Mr. Jefferson had a lot to say about him, *a lot*. Said he always liked a drink, but it got a whole lot worse when. Only he never said when what, so I asked if that was after their daughter died. He said it was, but he wasn't prepared to say anything about that, clammed up just like last time."

"Then if it's not her dad, you think it's her grandfather? Like really?"

"I don't know, Ruby. That's why I'm asking. And look I *really* do have to go. We'll talk next week. I'm sorry."

She hangs up before Ruby-May can even tell her goodbye.

Ruby-May doesn't know how long she sits in the classroom. There's a sudden chill in the air, even though the wall thermometer says it's still sixty-some degrees. Trees out in the yard are still. Sometimes she can hear Mr. Burke's wind chimes, but not today. She rests her hands flat on the table, looks at April's poem. What if something was happening right under her nose this whole time and not the semi-absent *alcoholic* father, but the man she has sat with in this very room, even felt sorry for him. Can't be easy trying to take care of a teenager and a wife with Alzheimer's. Could have been happening right there and she never even saw it.

She picks up April's poem, puts it into her bag and crosses the empty classroom.

Her eyes find April's book cover, the little blue bird, poems about love; she's bought the book to read for herself. She thinks about April today, the way she was with Kevin. Normal. *So normal.*

But April's poem – that's no love poem. She thinks about the second verse.

I saw that soldier on a street
Saw the broken man.
I saw that soldier with half a face
And from his ghost I ran.

April is troubled, whichever way you look at it.

She looks out and sees their silver Golf pull up outside. Her sweet Randolph. Only she's lost her appetite for seafood. Maybe Libby's right. Maybe April's not like Billy. Maybe April's friends are a reaction to something happening at home. She doesn't know which is worse. That's when she sees it shining on the classroom floor, a silver dime. She bends, picks up and thinks how she'll take all the luck she can get.

Chapter 6

I

May 23rd, 1977, Atlanta, Georgia

George watches Henry. He squirms on the back seat next to his sister who is all pokey tongues and giant pigtails. She looks a picture in that dress of hers. Pink with bright orange swirls. Everyone goes bold these days. Not George. Or Henry, both in plain blue T-shirts. He has not said a word since they pulled away from the school. Josie-Ann is Henry's protector, but next year they won't be in the same school. And he worries about that – he worries about that a lot. Josie-Ann is everything Henry Jnr's not. Of course, Molly says George worries about everything.

Josie-Ann leans forward, jabs his shoulder. "Put the radio on, Daddy." He reaches for the dial. Stevie Wonder – *Sir Duke*. Josie-Ann swishes her head from side to side and sings along. As for Henry, he stares out.

It takes them fifteen minutes in the afternoon traffic to get to Peaches Avenue. Between the songs, Josie-Ann talks; that girl talks a lot, just like her momma. She says what's she's been doing in class and how much homework she's got and what her friends are doing on the weekend. Today it's about making plans for the summer. School will be out soon enough. Henry, on the other hand, watches the world flicker past, quiet as a mute. When they reach the house, Josie-Ann helps her little brother with the door, though there's nothing little about Henry, he has the *Tucker long-legs* for sure. Four years between them but Henry's already almost as tall as she is. Josie-Ann is like her momma, though everyone says they can see George in the eyes and the shape of her nose. She has attitude too. She caught that from her momma. We all catch different parts. He worries which parts Henry'll catch.

He looks at Josie-Ann – she needs a haircut; her hair gets any bigger she won't fit in the car. *It's the fashion, Daddy* she tells him. George does not follow the fashion.

Henry is a mini George. But that's what worries George the most. Especially since Henry is one for mumbling. Seems like he prefers to talk to himself. His momma says George was the exact same way. That's why he worries.

George has good reason to worry. While those kiddies are at school and George is busy working at the library, he stares at that clock until he knows they're both home safe. Usually they go over to Marcie's or his momma's if George and Molly are working or if he's away, like he was last month in Jacksonville. Sometimes, like today, he finishes in time to collect them. Of course, they could walk. He worries about that too – you hear all kinds of stuff, about kiddies getting knocked down or snatched on their way home, or attacked because of who they are. Josie-Ann is only ten, not old enough to take care of herself or Henry; of course Josie-Ann would disagree. Sometimes Molly lets them walk with Margaret Howard from across the street; she always walks Lotty and Barbara home from school. He tells her: *what if Margaret Howard can't keep a close eye on four kiddies?* Especially when two of them are colored; what does she know about that? Only he doesn't say that last part. But he does say *someone could still come along and take 'em because she ain't payin' attention*. Molly tells him he is being paranoid and starts talking about the shrinks they have at The Gradies; she can fix him up with an appointment. She says she's joking, but sometimes he's not so sure. Last time she said it was after he came back from Jacksonville. That time she meant it, but like he said then and all those other times: *George is not seeing no shrink*. She doesn't have to know about what happened in Jacksonville either. Where he went or what he did is his own business – not even Momma wanted to know. And no way is he is telling a stranger.

Sometimes he thinks Molly does too much of the *jabber-jabber* to his momma – she was the one who wanted him to speak to someone a long time ago. He hopes there's no talk about that.

Sunday nights is the time for the *jabber-jabber* on Peaches Avenue. While George is out.

Molly is still working. Since she moved to the Burns Unit at The Gradies, she works longer hours. She also has to do a whole lot more studying but she says she loves it best. She has moved around a few times since her daddy dropped down dead in front of his congregation six years ago. When Molly came home from the hospital and Lydia took care of everything, she said she didn't want to work with the old folks no more. She never said it, but George figured there'd been enough of people dying. She cried every night for a whole year for her daddy. But in the end, life goes on and that's what she said. Like a switch got switched on Henry's first birthday. She got up that day and said, "That's it then, enough now." She said they were a family, couldn't be any more children, but they were enough. Because they had to be. It was just like her momma, same thing happened to Marcie only she had to have her womb taken away because of the cancer. That's the reason there's only a Molly and not a Molly and a Cissy and a Clara and all the other names Molly said she had lined up. She said at least she was alive with two beautiful children. She said you got to accept what God gives you.

Molly's momma'd stayed with them for a while after her husband died but even she got herself busy with the church. God's will she said. She even learned to drive Henry's car. She said Henry Snr was with God. She'd see him again when it was her time. Now she walks out with a man she met at the church. George thought that might restart Molly's grieving but all she said was *everyone moves on. Because they got to, George. One year of grievin', is quite enough.*

It took four years after Henry Snr died before Marcie Collins started to walk out with William Black. Molly reckons they might even get wed.

There was a big house fire last month, was on the front of the *Atlanta Daily Record* as well as some of the bigger *white* newspapers. They said it was racial, political. Cousin Thomas knew the family. Molly told him how she was nursing that one little kiddie who survived. Said he had burns all across his body. When she described how his skin was falling off and what they had to do every day, and how he was screaming out for his dead momma, George told her stop. STOP. Right now, stop. She ought to know better than to tell him about that stuff. Not often George raises his voice but when he did, Molly knew to stop. He does not like to raise his voice because if there is one thing George is not – it's like his pap. He told her save that talk for Sunday nights. Momma and Marcie, they like to hear all about what Molly is doing. Sunday nights is when George is at the library at his poetry club. He does not like the *jabber-jabber* or *The Jeffersons*. They all love that TV show. Even Marcie says God is okay about her missing church for *The Jeffersons*. They talk about the characters like they're real people. Of course, Molly had something to say about that when he pointed it out. She looked at him with one of her *is that so?* stares and she asked him what they talked about at his book club on Wednesdays when they're discussing *books*. He didn't answer.

This is different. And besides, everyone knows Sunday nights are more about the jabber-jabber. And the rum. After Henry Snr died, they found crates and crates of rum in his cellar. It got shared out and they still have some. George doesn't touch liquor. Well, except for special occasions. He is not like his pap.

George does not want to think about that poor little boy with his skin all hanging off. He gets enough of the talk about the wars and the politics from Cousin Thomas. He works for Maynard Jackson now. It wouldn't surprise George if he tried his hand at running for Mayor when Maynard Jackson's done. There was a lot of trouble back in March with the strikes, the sanitation company. Thomas said it was about inequality, unfair pay for colored folks. Only in the end Maynard Jackson went against his own, sacked all them people.

Far as George is concerned, everyone is out for themselves. Even the new president, although everyone says he is for the Negroes, Molly said the same. But George knows different. Molly reminds him they've come a long way. Josie-Ann goes to a school where she sits next to white children, just like Mr. King promised. But how many white friends does she have? And George works in a public library he wasn't even allowed to step foot in at one time. That much is true, but how many white friends does he have? And they live on an avenue. What's that mean? he'd said. An avenue, like they weren't good enough for an avenue? Like they should be living on a plain old street? Molly'd laughed, said it's a tree-lined avenue in a nice part of Georgia with white folks and colored folks living side by side. Only George knows what it looks like and what it is, is not always the same thing. Only white neighbor he's talked to is Margaret Howard and she acts like she's doing it to win points. Look what happened to that family in the house fire. Just like the Klan all over again. And last week Henry asked him what's a retard? They called him it in school. Now that was bad enough but then he said they called him a dumb nigger boy retard. He asked why no one sits next to him in class.

But Molly says how they all got to keep standin' up. Only it wasn't any of them he was thinking about when he put his cross next to Jimmy Carter. There were posters all across the South about his promise that discrimination was over – Hands that pick cotton… now can pick our public officials. Only all he could think about when he went in to vote, with Molly right there beside him, was how one hand that picked cotton, never got to vote. That's who he did it for, Grandpap Zeb and who he always does it for and who he always will do it for.

It is true, the world is changed. George knows that. But it's not a hill, it's a mountain to climb. Not even reached the first base yet. But that's as political as it gets for George. He is not like Cousin Thomas. Some things will never change. There will always be the haters.

Molly gets a ride home from The Gradies most nights. Its official name is Grady Memorial Hospital of course but it was named The Gradies because of the way its units used to be segregated. George thinks Molly ought to learn to drive like her momma did, so she can drive herself to work, but she says they don't need two cars; one will do just fine. They bought the new one last year, after George got his pay rise – not new but only a couple of years old – a top of the range station wagon – brown. When he was picking it out, it put him in mind of Cousin Thomas and that beat-up old car he drove them all back from Clayton in. Momma and Grandmomma sat there with boxes all around them. George thinking about Abe. About how much he ached to see him turn that corner one last time like he'd come to wave them off, or better: squeeze himself in amongst all the boxes and ride with them all the way to Atlanta.

But Abe is gone. It's done. He knows that now. He's done with thinking about Jacksonville. He has his family right here in Grant Park, Atlanta.

Henry is sat on the couch when Molly comes through that door with a clatter and another pile of textbooks she dumps on the table. Henry runs right to her, and she wraps her arms all the way around him. Henry is so lean she could wrap him up three times over. She asks about school and that's when he says, "I got somethin'." Next thing he is rooting in his school bag and handing her a manilla envelope. "Miss Winters says to give you this. Make sure you got it. It's real important."

Josie-Ann is already in her room doing her homework. That girl is bright, grade A student all the way. She talks talk that goes right over George, except for when they get to talking books. It was Lydia told him *not* to wait when Molly came home with baby Henry. Told him to take the job at the library. She said it would all work out; he just had to trust his instincts. In the end, it turned out when Henry Snr said they were getting their inheritance early for the mortgage, he wasn't telling the whole truth. As well as crates of rum, he left a whole other pot of savings for his only daughter not even Marcie knew about.

George always thought Lydia was a wise old woman in a young body. The house filled up with chicken stew in those months she stayed. Her own momma was not long dead and yet there she was, taking care of them. She said Aunt Ismene had taken Jimmy back to Dallas and had stayed on a while; she was taking care of her papa just fine. George's momma was getting busy with her anti-war rallies, Marcie was too full of grief to notice anything, and Molly had a whole lot of healing to do. Not just from the operation. After Cousin Thomas and Nettie came to help them move, Lydia was taking care of the baby, Josie-Ann *and* Molly. And when he thinks about it, him too. *Especially* him. It was like she knew him. Knew him even more than *his Molly* knew him. Some secrets you hold inside. But when Lydia looked at him, it made him wonder what she saw.

Molly needed a lot of healing but the scars that took the longest were the ones on the inside. She said the pain from the grief was worse than any pain in her belly. The scars from her operation had faded good by the time her daddy had been in the ground a year and Henry'd turned one. Lydia had long gone by then.

Lydia stayed five months and four days.

She said that's how long it took.

"How long it took for what?"

"For you to be okay," she said, "working at the library. And for Molly's belly to be all healed up good, and for…"

She seemed to get stuck so he had to coax her.

"For me to make up my mind."

And just like that, her stuff was all packed up and she was checking out times of the buses back to Dallas.

When he asked what she was making her mind up about, she said the same thing she told George when she made him write to accept the job at the library: *when a person knows their path and what they're supposed to do, they just got to do it. Only way to be happy.* She never said what it was, but later he heard Molly telling Marcie. Molly thought maybe it was something to do with job at Bessie's florist, only Marcie says it's the *other thing* – helping folks at the church. Not a church like Papa's church, one where she used her *gift*. Only her daddy, Benjamin, the preacher, was not so keen on that. He never approved, said it was against God: the wrong kind of church. That's what Marcie said.

All he knows is, if it wasn't for Lydia showing up like that and staying for that five months and four days while she *made up her mind*, he doesn't know what he would've done. He worried the most about Henry. Used to stand in that room and watch him, make sure he was still breathing. Lydia told him that wasn't healthy. She said Henry was fine. He would stay fine. He would always be fine.

Only is he… fine?

Now he's been sent home from school with a letter.

Sensible George says it's about a letter everyone got, about a school trip or… stop, George. Molly says the worst thing George does is overthink. She might be right. Only how do you stop?

Molly is reading that letter now while George flicks through his latest book *The Ardis Anthology of New American Poetry*. Black and green cover. He watches Molly as she reads. Waits, looks back at his poems and then back at her. She has her worried face on. It's not the face of a letter about a school trip now, is it?

When she finally looks over, she holds it out to him. "You better read it."

"Read it to me."

She looks at Henry, tells him to go get washed up before they eat. They watch him lope from the couch to the bathroom.

"Okay, it says they're worried he is not socializing right. He is very quiet, doesn't interact…" she looks at George, "but then we always knew that, right?" George nods. "Only they want him assessed, he's slow on the learning, doesn't pay attention."

"He's only six!"

Henry Jnr is no retard. He is not like Isaac Harrison's brother, Jacob. That boy was slow. But not his Henry. School is bad enough being a Negro. He heard Jacob Harrison got himself killed in Vietnam. He should never have been allowed to go. That was when Lyndon B Johnson was still the president, but it was Defense Secretary Robert McNamara who let the people of low IQ go to fight. He must've known most of them would never come home. Now Mrs. Harrison lost both her sons. He is sure Jacob never got a medal. George hates wars and he hates guns.

"George, you listenin' to me. I said they want us to come talk to them."

"In the school?"

She lowers the letter away from her face and looks at him. "Of course, in the school. George, and this time, I'm not goin' there without you."

"When?"

She glances back at the letter. "Next Friday."

"I'm workin'."

"So am I, George, but I'll change my shift, same as you. This is important. You're the one worries so much about Henry, now's your chance to help him and you'd rather be workin'."

"I never said *I'd rather be* workin'."

"Well then that's settled. And George, don't you be gettin' *the anxious*."

Next thing Josie-Ann, still in her bright colors, swirls into the room like a tornado. "What's for dinner, Momma?"

Molly rests her copy of this month's *Good Housekeeping* on the night stand. George still hasn't come to bed. What's he up to now? She was sure she heard the pan whistling on the stove, which usually means hot chocolate. And it usually means ten minutes and she's hearing the pad of his shuffly footsteps on the carpet, the trickle of his pee in the pan and then it'll be all a fidget, cold feet on hers and where's all the blankets gone? George likes to hog. But it's already been an hour. It's already tomorrow. Her shift starts in five hours.

This isn't the first time.

George doesn't sleep. He gets the nightmares.

He won't talk about them but she's heard him call out. Say names. And sometimes, in the day-time, of late, he's been talking to himself. He's caught *the anxious*.

She knows he worries about Henry. Henry is Henry: quiet, sweet, shy. Henry likes to talk to himself too. It's one of the things they talk about on Sunday evenings. Olivia, George's momma, says George was the exact same way when he was that age. Molly never said George is the *exact same way* of late. Especially since he went AWOL. Olivia said he got better, a lot better until he was a teenager. She went awful quiet and she wouldn't say a whole lot about that, but it's no secret teenagers are moody. Josie-Ann is already a handful, won't be too long before she's a moody teenager.

Now George worries about Henry and she worries about George. Everyone worries about someone.

George has his demons. Her momma says everyone has their demons. She says the best place to get rid of those demons is the church, but no way George is budging on that one. He's been twice since they were married – when the kids were baptized – Marcie fashioned their outfits from what George calls the *hush-whisper* dress. He only went for Molly. That was one thing she insisted on and *she* was not budging on that.

When George went missing last month that was like opening a whole new can of demons.

It was a work trip – George had worked hard on the exhibition at the library. American poetry by colored poets. It took a lot of persuasion, like having Negroes work at the library was one thing, a celebration of Negro poets was quite another. But whatever he did, he persuaded someone and it went ahead. Langston Hughes has always been his favorite and Gwendolyn Elizabeth Brooks. When they first got together, he was always saying how Molly should read Gwendolyn Elizabeth Brooks. He chose Audre Lorde, Alice Walker, Dudley Randall, Maya Angelou and a bunch more. Most she had never heard of. In the end, George's exhibition was a huge success at Grant Park; they loved what he did with the display. He had made signs, included lines from his favorite poems for folks to read. He'd even persuaded some local poets to come along, read some of their work. As a matter of fact, he did such a good job they asked him to do it at the public library in downtown Atlanta and later at Jacksonville Library. That day when they asked him if he wanted to take it to Jacksonville, she thought he'd be way happier about it. That was the first library he got thrown out of and sent to the colored one. How times are changing.

He was supposed to be in Jacksonville for two days, one night. They even booked him a hotel and not a cheap one either. But George was gone two days longer than that and no one had seen him. He didn't find a payphone or call from the hotel – he just booked himself out of that hotel but he never made the train.

George Tucker went AWOL.

Of course, it wasn't the first time – did the same thing the day they were supposed to get wed. But she knows why he did that. That was her fault. And he wasn't so hard to find.

This time was different.

This time his cousin was too busy to go look for him, busy with his duties for Mayor Jackson. Nettie's got quite enough now she's a baby machine – five children, all under ten, Molly does not know how she does it. Olivia said to leave it, if he didn't come home by the weekend to call the police then. "Besides," she said, "no policeman is gonna waste his time looking for a Negro – unless they plan on beatin' up on him." She said George would be okay. But Molly wasn't so sure she heard *okay* in her voice. Seemed like Olivia just didn't want anyone to fret more than they needed to. Besides, now she's got herself a new man, she hasn't got a whole lot of time for anyone. And who said the police would do that? Only they did, and she knew it.

Molly did call them. What if there had been some folks not like an exhibition of Negro poets? Things might be changing but look what happened to that poor family whose house got burned down. The police said there was no way of checking for sure if George got the train. All they knew for sure was he checked out of that hotel. But then he said George'd asked work for a couple of days' leave.

He did?

He told them something important had come up in Jacksonville.

What something important? So important he couldn't tell his wife?

It was Eddie his co-worker told them, and since he never took time off for anything the boss said yes right away.

"He didn't say what?" Molly said.

"Nope."

She has no idea what *something important* might had come up in Jacksonville, but the police said it meant George was not a missing person. They had laughter faces on like they thought he had another lady – or maybe they'd had a fight and he did not want to come home. But George always wanted to come home. *Didn't he?*

Olivia said the very same thing as the cops. She said it proved he was okay; he had not had an accident. Of course, Molly had already called all the hospitals in Florida. But no sign of George.

Like there's no sign of George now. Third time this week. She does not want to find him on the couch again. She'll give him five more minutes then she'd going down to get him. He won't tell her what's wrong. He never tells her. Not even when he went AWOL and she asked him enough times. Marcie and William said they'd drive her to Jacksonville the next day if he still wasn't home, it was all arranged. Molly'd even called Cousin Lydia since she heard she was good at finding missing people. Last she heard she started working for the Dallas Police Department, as a police psychic and getting quite a name for herself. She still worked at Bessie's, only now she's known as *The Clair-voy-ant Flor-ist*. She said she was busy on a police case, but if she *learned* anything, she would be sure to call. *Learned?* "Don't worry, Molly. He'll be back sooner than you think." And a couple of hours later, just like that, George's key was jangling in the door and he was stood right there. Like nothing'd happened. Only it was clear something had. She knows when George has been crying. But he said he needed some time to think. And he didn't want to talk.

"It's not me is it? You do still love me, George? You didn't find yourself a new woman now did you?"

But she already knew the answer to that one, even before his arms were around her and he was pulling her to him saying he was sorry, of course not, she was enough for him and always would be. That she had to trust him, he was okay. It was done. He would not be going back to Jacksonville.

After that, Molly knew better than to keep on asking. She called her momma and said they would not need to be taking that trip now, George was back. Only was he? Seems George's mind is in a whole other place since that trip. To her, he *is* still in Jacksonville.

That's why Molly suggested he speak to someone. She even got the name of a doctor at The Gradies. But she should've known – *no way he would speak to no one*. When she talked to Olivia, she said that's what George does. *Goes inside his-self but give it a few days and he's gon' be fine.*

Of course, Molly has been with George long enough to know about the *goin' inside his-self,* but this time he seems different and she is sure his momma knows something she's not saying. She knows that look.

That family have some secrets and Olivia is the worse one for it. But Molly knows how to handle Olivia.

So, that next Sunday evening, she made sure to get her on her own once her momma'd left. Now Olivia, she had a taste for the liquor, not the way Ezra did – George's daddy, not that he ever likes to talk about that, but he did tell her about the drinking. His momma, she likes a drink occasionally. So sometimes they crack open a bottle of something and if it's a special occasion Molly still has some of Daddy's special rum. Sometimes, like last weekend, she said it being Sunday was special enough. Now she already knew Olivia had been sneaking extra glasses. She'd seen her do the *rum sway* after all those trips to the bathroom. Molly knows Olivia and she also knows how enough rum loosens those lips. So, Molly persuaded her to take a "third" one. It did not take a whole lot of persuasion. Then she asked her, "So, where'd George go to, Olivia?"

She shrugged.

"His old neighborhood? You think we was visitin' folks in Jacksonville?"

When she didn't answer she got up close so she was looking right into her eyes, smelling that rum breath. "He doesn't have… an old girlfriend there?"

That made her laugh, that made Olivia laugh out loud so hard she got the hiccups. So, then she was gulping down more of that rum, emptying the glass until they stopped.

"He did tell me once he only had eyes for two girls, someone he was in school with and then me."

By now she had tears on her cheeks from all the laughing. "Chloe Johnson? You think he went to look for Chloe Johnson? Molly, honey, now let me tell you…" there was a definite slur, one finger doing a dance right in front of Molly's face. "Chloe Johnson was no more than a high school crush. Lasted five minutes. You, honey, are the love of his life. You the only one he ever loved." She shook her head, winked. "Except for his ol' momma of course."

"Well where'd he go? Who'd he visit?"

Molly poured another glass, with Olivia telling her she shouldn't but she was soon sliding it across the table towards her and Olivia was sipping. Slowly this time.

"Maybe he just needed time on his own, Molly. You know how he is. We all like to take ourselves off sometimes. That boy is fine."

But she was not giving up this time, no Sir. *That boy is a grown man and he is not fine. Olivia knows something.*

"What about old friends?"

It was only for a second but when Olivia looked away, she knew there was something. Yes, she did. Olivia took another long gulp of that rum.

"He grew up in Clayton. He must have friends there, right?"

"You ever hear him talk about… *friends?*"

"No but doesn't mean—"

"George is not one for making lots o' friends."

Of course, Molly knew that. "Well, he must've gone someplace."

"If he never told you, honey, means it's *pri-vate.*"

What does that mean? And why she say it like that?

She was about to say they did not have secrets only they both knew that was not true. She's seen the way George and his momma got all agitated anytime someone mentions his daddy.

She finished her glass in one loud gulp and next thing was reaching for her purse. She said Garfield would already be outside waiting in the car. Garfield is not unlike George, another one not so good with *the sociable.*

Olivia swayed as she stood. "George loves you, that's all you gotta know."

"I'm his wife, Olivia. There should not be secrets in a marriage." Maybe that last part was a step too far – she'd only been with Garfield a few months, but everyone could see he was different to the others – *she* was different with him.

"Please, Olivia."

George said it was about time his momma met someone who treated her right.

"Olivia, you know what secrets do to fam'lies. I won't say a word, but if you know something… we women, we look after our men, don't we?"

Olivia wrapped her fingers over the back of the chair.

"Where was he, Olivia?"

She had her thinking face on.

"Olivia?"

The sound of a car horn.

"That'll be Garfield."

"What place, Olivia?"

"Somewhere he used to go."

"Where?"

"Clayton Cemetery."

She was not expecting that.

"George might've mentioned something about his brother, and his brothers' friends, well, their families anyhow. Those boys all got themselves killed."

"His *brother*?"

Olivia was already turning back pulling on that front door handle but no way she was letting this one go.

"George has a brother?"

"George had a brother."

"What happened to him?"

"The Korean War."

"Why didn't he—"

"We don't talk about that. Or about his pap. Got that."

"But a brother?"

"One thing I can tell you…" She was holding onto that door like it was keeping her upright, which it probably was. "…is the past can haunt a person, so best you leave it right where it is, Molly. He'll never talk about what happened on his fifteenth birthday."

Then she was gone, tottering along that path and into Garfield's sedan.

And Molly was dialing Cousin Lydia.

Finally, Molly hears George's feet going shuffle on the carpet, only he does not use the bathroom. He is standing in the doorway. "About time," she says, patting the bed. Now George is lean but he looks thinner stood there in his blue pajamas, feet bare.

"I was about to come look for you." She had asked him about his brother. How could she not? It was last Wednesday when he came home from the book group because that's when he's usually in the best mood. She took a drop of Daddy's special rum herself before she did. The kids were tucked up in their beds. She'd looked right at him, her hand on his and she said, "George, honey. I was talking to your momma, and… all this time I thought you was an only-child, just like me… but your momma, she said…"

She will never forget the panicked look on his face or the way he tried to pull his hand away. "George, why'd you never tell me about your brother?"

It didn't come out as neat the way she'd been planning on saying it but there he was. And from the look on his face, she might have done the wrong thing.

He tried to pull his hand away again, then he'd looked at her. "I had a brother and now I ain't."

"Sorry, George, I—"

"Leave it. Momma never talks about Abe. Why'd she have to—"

"His name was Abe?"

He was squirming, trying to free his hand but Molly wasn't letting up.

"You *can* talk to me, George. I am your wife. You miss him, like I miss Daddy."

"NO."

Now George has been forceful before, but he only ever raised his voice and not often. Maybe if the kids were playing up, getting too boisterous, too noisy when he was trying to read. But right then, that was something different. Something she had never seen. When he's gotten angry with the kids those were moments, over as soon as they came, but what she saw last week was scary. For a second, she even thought when he pulled his hand free in one forceful yank, fists all bunched up, he was ready to hit her. Olivia told her that George's pap – Ezra – had a temper on him exactly the same as John Langton.

It's common knowledge that sons take after their daddies and in that moment, that iddy-biddy fraction of a moment, she was afraid, only soon as she thought it, it was gone. Next thing he was saying he needed to take a walk.

Last thing he said was, "My momma was right."

"About what?"

But he never said.

Words got cut off by the door slamming shut. And Molly sobbing on the bed wondering what was so bad he couldn't say it. But grief can do that. It affects people in different ways. She took long enough to deal with her daddy's death. His brother and all his friends died? That's a whole lot of grief.

By the time he came back from his walk, it was like it never happened. Now it's the thing they don't talk about – his fifteenth birthday, the day his brother died.

The bed sinks as George climbs in, feet icy cold.

Cousin Lydia said whatever was eatin' George would come out when the time was right. That he must have his reasons for not telling her about his brother. "You need to be real patient on this one."

As she leans over, turns out the light, thinks about those babies of hers asleep next door, the letter about Henry, she thinks maybe Lydia's right. She's right about a lot of things. When George is ready to talk, he will. In the meantime, they have to make sure

Henry is okay. She always thought it was a good thing Henry is just like his daddy… but what she doesn't want is for those demons to be catching.

II

May 23ʳᵈ, 2003, Jacksonville, Florida

April has been staring at the page for the past twenty minutes. The smell of burned pot roast drifts up. Grams should never be left alone. Pops said he had it, don't fret it, he was helping, only seems he forgets too. This is not the first time supper is charcoal. April ordered take-out – not the first time she's had to do that either. She told Pops she was eating in her room. Of course, she knows it's *against the rules* but so's burning supper. Besides, like she told him, she had something important to do for Mrs. Johnston. He'd watched her put three slices of pepperoni pizza on a plate, grab a napkin and head upstairs before he could give his lecture about rule-breaking. She only ate one slice. Now she looks down at her notebook. This is not the first time she's tried to describe her friends for Mrs. Johnston either. Last week, after class, she asked her had she gotten to it yet. She said she'd try on the weekend only she didn't. She has English tomorrow. She still has nothing for her.

The TV's on downstairs – muffled TV detective voices drift up with the smell of burned supper. Grams doesn't even watch it; it's not like she can follow it. Grams is getting worse but Pops says no way he is putting her in a home.

Jesse says his grams was the same way – he means forgetful. He says folks get old and then they die. And sometimes folks don't get old and then they die.

She told him stop.

Her mom was only six years older than she is now when she died.

She was only two years older when she got pregnant. No way is April getting pregnant at seventeen. Or dying at twenty-one. Jesse says she's being morbid. Like that book. He'd pointed at her collection of poetry books, the one on top with the black and green cover; the one she found in the big library downtown. An anthology – it's old.

"Poets like to write about death," he says. It makes her think about the war poem she wrote for Mrs. Johnston. Only she could never have written that. Just heard the words in her head.

She is propped up on the bed, legs stretched out all long, white sneakers kicked off. She fumbles with her pen, looks down at her notebook. All she has so far is one name.

Jesse: Loud, extravert, flirtatious.

He says he is none of those things. She ought to add *liar* to the list.

She rests her pen in the furrow, lays the notebook open on her bed and looks towards the window. Was that a car door? They never have visitors. It's against the rules.

Martha likes food. Cream pies are her favorite. She probably likes pizza too though she's never said it. She picks up the pen writes *Martha: likes pies.* It's something. *Grace: sweet, kind, Rose: chatterbox, nervous. Owen: likes history.* Describe how they look Mrs. Johnston said. Martha is… *heavy*?

It's as April is thinking on that, she hears someone knocking with a familiar beat on the front door. Only person she knows knocks like that is her dad. Now ordinarily she'd be off that bed and down those stairs so fast they'd be no time to catch a breath. He never surprises her like that. She gave up on wishing for surprises a long time ago. How many times had he promised to take her out for hot chocolate? And how many times had she waited for him *not* to show. But since their *almost* camping trip when she caught him slipping vodka into his Dr Pepper, she has not even answered his calls.

They'd been getting along just fine. He suggested they set up camp halfway and make it to Sugar Loaf the following day. Sure, she'd told him. She didn't care as long as they were together. But she knew once they'd got that big old tent of his up, she knew something wasn't right. Watched him slump more and more into that fishing seat as he sipped his Dr Pepper. She knew it for sure when he started talking. He's not one for talking, unless. April knows the signs; she's seen them enough times. Didn't take too long before she found the bottle, while he was taking a leak. Sure, it was a small bottle, in the pocket of his coat. But she knew enough about rule books to know it was against the rules in the AA Handbook.

That wasn't the worse part.

The tears. The *I'm sorry for what I did, April.* The *I loved your mom, you do know that, don't you, April. Look how pretty you've gotten, April.* Then the *You've got your mom's hair, your mom's fair skin, your mom's... I miss her, April.*

She hated it. Hated him for it. Heard it all before.

She told him she was tired, zipped herself into her half of the tent. Cried herself to sleep. Next morning, she was gone while he was still snoring. Left him a note. He didn't deserve it but she did it anyway. She hitched a ride to the nearest train station – some place called Winter Park. Pops would freak if he knew she hitched. She had enough grief off Jesse who said strangers can do bad things. Well so can dads. Besides it was a nice old woman. She must've seen the tears still wet on April's cheeks, but she gave up asking if she was alright when April never answered. The knock comes again, only softer this time. What does he want? They won't let him in. Pops will be real pissed with him now. She looks down at her notebook. Only she can't concentrate. Next thing Pops must've answered the door because she can hear voices and these are not TV voices. She swings her legs over the end, perched half-on and half-off and listens, or tries to. Rose has started her *jabber-jabber*. She tells her hush as she lowers her feet onto the rug and shuffles slowly to the door in her bare feet. That's when she hears Pops call out. "Someone to see you."

Like really?

No swinging shotgun and *get off my property.*

Not this time.

April's folks usually call her dad by his full name: Mitch Jones. April used to be April Jones. That was until her mom died, not that she remembers but since the judge said she would be living with her grandparents, they changed it, so's they all had the same name. Pops said it was better that way. Less explaining to do.

April hangs in the doorway and looks at her dad. Doesn't

deserve the title. Maybe *she* should call him Mitch Jones, like he's a stranger. It's easier to pretend he is no one when he doesn't have the same name. Maybe her pops was right.

Only he's not no one, is he?

April wasn't going to come down only Pops raised his voice. So she was pushing her feet into her sneakers. What does he even want? He lives like thirty miles away. He drove?

He has his smart jeans on – the ones without the holes, and his best cowboy boots. Even his shirt is white and it's clean. He's not drunk – least he doesn't look it. He's even had a shave. Still needs a haircut but looks clean and seems like he's gone a little crazy on that cheap aftershave.

He's said he's sorry for like the tenth time.

She can't believe Pops has not made him leave already, though he hasn't come inside. That's one rule he never breaks. Not after what happened. But why's Pops being so nice? Only when *Mitch Jones* says, "Thanks for letting me come" she realizes he was expecting him. Why? He hates him.

She hadn't planned on telling Pops about what happened, give him another reason to hate Mitch Jones, only when she got home early from that trip, it must've been written on her face. And Pops had probably seen that disappointed face one too many times. She told him she never wanted to see her dad again and now, well here he is. *Mitch Jones*. It sounds so alien when she says it. Well maybe that's because he's a stranger. If she added up how many days she'd actually spent with him in her lifetime she reckons it wouldn't even reach double figures. All those times he wasn't allowed to come and she wanted him to, and now she doesn't, here he is and Pops is even being… *polite?* Jesse is right. The world is fucked up.

"April, I just wanted to say sorry."

"You spoiled everything."

"I know. I'm back on the program. It was a blip. I'm sorry. I've got a new sponsor… it'll never happen again."

It means jack shit. He's said it before. Why can't he keep to *those* rules?

"Well," her pops says, "you've done what you came to do, and you promised you'd leave when you'd done."

About time.

"Mr. Jefferson… Sir?"

What's with the formality?

"If April agrees, I'd like to take her out to that diner up the street, buy her a hot chocolate?"

Now he wants to? Now, when she's pissed at him for spoiling their trip. *No. No way.*

But maybe it's the look on his face. The way he promises he has not drunk again since then and they can walk there, *if she's worried*. It's only two blocks. Maybe it's the set of his eyes, the softness in his expression or the way he lowers his head. "I understand. I messed up. Another time."

He's already turned around and halfway back to his car when she says, "Okay."

She looks at Pops. "An hour," he says. "It's getting late, you have school." He adds, "Walk."

And just like that April is walking to Rick's Diner with *Mitch Jones*. Maybe not arm in arm how she pictured it all those times, but she is. Only it doesn't mean she's not still mad at him.

Rick's diner is the all-American kind, but it's homey, not for tourists, not that you get many in Clayton. Not much to look at from the outside but inside it's clean enough, red seen-better-days leather seats. No air con, just big ceiling fans whipping up warm air. Not too many people in, a family who were singing *Happy Birthday* when they walked in, couples mostly. Place smells of home-cooking. It's known for its mean breakfasts and its pies. And she heard they make the best hot chocolate. She has only been inside once. That was like three years ago. She persuaded Grams. It was before she started freaking out in public places. Before she was diagnosed with the early-onset Alzheimer's.

Grams ordered the biggest Mississippi mud pie you ever saw. It sat between them and Grams's eyes lit up so bright you'd think they'd won the state lottery. Next thing they were sat there with the spoons poised.

"Ready?"

"Yes, Grams."

And there they were digging in. Oh my God it was the best. She had to promise to keep some for Martha later. Which was no problem with eyes bigger than bellies – Grams's saying – and they asked for a doggy bag. But they laughed so hard that afternoon. She remembers it most because it was one of the rare times, strike that, *only* times when she asked her to tell her about her mom, she actually did. Maybe because Pops wasn't there. It's against his rules. She said Mississippi mud pie was her mom's favorite. She said she liked to play Snap when she was small. She said she liked to read but not as much as April does. She said she was good at dancing; she did not know that. April had wished she had a notebook with her that day, so she would remember. Only she didn't need it because she does remember. All of it. Her favorite color was purple. Her favorite animal was a horse. Her favorite dress was yellow with purple buttons. She liked spelling bees, warm rain and coloring books. Grams's face had been so bright it was like the memories washed all the lines away. She said they waited a long time for Catherine to come along, almost gave up hope and then just like that, when they were looking into adoption, two days after her thirty-fifth birthday she felt the nausea, the tingling and she just knew. She had never spoken so openly. She said April was so much like her mom – not just how she looks. She said they even had the same laugh, same way of walking (she didn't know people had a way of walking) and the same dark moods.

She lost the glow as soon as she said that part. Next thing she was reaching for her purse, asking the waitress for the check. She never talks about what happened to her mom. Like those memories got washed away before all the others. Only she knows that's not true. She's seen the looks, heard her crying at night, saying her name. Later when Pops asked what they did that afternoon, Grams said how she and Catherine had gone out for Mississippi mud pie.

"April," he said. "You mean you and April."

"That's what I said."

When he found the doggy bag later and asked if he could have some of the pie, she said, "What pie?" They thought she was joking, but turned out she had no memory like she got herself stuck in the Mississippi mud. And still, every time they drive past Rick's, she says how she's always wanted to try it, being so close to the house and all, that it was about time they did. But that day was when it all started; not long after that Pops was taking her to see their GMO.

But April will never forget. As she shuffles into the booth now, she looks across at the empty table in the corner. They'd left before she got to try the hot chocolate. But she'll try it tonight. With whipped cream, marshmallows and sprinkles.

They were right about the hot chocolate. April sits across from Mitch Jones with his sad face and his twitchy eyes. He has this tic that looks like he's winking. She has always loved that tic; she always forgets he has it until the next time she sees him. He has both his hands gripped tightly around his coffee, with extra cream and sugar. He's twitching for a cigarette – he's supposed to have given them up too.

"Good?" he says as she spoons off more whip and marshmallow and shovels it in.

"Yeah."

Her friends say drinking liquor is a sickness, in the head, same as her mom, only this is not the same. He had a choice and he blew it. He told her on the walk here that he'd bought the vodka when they stopped for gas. That he hadn't planned it. That it was sat there looking at him, like it was calling his name. That he hadn't meant to drink it. Bullshit. She knows he'd probably been back drinking for weeks.

"I made a mistake, Ape. I'm sorry." He is the only one she has ever let her call her that.

She lets the sugar sink in, rolls the marshmallow over her tongue.

"And when you'd gone like that and I read that note, saying you never wanted to see me again, I—"

"I don't want to talk about it. I just want you to stop."

"And I have, honey. I swear to you."

"I came here once. With Grams."

He nods, takes the hint, sips his coffee.

"I asked her to tell me about Mom. No one ever wants to talk about her."

He lowers the cup. "I do."

"When you're drunk."

That seems to hit him like a punch but she doesn't care. He hurt her; now it's her turn.

"I remember that day." She stirs her chocolate with the long spoon.

"What day?"

"When the cops came."

"You remember that? You were so young."

"Hard to forget a shotgun."

"Jesus, Ape…" Now he's looking in the direction of the waitress tending the couple at the next table. She glances over. Maybe April said it too loud but she doesn't care. He deserves it.

He sips his coffee while she finishes her marshmallows and starts on the thick chocolatey drink.

"It wasn't my bad." She looks back at him. He always mumbles when he's upset. "I was trying to get it off Cath… your mom. She was sick; she didn't know what she was doing. I swear that's all I was doing when Ted came home. Jesus, she could've shot you, killed us all. You think I'd let you live in that house with your mom and your grandparents if I knew there was a shotgun in the house? And live ammo, Jesus Christ."

April takes a long sip of chocolate and holds it in.

"He blames me but what the fuck… hell, what was he doing with a gun like that? All I did was wrestle it off her. It was him who took it off me, it was him who…"

She swallows, watches him squirm as she savors the flavor only now it seems like the moment is bitter sweet. He doesn't even know it's bad to swear like that. Only… you don't get to choose your family.

"He was a soldier," she says looking back at him. "It's historical. He collects stuff."

"I know, but Ape, it should've been locked away. Cath should never have been able to get a hold of it. Not when she was so…"

He's fidgeting. He looks unsure.

"So?"

"Unstable."

The first shot was an accident. He didn't know she'd loaded it.

Before they knew it, the cops were outside saying a neighbor had heard gunshots.

They go quiet when the waitress walks past.

"Jesus, I thought he was gonna kill me, the way he was wavin' that gun, tellin' me to get the hell off his property."

The bad man. The bad man with the gun. She doesn't realize she's mumbling, that she has her hands pressed to her ears to shut it out until he reaches for a napkin and wipes his eyes. "I'm so sorry. Jesus, what did we do to you?"

"It's okay… Dad."

"It's all my fault."

Her mom was the one who unlocked the gun, loaded in the bullets, not him… Pops was the one who fired it, first bullet blew a hole in the grass. Second, the warning, shot a huge hole right in the fence.

"It's all my fault," he says.

Only now as he looks at her, she realizes he's thinking about the other time. The other gun. The other house. The secret she must never tell.

Chapter 7

I

May 31ˢᵗ, 1984, Atlanta, Georgia

Molly fumbles for her new reading glasses. George is at the kitchen table; his glasses propped on his head. He was trying to finish a poem and now he's not. He's waiting on Molly to finish. The letter says Henry has gotten himself into trouble *again*. And this time it's George's fault.

The letter has George all *a dither*. He's got *the anxious*. But not because of what he did, because of what Molly is going to do.

Henry has been in his room since supper. George left the letter on the table. Now Molly takes extra shifts he does the cooking; she never gets home before eight. He's gotten good at pot roasts. Josie-Ann is in her room. Soon as she finishes her homework, she'll be on that telephone to Jerome. That girl is so grown up. She says Jerome was her sweet sixteen. Noticed him at fourteen, went out on dates at fifteen, agreed to *go eternal* at sixteen – on her birthday. He gave her a special ring. Not *that* kind of ring, she wears it on the other hand. *Go eternal?* He doesn't even think it's a thing, it's a *Josie thing*. Go steady? Exclusive? No – *go eternal*. What does George know? Only one woman he got to *go eternal* with and she is about to *go crazy*.

Kettle squeals. George pushes back the chair, walks over. He reaches for the towel, wraps it around the handle.

It's the last line of the letter.

Clearly Molly hasn't gotten to the last line. He'll know when. The whole house will know when.

George pours hot water into two cups, one eye still on Molly. She's taking her time but when she sees it, it might even put her off her pot roast that's all plated up, oven on low. Though it takes a lot to put Molly off her food. Even if it is the third time this week for pot roast.

Molly has put up with a lot. He is not so sure what she'll say about this one. If there's one thing Molly cannot abide, it's violence. Only what something looks like and what it is, ain't always the same. Molly always stands by him. She stands by him even when. There ought to be a wedding vow for all the things George can't say: *I promise to love you even when.* They've been a lot of *even whens.* He looks at Molly. She must have gotten to it by now?

Over the years there have been a lot of letters sent home with Henry. Now he has his problems but one thing George knows is Henry is no retard – he's just slow at the learning. Used to be the other kids picked on him. Called him names. Bullying is the word they use for it. Only now… he pours some milk into that instant coffee, seems the bullied just became the bully. But it's not what it seems.

They taught both of them good manners. Look how good Josie-Ann turned out. Never brought one ounce of trouble to their door. Only letter ever comes home with Josie-Ann is the one that says how well she's doing, how they want her to stay back after school for extra classes as they want to fast track her, get her on a special program. Josie-Ann might even be good enough to try out for one of the ivy leagues. Only anxious that comes with those letters is how they'll pay for that. Josie-Ann says they have funding for people like us. Now she doesn't mean for people on low incomes, they got funding for that too. With Molly being a specialist burns nurse, taking all those extra shifts and with George newly promoted in charge of the poetry archives and the summer programs, they do okay – only college costs, more than their okay. Costs up to $15000 a year. Josie-Ann says there are scholarships for black people, they come under minority. Only there are a lot of black people, so how are they a minority? Pell Grants, Supplemental Grants, the college Work-Study Program… she says she can apply for them all. All George does is smile, cross his fingers and thinks about his grandfolks. Look where they came from?

143

There have been lots of talks about what to do about Henry. Henry doesn't fit anyplace. They say he is not bad enough for a special school but he is way behind the others in the special class. Henry is special – they think they can add bully to retard and all the other names they've got for him, but George knows different.

No one would think Josie-Ann and Henry are cut from the same.

One thing he knows, when Henry gets to seventeen, this is not one of the discussions they'll have. He has no idea what Henry'll do. Never been good at anything, except for maybe his art, only he never sits still for long enough to finish anything. But university? Not Henry.

Maybe not Josie-Ann too if she can't get funding.

That movie star they've got for President has a lot to answer for, or so Cousin Thomas says. All George hopes is he is not still President after the elections in November. Cousin Thomas says everyone should be voting for Jesse Jackson. Since Cousin Thomas stopped working for the mayor's office, after Andrew Young came to office, he's been working for Jesse Jackson. George does not know exactly what he does only that in a few weeks he is going with Mr. Jackson to San Francisco, something about the Rainbow Coalition. George thinks it's one thing having a black mayor, having a black president? In his lifetime? Now that ain't gonna happen.

Marcie says no one is gon' vote for a Negro. She says William is voting for Walter Mondale. Long as it's not Reagan she says. Says it's his fault there is so much unemployment and it's hit the black folk much harder than the white. And what George does not tell Josie-Ann, is what William told him – Mr. Reagan cut a lot of the finances for the black folk.

"HE – DID – WHAT?"

There it is. Looks like Molly's got to the last line.

"I'm gonna kill that boy."

He walks to the table and sets down the mug, the one with the roses on that Momma bought her for her birthday. She has the face, the what-we-gonna-do-about-Henry? face.

"When he gets to Junior High, he'll make friends. They have better programs. They'll help him."

"George, what was he thinking? He fights now?"

She looks again at the letter, shakes her head.

"Maybe it's not like you think."

She looks at him, face all fixed in a scowl.

"Only reason he ain't been suspended is school's out next week, and his IQ." She must've seen the shock on George's face when she says that because she adds, "If he didn't have the learning difficulties I mean, George. They make allowances, but maybe they shouldn't. How else he gonna learn?"

Her hands reach for the mug.

"He'll be alright."

"George, you been sayin' that since he was six years old. He's thirteen now, and if things don't change Henry's gonna get himself into big trouble. Fighting? In class? Who taught him that?"

But George already has his back to her and is heading back to his poem. Seems them Tucker genes have a lot to answer for. Josie-Ann is a Collins through and through. But Henry, he has a temper on him. But it was George told him to stand up to the bullies. He is the reason for Molly's look now. All he needs to tell him now, is how to control the Tucker temper.

"George, you listening to me? Who told him it was okay to use his fists, we taught him better than that. If you gotta fight, you use words. That's what we taught him."

He sits down, stretches out those long legs of his under the kitchen table. There's a radio on soft. They're playing the new number one. Josie-Ann's favorite, about crying doves and that singer, he's a whole other kind of strange. Josie-Ann says if she wasn't promised to Jerome, she'd be going eternal with Prince. Sometimes he wonders if her intelligence is all an illusion.

"George, are you even listenin' to me?"

He looks down at the first draft of his poem.

"Who taught him it was okay to fight with his fists?"

Now George does not know why he says it. Not like it was

145

planned but right there with Molly blowing steam off her coffee cup he says, "I hit my pap once. So hard I made him fall down."

He does not know what he sees on Molly's sweet face; it's not sweet now that's for sure. He expects something but when she don't speak, he thinks maybe he shocked the words clean out of her head. So he adds, "Sometimes, it's the only way. Maybe Henry was standing up to the bad man."

She lifts her glasses off her face and lays them down on the table. "The bad man?"

"It's a metaphor."

That's not exactly true. So now he looks across at where he's left his coffee on the side. He expects her to be mad at him now. Maybe he shouldn't've told her. Only he hasn't told her what happened after his pap fell down.

She sets her stare on him before she says, "I am sure, George, you had good reason."

"And maybe Henry did too."

She looks down at the letter, folds it over. "Well let's hope that puts an end to it."

It worked for George – it put an end to Pap only that's not what she means and that's one secret too far. If he told her, he's not so sure she'd still love him even when. But the conversation's done. Done as that dinner dried out in the oven because that's when Josie-Ann appears, perhaps with not quite the usual spring, like maybe she heard, but there she is. Josie-Ann walks right across to that phone and is calling her eternal. Used to be she only had eyes for her daddy.

Josie-Ann is in her room; it's been forty minutes since she spoke to Jerome. Told him what's been eating into her of late, the reason for the moods. Now she's standing at the window waiting. Jerome said he wanted to come talk to her. He said it in his loud voice. The voice he uses right before a fight: why'd she have to do it over the phone? She told him because. That's all she had. Then she said: no, don't come over. He told her: yes, he was coming over. Now he's coming over.

She rolls the silver ring between her fingers then sits it on the window sill; sucks in a long deep breath. Her nose is full of snot.

The palm tree out-front is doing its hula dance. All swish and sway. Sky is rose pink. The black and white stray, the little cat she knows her dad secretly feeds, is stalking something. Looks like a red cardinal only it's a paper napkin. Lotty Howard from across the street has *one of her boyfriends* over again – her momma must be out. She thinks she's Madonna, from the way she dresses. She sneaks the boy in the back. Now Michael Jackson is playing from the open window. Sounds like she's getting down to *Beat It*. She wonders where that stuck-up sister, Barbie, is at... and what Mrs. Howard will think if she comes home early.

There's a new lady at the house three along from Lotty Howard – where Erica Halls used to live, that crazy old cat lady. She used to walk around butt-naked. She thinks maybe that little cat, the one Dad has been trying to coax in, was one of hers. Now she's dead and that poor little cat is all alone. She feels the roll of another tear. She's being over-emotional which is *not very Josie-Ann*. Momma says Erica had a touch of the dementia, that's why she walked around her yard butt-naked. It's what Garfield thinks Grandmomma Olivia's got – her daddy had it, says it runs in families and she's been getting awful forgetful. She says it's old age – only she's not quite sixty. He says he's making her an appointment at the doctor's office.

She looks at Erica's old house. In all the years they've lived on Peaches, this is only the third time there's been another black family. She wonders how they fit five kiddies into that place, looks smaller than theirs. They had a party over there yesterday – plastic cups and paper plates, maybe someone's birthday. Loud music, her momma said. She never saw it – she was at the Pattersons' house with Jerome after school.

She had planned on telling him then, only in the end he needed to help his dad clear the garage and then he told her his grandpa was sick and she couldn't do it.

She didn't see him in school today, only in math but she couldn't do it then. She couldn't do it, period. She should never have said it over the phone, blurted it out like that. But seems when you have choices rolling around inside your head like that, once they settle, once your mind is finally made up – it just has to be said. Like holding it in your hands too long will burn the skin clean off.

The family in Erica's house have put wind chimes in the orange tree. Wood. Their flutey jangle carries and one of those plastic cups is blowing into the street.

Josie-Ann notices all of these things. She notices the detail. Like her senses got heightened, like she can hear inside heads. Maybe she's more like Aunt Lydia than she thinks. Momma says her aunt used to help the police look for missing children, one time she was even on the national news. Her momma says she stopped doing that after her papa, Uncle Benjamin, died. But she remembers when she told her how she could hear right inside folks' heads: people's whispers, people's prayers, people's dreams. All those decisions being mulled over, like hers – will she, won't she? Get the funding, not get the funding? Study for her college degree in DC, stay right here with Jerome?

The music from an old radio is playing soft next door – that'll be Clive. He likes country. Johnny Cash twangs compete with Wham from Carl's car stereo. He lives the other side. Dresses like George Michael. Thinks he's quite a catch. Yeah right. *Wake me up before you go go.*

Somewhere a dog's barking to be let in and a baby's crying to be fed – might be the house next door to the Howards, opposite: Amelia and Frank Washington. She heard she had a baby boy. Quite a chorus going on. A waft of smells too. Cooking smells: chicken frying, Daddy's pot roast, and someone's burned something, smells like toast. She senses it all.

Details. It's all about the details – that's what she learned in class, that's why she does so well. She pays attention. Only it seems not always to the things that matter. Like what Jerome wants. He says he loves her. Says he'll do anything for her. Except let her move to DC. He says she should go to school in Atlanta. Why the ivy league? Or DC? *Don't leave.* Only he never actually says that last part, but she hears it, in every conversation about school and college applications.

Uncle Thomas says *she's gonna go far, maybe be the first black female president.* Yeah right – no pressure. She won't be anything without funding, or maybe she won't be anything anyhow. Her uncle bigs everything up. He is the one who likes to talk politics. Says she ought to study Law. She already told him Psychology is her thing, *a Josie thing* – unravelling why people think how they think, act how they act. Like her dad and his moods. Her uncle says Law is about why folks act like they act. She told him it's more about folks being *allowed* to act like they act. It's not the same. That's when he said he wanted her to go to San Francisco hear Jesse Jackson speak. It's the week after next. Jerome says they ought to, but no way her momma will let her go.

And now… she's not so sure anyone is going anywhere.

She should have handled this whole thing better.

Josie-Ann'd had to drag that telephone out into the hall, tugging on that long cord; she told them they make them cordless now, but Momma says *if it ain't broken, no need to pay for a new one.* She doesn't think her momma or her dad would've heard anyway. They were too busy talking about Henry. He might have his problems but head-strong Josie-Ann is the one who will make something of herself. Dad worries there's no money for college – Uncle Thomas says he's working on that, says he knows where to find her funding. There are pots of money for black folk if you know the right place to look. She's made her decision; she can't unmake it now and that's why she's mulching that tissue to nothing between her fingers. The ring on the sill glints orange as the sun sinks.

Her grandfolks, especially Grandpap William, act like she's already gotten into Harvard only she's got her heart set on Howard, in Washington DC which is mostly for black folks. Jerome said that's too far. She told him it's like a two-hour flight. The Pattersons can't afford flights but he wants to be a car mechanic – he can get that apprenticeship at Lou's then he'll make good money *in the end.* In the meantime, it's a ten-hour drive. He'll have his driver's license soon enough. He did not look too pleased about a ten-hour drive. Or there's the bus? The train? They'd make it work. Only his face said different.

Since then, every time they talk about it, it ends the same way. You can have one *too many* fights. She's been talking to Grandmomma Olivia. She says *differences of opinion are normal.* But the next time she visited she didn't remember they'd even talked about it. Maybe Garfield's right about her memory, only when she saw there this week, she knew exactly what she was saying. That's why she told her – that she'd made up her mind. She won't unmake it. Even when Jerome is standing right in front of her.

She looks out; the cat's lost interest in the napkin and is probably getting fed pot-roast leftovers by her dad. Her momma is still in Henry's room. She expects Jerome to walk around the corner any second. They ought to go out, only it's getting late but she doesn't want Momma to hear. She'll tell her when she's ready. That's what she told Grandmomma Olivia. Her dad says since she's grown up, Josie-Ann looks just like Grandmomma Oliva; says it's the shape of her lips. The thing about Grandmomma Olivia is she might forget it's a secret. Only it's not now. And everyone will know soon enough. That's when she sees it.

Shit.

The car.

That blue Golf.

The Pattersons' car?

Like come on. Seems Jerome didn't walk. He's in the back, with his sister – he told Kimberly too? His folks are in the front. Billy Patterson does not look happy. She's not sure what it is she sees on his wife, Dionne's face. She'll know soon enough.

Her momma will be all sweet when she sees them and *how nice to have visitors,* only she hates it when people turn up unexpected. And on a school night. She'll be worrying about the shoes and socks and other mess that her and Henry have not put away. Only soon, she won't care about any of that.

She should never have told him, not like that, not over the telephone. But if there's one thing Josie-Ann's not – is a liar. And she is no good at keeping secrets. Her momma taught her secrets have a habit of being found out, and it doesn't matter what it is. *You got a secret, Josie-Ann, then you tell it.* Makes her think of Grandmomma Olivia. When Josie-Ann was a little girl she told her how a secret shared is *like lemons.*

"Lemons, Grandmomma… how's it like lemons?"

"Lemon cordial. Pour in the water and it gets diluted out."

She still wasn't so sure what she meant; then she added, "Takes away the bitter."

She wishes Grandmomma Olivia was here right now when her momma finds out, to help take away the bitter.

She sees them park up, hears the doors slam, sees them walk along the path in single file, Jerome paying real close attention to his sneakers.

She'll wait for her name to get called out before she faces them. But doesn't matter what anyone says. It's her decision. She always wanted to go to college, make something of herself and she still can. It's her body.

It's not just the shape of her lips she has in common with Grandmomma Olivia. She was seventeen when she got pregnant with Abe. But this is different. She doesn't have to have it. She won't have it. They never talk about her dad's brother, the soldier, but Grandmomma Olivia told her last week. It's a big family secret. And now there's another and this one they *will* want to talk about. She slides the silver ring onto her swollen finger just as her momma calls out. Only it's not her name she hears.

"SHE – IS – WHAT?"

II

May 31ˢᵗ, 2003, Jacksonville, Florida

Starbucks might not have been the best choice for a busy Saturday afternoon. Especially not with three four-year-olds: talkative chattering four-year-old girls.

Randolph was meant to help only something came up. A favor for Lenny, his old boss. Of course, something would come up today. An interview with an old war veteran – Howard T Bowers – celebrating his one hundredth birthday. Got medals in the Second World War and the Korean War. So, looks like Ruby-May's got her hands full with Lilly, Lotty and Lou. Yeah, that's their names – couldn't make it up. Sounds like something Walt Disney created. Only no medals for Ruby-May. She deserves medals. That's for sure. She is one of the few people who can tell the girls apart. She's only known two sets of triplets in her school but there's been a lot of twins. You get good at this; no two people are the same, even if they look it.

Libby said she did not plan to have the meeting on a Saturday. It was supposed to be Friday, only Ted Jefferson had called. He had another appointment, for his wife, something about a clinical trial. And what with only one week left before school's out he said he really wanted to talk to her. Ruby-May has been wondering what will happen to April over the holidays. She's suggested summer school.

Libby said her ex-husband's out of town with his new girlfriend. Her mom is sick… her usual childminder's away… So, there she was saying *okay, of course she would*. She loves Libby's girls even if they are a handful – more than a handful. That's the reason she is in Starbucks because when Randolph gets home, he'll think a hurricane hit the house. That's why she decided to come out. She left a message for Libby to meet at her *their place*. There have been a lot of chats in this Starbucks. There are more kid-friendly places but no way she was taking them to McDonald's. Besides when a girl needs her Starbucks mocha latte with whipped cream, then a girl needs her Starbucks mocha latte with whipped cream. No surprise little white fingers been poking that whip of her Starbucks mocha latte, even though they have their own drinks – juice. And cookies. And she tells them it's not good manners. And Libby is late. She messaged to say she needed to visit a doctor's office. *What doctor's office?* Only she never said.

The girls are sitting quiet, which is something, but that's only because they're busy enjoying their cookies. Licking the icing off the top and eating around the edges. Libby is over an hour late. Now she's worrying about why she's been to a doctor's office. She never said it had anything to do with April Jefferson.

Libby's already made Ruby-May promise not to ask anything about her latest meeting with the Jeffersons. Of course, she'll ask and Libby knows it too. She's noticed a change in April these past two weeks. Last week, she asked her if she'd gotten to the descriptions of her friends yet. She said no. She'd been busy. Been seeing more of her dad. She said her pops did not approve, didn't trust him.

"Do you?"

"I want to."

Then she looked at her and said, "The bad man has a gun."

Just like that.

"What bad man? What gun?"

But the moment was done, like she didn't even know she said it. Next thing Ruby-May had dialed Libby's number.

She said maybe it was nothing, April says lots of crazy things. But now it's sitting right there inside her head, digging in like an ache. Oh, you bet, she'll ask what happened today.

The noise levels rise, the girls are fidgeting and Ruby-May is looking at her watch again. And finally, when she thinks surely she can't be a whole lot longer, the door opens and Libby is standing there. Her face all flushed. She is holding what looks like a bag of groceries.

The girls with their cute blonde curls and their sweet cookie smiles are out of their seats so fast, and Libby clearly has no plans to stay because she is telling them, "Thank Auntie Ruby for the..." her eyes on the table of crumbs and cartons "...*cookies?* She shoots a glance at Ruby-May. "And for the juice and for... taking care of you."

"It went okay?" Ruby-May says.

"Fine." Which she can tell she doesn't mean.

"What happened?"

"I said it went fine. Come on, girls."

The girls are now holding hands walking towards the door. "You still think something's going on with Ted Jefferson?"

"We'll talk next week."

"What did you find out?"

She looks at the girls who are now talking to one of the staff. She says she has something for them, wait there. She's the one who said earlier how she'd never seen real triplets before.

"Well?"

"I know what April said and it's not what you think. I asked him about it."

"The gun?"

"Something did happen but it was years ago and it was nothing. A misunderstanding." Her eyes find the girls. "I can't do this now."

"A misunderstanding about a gun?"

"Her grandfather collects military guns. Look, just know it's not what it sounds like. Another time, Ruby. Trust me."

"Then what did you learn about her mom?"

She shakes her head, looks again at the girls before she takes a step closer to Ruby-May. "I think I might have been right to start with."

"About Ted Jefferson?"

"About it being clinical."

She sees the girl now talking to Libby's girls, handing them a white paper bag.

"I'm sorry, Ruby. April does behave like her mom did. That's what he wanted to talk about."

"And?"

"Look, this isn't the best place, I—"

"Just tell me."

Libby has a real serious look on her face now when she looks at her. "Catherine Jefferson suffered from psychosis – very possibly schizophrenia."

Ruby-May feels herself slide right back down into her chair. Libby's head turns to look at the girls who are now on their way back holding out a large bag of… *more cookies?* No… muffins.

"I've spoken to Dr. McGarrigle and he wants to see her next week. He'll be able to get a hold of Catherine's notes by then too."

She doesn't know what she says after that, just that the girls are coming in for another round of sweet little sucky kisses and then they are all clattering out of Starbucks, Libby with her bags and the girls holding onto one another. But all Ruby-May does is stare into the foamy dregs of her mocha latte.

She knows about schizophrenia.

It's what they said Billy had.

And look how that ended.

Chapter 8

I

June 11ᵗʰ, 1993, Atlanta, Georgia

George watches. It's gotten busy this Friday afternoon on Peaches Avenue.

The new family across the street, where the Howards used to live, have put a swing set in the front yard, metal frame, there's a little kiddie in it now; the swing needs oiling. Sound sets the nerves all a-jangle. Molly is watering her roses, talking to the cat, Archimedes, Archie for short. It was Josie-Ann's idea – wonder what she was studying in school at the time? Given how she never liked cats she soon took to Archie. Don't know his age but he looks like he's getting old – legs all stiff after he's been sleeping, which he does a lot – George knows the feeling, age creeps up. Molly's started calling Archie a *grumpy ol' man* first. Now it's her new name for George. Well, maybe *he is a grumpy ol' man* and the sound of that *rusty ol' swing* is turning up the grumpy. It doesn't seem to irk Molly but then nothing seems to irk Molly. Except for last year after the letter came.

The kid on the swing looks about the age for pre-school – like the twins. The grandbabies will be here soon and now he thinks they'll be asking him for a swing set – that's how it works. Next thing Molly'll be asking him to get that old tire and make one in the tree outback, like he did when Henry was little.

Of course, Ella – otherwise known as "Biddy" – won't be so worried about a swing set. That girl always has her head in a book, just like her momma and just like George. Last year, on her eighth birthday, she told George how she was changing her name to "Biddy". *What kind of name is that?* She said she it was in honor of Biddy Mason.

"Who's Biddy Mason?"

She was already getting good at the attitude, hands straight onto her hips. "Grandpa, that's the first ever black landowner in 1866.

Was a nurse like Grandmomma, and a whole lot more besides." George's grandpap was picking cotton when a Negro woman called Biddy Mason owned her own house? He'd heard it all now. He made sure to tell her about his grandmomma and grandpap, cotton pickers and about how he met her grandmomma, registering for the vote. Sometimes she asks about Grandmomma Olivia and the *other* grandpap she never knew. All he had to say about that was he's been a long time dead and Garfield – husband number three – this time no eloping in secret to city hall, is more of a grandpap to her than Grandpap Ezra would ever be.

Biddy has already decided she's gonna be a doctor, and own her own house in California. She's got some fanciful notions. Josie-Ann used to be the same way. Molly says she still is, there's still time – twenty-six is still plenty young enough for dreams. Of course, she would be a psychologist by now if she hadn't changed her mind.

The letter was from Jacksonville. Arrived on a Thursday.

The house smells sweet – coconut cake is everyone's favorite. Of course he prefers lemon. Molly has made two coconut cakes, a chocolate cake and a bunch of oatmeal and raisin cookies for when they all arrive. Maybe she thinks she's feeding the whole street. As he watches from the window, George sees the "For Sale" sign is up. That house has had a lot of folks in it since Erica died. White guy owns it now and has rented it out to one family after another: all troubled. Robert Adams, from next door, moved in after Clive died, says it's bringing down a nice neighborhood; *having families like that.* George didn't know if he means renters, poor folks or black folks or maybe all three. He never even gave George a sideways glance until he learned that he works at Grant Park Library and runs the summer programs and that Molly is a head nurse at Grady Memorial. That's when he said he was a cop. Said George is proof not all black folks are bad. George hasn't spoken to him since. After "the incident" last month. Robert Adams might not have been the cop on duty but you can bet he saw Henry come home in a cop car. And it wasn't the first time.

George told Molly it's not Henry's fault, he's gotten in with the wrong crowd. Molly *does* get irked over Henry. Only Henry said *he never hit no one*. Cousin Thomas is the one who posted bail and later got the charges dropped. He said it was on account of Henry's "learning difficulties", but they all know it wasn't that. Henry did nothing wrong: wrong place, wrong time, all they saw was the color of his skin. He said he did not throw a single punch. Says he's learned to save his tempter just like George told him. Since Cousin Thomas stopped working for Jesse Jackson, he is back working for Maynard Jackson since he was re-elected Mayor of Atlanta. Now George might not like the politics, but whichever way you look at it, Cousin Thomas is a good man to have in your corner. He tells Henry to keep his head down; some folks look for trouble even if it's not there.

Everyone knows what happens. They all saw what happened to Rodney King in LA only last year. And the president – worse than that actor. George H W Bush is another republican who says he's on the side of the black folk to get the votes. All these presidents are exactly the same. No better than the cop they've got living next door. They might've come a long way but not far enough. Cousin Thomas knows it too. They have good reason for the anxious about Henry. Wrong place, wrong time. Bang.

But George does not want to think about that.

While those folks were rioting in LA, he was battling his own demons. And Molly was the one who held it all together.

He went to the doctor, but only because she promised to stop asking about that letter if he did. She still wants to ask; he sees it right there on her face. But she knows better. Besides, what's to tell? The past is the past.

They grounded Henry for a month after "the incident" – not so easy for a twenty-two-year-old. Now Cousin Thomas says he's trying to get him onto a program, something in the community. His oldest daughter works for "the project". Of course, if he was able to hold down a job it would help. When he says it, she's sure Thomas remembers that George was the exact same way.

Thomas had his sixty-second birthday last month. He plans on retiring soon as Maynard Jackson finishes his term, so Henry needs to get on the program before something real bad happens.

George looks further up the street. They'll be here soon... Josie-Ann, the twins and of course Biddy *Ella* Olivia-Marcie Patterson. She won't even answer to Ella now.

"What's wrong with the name Ella? Grandpap Henry's favorite singer was an Ella." She's perfected the *rolling eyes thing*. She's just like Josie-Ann at that age. Seems like age creeps up and one second your babies are in diapers and the next you're changing your grandchildren's diapers. And your momma is in a nursing home because she's forgotten who you are.

Molly invited Garfield over too. And Marcie and William. "What's the occasion?" Not like it's any of their birthdays, only she just tapped the side of her nose. She learned that from her cousin Lydia. No point in speculating, probably just wants an excuse to see everyone, bake some more of that coconut cake.

Garfield loves George's momma deeply but he worries that pretty soon she won't remember who he is either. Last time George went to see her she called him Abe. He's not been back since.

Getting old means more funerals, but not getting old is worse. Last year they lost four friends, and the neighbor.

The letter was from Mrs. Harrison, Isaac and Jacob's momma – now close to eighty years old.

He sees Molly in that pink dress of hers as she kneels and starts tugging at the weeds. He does not know how she does it all. She's on the night shift this week. At fifty-four when she ought to be slowing down, she's taking on more shifts – she says she wants to get that mortgage paid off once and for all. Of course, it doesn't help that since his "problems" last year, he's still only working three days a week at Grant Park Library. At least he has more time to work on his poetry collection. And Molly, she just says she loves her job now she's in charge of all those nurses. No sign of her slowing down just yet.

Molly is the glue. Everyone knows it.

And "Biddy" is just like Molly... and her momma of course.

Full of feist. And like her momma she's a grade A student – gifted they said at school. They got high hopes for her, that she won't waste all that education the way her momma did. Josie-Ann was always planning on going back to school. She was planning it right up until Biddy started school, only next thing she knew she was pregnant with the twins. George was never too sure about Jerome; Lydia was the one who planted the seed on that one, saying how sometimes people settle. George couldn't shake the thought away – had she settled? He might've had his reservations but that boy came good in the end, provides, works hard for his kids, did a whole lot better than they thought he would, now he owns the mechanics business, takes care of all the politicians' cars, thanks to Cousin Thomas. He did okay.

Just like George did.

And Henry will.

Jesse Jackson never did get voted President but he did make it to DC – Shadow US Senator for the District of Columbia. Shame Josie-Ann never made it – she gave up her dreams of DC and that Psychology degree soon as that baby started to kick. Ordinarily when she makes her mind on something, she don't change it, but this time it was different. She had her heart set on Howard in DC, no one was changing her mind on that – and definitely not the Pattersons no matter how hard they tried. Cousin Thomas said he'd got her the funding for Howard University. It was all set to happen. Only when her and Molly came back from the hospital, she'd looked right into his eyes, told him, "I'm sorry, Daddy, I couldn't do it." Like it was supposed to make him mad, mad that she wasn't moving 700 miles away now. That she wasn't getting rid of his grandbaby now, that she wasn't leaving Jerome now. He never told her how he'd been all blubber-blubber thinking about what she was doing, and how happy he was when she said that, there he was all blubber-blubber for a whole other reason. In the end she said she was happy, she wanted a baby, even if he did hear her crying herself to sleep every night before that baby came.

They got wed at City Hall.

Grandmomma Olivia was there with Garfield; Grandmomma

Marcie with William but no Cousin Thomas or Nettie. He wasn't too happy that she was not going to DC, although he came around in the end.

Sometimes he wonders what would've happened if Josie-Ann'd gone to DC, but he does not like to think about that because if she had, there would be no Biddy Ella Olivia-Marcie Patterson and maybe no twins either. Those boys are sweet as mud pie: Joshua and Jake, known affectionately as Bean and Button. They're not identical. As a matter of fact, since Joshua has the Tucker long-legs, he's like a whole inch taller than Jake and Jake is not so happy about that.

When Molly called yesterday to invite them all over, Josie-Ann said she'd had the phone right there in her hand. She was about to call, she had news – something important to tell them. Now he wonders if she's pregnant again. That's what she said last time she said needed to come over because "she had news". He stares out some more, sees the car. Josie-Ann and the kids, but no Jerome? That boy works some long hours. Looks like she gave Garfield a ride over. As they're parking up, not far behind them are Marcie and William. Looks like Molly got herself quite a family reunion even if he doesn't know why.

No doubt about it – Molly certainly is the glue.

The twins have chocolate-cake smiles. Molly wets a napkin and rubs hard but Bean's not having any of it and wriggles away. Biddy is looking at the family photograph album. Josie-Ann looks like she has a touch of *the anxious*. Though George has already told Molly he thinks she has good news to share: baby number four. Molly says nothing. She has other things on her mind. Besides she does not look like she has that kind of news. If she did, she would have said it already.

Bad news takes some working up to. And she knows. Cake is a good softener.

Maybe Molly ought to go first.

Henry is his usual quiet, only when Molly suggests he does

some drawing with the twins he seems to come to life. So now they're making space on the kitchen table. Those boys are all *chit-chat* and smiles. So, Henry is keeping the boys busy and Garfield, well he looks thinner every time she sees him. She watches him now, sitting alone. She's already put some cookies and one of the coconut cakes in a tin for him to take home. He needs to take better care of himself. She tells him he needs a hobby; that visiting with Olivia every day like that must be hard – especially since she has gotten so much worse. He says if he didn't go, he doesn't know how he'd spend his time. And that's a worry. Olivia is a worry. Not even George goes to see her these days. He said she told him not to.

She's gotten a whole lot worse than she was when Molly visited her last year.

Momma and William like to speak church which is usually George's cue to go play with Bean and Button or talk to Biddy. What kind of crazy names are they? She hopes they don't stick.

Molly nurses her chamomile tea with both hands and waits... for the right time.

She hopes George's cousin Thomas will let them know soon about "the project". Henry knows how to do the yard, prune the flowers, so if they can get him into the community gardening program, maybe that will suit him. He needs to find himself a good woman to take care of him. When he gets to mumbling, all she can think about is George. She came along and rescued him and someone will do the same for Henry.

George is watching the twins make a mess of the kitchen table, Henry laughing along with them. You'd never think there was anything wrong to look at Henry like that. He has felt tip marker on his cheeks. Or anything wrong with George. But those demons are still there.

Last year, Molly made an appointment with the doctor for George and that time she made sure he went. Josie-Ann drove them. She did not think he would go; but something was eating into him worse than last time he got the depression. Of course, being

George, he did not let her and Josie-Ann go in to see the doctor. He could have told him anything. But he did come out with a prescription for sleeping pills. She was looking them up soon as he got the prescription filled. She wishes she could have spoken to that doctor herself. He is *private*. Another word for that is *secretive*. She always remembers what Cousin Lydia said about when the time is right but sometimes, she thinks, the time will never be right. And as for Lydia, she made a big mistake years ago that got her kicked off the Dallas PD. Marcie says how everyone said she was a fraud. But that's not what Molly thinks.

George won't talk about what happened. All she knows is a letter came to the house. When she asked, he said it was nothing – but she could see on his face it wasn't nothing. The doctor's visit was six weeks later, after George'd starting missing work, sleeping on the couch and the mumbling had gotten a whole lot worse. She looked everywhere for that letter – but seems he hid it good.

She planned to talk to Lydia at Ismene's funeral last month, only it was like she was avoiding her. Now she realizes Josie-Ann is trying to get their attention. She looks tired. She's got her jeans on, that blouse she bought her last birthday, clothes seem looser, and her hair is pulled back. No make-up. How can George think she has *the baby glow*? But George always did love a baby. His moods are definitely better now he sleeps. But will it be enough? She needs to tell them her news now, while she has the adults' attention – well except for Henry who is still playing, she can tell him later. She ought to say it now, before Josie-Ann. But she doesn't. Josie-Ann has something to say and George's face is all lit up, waiting for the *baby* announcement. For a moment she hopes it is, really hopes it is. Isn't that what they say: good news first. But that is not a good-news face. Josie-Ann shoos the twins outside along with Henry and lowers her voice. "I thought you ought to know…" She looks at George then at Molly. "…Jerome and I have decided to file for divorce."

George's lips have that gaped shocked look where he was supposed to do the new-baby smile. It comes as no surprise to Molly. She knows they've been fighting. She's just happy Josie-

Ann made up her mind and she said it with all that confidence, like the old Josie-Ann. Only now she's said it out loud, that child's got tears on her cheeks. Molly pushes herself up from the armchair and next thing she has her arms around her baby. She smells sweet like talcum powder. "It's okay, honey. It's all gonna be okay. I'm proud of you."

Josie-Ann pulls away. "You are?"

"It's the right thing."

"The kids know," she whispers, "and Jerome's telling his parents now. Kids'll see their daddy every other weekend. We'll make it work; we won't let it be bad. We just..."

"Want different things?"

"Yes."

"I know. You always did and you tried. And you have three beautiful kids to show for it. So, you listen up." She runs her hands under Josie-Ann's chin and softly tilts her head so she is looking into her eyes. "No regrets, you hear me. It's the right thing. You'll both realize that one day. You were too young. But it was meant to be because you have these children. No regrets."

"I know, Momma. No regrets."

Molly reaches for the napkins on the table. "Here. Now blow your nose. You'll feel better now it's been said. Secrets are always better on the outside." Of course, she looks at George when she says that.

"Mom, if you can help with the kids, maybe after school," she says, "I'm going to back to school, in the Fall. Atlanta University to do my degree in Social Work. I can work at the same time."

Molly looks right at her. "About time."

Molly's momma is crying but then she believes those vows they made should never be broken. Molly knows different. No point is wasting a life being unhappy. She watches William offer her a tissue.

Garfield doesn't say anything; maybe he's thinking about how he'll tell Olivia, only she won't remember even when he does. She would support her, that much she knows. Olivia knows if you're not happy then you leave. She might not have done that the first time, but she sure did with that second husband of hers. She found a good one in the end. And she knows Olivia was the one who told Josie-Ann to follow her dream when she was seventeen – that there was plenty of time for babies. She wonders now if that's what she thinks she should have done when she was pregnant with Abe.

Josie-Ann says she'll make more coffee and she heads for the kitchen.

"Maybe they'll change their mind." It's George's sweet voice.

"It'll be okay, George. Now go help Josie-Ann."

She watches him walk towards the kitchen; then she sees Biddy. How long's she been standing there? It's only as she turns her head, she sees the shine of tears on her cheek. Molly pats her lap. Biddy doesn't move. So, Molly does it again.

This time she shuffles over. "Sit," Molly says. "Everythin's gonna work out. No one's fault. They love you just the same as they always did."

Biddy nods but seems to hold on to Molly's stare. "You got that, Ella?" She doesn't even say anything about her using her real name. "Things will be different but they will work out."

She leans in so now Molly can feel the warm tickle of her cookie breath. "Your turn, Nana."

Molly nudges her gently away and looks at her. So much like Josie-Ann. Sweet lips, sweet nose, even her hair when she was little, Josie-Ann even had a little pink clip with a butterfly very similar. "My turn for what, sweetie?"

"Your secret, Nana."

Those words are the reason for Molly's shiver.

"I know, Nana."

But Molly never told. *Never told no one.*

With that Biddy's small fingers find hers and press down like soft kisses.

"Are you telling?"

"No," she whispers. "Not yet, Biddy."

How can she say it now? Biddy smiles and now she leans in and holds onto Molly. Wraps her little arms around her and holds on good 'n' tight. *Another one has the gift in the family?*

165

Maybe Lydia was right – you just have to wait for the right moment.

Like George – and his secret.

Like Josie-Ann – waiting to go back to school.

And like her – telling those you love how two weeks ago you found a lump in your breast and that the doctors say it's cancer.

II

June 11ᵗʰ, 2003, Jacksonville, Florida

They need rain.

Pops says it as they watch the sprinklers made rainbows. Air is too dry, saps the life right out he says, slapping a handkerchief over his face. He says there's a storm coming. He's wearing his shirt – the gray one – the one with the short sleeves. A gray tie. His favorite black pants. He's shined his brogues. Always does. April watches him look skyward into the blue. It's almost 1.30. The appointment is at 2.30. Grams is staying home. Pops has asked one of the neighbors, Mrs. Drake, to sit. He hates to do that but Grams is not so good with hospitals.

Water droplets cling to the big palmy leaves of the cycad plant. Grams says that's what it's called, or she did. Hard to know what she remembers these days. The plant with the big red blooms is wet through. Water drips onto the square of grass. Air smells fresh, leafy. The palm stands in silent salute, no zephyr, no dance. April doesn't know the names of the plants – Grams was good at that only Grams's memory has gotten worse. When she says it, all Pops does is shrug. He's in denial. One of the stages of grief Jesse says.

"Grams isn't dead."

"She is going… just slowly."

Doesn't matter how wise Jesse sounds, April does not want to think about that. Jesse says maybe she needs to go into a home – like his grandma. She does not want to think about that either.

What she knows is Grams drifts between *now* and *then* only lately she spends most of her time in the *then.* Last night she was sure April was Catherine. Usually it's once or twice. Last night no amount of correcting was changing it. Pops had her assessed for a clinical trial only turns out she's a stage too far on for *the new wonder drug.* She saw the way Pops's expression changed when he told her. Like a balloon deflating, the hope getting sucked right out. There is no cure. Some losses are sudden, some are gradual,

167

all are inevitable. Maybe Jesse was right but some things you're best not to talk about. One of the first things Pops taught her.

Mrs. Drake has brought cookies. They're both set up in the back yard, at the big table under the umbrella. Pops says she used to love to sunbathe. Got to be careful now, it causes cancer. He won't let her anymore. Maybe it ought to be in his book of rules.

Secrets are like cancer.

The air smells sweet, damp, and April has a sudden urge to run into the sprinklers. She used to do it with her mom when she as a little girl. But not today – she's dressed up *so pretty*. That's one of her mom's expressions. *April – you're dressed up so pretty*. It's the last thing she remembers her saying to her.

Pops says April has to make the right impression. It's the floaty dress with the pink flowers and those white sandals; she even painted her toe nails and her fingernails – coral. She has her pink purse with the glitter-butterfly. Matches the clip in her hair. Grams bought her the dress and the shoes the last time they went to the mall. Like she thinks she's eight not fifteen. The purse and the hair clip were for her birthday. Grams can't go to the mall now; it freaks her out.

April wonders why can't she wear her jeans. It's not a job interview, it's a hospital appointment. Only she knows why – this is no ordinary doctor. They think she doesn't know what this is and what they say? *April is crazy – just like her mom.* Well she's not. They all say she's not – Jesse says it, Grace says it, Owen says it, Martha says it and Rose is saying it right now and she stands in the doorway watching Pops unlock the car. Rose says, "Just act normal." So does Pops, only his idea of normal is different.

"Be yourself, Peach," her dad says. He is not happy about any of this. Says if they want this to be a "family session" then he ought to be there. He knows about therapy, seen enough doctors. But Pops says it's best he's not there, not today. Same as Grams. She won't remember things right.

"Dad will."

But even when she said it, she realized. Grams spends most of her time in the *then* and her dad spends most of his time in *an alcoholic haze*. Or he did. Pops says he isn't ready. When the time is right. It's a dumb expression. It means *never*.

Mrs. Drake's oatmeal and raisin cookies were still warm when she arrived. She can still smell the waft, sugar-coating the air. Grams is the one with the sweet tooth. April not so much but last night Grams said her mom had it. Mississippi mud pie. Told her the story all over again, only last night she remembered Rick's Diner, said she took Catherine there but she couldn't have. Rick's Diner was only ten years old last year; she remembers the balloons and the banners. So now they're sat out back, with cookies and a pot of coffee and April wishes she could sit with them, maybe even try a cookie. Pops is looking at April and then at his watch. She looks down at her dress, her shoes, the nail polish is smudged on her little toe. She straightens up. Adjusts her pink purse so its sits straight on her shoulder. Okay – she's ready. *But is he?*

On the ride to the Ellison, Pops will not want to talk. He gets a look, like his face is all closed up, the way it does when anyone talks about April's mom. Same face when *she* talks about her dad. How she wants him to come over and he says, "No. No April, you know the rules, April." Rules get broken, they all know it, Jesse says it all the time. Jesse hates Pops; they all leave when he comes into the room. They hate the rules.

Don't tell folks your business – that's the first rule she learned. Though her pops did say one thing a couple of weeks back. That he told Miss Gerard about the night her mom went crazy with a shotgun. That the cops came but it was a big misunderstanding. Gun fired by accident. That's one way to say it – maybe the first shot. He missed out the part about waving that gun around and telling her dad to leave and never come back. And the part about how all that did was make her mom so mad they all moved out and went to live in that trailer park. She doesn't remember much, she was three; her dad sometimes talks about it. The only thing she does remember about that trailer park, was the way it ended. It's one thing Pops will never talk about. Not to Miss Gerard and especially not to a shrink.

But why did he have to tell Miss Gerard about the shotgun?

Pops said he only told her in case it comes up. They can check police records. You can bet it's *coming up* now.

What makes him think the other incident won't come up? But she knows he never told her about the other gun; of course he didn't. He never told her about the gun that killed her.

They have to park way at the back of the lot. Ellison Children's Hospital is downtown. They left extra time for traffic but since the schools are out, they're early. It's a Pops thing – he always likes to be early. It's a massive hospital, clean lines and open spaces.

Pops walks slow, then he has to use the bathroom *again* while April waits, watches. A mom and a little girl on crutches and another little boy with burns on his face. April does not belong here and soon as that doctor talks to her, he'll know it too and the only thing that will be crazy about today, is this – *this* is the misunderstanding – *one big misunderstanding.* Just like her friends tell her it is.

She thinks about what her dad said. "Be yourself, Pumpkin."

Isn't that what she'd been doing this whole time?

Dr. McGarrigle is only about five foot two, three? Small round glasses, not much hair. He's wearing a white coat, and sneakers. The whitest sneakers you ever saw. He speaks slow, smiles too much and says he is happy to meet with April, only he says it too much. April knows insincere. They're in a room with more toys than books. It's way bigger than Miss Gerard's office. Even with the air con, she feels her skin goose up. White walls with colorful murals, jungle animals. Huge window that looks over the parking lot. Five soft chairs facing one another. Still smells like a hospital even if it doesn't look like one. He sits and waits for her to say something. It might be a long wait. The less she says, the sooner this will be over. She's already told Miss Gerard everything she wants to tell her and she'll only tell Dr. McGarrigle the same damn things: she loves school (except all of it sucks), she loves her friends, she loves her teachers, she loves her grandparents, she is not crazy, her dad likes his liquor but not now, her grams has Alzheimer's, her pops is ex-military, has a gun (well maybe not that last part). But seems he isn't asking any of those questions. He's watching. Talking about the weather, Pops's cue to say how much they need rain, a storm's forecasted. Chit-chat. Now he's asking April's opinion. *On the rain? What is this? Just get to it.* She leaves them to the chit-chat. When this is done, he is sending a report back to Miss Gerard and to Mrs. Johnston that says there's nothing wrong with April Jefferson – she is well adjusted – intelligent – has the best friends – does not have an opinion on the weather.

It's twenty in before April realizes she's been mumbling. What's more, her cheeks are wet and Dr. McGarrigle is offering her a Kleenex. What just happened? She's been mumbling bad from the look on Pops's face. She takes the tissue and softly dabs her cheeks. April has lost time before – maybe they'll take her to CT, see if crazy shows up on a scan. But she doesn't want to lose time while she's trying to prove how normal she is.

So, she sits, feet crossed over, looks at the clock on the far wall again.

The doctor finally speaks. "I know this is difficult, but I need to find out when all of this started. When you first spoke to your friends."

He knows. Miss Gerard would have told him. She's not saying. So, Pops says, "She was three." And the doctor is staring at April when he says, "And was that before or after your mom died?"

He won't like it; Pops won't like it. Don't tell them what happened.

"After."

She keeps her mouth zipped. Pops ought to do the same.

"Do you remember your mom?"

Of course, she remembers. Sprinklers. She remembers sprinklers, wet toes. Shotgun, moving in with Daddy, lots of fights. But seems the one thing she had to do, keep it zipped, she has failed on and Dr. McGarrigle is nodding.

171

She bunches her fists into the sag of her dress. Must try harder. Pops is all a fidget now.

"April, you remember when your mom died?"

No. Yes. Not telling.

This time she does keep her mouth zipped up tight.

"What about how you felt, you remember how you felt?"

She was three. All she knew was one day there were all living together in a trailer, and three weeks later she was back at Grams and Pops, and Daddy was gone.

Fuck.

From the looks on their faces she said that.

And now the doctor is handing her the whole box of Kleenex. This is not going well. All she had to do was keep her cool, just the way her friends told her. And Pops, he is out of the seat, saying he needs the bathroom. Oh, this is going great.

Ten minutes later April has regained her cool.

Pops is talking to the doctor outside; whispering. They have a lot to talk about. Jesse is back, says April is doing good. Just stay calm. She does not feel like she is doing good but Jesse has a way of making her feel better. She can do this. She listens to the buzz of the air con, closes her eyes and waits for them to come back in. When they do, Pops looks anxious. Soon as he comes back in, Jesse leaves.

This time the doctor asks easy questions. So, she tells him straight – her friends' names, when he asks if they tell her do things she says yes. See, being honest? This is better. Much better. It's easy to lose another twenty minutes talking about her friends. Sure, she hears them, sure they talk to her (he's as bad as Miss Gerard, does he know what a friend is?), yeah, she recognizes their different voices – what is this? Yes, they ask her to do things, what friend doesn't? Yes, she usually does it, she's a good friend, even if she doesn't want to. What bad things? They never make her do bad things.

Questions – too many questions. But she's answering them, but only because her friends told her she had to.

172

Pops has sweat on his face, even though it's freezing in the room.

Clock ticks round and April's sure she's aced this last part. Maybe it's like a test, overall it's a pass even if she messed up the first part.

They're almost done because now Pops is pressing his hands into the arms of the chair, slowly standing. Then he's holding out his hand and so April scrambles to her feet, tugging at the strap of her pink purse. How'd she do?

"I'm very sorry you lost your daughter so young," the doctor says as he shakes Pops's hand. Even sounds sincere – for a moment. Pops nods. "It can't have been easy. For you to talk about what happened. A terrible tragedy."

He told him what happened?

That's what they were whispering?

Shit.

Heads turn back to April. "I'm not like her," she says. "I'm not." She tugs her purse onto her shoulder and now she walks slowly towards the door. Keep it zipped. Don't say anything else.

"Make an appointment," the doctor says. "I'll see you next week, April."

Another appointment?

Now Jesse is back, they all are, even though Pops is here and Martha has started with her jibber-jabbering. Shut up. Shut up. Shut the fuck up!

Of course, she did not mean to say it so anyone could hear, and she definitely didn't mean to shout only sometimes Martha gets way too loud and…

Pops does not look happy. And for the first time seems the smile has slipped right off Dr. McGarrigle's face. "You okay, April? You want to come and sit back down."

No, she does not want to come and sit back down.

Shut up! Will you quit already!

Pops shuffles closer, his hand reaches for her arm. She snatches it away. "Come on."

She's embarrassing him now? He's the one who told the doctor

173

the thing they're not supposed to tell. He looks back and thanks the doctor and nudges April into the doorway. But she's not done. Martha is not done either telling her to say it. Say it, April. Just say it. So she does. She spins around in those pretty sandals of hers and she looks at the weedy little shrink with the fake smile and his too-white sneakers and she tells him. Just like Martha tells her. Only way to shut her up. She says, "Stay away from the bad man with the gun."

She feels the grip of Pops's fingers pinch hard on her arm.

The doctor is staring, not saying anything.

She pictures the trailer park; it was a whole other time, gun was smaller, much smaller. They'd gone out for ice cream. She changed her mind. Popsicles were her favorite. Daddy was holding onto her hand as they turned the corner, walked back past the trailers. She had the Popsicle in her right hand, only it was so hot it was dribbling along her fingers.

It was so loud April dropped the Popsicle. It sounded like a car back-firing but it was not a car back-firing. It was a gunshot only she didn't know it at the time. Only that Daddy was running, telling April to stay there. Stay right there. Don't you move, Ape. Her fingers were sticky. Daddy was shouting. She had bent down to pick up the Popsicle only it had flecks of dirt on it and she remembers frantically trying to wipe them off not knowing her momma was dead. That she'd found her daddy's handgun when they went out for a Popsicle. Blamed himself. Moved out because Pops had a shotgun, yet her daddy was no better. He never believed she'd find it. Said it was hidden away good. Only not good enough, was it? He cried about that enough times when he was on the liquor. But sorry loses meaning the more you say it. Everything changed that day.

April would never eat another Popsicle.

Daddy would start drinking beer for breakfast.

And twelve years later, April would be standing in a doorway at Ellison Children's Hospital while a shrink looks at her like she's the crazy one. Just about the same time a fist of rain hits the window. Looks like that storm came.

174

Chapter 9

I

July 19th, 1997, Atlanta, Georgia

It's the perfect day for a picnic. Molly found just the place: Winn Park in downtown Atlanta. And now, as Molly packs away the paper cups and plates, it seems it's the perfect place for softball. Cool afternoon air flaps Molly's purple dress as she bends and catches a rogue cup before it blows away.

Sounds drift from Biddy's radio. As Puff Daddy sings about *missing you* and Biddy sits mouthing the words; Jerome and the twins are busy recruiting. The softball was Jerome's idea. George is not sure, for all his *co-ercin'*, Marcie, who turns eighty next year, is up for that. William has to watch from the side lines anyhow, since his knee operation.

Josie-Ann is sat on the blanket – the big green one, head poked into a book. Biddy is leaning into her, their legs stuck out in front. Same pink toenail polish. It's hard to believe Biddy'll be in her final year of middle school when school starts. She still has her heart set on being a doctor – only now it's a surgeon. Cardiothoracic. That girl has some pluck.

Bean has already helped Button mark out the plate and loaded the bases with backpacks, sweatshirts and whatever else they can find. They have a baseball bat and a tennis ball. No one wants to get hit by a baseball. They don't have enough for two teams but looks like Bean and Button have asked other folks in the park: recruited two dads, a mom and a handful of kids all eager to join in.

Garfield has perked up right out of his usual quiet, as eager as those kids. He's already making air pitches like he thinks he's Bob "Hoot" Gibson. Even has his hands around the imaginary ball in a cutter grip as he leans back, lifts his leg. Even the twins have stopped to watch him. Makes George think about Abe, when they were kids playing ball at Clayton Ballpark, before it became part of Memorial Park.

Henry is sat on one of the foldaway seats but he doesn't take a lot of notice of the twins and their rallying; seems his eyes have a whole other focus. It's the first family celebration when Henry has brought along a girlfriend – and at the age of twenty-six too. Small, curvy figure, long hair looks like it's been ironed out straight and the biggest smile, not quite as radiant as Molly's because no one has *that* smile, but George thinks it's good enough. She has a pretty name too: Nia. Nia seems to like Henry a whole lot. They met at "the project". She has learning difficulties too only she seems bright enough to George. She likes to read his poems, though she says she cannot think why he hasn't gotten them published into a collection yet. Like it's easy. He tried but letters always said the same thing – *not for us.* Doesn't seem like anyone wants to read poems by a fifty-nine-year-old black man. In the end he thought maybe he'd get them made into a book himself – his legacy – for the grandkids, for when he's gone. All Molly said was not to talk so morbid. She calls it *the morbids.* That was after she got diagnosed with the cancer for the second time. In her other breast. Only that time it had spread. He had good reason to have *the morbids.*

George slowly wanders towards Garfield in his knee-length khaki shorts and his bright white T-shirt; he still has some muscles – George never saw that before. He's even wearing a Braves baseball cap. He looks so at home it's like he's grown a whole inch taller, almost caught up with George. Now he's showing Bean how to hold the bat, hands on his as he guides the movement, just like George taught Henry once, just like Abe taught George and just like Pap taught Abe. There's an area Button says is for the batters and Jerome is flipping a quarter to see who hits first. Girls win. Seems someone made it boys against girls only there are more boys. Nia is laughing at something Henry is saying as she presses her hand onto his knee and pulls herself up.

She told George her momma used to work for a publisher; she

176

still does from time to time. A small one. Black Oleander. An African-American press. Based in Jacksonville. Must be small as George never heard of it, not even from all these years of working at the library. He was quick to look it up though. They've published two books of poetry – he ordered them both for the library. Now George has lots of questions to ask Nia's momma, only Molly says he has plenty of time for that. *Let it grow. Don't scare her off. You'll meet when the time's right.* But seems the time is not right to invite her to the picnic. Molly says they have only been dating for three months. *Be patient, George.*

Nia now reaches out and pulls Henry from the seat. Then she brushes grass from her jeans, her T-shirt is yellow, canary yellow just like that *shimmer-shimmer* dress of Molly's. Nia says something to the twins – she is good with them; you can tell she works with children. She works for the art projects, and is hoping to start working at a school soon. She says Henry likes to help out and that's how she suggested Henry did the paintings of the plants: the ones he puts into pots at the center and the ones he plants for old folks when he does his gardening jobs all along Peaches Avenue. He is the reason there are paintings and sketches of plants all over the house. George told him maybe he ought to try something else. Last month he said he was working on a sketch of Archie, asked George for some photographs. He says it's a surprise, for his momma, since she was the one who cried the most when that cat died. Now they've got Socrates, shortened to Socks and Descartes shortened to Des. It was Biddy's idea to get the kittens last year – two brothers, and of course she'd already named them. Not like the kind of names George would've chosen. But then he wouldn't've chosen to have more cats. George cried the most; he just never showed it. He wonders if Henry'll draw Socks and Des next.

Now Nia's saying something to Garfield. He is definitely standing taller *and* younger. George does not know how old he is; he knows he was older than his momma, at least ten years, so must be eighty-five if he's a day. He's usually as quiet as George, but he looks like he's giving Nia some pitching tips. Arm around her, now they're laughing. Everyone likes Nia. Doesn't matter if she's slow like Henry, he's seen the way she makes the doe-eyes at Henry. And he looks at her the exact same way. Henry has even sold two paintings. Okay so one was to Marcie and William – the one of the cycad plant, painted from the plant growing in their own back yard, right next to where Archie's buried and the other was a fancy one with red blooms – sold that one to Garfield. But a sale is a sale. Garfield says his grandmomma Olivia would have been so proud of him, she loved camellias – then he got this faraway look. Grief is a terrible thing, and George knows it. Three years and George still looks for Archie. Only been two years since Momma went – only a blink – but everyone knows some grief lasts a lifetime. George does not want to think about that – not today. Today is meant to be a celebration.

The air is full of happy sounds. Even the radio has moved onto something all *Mm-boppy*. Biddy says it's Hanson. They have a lot to be thankful for and today is not just a celebration, it's a double celebration. For Molly and for Josie-Ann – but he always knew Josie-Ann would get that degree, even if it did take her four years. Now she works as a social worker. He's heard her speak to Molly about some of the things she sees – some folks should never have kids. Molly still works but she doesn't take extra shifts since the cancer. Just as well she has such good medical insurance – some poor folks can't afford to get treated. Cousin Thomas was the one fighting to get better healthcare – especially for African-Americans. It was the last thing he'd been working on.

Seems they are almost ready, batters lined up and what George thought was a fun game seems like it took a serious turn, as Jerome organizes them, gets everyone into huddles to talk tactics, that's something Abe would've done – but right now George thinks the only strategy he needs is to hit that ball and run – neither of which is likely. George's stopped listening. Josie-Ann was the one said to invite Jerome; it's not like he hasn't met Luis, and she's met Aisha plenty of times. Seems like they were working it out just fine. Of course, Aisha's had to go already – she has to work, she paints nails. George was not so sure about Josie-Ann dating a man whose family is from Cuba. *What's wrong with that, Dad?* Nothing. *He's brown, not black, so what?* And Molly – she gave him dagger stares and told him to *be quiet, George.* He didn't mean it the way it came out; got his words muddled when he tried to say it. Cousin Thomas said something once, about the way society always wants to be integrated, all mixed up, but he said in the end we need to stick together. "No one understands it better than us," he said. "Sure, we all got white friends, but when you grow up in a world that looks down on you, and they still do, you know it, George, then you need friends who've got your back. Only we know, only we fully understand the struggles of the Negro, colored, black, African-American – they're so scared about what to call us, about being *politically correct* and all that bullshit, they miss the point. Take the word out of the sentence and you got man; not black man or white man or any other damn color. Soon as we got labels, we're segregated just the same as we always were."

And all George said to that was, "All they gotta do is call us by name."

Cousin Thomas liked that.

There were times George mighta rolled his eyes when Thomas started with the politics but now he misses it. Now who'll tell him which is the best president to vote for?

The last time George played baseball he was in high school. He and his friends played after school and all through the summer holidays when Abe was away fighting in Korea. Used to play with his glove. Abe always said softball is baseball's lazy cousin. He would not approve of softball – especially without gloves and especially not with a tennis ball.

Radio battery winds itself down. Noises come in slaps of sound: cheers and whoops and every now and then the hollow pop of a tennis ball sent across the park. George misses another flyball – Jerome's already moved from first base to midfield but it doesn't matter. Right now, all of them are here, everyone he loves, only that's not true is it. Every year there're fewer of them.

He watches the white family who are joining in. When Jackie Robinson played baseball, he said it didn't matter what color your skin was, all that mattered for those nine innings was who was on your team – who'd got your back. Makes him think about what Cousin Thomas said. Only what happens off the field can be a whole different thing. Cousin Thomas died fighting for his beliefs.

George's team is up to bat.

Henry is first. The bat connects and the ball skims hard and low to center field where Marcie scrambles for it. She's still pretty nimble.

"To me!" Josie-Ann shouts from third base as Henry passes second. That boy can run. His legs are *all antelope.*

He makes the home plate and fist punches the air. Jerome howls and the boys cheer. Henry has got them a point.

Button is up next. Hits first time and balls goes high, he whoops in victory only it's short-lived as the ball goes right into Luis's clean snatch. He stomps his feet and the bat clatters to the ground.

Bean next, he looks the part, eyes fixed hard on Nia.

Misses.

Nia throws again. Does all the actions like a pitcher, like she's doing a dance, runs up and then slows and throws it underarm. They say baseball is for theatrics.

This time, straight to the dad whose been put as catcher.

Three – and out. Now Bean begs for more throws but Jerome gives him *the dad stare* and he joins his brother on the side line.

George remembers how to hold the bat but not how to hit. He is three strikes and out just like Bean.

They are not going to beat the girls' score.

Jerome is up last. Ball flies past Molly and way back as far as the ice cream vendors. Whoops and squeals and they are only two behind the girls.

George has lost count of the innings. All he knows, is he's as bad at batting as he is fielding. Garfield and Jerome are the battery and most of the balls didn't even reach George in the outfield. The girls are still doing better than the boys. Garfield is the best pitcher – no underarm. His pitches are something to watch: fastballs, curveballs, change-ups. Wasted on these guys, and with a tennis ball, he is all *nifty-fingers*. In one of the lemonade breaks he heard Jerome saying Garfield used to play for the Jacksonville Red Caps, in the Negro American League. It explains the reason for the grin on his face: all teeth and lips. George does not think he has seen him that happy since before Momma got sick. And why did he not know this before? But he knows why. Neither of them are talkers. His grandmomma told him once how there's a whole lot more to people than what you see, everyone's got a story. Just that some people leave it tucked inside.

George is drifting further into outfield, edging towards that ice cream vendor thinking he wants it to be over. He can almost hear Abe in his head, saying *what the hell, George? You were never this bad. What happened to you?* Getting old is what happened. Only not everyone gets to do that now, do they?

Biddy's laugh is so loud it stretches out as far as George. She's laughing at something Luis says. Luis is good for the kids, doesn't try to be their dad, there if they need him. It was Molly who said all you had to do was look into Josie-Ann's eyes and see the light had come right back on – that's how she knew she'd made a good choice. And as George looks over at Molly all radiant in that purple dress of hers, he realizes what's different. Since they said she was in remission – for the second time – the real reason for today's celebration, her lights have come back on brighter than they ever were. She's okay, just like his momma said she would be, in one of her lucid moments. That was the last time he went to see her.

Whoops and cheers and looks like Biddy makes a home-run and thankfully the ball has gone in a whole other direction to George. Now Molly is up to bat.

George is a worrier. A whole lot better at worrying than he is at playing softball. Worried after Molly had her operation the first time. Worried during that radiation therapy. Worried even when Dr. Carter said the cancer was gone. It was three years before the cancer came back. Just like he worried it would. Molly told him: *George, you want to waste your life away worrying 'bout somethin' bad that might never happen?* But bad things do happen. Terrible things happen. The cancer came back, and what if it comes back again? *Will you stop with the worrying, George? I'm here now, and that's what counts. We all got to go sometime.*

Garfield didn't meet Momma until she was in her fifties. George's had a lifetime with Molly but it will never be enough and he knows it. Molly has rescued George from his demons so many times – but what if she's not there? She says she has no plans to go anyplace – not yet. But no one ever knows. Looks what happened to Cousin Thomas.

Jerome is the reason for the sudden whooping. The ball is low and fast and slips right through everyone's fingers. He gets round so now the game is tied. The boys need one more to win. Henry was struck out, the twins had extra goes and still never hit the ball. George is up next. Molly is standing way back.

He misses the first two. *Focus, George.* Abe used to say his head was always buried in a book – even when it wasn't.

Henry gives him a thumbs-up. When he looks at him, he thinks how Nia saved him just like Molly did him. He has not come home in a cop car since. At one time he said he wanted to join the army. George soon put a stop to that. Now soldiers go to Iraq. They always go somewhere. And young men get themselves killed for their president. President Clinton *has* done some good things for the African-Americans but then he is a Democrat, first one since Roosevelt. Cousin Thomas said he was worth the vote, he was still talking about how one day, there'd be black president. If there is one, he won't get to see it now.

Focus, George.

Nia throws easy this time, George swings, feels the ball engage and up it flies. And this time it *really* flies. George is so shocked he almost forgets to run. Only now everyone is shouting. Garfield shouts, "Run, George! Run!"

Luis is on first base; he whoops and shouts out to Molly to catch

182

the ball. The ball has gone that far? He needs to get to the red T-shirt that marks out first base. George is running. He makes the red T-shirt and all he can hear are the twins squealing. "Go, Grandpa!" and Josie-Ann is screaming, "Catch it, Momma! Catch it!"

Passing the crumpled gray sweatshirt that marks second, willing his legs faster. He scored one home-run in his life. That time he hit that ball so high it was almost over the fence.

George is passing the water bottle that marks out third; he has no idea where the ball is but he's running anyhow like suddenly he *does* care. He closes his eyes as he makes it home expecting any second for Nia to run him out. But he needn't've worried. When he looks back all he can see is Molly way across the park still looking for the ball.

Second home-run in his life.

What's more and you can tell from all the screaming – thanks to George the boys have won, no point in Garfield even taking his turn to bat. They tell him he is the hero of the moment. Just like that day with his friends. Hands pat his back but George flinches. George is no hero; George is a coward – was back then – still is now.

As the twins do the victory dance, George stands still. For a second, it's like all the sound got sucked right out of the air. This time it's not Winn Park on a Saturday afternoon in July. It's Clayton Ballpark. Bases are loaded – Grandmomma Josie on first, Grandpap Zeb on second: young again. Pap is on third, a menthol Kool sat right between his lips. Seems like his eyes got softer, like he's smiling at George. Cousin Thomas is pitcher, he's on the mound, looking right at George. This is baseball not softball. He wrote a poem for Cousin Thomas, about fighting for the black man. He gave it to Nettie and she put it in his coffin. Said he was beautiful, that he had a gift. He's not so sure about that.

It's in his collection hoping to get published by Black Oleander Press.

"George!"

He stares out, wants to stay right here for a second longer.

"George!"

Abe is in to bat – he looks strong, focused, hands grip on good and tight. Henry Snr is catcher. Cousin Thomas pitches a forkball, one Garfield would be proud of. Abe hits the ball up so high it disappears into the blue.

"George!"

His momma stands in midfield. George wrote a poem for her too; Biddy read that one out at her funeral. It was Molly who made him go visit her that last time, when she got the pneumonia. The time before that she thought he was Abe, but not that last time. She said Abe had already been.

A big warm hand on his arm. Molly is standing in front of him. "You know I missed so you could win," she says. Behind her everyone's packing up, twins gathering up the backpacks and the sweatshirts from the bases and Biddy and Josie-Ann are shaking out the big green blanket. And it's as he stands there, only for a second, George is sure those *friends* of his, ones he has not heard in his head for a lot of years are here too. Jesse always did love a ball game. Not so much Owen. The girls – Rose, Martha, Grace – would take it or leave it. He closes his eyes, pinches his lips shut so he doesn't get *the mumbles* – then just like that they're gone.

George watches as the others walk back in the direction of the parking lot. Molly joins Biddy, Josie-Ann and her momma, next to William with his walking cane, as they make their way slowly back across the park.

But George stands still.

He realizes, as he stands and looks back at the empty space, he's not the only one.

George has never really spoken to Garfield about his past. Garfield is not like Pap – Garfield is a good man.

"I never knew you played for the Red Caps."

Now they're stood side by side, toe by toe.

"That was a long time ago, George. Ain't played in years. For a second I was back there at Durkee Field in Jacksonville – you know it?"

George nods. "I didn't know you were from Jacksonville."

184

"I wasn't. I went because everyone said Jacksonville was a blackball town. Played with the Caps for a year, before they moved to Cleveland, then came back."

"You win many games?"

"Hell no. We were never any good, George, but I was." He laughs. "People told *me* I oughta try out for the Major League."

"Did you?"

"Hell yeah."

"That must've been before Jackie Robinson?"

"They even said yes. You know I was signed up for the Blue Socks – I was scheduled to play for the Major Leagues, George. Date was all set for that first game at Durkee Park. Turns out no one wanted to play against a team with a Negro in it. Eight years later Jackie Robinson was playing for the Brooklyn Dodgers."

"So, *you* could've been the first?"

The others are way across the park now, though George can still see Molly in purple.

"I would not have been the first, George. Jackie Robinson weren't even the first.

Moses Fleetwood Walker. Played in the Major Leagues for one season. It was sixty-three years before Robinson. There wasn't another black player in the majors for six decades."

"For real?"

"But he wasn't the *very first*. That was William Edward White, a former slave. Played one game. Then came Moses Walker and after that his brother, Weldy Wilberforce Walker, joined him on the team – so Jackie Robinson was actually the fourth to play for the Major Leagues. Now Jackie Robinson made history, ain't taking nothin' away from that. But imagine being the first and no one remembers you, like you just fell right out of history."

But now all George can think is Garfield is rewriting *a whole slice of history*. He only wishes Abe was here to tell him that. Pity you can't rewrite his history.

Garfield looks like he shrunk, like he's got lost all over again. His face was the same that day. He was stood a long time at Momma's graveside while George waited his turn over by the trees. Watched his family leave. He'd told Molly he needed some time alone, to sit quiet where she was buried. As he'd watched Garfield, all he could think about was standing at Molly's grave one day wondering how to live without her.

He watched Garfield mumbling words he didn't hear. And then he was on his knees, dirt on his black trousers, bent over and that's when George'd looked away. The sound he made next wasn't meant for him. Grief is a private thing. Not so much a celebration of life, an ending and there had been too many of those. Older you get – the more there are.

Too many *what-ifs*.

George heard Lydia say it to Nettie at Cousin Thomas's funeral. What if he hadn't gone that day, what if Noah Washington hadn't died in that police cell. No point in *what-ifs*. His grandmomma taught George that when he was fifteen. Lydia told Nettie Thomas'd died for his beliefs. That he would've wanted that – but the way he sees it: wrong place, wrong time. It was supposed to be a peaceful protest. Noah Washington had died in police custody, kicked to death in his cell the *Atlantic Daily Record* said. Didn't make the news like Rodney King, but there was a protest, downtown, not so far from Winn Park. Cousin Thomas got caught up when the violence started. No one knows exactly how it happened, called it an accident; that he tripped and hit his head, only he hit it all wrong and bled out in the street, while the cops trampled right over him. They denied it all, said no one could prove it. Just like no one could prove Noah Washington's death was because of his color.

Nettie is fighting for justice for her husband, but all George knows about that is sometimes you can't fight it – all it does is make you relive it over and over – it's not bringing him back.

Lots of folks died for their beliefs – the ones everyone knows like President Kennedy, his brother Bobby, Martin Luther King Jnr, Malcolm X… and the ones you don't: Reverend George Lee murdered for helping folks to register to vote, Lamar Smith, shot dead outside a courtroom by a white man, Emmett Louis Till aged fourteen beaten to death for flirting with a white girl… Willie Edwards Junior, Mack Charles Parker, Herbert Lee, Cynthia Wesley… one long list

Cousin Thomas had in a notebook. That was only some of the names – the real list is so long George wonders if you stood and read out all the names how long it would take, not hours, not days, years, maybe decades. And now – added to that list of names – is Thomas Virgil Louis Brown, Momma's nephew, George's cousin.

George follows Garfield's wistful stare. Ice cream vendor way across looks like he's packing up ready to leave.

Momma was buried next to her momma. There were so many flowers. Most of them red, her favorite.

It was hot that day, lots of flies. Most of the service George had been whipping up a draught with that service sheet, shooing away flies at the same time. They all said lots of nice things about her and Biddy read his poem.

It was as George was standing there, at her grave, he felt the shadow pass across. Next thing he was looking down at two sets of feet side by side. Two sets of black shoes, toe by toe. At first, he thought it was Garfield come back. But there was a walking cane.

Same height as George, same stooped shoulders, same build. Not Garfield. He knew who it was. Two shadows falling across their momma's grave.

"How've you been, George?"

"I never thought you'd come."

II

July 19th, 2003, Jacksonville Florida

It's the perfect day for a picnic. April found just the place: Memorial Park in west Clayton.

They're in the shaded part, by the trees. Knee-length denim shorts, calves smeared in suntan lotion. She's slipped her feet out of her gray Sketchers, flipped them under the table, bare toes dug in. She likes the coldness of the grass. She watches her dad root through his backpack. He lifts out more plastic boxes and sandwiches wrapped in tin foil. So much food, looks like maybe he's trying to make up for all the times he never showed and all the birthdays he missed. Only today is not a birthday – all he said was *choose somewhere nice for a celebration*. He still hasn't said what they're celebrating. He sets the chocolate cake down next to the plate of sandwiches on the picnic table. He's even bought napkins.

Some kids are gathering across the park, looks like they're getting ready to play ball. She can see the dusty outline of a ballfield. Her dad looks over and now he's shaking potato chips into one of the plastic bowls. He's wearing navy shorts, a Marlins T-shirt, new sneakers: blue, Nike. That's a first. Looks like he's had a haircut since last week though it's still got a curl, it's thick and brown; at least it looks clean.

When he first showed up at the house, she did a double take; told him she thought she'd gotten herself a new dad. He said he wanted to *make the effort*. Pops'd rolled his eyes. Maybe because he thought he ought to have *made the effort* way before now or maybe because he wondered how long the *making the effort* would last this time.

She's always thought he could pass as handsome, though most of the time he looked like he needed a good scrub clean. But not today. Grace was the one told her to give him a chance. *Last chance.* April's lost count of how many *last chances* and how many times she dreamed about something as normal as a picnic in a park.

She nearly ruined it. On the ride over. Why did she have to bring up about the doctor?

She looks at the table, the red plastic plates – they have chicken and looks like bacon wraps, pizza slices, even a salad bowl, he's gone all out. Martha's already eyeing that slab of chocolate sponge with its *oozy-squidge* buttercream. She is sure she sees a bottle poking from a brown paper bag, looks like champagne but even he's not that dumb – is he? Wouldn't be the first time he said *what can one hurt? It's an occasion.* Only one *can* hurt and there's *always an occasion.* Be good if she knew what *this occasion* is.

She looks at all the plates. "You did good, Dad."

He fumbles with plastic forks and bowls for the cake, sets them down. "This is fun, right?" He says it like he needs it to be.

"Yeah, this is *fun.*"

She knew Pops had spoken to him from the way he was on the ride over. Like he was trying too hard, like it was sat there between them. So, she told him straight: "I'm not like her." He'd carried right on staring ahead as they turned onto Clayton Avenue.

She'd wound down the window, no air con in his beat-up old car. Radio blasting out Eminem and her dad tapping the wheel.

"I'm not like her, right?"

He stopped tapping, carried right on staring.

"Doctor thinks I am, some fancy name for it, and he wants me to take the pills – but he's wrong. They all are. They all said it – not to take the pills. All my friends. Jesse, Owen…"

That's when he turned his head, looked at her then back at the road. "I used to hate doctors." He flicked off the radio. "But sometimes you gotta listen to what they say, Peach – okay. Let them help."

"But there's nothing wrong with me."

"I'm just saying try, okay."

"They mess with my head. The pills. Like I can't think straight. Can't…" It was a mistake; she should never have said something. She thought maybe he'd be different.

"Can't what, Ape?"

But how could she tell him, it was like she was in another room, couldn't even hear what her friends were saying. Like it all got distorted.

"I'm not taking the meds. I flushed them anyway."

"Yeah, I heard."

She'd folded her arms across her chest. Why did she have to bring it up, spoil the day?

"They tried to medicate your mom."

She looked back at him.

"You know she did the same thing. Never stayed on her meds for long. But when she took 'em, Ape, they *did* help. She was off them when."

Only he never said when what. Didn't have to.

"I'm not like Mom. It's not the same."

"I'm just sayin'."

"I wouldn't, I'd never do what she did."

"There's chocolate cake," he said. "You like chocolate cake, right?"

He flicked the radio back on. Eminem replaced by Puff Daddy.

One way to stop the conversation, one way to sweeten the bitter.

She watches him now; pushes her sunglasses up on her head, looks down at her pink cropped top. She needs some fun. Fun is not something she knows. But after the week she's had, she needs something. She had to get out of the house. Since she flushed those crazy-ass pills, Pops has been so mad. Mean, bad-temper mad.

Her dad is staring at the cake. It's huge. Must be some celebration. Another month of sobriety?

She doesn't know how much Pops told him – apart from how she flushed the pills. And he must've said that Dr. McGarrigle wants to talk to him and they're talking about having her stay so they can make sure she takes the meds. Pops thinks it's the best way, the *only way. No way. No FUCKING way.*

He leans forward and hooks out two plastic glasses from the backpack and then comes the brown bag, *the bottle.*

"You wanna play ball?"

They both turn to see a spotty kid with greasy black hair, red T-shirt and shorts – looks about eleven, twelve.

"We need to make a team."

Does she look like she plays ball? She shakes her head. "Er... no."

Now she watches as her dad opens the bottle, holds out a glass and she can see the bubbles rising.

"You sure? It's softball."

So? "Kind of busy here…" she gestures at the table, looks back into the fizz. This time the kid walks away.

"Here," her dad says. "Try it."

He really bought champagne – he really thinks this is okay?

"It's not what you think."

"What isn't?"

"It's grape juice. Look at the label."

"Oh."

"You *can* trust me, Ape."

She reaches out, takes the glass. Sniffs – to be sure.

"Time for a toast," he says.

Only now Jesse is nagging – *You should've said yes to the softball. Let's play softball!* She tells him, she is not saying yes, if he wants to play then go right ahead, she's not stopping him. Her dad's gaze finds hers. "You think I should play?"

"No, I was talking to Jesse."

She doesn't know what that look means; he's probably thinking about what Pops said – about the doctor. But she's not crazy. She does not need meds.

"I never said you were crazy."

Shit. "I never meant to say that."

He lifts this glass, holds it up.

"So, you gonna tell me what we're celebrating?"

He breathes in deep, like he's savoring the moment. "I'm moving."

"To another trailer?" It's like the third trailer park he's lived on. How is that a celebration?

"Nope. An apartment. Signed the lease yesterday."

That's a first.

"Close – like fifteen minutes from you. And there's a room for you. Maybe stay over some weekends. I know the guy who owns the building – Joe Miller – he's my new sponsor."

She takes a sip of the grape juice, looks at him. That's some grin on his face.

"They do that? Help with stuff like that."

"Joe does."

"Oh."

"Place is on Albany."

"Albany Street, Clayton?"

"Yep. Not the best neighborhood, but it's okay, right?"

"But how—"

"Got a job too – working at the university. Only cleaning, but the pay's good, best of all it's regular. Keep my head down and there's a ton of overtime too. Joe helped with that as well, knows the manager. They know, about me... got faith in me. I need that."

She sees there are more kids now gathered around the baseball field.

"I won't mess this up, Ape."

"That's great, Dad, like really great."

She can hear Pops in her head saying *if he stays sober this time.* But this is the first time he's gotten an apartment. Or a regular job.

The spotty kid is back. "Look, you sure you can't play? We need two more. In like ten minutes – you can eat first."

"Sure, why not. Wanna play, April?"

Does he know her at all?

"Let's show them, right?"

Show them what? April has never played baseball or softball or *any ball* in her life.

But now Jesse is like going crazy telling her: *Play... play, April. It's gonna be so much fun, April.*

She looks back at her dad. "Let's do it, Ape."

"Yeah, so much *fun*."

The kid misunderstands her sarcasm and is saying, "Great!

192

Come over when you're ready." He points to where a girl in a purple T-shirt is swinging a bat in mid-air. "My sister – Ceci. I'm Oscar."

So, looks like April's agreed to play ball.

"It's gonna work out great," her dad says. His gaze is distant. He doesn't mean the game.

Now stuffed full of chicken sandwiches and *oozy-squidge* chocolate cake, April is standing on a baseball field in Memorial Park on a breezy Saturday afternoon playing softball for the first time in her life. If you can call it *playing.* With her dad – her friends – and a bunch of complete strangers. Her dad's explained the rules, though it's supposed to be just a game for fun, mostly kids, a few dads. Lots of whoop-whoops, handclaps, the occasional thwack when someone actually hits the ball.

There's a first time for everything. Even softball.

And the picnic. Her dad signing a lease on an apartment. A full-time job.

So, April who does not do sports, is now in the area Jesse calls the outfield, running for a ball. Jesse is shouting, he shouts every time she misses a catch or is supposed to be running. She's all *fumbly-fumbly butter fingers*, can't catch a cold, but if her dad can *make the effort,* so can she. She might even be liking this if it wasn't for Jesse. She tells Jesse to shut the fuck up again as she runs. This time the ball's dropped down and is rolling. She can hear her dad. "That's it! Back to me." She ditched the glove; it doesn't help and it smells. She bends to scoop up the ball with her fingers, when she hears her name. This time not Jesse or her dad. She feels the weight of the ball in her hand, looks back at her dad and throws a hard overarm, hears the ball slap right into his glove.

"Great throw, April!" Who said that? Not her friends. Not her dad, he's too busy throwing the ball in the direction of third base.

"April?"

This time she turns. And right there, waving from behind the metal fence, is a woman in a pink dress. She's with a man dressed in blue. She doesn't know him but there's no mistaking her.

Of all the people to be watching as she makes a fool of herself in Memorial Park, it's someone she hasn't seen in over a month – since school's out for the summer – her teacher, Mrs. Johnston.

Game's stopped for drinks. April doesn't know who's winning. Jesse thinks the boys and they're three ahead. Her dad had wandered over, must've wondered who she was talking to. Her teacher shook his hand, then introduced her husband. Turns out his name is Randolph. Next thing her dad asked them if they wanted a glass of grape juice. Now they're all standing in the shade by the picnic table.

"I didn't know you played ball," Mrs. Johnston says.

"Me neither."

Mr. Johnston's tall, slim, small glasses propped on his nose. "It's good to meet you, April."

They make polite chit-chat. Her dad clasping onto the stem of the plastic champagne glass, lines of sweat rolling along his cheeks. He seems breathless, all a fidget. It's the first time he's met her teacher. April steps further under the shade.

"You've got a good throw." She looks back at Mr. Johnston. "Practice the catches, better with a glove."

Someone shouts over – they're ready to start again.

"April…"

Mrs. Johnston is now looking right at her. "Your dad said you were working on something for me? Last time you were with him… homework?"

"Oh, yeah. The character thing, like you told me. Write down about my friends. I did it last weekend. It's at home. I can give it to you at the start of the new semester?"

"Thank you, April." She looks disappointed, but at least she did it for her, even if it did take a while. She sees something in her dad's expression but next thing spotty Oscar waves over. "Be right there," her dad says. He turns back to Mrs. Johnston. "If you give me your address, I can bring it over, save you waiting? If you think it'll help."

Help how?

194

Mr. Johnston gives Mrs. Johnston the look. April knows the look – it's the warning *don't-tell-them-any secrets* look – only now it's the *that-is-not-appropriate* look. But Mrs. Johnston is already fumbling in her purse. She pulls out a pen and scribbles her address on the back of a bill. "It's not too far from the school."

April glances over. Ceci is waving.

"Great I'll do it after I take April home."

April looks at her teacher, then Mr. Johnston and next thing her name is being shouted.

"Go enjoy your game," Mrs. Johnston says.

She'd rather stay and talk to her teacher. But looks like she's got no choice.

April stands in line to bat, doesn't speak to anyone. She sees the floaty pink of Mrs. Johnston's dress; they're back standing by the fence. It's as she waits; she sees something else. Stands real still, hands lifted to her eyes. Feels like someone turned the volume down. A shadow passes across – like she just stepped into a whole other ball game.

"April – you're up next."

Who are they? Like shadows. A pitcher, a catcher...

"April, honey." Her dad's voice this time.

She's sure she smells something too – is it menthol?

Ceci now thrusts the bat into her hands. "You got this."

April stands on the plate.

Mrs. Johnston and her husband are still watching but the shadows are gone. All that's left are the goosebumps, yet it must be eighty-five degrees.

She hears Jesse say something but she's not paying attention. She misses all three pitches – doesn't even try. This time when she looks back Mrs. Johnston has gone.

———————

"What's that?"

Ruby-May holds the piece of yellow lined paper in her hand: April Jefferson's scribbles. Randolph is at her shoulder. He won't like it. He already told her she should not have given out her home address, it could have waited till school started. It was part of the *you're-getting-too-close-Ruby* speech. She told him she was curious. Of course, they both know it's more than curiosity.

He flicks his eyes over the note. She thought she'd heard a car, the metallic clank of the mail box but she didn't see him. The paper was folded over, *For Mrs. Johnston* scribbled on the back. She wanted to tell him maybe April needs a second opinion; Libby would have something to say about that. But once she's in that hospital, once it starts, she won't be April anymore.

She reads the note again, but it's not what she's written about the children. Although it's the first time she knew they had last names. It's the last line. The post script.

> *Martha Woodruff: likes pies. Chocolate cake and burgers. Food is her comfort. Favorite: Pie. Folks from Kansas originally.*
>
> *Grace Robinson: sweet, kind. Never says bad things about anyone. Has a baby brother.*
>
> *Rose Johnson: chatterbox. Gets easily freaked out. She's got an identical twin sister.*
>
> *Owen Edwards Junior: Spooks easily, has a temper on him. Likes history.*
>
> *Jesse Butler: flirt, likes girls and baseball.*

"Told you," Ruby-May says. "Read the bottom."

The post script is in blue pen, not black, like an afterthought. She has written: *Mrs. Johnston, I know you said to describe how they look...* she feels the skin on her neck goose up... *but you should know that I don't see them, I feel them.*

"Tell me you see it now, Rand? It *is* like Billy. That's exactly what he said. And look what—"

But Randolph's already gone. All she hears is the door to the den click shut and the pad of feet on the stairs. And now all she's got in her head is: *I don't see them, I feel them.*

196

Chapter 10

I

August 7th, 2001, Atlanta Georgia

Everyone's left. House is quiet. A full moon shines bright as a flashlight.

George is sat at the table, scribbling, probably more poems. He's already planning out his second collection before the first one's published. September 15th is a big day for George. Been a long time coming. Molly only hopes she's here to see it.

Henry and Nia were the first to leave, got their hands full with a six-month-old. And Henry says she wants another. Molly told them to wait – plenty of time for making more babies. Cousin Lydia had a face on her when Molly said that – like she knows something. Wouldn't surprise her if she's already pregnant again. Now Lydia is washing dishes while Molly has her feet up – the weight of two cats pushing down. Lydia told her cats know things. They've not left Molly's side since the news.

Lydia says she's got five cats now. The newest just adopted her, calls it Missy cat. Her neighbor is minding them. But Molly tells her she ought to get back, if she needs her, she'll call. Lydia nods, says she'll go back to Dallas the day after tomorrow. They both know she doesn't have to call. Lydia has a way of showing up, when she's needed.

Blades of the new ceiling fan whip up warm air. When she looks up George has his eyes on her but soon as he sees her, he looks back at his notebook. Lydia's already asked her if she's had *the talk* yet. Of course, she knows the answer, just her way of making sure they do it. She wonders if that's the real reason for the visit this time – make sure Molly has *the talk*.

George is off to Jacksonville next week, see his publisher. Last time he went she thought he'd come back full of excited book chatter only he came back with the darkness. That was *before* Molly went to the doctor about the headaches.

She knows his visits are more than a trip to a publisher – it's about his brother, his friends, he probably goes to that cemetery. She looks over at him now, eyes fixed on the page, but he's stopped with the writing. It doesn't matter about the secrets – everyone's got those – but lately she's seen the weight of them, in his movements, in the creases screwing up his face, in the way he cries out in his sleep. *Why can't you tell me, George?*

Last night Molly told Lydia she worries most about George.

And she told her the same thing she always tells her: *he'll talk when the time's right.*

"If you know what's eatin' George, why don't you just say it? Things are different now; we're running out of time. You know it."

"Who says it's different? Everything always happens just the way it's meant to."

She made it sound like even the cancer was part of the plan.

"Molly, honey, some things folk bury so deep inside, like it's the only way they can protect themselves, and the people they love the most. I need you to trust me. You think you can do that?"

"When ain't I trusted you?"

All she knows, is whatever it is, been eating George all these years, if he don't let it out soon, it will eat him alive worse than the cancer that's eating her up, organ by organ.

The TV is on silent – news update – more talk of fighting in the middle-east and Iraq. She reaches for the remote and switches it off. She wonders if in that list of poems is one about his brother and the Korean War; he writes poems for everyone that passes – she wonders if there's one for her momma – and for William. Died three days apart. She wonders if he'll write one for her. Seems like soon as one goes, another one pops right out. She thinks about Nia again. People said they might not cope, being parents and what with their learning issues – but they coped just fine. She's never seen two people so happy. Except for maybe

Josie-Ann and Luis, now that was some wedding. Now Biddy is all about college applications like her momma was at sixteen. Still got her heart set on medical school but why so far away? Why California? Why UCLA? But seems when that girl sets her heart on a dream, there's no stopping her. Even got her on an accelerated program. Of course, her momma and William's college fund's gonna help.

Henry and Nia's wedding was a much quieter affair, City Hall, no fuss. Just like they did, only they had more people than when she married George. Josie-Ann saw to that, she said no way was her brother getting wed without the family there. She paid for the party afterwards.

Molly shifts her legs, both cats sinking their claws in deep.

It's been a good day. Seems like everything's lining itself up just like it's meant to. She's even stopped worrying so much about Henry. Of course, he took it bad and she's still not so sure him or Nia understand it right, but something tells her they'll be okay. Same with Josie-Ann, hands full with the boys, the job, Biddy. She saw the way Biddy was looking at her today, even saw her whispering to her aunt Lydia. Biddy is so much like her aunt and she doesn't mean in looks.

Biddy knows it's coming.

Lydia knows it's coming.

Everyone knows it's coming – even the cats know it's coming.

It's just George.

Tonight, she'll have the talk. Sit out back, bring the blankets, get her propped up comfortable, with hot chocolate – the way he likes it with the whipped cream and the marshmallows. Air nice and still, coolest part of the day. She'll ask Lydia to boil some milk. Because right now as she sits she feels it. Something stirs. Maybe it's what the cancer's done to her brain, like sometimes she thinks she's growing more like Biddy and more like Lydia each day, or maybe it's what Lydia said or it's just because.

The time is right.

"It is."

Molly looks up.

Lydia is standing there with two mugs in her hand. "Hot chocolate?"

George's got the fidget knees. Des did try to sit on him but that cat does not like the fidget knees and is now back on Molly with his brother.

It's been a long time since George and Molly came out here, sat in the moonlight, drank hot chocolate, especially with the whipped cream and the marshmallows. Last time must've been his sixtieth birthday, more than three years ago, before the kids' weddings, before the cancer came back. Molly's not touched her hot chocolate. It's another one of Lydia's crazy ideas. Had him help Molly out here, no matter how many times he said it was not such a good idea, she gets tired. Molly saying, "What d'ya thinks gonna happen, George, catch my death?"

Why does she always joke about it; dying is not something to joke about.

Now he's sat here with the fidget knees and trembly fingers trying to keep from spilling his marshmallows while Lydia's in her room – which used to be Josie-Ann's bedroom, catching up on her reading she says. Said to call up if he needs help getting Molly back inside. The light from the bedroom shines down. The yard with its plants and its flowers looks pretty – it was Josie-Ann's idea all them years ago to string fairy lights in the trees and along the path. Over the years there seem to be more and more of them.

There's a kind of magic to it, but there's no magic in the way Molly is looking at George right now. That's the reason for the fidget knees and the tremble fingers.

Since Dr. Carter told them Molly's cancer is everywhere, she has wanted to talk about it, only George does not want to talk about it. All he knows is no amount of *talking about it* will help. She got better last time, and the time before that.

"George, did you hear me?"

This is the conversation he does not want to have.

"I need to know you're gonna be okay, George. When I'm gone."

It's the *I'm-dying* speech.

He takes a sip. He has whipped cream on his lip. Next door's dog scratches at the door to be let in. A baby cries somewhere on Peaches Avenue. A brown thrasher bird sings; sounds like someone smacking their lips.

"All of us gonna die, George, just some do it sooner than others. Some do it before they even get a proper chance to live."

Of course, he knows that… what is this?

Now every full moon will make him think about this, the *I'm-dying* talk he never wanted to have – with hot chocolate to sweeten the moment.

"George, sixty-two ain't so young. I'm happy with what I got, George."

Now who's got *the gloom?* It's usually her telling him he has it.

"When I'm gone, I want you to still talk about me, remember me. Not close it off, act like I never lived."

"I'd never do that, why would you even—"

"It's what you did with your brother."

This is about Abe?

"Had to learn you even had a brother from your momma and even when I told you – you still never talk about it. If I had a brother who'd died—"

He closes his eyes, focuses on a car horn someplace, the dog still barking. *Why'd she have to bring up Abe? And someone let that dog in.*

"George?"

"Don't do this, Molly."

"Do what George? Talk about your brother? My cancer? That's exactly what we gotta do. What he ought to have done a long time ago."

It's not quite the *I'm-dying* talk he imagined.

"It must've been a terrible thing, him dying so young…"

"He didn't."

"Before he got to live his life…"

"I said he didn't."

"Before he got to… say what?"

"He didn't die young."

"I don't—"

He closes his eyes. "Abe didn't die."

Molly leans forward, sets her mug down on the table. He holds onto his mug tight, stop his hands from shaking. He doesn't want to talk anymore, but no way that's happening now.

"He came home from Korea?"

"The only one outta him and his friends who did."

"The ones buried in that cemetery in Clayton? Your momma said you like to visit all the time?"

George promised Abe he wouldn't tell her. He remembers the day Abe came home, Momma fussing, Pap could barely bring himself to look at him.

"It's complicated," George says. "He did come home but didn't stay. He was missin' a long time. I only found him a few years back. It was easier to say he was dead and it's what Momma wanted everyone to believe."

"I don't understand, why would—"

"Half his face was blown off in the war, and he was badly burned all the way down one side. He needed a whole lot o' surgeries."

"Oh, George—"

"I was fifteen. Two men came, told Momma the news. She thought when she saw them it was gonna be the other news, like when they came to tell Mrs. Morrison Benjamin was dead, but they said Abe was alive but they didn't know if he'd survive his injuries. Momma fell down on her knees, Grandmomma had to hold her up. All I remember is when he came home a few months later, he weren't the same. Said he was better off dead – like Benjamin Morris and by then Isaac Harrison too. He was the only one of them that came home and he wished he never. He went out there a man, still came back a ghost."

George sits with his mug rested on his knee; all that's left is froth. Molly looks tired and for the past ten minutes has been staring into the *twinkle-twinkle*. The sweet scent of the acacia, planted in memory of Marcie and William last year.

He looks at Molly, wrapped up tight, she looks tired. It's ten minutes since he told her Abe is still alive. And he told her the reason why he never talked about him. Of course, now they know it as PTSD – back then he had *the war crazies* – least that was his grandmomma called it. It was the reason why he drank, why he tried to kill himself after he came back, why he couldn't live at home. It's why Pap threw him out all those times. Took George years to find him. Always hoped he'd show up. He knew he was near Jacksonville someplace. Mrs. Harrison had seen him living on the streets, picking trash in dumpsters. He made sure she had George's address all those years, of course she's dead now. But she had it – just in case. A just in case came a few years back – she wrote how he'd come to visit, after he'd gotten himself on a program, rehab and was doing good. He wanted to see George. George was coming to Jacksonville anyhow, for his exhibition, three weeks later. It was all set up only by the time he went, he was missing again. The real reason George went AWOL. Took a day to find him living at the YMCA. He was back on the drink and told George never to look for him again. That he was dead to them all, just like his momma said he was. And George tried to do that. Told himself that's exactly what he would do. But blood is blood. Now he knows where he is and gets the urge to see him, in the hope he's changed, that he's the brother he remembers. Only it's all wishful thinking. That war broke him, but the scars that run the deepest are not the ones you can see.

Molly cried, tried to reach across but George moved away – it was just something had to be said – didn't want no fuss.

He even told her the part he never wanted to say, about what happened the night he knocked his pap down on the stoop. It was like once he started to tell her, *his sweet Molly,* he had to tell it all.

Pap was a bad man but it didn't mean George wanted him dead. For a long time, he blamed himself for what happened that night.

Abe was there. Always showed up liquored up. Been staying at the Harrison's. Pap was sitting in his rocker, a Kool between his lips. Momma and Grandmomma were inside the house. First thing they heard was the hollering in the street – everyone knew it was Abe. Wasn't the first time – but *it was* the last.

Abe was not welcome at the house, yet to George he was always his brother, always his hero. He even had that baseball poster on the wall reminding him every day. Somehow Abe'd gotten up close and was right in Pap's face. Now Pap, he could never bring himself to look at that face of his, all messed up with the scars, he hated what Abe had become, even said it too: would've been better if he died like those boys – at least they got medals for their bravery. Next second, he called him a *crippled nigger boy* and spat right into Abe's face. Just the way he's seen him do to Momma, right before he gave her a good hiding. Something about that just switched something on inside George's head and next thing his fist was balled up. Looked right at Pap as he swung. Punched, hard and clean, harder than when he fought over Chloe Johnson – much harder. And told him straight, "That's for all the times you hurt Momma…" Then he added, "and it's for Abe."

But Abe needed no encouragement; he knew how to fight and seemed soon as Pap fell down hard on that stoop, Abe had him – the left side of his body might not work right, but the other side made up for it. Momma was screaming at him to stop. Stop right now! STOP! Someone must've called the cops; none of them had phones in the house, maybe it was Grandmomma went to the payphone – all he does know is by the time anyone came – Abe was gone and Pap was dead.

And that night Momma told Abe never to come back – that he was no son of hers.

She forgave him in the end, but that was too many years too late.

Pap was still alive when Momma told Abe to go. Somehow Pap had gotten himself back into his rocking chair but he was bleeding bad. Momma and Grandmomma were fussing, asking George to help them look for the first-aid kit. They were still in the house when George heard his pap call out. He thought Abe'd come back. But Abe was standing across the street. Pap had stood himself back up and was groaning; making *snuffly* sounds as he shuffled his way across the stoop, like maybe he was wanting to come back into the house. Next thing, just like that, he fell – dropped down dead with a *clunk-thud*.

His momma never told the police about the fight. Said he was always coming home drunk like that. It wasn't the fight that killed him, he suffered a massive coronary – but George knows if he hadn't thrown that first punch and if Abe hadn't got *the crazies* – maybe he wouldn't have died. Only later Momma said she didn't blame George, that he was defending her, she heard what he said. But she said it was different with Abe. He didn't know when to stop, trained to fight. She said he was the one who killed him. But like George told Abe when he was stood at their momma's graveside – and like Momma told him that last time, when she was lucid enough to know who he was – it wasn't his fault. Pap was getting what was due, just took her a long time to realize it. Besides, if Abe hadn't done what he did, Pap's heart would've given out sooner or later anyhow. Only Abe still blames himself.

George told Molly all of it, while she sat, one hand under the blanket, the other slowly burrowing into the cats' fur. She never said a word until he was done. Even told her how he'd gone looking for him the day of their wedding, because of a promise they made except it was years before that letter came. He'd given up hope of ever finding him by then. He said the day they all left Jacksonville for Atlanta when he was twenty, he'd hoped he would show up. But of course, he knew that would never happen, but he was sure deep down his momma was hoping it too. Then all Molly said was, "I'm so sorry, George. Where's Abe now?"

"Still in Jacksonville. Still drinks. Still messed up. He tries, gets sober for a while then he's right back where he started."

She looks down at Socs, rubs his chin. "He's still your brother and you still should've told me. I would've liked to meet him. Does he know about us?"

"Yes. He didn't want me to tell you, or them about their crazy uncle. Says he only brings the bad. That's how he says it."

"I would still've liked to meet him."

"Maybe you will."

But her look says he left it too late for that.

The sound of a door opening, next thing they see Lydia. "Came to see if you're ready to go in."

And just like that it's over.

Molly shoos the cats off her legs and folds the edges of the blanket together. Then she makes ready to stand, Lydia is waiting to help but George's got this and he tells her so. Molly wraps her arm into his, Lydia instead collects the mugs, though Molly's is still full; the whipped cream and the marshmallows have melted.

As they shuffle across the yard, arm in arm, George thinks about his pap. His momma, his grandmomma, Abe. Now Molly knows.

"George?" Molly whispers. He catches the look in Lydia's eyes; it's there for a moment before she turns away. "George, I just wish you'd told me when there was time to do somethin' for him. Those poor boys, and him with those injuries, I can't imagine finding out something like on your fifteenth birthday, that's gotta haunt you."

He doesn't say a word.

How can he tell her that's not the thing that haunts him; or the real reason for his trips to Clayton Cemetery. What happened to Abe didn't happen on George's fifteenth birthday. He never said that; he doesn't know why she thinks that. That's not the day the soldiers came with their bad-news faces. That was six months after his birthday.

He can't tell; he can't put that into her head. Not his *dear sweet Molly*.

Because the thing that happened on his fifteenth birthday is worse – *far worse.*

206

II

August 7th, 2003, Jacksonville, Florida

Randolph is still in his office.

Ruby-May hears the judder of the printer as she shuffles past in her slippers. He declined the offer of hot chocolate. He never declines. She makes her way back to the den. Window's open; air fresh, smells like rain. Wind rattles the screen door. It's only 8.45; too early for her bed.

She sets the mug down and looks at the book on the table; she's not in the mood for any more reading. She's not in the mood for anything. All she's got in her head is what Ted Jefferson told her a couple' nights ago. Almost puts her off her hot chocolate. And Randolph's no help – she tried to tell him – but he's got a story on his mind. These past two days she's barely seen him. He has not been like that about a story in a long time.

Curtain flaps, puffs cool air into her face. She closes her eyes. She can still smell the lavender bath oils.

In truth, Randolph's been distracted the past couple of weeks, but since the weekend it's been the story– it's just like the old days. Though in the old days he'd tell her what he was working on. They'd sit and bounce ideas: the best angle, *now this is interesting, Ruby. What you think of this, Ruby?* But not this time. Used to be all she had to do was offer up her *yes* or *no* or *that's great, sugar* and keep the coffee coming. Now he doesn't drink coffee – not since the cancer, and now it seems he doesn't even want hot chocolate and he certainly does not want her help. She knows why: he's still mad at her. About April, about giving out their address, about getting too close.

Must be a big story because yesterday he even went to Clayton Library and when he couldn't find what he wanted he went to Jacksonville Library; even paid a visit to the offices of the *Jacksonville Daily.* But why so secretive? All he said was, "Tell you later." She knows there's something not right. If there's one thing about Randolph – he's never been one for the secrets.

A flash lights up the room.

No thunder – must be too far off. Probably over the ocean.

Randolph won't talk about his new story and he won't talk about April or what she wrote on that yellow paper. A couple of nights ago she was looking at it again, wondering if it's normal to give imaginary friends last names and maybe she should've mentioned that to Libby. She'd kept it with her books, her lesson plans for September but this time must've left it on the table – next day, she found it in Randolph's office when she went in to clean. When she asked, he said he must've picked it up by accident. With his notes. But she knows different. She knows when he's fibbing. She knows he must've been reading that post script again. With Billy the voices got so bad they took him out of school. He always said his *friends*, he had three of them, told him to do things, but it was one in particular spoke to him most. He never saw him – never saw any of them, just heard them and before he was taken into the hospital, he said he felt them when they were close by.

Randolph remembers what happened just as much as she does. Hit him just as hard when Billy died.

She sits, legs up on the couch, sips her hot chocolate and wishes she had whipped cream. Last week she spoke to Libby. Told her she'd seen April with her dad, playing ball at Memorial Park, acting like any normal kid. Which is not quite true because she wasn't talking to any of those kids, she was mumbling to her other friends, but she never said that. All Libby said is the same thing she always says: it's out of their hands now. Ruby-May wishes she'd spoken more to Mitch Jones – though is a recovering alcoholic really the best person?

She reaches over, holds the mug in both hands and blows across her chocolate.

She knew she shouldn't've called Ted Jefferson. It was overstepping. At first it went to answerphone. Maybe that was a sign to leave it, only she couldn't. When she called a second time, he did answer, only it took him a while. He sounded out of puff.

There's another flash. She counts twelve before the rumble.

All she said was she was calling to thank April for the *assignment* a couple of weeks back. She was sorry – ought to have called before

– *blah blah*. Of course, it was only an excuse to call. And of course, she did some digging. He sounded angry, said April was *acting up*, maybe she was spending too much time with her dad. He said that April had helped him move on the weekend – to Albany Street. Ruby-May told him she heard that neighborhood was much better since the renovation.

Lightning cuts the room in half. This time the thunder is only six seconds later.

It's what Ted Jefferson said, right before he hung up, that sits uneasy. He said April had another appointment with Dr. McGarrigle on Thursday – which is tomorrow. They plan to get her admitted to the hospital and started on the meds. The plan is to get the meds right before the start of the next semester. Seems unlikely – it's only a month – but that's what he said. "Hospital is the best place for her now; I'd appreciate if you didn't keep calling."

"But Mr. Jefferson… you sure you want her on those kinds of drugs?"

Maybe she shouldn't've called, shouldn't've said it. A first, he was quiet then he said in almost a whisper, "I do not appreciate your sort calling here."

What sort? The *interfering sort*, the *caring-about-April sort?*

That's when the phone clicked off.

She shouldn't've told Randolph; she never told him how she knew, but later, cozied up in bed, neither of them sleeping, she said April would be on the children's psyche ward at Ellison this week, that it had started. He'd taken a hold of her hand. "When this week?"

"Thursday."

She didn't see what difference that made – not like she had any power to stop it – once that ball starts to roll…

That was it; then he'd turned over but she knew he wasn't sleeping. She knew he was thinking about Billy. Once they used electric shocks, his brain was fried.

The whole room lights up and a long low rumble a couple of seconds later. As she sips, she feels the cold splash on her arm.

Something real nice about the rain. She hears its soft patter on the roof. She closes her eyes; sinks into the sounds.

"Ruby."

Her hand jerks so now there's a line of hot chocolate splashed on her dressing gown. She never even noticed Randolph come down. He's standing in the doorway. She does not know what that look is but it does not look like he's still mad at her – this is something else; she thinks maybe he's had a breakthrough on that story of his. He's standing there in his gray sweatpants, his favorite white sweatshirt, bare feet and he has sheets of white paper in his hands. "I need to show you somethin' but I don't want you to get all… freaked out on me."

Now she's setting that mug back down, now she's sitting upright; now he's got her attention. Get all freaked all out on him about what?

Clock says 9.10. The rain is more a hollow roar as it rushes down; beats hard on the roof; slaps at that screen door. As she shuts the window, she savors the earthy smells. Now only a second between the lightning and the thunder claps, real loud. But that's not the real storm that's hit Tabebuia Drive. Ruby-May fingers the paper; the other sheets fanned out on the kitchen table.

Randolph showed each one to Ruby-May and waited for her to read, take it in. She's not so sure she *has* taken it in. Said he knows tomorrow is Thursday, that if he was going to show her it had to be now. He has done a whole bunch of research but this is not for a story. He says he had to use archives; that it was hard to find anything on the Internet; not from so far back. Now her hands are all a quiver as she looks down and reads it again.

"I recognized the names," he says. "But I was sure I had that wrong. Was a long time ago. Took a lot of diggin' but there it is. Bloody Thursday."

Randolph always had a memory for names, places, dates.

The paper dances between her fingers. She looks along the line of printouts, not many, some only mention it, but this one, this one she has in her hands has it all. She looks back at Randolph.

"I wasn't gonna look, only when I saw them names again…"
"You got curious?"
"I guess I did."
"So, what do we do now?"
"I have no idea."

BLOODY THURSDAY
MASSACRE IN HIGH SCHOOL
SIX DEAD

Just before 9 am yesterday police were called after gunshots were heard on Williams Ave at Eastfield High School. Five school children and their teacher were found dead. Janitor Wesley Izaiah Hart (38) is said to have opened fire shooting dead the teacher and the children. Hart had worked at the school for six years. High School Principal, Jackson Brown (45) from Clayton broke down, claiming it to be the worst thing he'd ever seen. The blood was in the classroom and in the corridors. He said the janitor had been having some marital problems but he has no idea how or why he did something so evil. Arrested at the scene, Wesley Izaiah Hart, has been charged with the murders of:
Teacher, Samuel Lewis (27)
And five minors:
Jesse Butler (15)
Owen Edwards Junior (15)
Rose Johnson (14)
Grace Robinson (15)
Martha Woodruff (14)

It's dated March 12th, 1953.

Ruby-May feels the paper slide from her fingers. Whispers the names. Jesse Butler – baseball. Owen Edwards Junior – history. Rose Johnson – chatterbox. Grace Robinson – kind. Martha Woodruff – pies.

Ruby-May looks up at Randolph.

"I couldn't tell you what I was doin', honey."

"But how did she—"

"Coincidence?"

But his face says he does not think that.

"She read it someplace, a school project, some people retain things."

"But you don't think that, do you?"

"I did."

"So what changed?"

"What April wrote next to the names. Rose Johnson did have a twin sister – Chloe Johnson, she was sick with influenza like a lot of the class that day it happened. Grace Robinson did have a baby brother. Martha Woodruff was originally from Kansas but I had to call in a favor to find that out; that wasn't in the newspapers. None of this was so easy to find. It might've been a big thing for Clayton, a terrible thing, Ruby, but this happened in Jim Crow. Times were different. We were only babies; we never knew the worst of it. Our folks did. I remembered reading somethin' about it a long time ago. But Bloody Thursday got lost, buried. A Negro killed Negro children and it got swept out of history like it never happened, because they were Negros."

"So how *could* she have known?"

She closes her eyes for a second as another lightning flash comes but this time, she feels the laughter bubble.

"What's so funny?"

"This! The storm, like something out of a movie."

But Randolph does not smile.

No thunder this time. Rain's easing but this storm is far from over. She pictures April, all those times, all those things she said about the children.

"What are we supposed to do with this, Randolph?"

Randolph shakes his head.

"What does it mean?"

Next thing she feels his arm around her, and he's pulling her to him.

"It means you were right, Ruby. It means April ain't sick."

Ruby-May finally lets the tears come. April might not be sick in the way those doctors think she is – but this might just be worse.

Ten minutes later Ruby-May stands at the window. It's almost dark, rain has eased, roses are wet through. She looks at the clock, looks at the phone. And what's she supposed to say? *Hey, Libby, turns out April doesn't have schizophrenia after all – she talks to ghosts!* And now she's just read something else. In one of the printouts. Seems Eastfield High School burned down in 1964. Though it was never rebuilt, another school was built ten years later close to where it was, further along Williams Avenue, this time not a colored school. A school she knows very well. Who'd've thought… She stares out some more. Looks along Tabebuia Drive. It's 9.45 – not too late, is it? She fumbles with the telephone and dials again before Randolph comes back from the bathroom and tells her not to. It's the fourth time. She doesn't want to leave a message, what she supposed to say anyhow – *don't take April to the hospital?*

Phone clicks. Thank God.

"Mr. Jefferson?"

"No… this is Mitch."

He's answering their phone? April says he never goes into the house.

"Sorry, this like a really bad time."

"This is Ruby-May Johnston, April's—"

"The teacher?"

"Yeah."

"Look, something's happened, I really need to—"

"Is April okay?"

"Yeah, it's—"

"I need to speak to you all. Tomorrow, early, before April sees the doctor. I don't know how to say it, best if it's face to face."

"Look I'm sorry, I have to go; we only came back for April's stuff. She'll be staying with me for a while…"

"What happened?"

"We just drove April's grandma to Birchwood – they had a room and better she stays there."

"The nursing home?"

"Look I'm sorry, we need to—"

"Is there something I can do?"

She hears him breathing hard, sounds like April says something.

"Mitch – I really need to talk to you before you take April to the hospital. It's really important. Something's happened. Don't take her; let me talk to you first, please."

She hears April again, muffled voices in the background.

"If you tell me what happened, maybe I can help."

"It's Ted."

"Ted?"

"He's in the hospital – he's had a massive heart attack. We don't know if he'll make it."

Chapter 11

I

August 15th, 2002, Atlanta, Georgia

Molly died on a Thursday.

There was nothing special or remarkable about that Thursday – like a regular sunny day in Atlanta, temperatures hit eighty-three. Sounds of balls slapping sidewalks, kiddies' laughter, a radio playing in someone's yard. Just like any other day – except by 1 o'clock there were extra cars parked up outside 131 Peaches Avenue. To anyone else it looked like they were having family over for a get-together. But everyone knew it wasn't quite that. Curtains twitched: the Hunts next door, the Jacksons across the way – Amelia Washington opposite.

By three o'clock, all their cars were gone.

By four o'clock, so was Molly because Grandmomma was right about bad things happening on a Thursday.

After that, folks came. Neighbors shuffled in with their casseroles and their long faces saying how sorry they were for his loss. Doesn't matter how much you know it's coming – you can never be ready. It wasn't loss. It was the end.

In two weeks, it will be a whole year on. Only George does not plan to see it.

George stands at the kitchen sink with his hands in dish bubbles. He shooed the cats outside. Molly said all it ought to take, the grief, is a year. But Molly's wrong. A year doesn't change a thing – just makes him miss her more.

Henry comes by most days, since most of the people he gardens for live on Peaches or one of the streets off it. He's got his hands full with Alfie William and now baby Harriet Olivia. Comes for the peace. They've got a lot of that – sometimes the house it too quiet.

If it wasn't for Henry, all the plants out there in the yard would be as dead as his *dear sweet Molly*. Sometimes, as he digs and trims, he hears Henry talking to his momma like she's still here. He reckons that's the real reason he comes. Her ashes are buried right alongside Archie, near the cycad plant and next to the sweet acacia. She said she didn't want to be buried like all the others at the cemetery in Grant Park.

"Does no one no good sitting by a grave," Molly said. "That ain't where I'll be, ain't where any of us end up. No one leaves – they hang around, they're everywhere, inside us and all around us." When she said it, all he could think about was his friends, how he used to talk to them. Like they were still there. Like he was sure they came when they were playing ball that day.

George has woken up 343 mornings without Molly. But not many more. A tear rolls itself right across his cheek. Lydia was here for it all; with her chicken stew and her apple pie and her fussing. Stayed for a month after Molly died. Said she had folks looking after Missy cat and King Marms and all those other kitty cats of hers. Then just like that she was gone again.

When she showed up a couple of days before Molly died, he knew. Saw it her eyes; he knows Molly saw it too. Later Lydia told George, "This is it, gotta find your brave now, George."

He tried to act like she was wrong, like Molly would beat the cancer again, only he knew and everyone knew different. Death was coming. Once it starts – no way to stop it. And it came that day to Peaches Avenue. It stalked them – while everyone else was going about their business. The whole family came but when the time was close, Lydia asked all of them to say their goodbyes, so it was just him and Molly for the ending. Josie-Ann had held him, stood at the door and told him, "Let her go, Dad."

But how can he *ever* do that?

Hard to believe this time last year she was still here, only soon he won't be able to say that. He won't be here to say anything at all.

George steps away, hands all crinkled, dripping water. He counts his steps to the doorway. When he was a kid he always counted. It was a game his momma taught him, listening for Pap's footsteps when he came home liquored up. Along the wood, if he got to three, he was stopping outside their room, if he got to four, he was walking right on past. Him and Abe hoping he'd not stop at three; come inside, start on them for not tidying the room. Then they'd count them to his momma's room – hoping he wasn't in one of his angers, Momma probably praying for the same thing. Later as he counted, he wrote his poems, used the beat, and after that, after the bad things happened, he counted whenever he got *the anxious*. Now all he has is empty spaces and he counts a lot. Seven steps to the couch. Nine steps across the bedroom. Ten steps across the yard to the seats – where he sat with Molly and told her about Abe. He doesn't even turn on the *twinkle-twinkle* lights now. They'd drunk hot chocolate – he did, she didn't. She never drunk hot chocolate again, or ate a single thing. That night, that was three weeks before she died. She never got to meet Abe, like she said she wouldn't and maybe that's one regret, if he'd told her before then maybe she was right, maybe she could've helped only what he's learned, is folks can only be helped if they want it.

Abe doesn't even know Molly's dead. What was the point? Never met her, never knew her, never will. He did think about him at that funeral, imagining him turning up like he did at Momma's – seeing his feet next to his but how could he if he didn't know? Abe is the only one left who knows what happened at the school that day. Only not the details because George will never tell. Just that on his fifteenth birthday he'd come home with two policemen, who were stood at the door telling Momma something terrible'd happened. His pap knew. Grandmomma knew. The Harrisons knew. The neighbors knew. Cousin Thomas even knew. He was the one suggested he go stay with him and his other cousins.

Now all of them are gone.

George was the one who came home – no one else in his class did.

Molly's funeral was nothing like the others and there've been a few over the years. Josie-Ann called it a celebration. A celebration of

Molly's life. No body, no coffin. Had her cremated privately just like Molly wanted. All they had in that little chapel was a pot in the shape of a heart with her ashes and a photograph. Like that's all that's left – we're here and then we're not.

Josie-Ann read the poem. How d'you choose when he's written so many? He could fill not just one book but a whole library of books of poems about Molly. But in the end, there could be only one. The one he wrote the very first day he met her. No way George could read it out – not like he read his poems out at the library when that book of his came out. Molly had been dead six weeks; in the end the launch was delayed by a whole month because four days before they were meant to have it, two big old airplanes flew right into those towers in New York City. It was the only thing anyone talked about – but not George – might not have been on the news, but there was a loss inside him bigger than Ground Zero. He thought about cancelling the book launch only Lydia and Molly'd already told him, *no matter what happens, George, you launch that book.* He doesn't think even Lydia saw that one coming though. Airplanes crashing and buildings falling out of the sky. This time they call it a war on terror – George W Bush's war. Always a war – some will never be over.

Sometimes he thinks how that book of poems is the part of him he never says out loud. He did start to write a poem that day, about the crows, but it's one poem he'll never write. Only got as far as the title. Some things should never be said. What happened that day will never be spoken or in any book of poetry because now he's done. Maybe years from now – or maybe even next year – someone'll borrow that book from Clayton Library and someone might say how the poet used to work at this very library, retired in 2001, dead now. And they will meet the real George between the lines. He thinks about all the things you leave behind – not just in your kiddies' smiles and your grandbabies' smiles but in your words. And all the words never spoken; left unsaid. Maybe they fly away, like them crows.

Not like Langston Hughes.

Gwendolyn Elizabeth Brooks.

Maya Angelou.

Audre Lorde.

Lucille Clifton.

Rita Dove – first black poet laureate.

So many more – and right at the end in small letters – George William Tucker. And in even smaller letters – descended from a slave.

Black Oleander Press made it book of the month. Now they want his second collection – but there will be no second. Those poems are in a notebook, for someone to find when he's gone. He did mail a signed copy of his book to Abe. There's a poem in there for him too, about the three friends who went off to fight in the war and only one came back. The real hero.

He doesn't know if he got it. He doesn't know if he read it.

House is quiet. Josie-Ann says she's coming over later with the boys. She says it's about time he had an email address and the boys will fix him up with one. Biddy's idea. Now he has Luis's old computer for writing his poems though he still writes them by hand. The main reason for email is so Biddy can email him, tell him all about her studies and her fancy new life in California.

But George doesn't need any of that. No emails will reach him where he's going.

They all have their busy lives and their families.

George has done his job, raised them good. But without Molly, there's nothing left. Now everything is an ending. His year is almost done.

From the open doorway, George watches one of the cats run along the fence. He looks at the kitchen; a magnet from Hollywood. Biddy bought it when she went to check out UCLA. It's holding his prescription in place.

House rattles with memories – a lot of memories and soon it will be for another family, maybe a new one starting out.

Molly said lots of things to George in those last couple of weeks. Every day it seemed she was more and more like her cousin, like she knew things. But she never knew what happened to him on his fifteenth birthday because what was the point in weighing her down. All she said was he had to find a way to conquer his demons. "Let go of the past, George. Let it all go."

There's only one way to do that.

He's almost ready.

And then there's the other thing she said; said it to him right before she closed her eyes that very last time.

He looks out at the white roses; Henry said they'll need planting out of the pot. Those roses seem to bloom all year, even though Henry says they're not supposed to.

There was one other person there to hear what Molly said to George. That was Lydia, only she was the other side of the room. But he knows she must've heard it.

He scoops cat chow into a bowl and wonders what time Josie-Ann is coming over. After she finishes work, picks up the boys. The poem she read out is still pinned to the fridge; next to his prescription.

Molly's Smile

Molly's smile is
Spring's scent
Summer's warmth
Fall's glow
Winter's sparkle.
Molly's smile is the question.

Molly's smile is
Joy
Peace
Love
Hope.
Molly's smile is the answer.

Moly's smile is
Soft blankets
Cool breeze
Warm hands
Gentle kisses.
Molly's smile is the beginning.

Molly's smile is
Yesterday
Today
Tomorrow.
Forever.
Molly's smile is every day in between.

Molly's smile is
Here.
Now.
Always.
Molly's smile is the ending.

Enchantment begins where love starts.

George William Tucker, April 10th, 1961.

He had that smile and carried that heart for forty years.

He thinks about what Molly said. He thinks about it every day. She said she did not want him to be lonely; told him she was setting him free, that there was plenty of time.

For what?

Love? The way her momma found William after Henry Snr died?

No.

There was only one person for George. Only one heart. One smile.

She said four little words – the very last words. Her hand in his, he had to lean in real close to hear it, feel the tickle on his cheek.

Door must still be open because next thing he hears the tinkle of two little cats' bells and now they're both on the table, pressing their sweet little faces to his, cold wet-nose kisses. Des pushes so hard he near knocks his glasses off. Now they're purring louder than that ceiling fan. "Good boys."

Four words.

He closes his eyes, presses his face into the softness.

Doesn't matter what she said – he has everything he needs right here and soon all of it will be gone.

Four little words.

Count them.

You. Must. Find. Her.

II

August 15ᵗʰ, 2003, Jacksonville, Florida

Randolph stands at the window and looks out at Tabebuia Drive. Ruby-May watches from the dining table, elbows rested on her pink notebook. The rush of another car on the wet road. Still not them.

Randolph says maybe they won't come. Ruby-May says they will.

She spoke to Mitch Jones last night. They will come. They're only ten minutes late. She pinches her fingers together. *They will come.* Tomorrow April is supposed to see Dr. McGarrigle – can't put it off any longer Libby said. They had to delay because Ted had a heart attack, she gets that – but he's had surgery, and looks like he'll make it, so now they need to do this. April needs to stay in the hospital.

Ruby-May did not say a word.

Nor did she tell Mitch why they need to come – just that it's *real important.* She'd heard the hesitance, heard the panic, saying Ted had insisted April get started on the treatment. It was April she heard telling Mitch *My friends say you must let Mrs. Johnston help.* Made the hairs along the back of Ruby-May's neck perk right up. He said they'd come. At four.

Maybe they hit traffic.

Mitch Jones had passed on his phone number the night he told her about Ted. She told Mitch it might be best to say nothing to Ted, while he's so sick. Mitch is April's dad and that's who she's staying with. It's his decision now.

Randolph has got the jitters – she has not seen him like this in a long time. It was Ruby-May's idea about the photographs. But there were no photographs in the newspapers of any of the children. Maybe to protect them, they were minors – maybe the parents didn't want it – just one in the newspaper – of the teacher. But Randolph called in another favor – this time from cop Charlie

223

Wilkes. He told Charlie it was for a story he was writing. Even when Charlie agreed, Randolph was not so sure. Not so sure about any of this – like he should have left it alone, never started with this in the first place. He said he was only doing it for Ruby-May.

"Don't do it for me," she said. "Do it for April. And do it for Billy. Because last time we failed."

He went on Monday, to Clayton Police Station. When Randolph came home, after looking at that file, he was almost as pale as a white man. He didn't only see the photographs their mommas had given to help with the identifying – he saw the file on Bloody Thursday – the *other photos.* Even Charlie said it was enough to bring your lunch right back up.

He's had the jitters ever since.

The only thing he would say about that was, "Once you see it, Ruby, there's no way to unsee it." Then he cried. Only time he ever cried that hard, since they lost their baby, and when his parents died, was the night they got the call about Billy, when they found him.

The photographs – *the good ones* – are tucked inside her notebook on the table. Next to that yellow note with the names. Randolph says if she doesn't *see* them, then how will she know. All she says is, "She will." He has the newspaper clippings in the den.

"But even if she does, what's it prove? She speaks to ghosts… then what?"

Ruby-May did not know how to answer that. If she thought a phone call to Ted Jefferson a couple of weeks back was overstepping – what the hell is this? She couldn't lose her job for this, *could she?* Friend or not, Libby would probably have something to say about that.

Getting too close again, Ruby.

Randolph was reluctant, of course he was. She had to agree that if it didn't work, and if they couldn't convince Mitch Jones, then she'd go to Ellison, tomorrow, get herself checked in – start the meds.

"They're here."

Randolph steps away from the window. "Ruby, they came."

"Told you."

Only now she feels sick.

"This has to work." She looks at Randolph as she says it.

"And if it does – what then?"

April looks tired, thinner, shuffles in with her head down. Hair looks like it needs a cut. She's in jeans, a purple T-shirt, sneakers. Mitch Jones looks scruffier than he did that day at the park. He shakes her hand, but there's a tremble there. Liquor? Nerves? Randolph fusses, fixes them lemonade even though they say no and now April lifts her head, looks around. "Nice house, Mrs. Johnston."

"How have you been, April?"

"Okay."

"You like Albany Street?"

"'S'okay."

"You like livin' with your dad?"

She looks across at him. "Yeah. Pops is mad though; says I should stay at the house, bring Grams home. But we like it better with Dad – even Rose doesn't freak out at Dad's. She hates Pops. They all do."

That's a new one on her.

She catches Randolph looking at her, turns to April. "Take a seat, sugar. We should get started."

They're all seated though Mitch is fidgeting. There's a tall glass of pink lemonade in front of each of them. April stares at the bubbles.

"I need to show April some photographs," Ruby-May says, pointing at the notebook. "And tell me who they are."

"That's it?" Mitch says.

"That's it. Like a test." She looks at April when she says that.

April is sat across from Ruby-May. Ruby-May is fingering the edge of the notebook. "All I wanna do, April," she says again, "is ask you if you know who these people are."

225

She slowly flips open her notebook and slides the first photograph across the table. "Can you tell me who this is?"

April leans in and red curls flail across her cheek. She runs her finger softly across the face of the teenage boy.

Silence, except for the hum of the refrigerator. And Mitch's fidget fingers tapping the table. And Randolph's deep breaths puffing out, like this is all way too stressful.

They wait.

Finally, April looks up. "No, don't know him."

She swears she sees relief on Randolph's face.

"You sure? Look again."

Randolph gives her the stare. He already told her – *no coercin'.*

"No. Should I?"

"What about this one?"

She does not look at Randolph as she slides the next black and white photograph to her.

This time she seems to stiffen up, something changes in her posture, her face. She knows this one? But it's wishful thinking because all she says is, "No, don't know her either."

"Any of these?"

She now sits all five photographs in a line in front of her.

First her eyes flicker over each one, next her fingers hover. She hesitates over one. Ruby-May holds her breath; still she can't look at Randolph. He'll say he was right – this is a terrible idea. It's just a coincidence or maybe she knew the names from someplace else.

"I'm sorry, Mrs. Johnston, I don't know any of them."

"Okay, April."

"Is that it?" Mitch says.

Randolph fingers his glass of lemonade; he definitely looks relieved.

"Yep – that's it. If she doesn't—"

"Mr. Lewis."

When she looks back, it seems the other photo, the one sticking out, the one she hadn't planned on showing her, April now has in her hand.

"Jesse says he's the teacher."

226

She seems to look again at the other photos. "They're all here now," she whispers and something about the way she says that has Ruby-May reaching for that pink lemonade, holding the glass to steady the fidget in *her* fingers.

April pokes the third photograph – another boy.

She sees Mitch take a long gulp of his lemonade. Probably wishing it was something else.

"He says that's him. That's Jesse."

Ruby-May sets the glass down, too hard so now she has sticky lemonade on her fingers. She rubs her hands on her skirt; turns the photograph over. Scribbled on the back in Randolph's scrawl is a number *3*. He didn't want the names there; no cheating he said. *No cheatin', no coercin'… should we even be doin' this, Ruby?*

Ruby-May turns her head to meet Randolph's gaze head-on. "Three," she whispers as he teases the list from the pocket of his pants. He nods. "Number three is Jesse Butler."

"Correct," Ruby-May says staring at Randolph. Someone just turned up the notch on her heart rate.

She identified the teacher and Jesse. That cannot be a fluke.

"She got it right?" Mitch says.

But Ruby-May doesn't respond because now April says, "That's Grace, there, she says that's her. Her papa took this." Now she is looking at the first photograph. A tear spills onto April's cheek.

"What it is, April?"

"I never saw their faces before. I never knew."

"Knew what?"

She looks hard at Ruby-May, like she's really studying her features carefully.

"That they were black like me?"

"Look at them. Grace has beautiful eyes, and Martha, she's not fat, she just has chubby cheeks. Look how pretty Rose is – those cheekbones. And Owen, he's… cheeky, look at his grin, and he's a looker – like Jesse, look at *those* eyes."

Ruby-May turns each one over, says the number and Randolph checks. "Grace Robinson. Martha Woodruff. Rose Johnson. Owen

Edwards Junior." All correct. Now she's got goose flesh on top of goose flesh.

"I don't understand," Mitch says.

"I passed," April says, "didn't I?"

Ruby-May nods.

"I never saw them before, how did you…"

"So, what's it mean?" Mitch says. He clunks his empty lemonade glass down on the table.

"It means…"

But how can she say it? What *does* it mean? What does it mean now for April?

"It means April's friends are not imaginary." It's Randolph who says it. He looks at Ruby-May, pushes back his chair, stands up.

"These are real children; she identified all of them," he says.

"Real children like where? In her class? I don't—"

Now April sobs, awful terrible sobs, but does she know what happened to these children… *can she know?* Ruby-May leans forward, reaches for her hand but she pulls it away. She slides a box of tissues in her direction.

Randolph looks at Mitch. "Come with me. I need to show you something."

Reluctantly Mitch stands, looks at April. "I've got her," Ruby-May says. "Let him show you." He looks like he really does not want to be doing this but he follows Randolph through to the den. The door clicks shut behind them.

April is now gathering all the photographs.

Ruby-May wonders how he'll say it – *they are real children – only they all died in 1953.*

Randolph said he'd show Mitch the printouts, the newspaper clippings, tell him everything he found out. But only if she identified them all correctly – she's pretty sure he never expected to be doing it.

April sits staring at the photographs. "Are you okay, honey?"

She looks at Ruby-May. "Is this it?"

"Is this what, April?"

"It is, isn't it? It's happening. They said it would, they said you would help." She looks right at her. "They all died in a terrible way, didn't they?"

"Yes."

There's something so sad in her eyes Ruby-May wants to take her in her arms, but April now takes a hold of each photograph in turn as tears drip along her nose. "It's almost time, isn't it?"

She doesn't say for what. She doesn't say anything more. All she does is stare at their faces.

When Randolph and Mitch finally come back in, she does not expect what comes next. Mitch looks sweaty, fidgety, he sits back down, throws his head back and next thing he's laughing. Laughing the craziest hyena laugh you ever heard.

It's been ten minutes. Ten minutes since Mitch had his laughing fit, saying it was like a joke – someone would jump out any second and say it was all a prank. Because how could it possibly be true? *Like how?*

All Randolph says is, "I wish I knew."

The laughing was over quick because right after that he was crying and Ruby-May was plucking Kleenex from the box and pressing them into his hand telling him it was okay. *It will all be okay.*

But will it? Will it *all be okay*?

April sits quiet; her eyes have not left the photographs. And all Mitch keeps saying is, "What the hell are we supposed to do with this?"

But no one answers – because *what are they supposed to do with this?*

"You think you should come to Ellison with us, show the doctor this, what you just showed me… maybe there's a medical reason for it? Gotta be a plausible explanation – right? Like a brain thing."

"They won't believe us," Ruby-May says.

"They might."

"They'll say it's part of the psychosis."

"Maybe because it is."

"No."

"How can you be so sure?"

"Because it happened last time."

She shoots a glance at Randolph. He said not to bring it up.

"Last time?"

April is rocking, like she's seen her do in class, only now she's clutching the photographs to her chest.

"What if the hospital is the best place for her? If Cathy'd stayed on her meds, maybe she wouldn't't've... Jesus. She never spoke to ghosts, did she? She heard voices."

"Maybe she did. We need to think about this, before they pump her full of drugs. Speak to someone."

"Like who? A priest? An exorcist?"

The laugh is back.

"Someone who knows about this – a clairvoyant?" Ruby-May says. Randolph glares. Well has *he* got any better ideas?

Mitch stands, looks at April. "Come on, Ape, we need to leave."

"Please. At least think about it. Once they get her on those drugs, you'll lose her; do you really want that?"

"Look at her! I don't want the same thing to happen that happened to her mom."

"Who says it won't anyway?" Maybe she shouldn't't've said that.

"Ape – honey, come now."

Only April is sobbing, still holding on to the photographs.

"Billy was like her."

Mitch looks at Ruby-May as she speaks. She presses her hands flat to the table, one eye on April.

"Billy was one of my students."

She feels the burn of Randolph's stare.

"His mom thought he spoke to ghosts but the doctors said it was schizophrenia."

She does not know what the look on Mitch's face means, but she knows what Randolph's does. Only they have to know.

"Billy was bright, just the same as April is. Best kid in his class."

Mitch slowly sits back down.

"It was back in the 80s; I was still young, not much experience. Billy had the same problems; he had three friends, one in particular. No real friends. He was troubled, disruptive in class – blamed it on *Harry* – just the same as April blames her friends."

April mumbles something, can't make it out. Ruby-May continues.

"We got to know him well, probably got too involved – he even stayed with us one time – it was after he left school. I was the only one who could calm him down. And Randolph – soon as he met him, he loved Randolph. We thought we were doing the right thing. He was the one who told us he didn't see him, same thing April said. He *felt* him. His mom said it all the time – she said they were ghosts; Harry was a ghost. Only no one believed her. Billy was in and out of hospitals from the age of fifteen. Sure, he had serious problems but what they did to him was brutal. They pumped him with drugs, did surgeries on his brain. By the time they'd finished with him, he could never have lived a normal life." Now it's her turn to reach for the tissues.

"But they've got better treatments now."

"Treatments are different but doesn't mean they're better, so before they pump her with drugs, before April disappears in front of your eyes, let's make sure."

"Make sure of what?"

"Make sure we did everything we could."

"And if you're wrong?"

"Then sure, take April back to the hospital. Just give her few more days while we look at alternatives."

Mitch sucks in a long deep breath and blows it out before he speaks again. "So, what happened to Billy?"

She looks at Randolph.

"Help them."

All heads now turn to April. She's clasping the photographs to her chest. "They all say you have to help them."

"It's my fault she's like this," Mitch says.

"This is not anyone's fault."

"But what if we're wrong – about this – if it is a brain thing – what if she needs meds. What if—"

"NO!"

"Ape, we—"

"I SAID NO MEDS!"

"It's not your decision, Ape."

"Jesse says no meds. You're supposed to help them." This time she shifts her gaze away from Ruby-May, fixes it on Randolph. "Now is the time."

"Ape, come on, this is nuts."

"Now is the time…"

"Ape?"

"…to make justice ring out."

Mitch now looks at Ruby-May.

"And you can help… you." She points at Randolph. "We cannot walk alone."

Mitch his now standing. "Ape, what's all this?"

"Mr. Johnston – help them."

"Help them how?"

"There's one missing."

She lays the photographs back down on the table. "They say one's missing. All of them say it."

"One what – photograph?" Ruby-May says.

"He knows."

"Who, April? Who do you mean? Randolph knows?"

April's fingers are clamped around the six photographs. Eyes still on Randolph when she says it. Four little words: *You. Must. Find. Him.*

Chapter 12

August 20ᵗʰ, 2003

Atlanta, Georgia and Jacksonville, Florida

It's quiet on Peaches Avenue.

In the front yard, sprinklers dance, making rainbow arcs over the white rose bush. A mockingbird trills as it flits across the long grass. The "Sold" sign casts a long shadow. The "For Sale" sign was there almost a year, seemed no one was buying houses. Now there are U-Haul boxes stacked up by the door and a radio plays somewhere inside. On the table, just inside the front door – the pile of letters – all unopened.

The time is 5.44 pm.

───────────────

Ruby-May leans over the pan and lets the smell of the onions waft up. Randolph should be home soon. She walks to the window. He's back at Clayton Police Station, third time this week. Charlie says he might have something for him. Now she waits, looks out onto Tabebuia Drive and wonders if they found him.

The time is 5.44 pm.

───────────────

Josie-Ann lets the air con breeze stroke her braids, lets the cool air wash over. The smell of popcorn and sugar coats the air. A momma with a stroller rattles past; a bunch of teenagers block her way. But Josie-Ann stands still.

She stands still right in the middle of the shopping mall and lets the empty bag drop to her feet. She had the same feeling last year – about this time, a few days before her momma's first anniversary. Maybe anniversaries heighten the senses. Only that time it was fleeting. It was nothing, or so she thought until there'd been three missed calls, all from Biddy. She hasn't checked her cell today. But she feels it. Something's wrong. Biddy has it – the same thing Aunt

Lydia has, even her momma did right before she died: she knows, she senses – but this one is all hers.

Only time she's had it, it's usually the kids – no more than a momma's intuition, usually she's wrong. But this is not about the kids. And she's *not* wrong… but something is. Something's wrong.

She says it out loud, reaches down for her bag. *Something's wrong.*

The time is 5.44 pm.

Randolph's still not home. Ruby-May adds more water to the pan of rice. The house fills up with risotto smells, but she's lost her appetite. There are four missed calls on her cell – all from Libby. One message – asking if she knows what's happening with April Jefferson. She has not called back. She has avoided her all week.

For Randolph, it's like he's the big hot-shot reporter he never quite was, only this is no regular story, this is personal and that's what he told Charlie when he said he needed his help again. He's known him long enough to know Randolph Johnston does not ask unless it's important. He didn't probe, just said *okay. Whatever you need.*

She hears a car engine, looks over at the window. The silver Golf pulls up outside. She can't see the expression on his face from here.

The time is 5.58 pm.

Josie-Ann rests her hands on the wheel, looks out at the parking lot. She came for a birthday gift, for Luis. Macy's have polo shirts a third-off. She never even made it to Macy's. She's staring at her cell – Biddy *has* called; it's like a rerun of last year. But this time, all she says is, "Did you speak to Henry? He needs to check the house."

Whose house? Does she mean their house? Did she leave something on? The boys will still be at soccer. Luis won't be home yet. Or Henry's house?

Should she call her back?

She should call Henry.

She scrolls through, stops. Then she throws the cell on the passenger seat.

She reverses out. Something tells her: don't talk – just drive.

The time is 6.01 pm.

Peaches Avenue gets busy as cars bring folk home from work. Doors slam and voices lift. Happy sounds. The Hunts next door are having a barbecue. There are already greasy fat smells clinging to the air. The Stewarts' kids, all three of them, are playing out; the boy is throwing a ball through a hoop. But Amelia Jackson from across the street is standing still, looking over at 131. Maybe looking at the U-Haul boxes, or the open window. Or maybe it's the radio. She has a card in her hand.

But she doesn't move. She watches. Like she's remembering.

She's not lived on Peaches for anywhere near as long as the Tuckers – but twenty years is long enough. Maybe she's wondering what the new people are like. She clutches onto the card and makes her way slowly across the street.

The time is 6.01 pm.

Ruby-May listens for Randolph's keys to jangle in the door. She hopes he looks better than his first visit four days ago when he looked again at the Bloody Thursday file – it scooped him out. Took him a couple of hours before he was ready to tell her what Charlie said. How they'd been looking at the case.

"There were no more children," he said. "I know April said one was missing, but that was it. Five children, one teacher. Lots of children were sick; it was a small class. The janitor said he didn't do it. So, I thought his fingerprints must've been on that shotgun; there was no shotgun – no one even found the shotgun they claimed he used. Only the spent cartridges, but no gun to match 'em to. We searched that file, Ruby. We all know 'bout Jim Crow; well I think we found him right here in Clayton."

And that's when he'd grabbed her hands. "So maybe it's him – he is the one we're supposed to find – the one who really did this. Maybe that's who April means. The real killer."

The front door opens.

Randolph is standing in the doorway.

The time is 6.01 pm.

Josie-Ann fists the horn. Makes no difference – traffic's going nowhere. She fiddles with the dial on the radio: *Destiny's Child*, Biddy's favorite. Radio guy says Clay Aiken is coming up in the next half-hour. She likes Clay Aiken. Her fingers tap in time to the "Bootylicious" upbeat – she needs the distraction, needs something to take the tremble out. Maybe he should call Biddy back, or maybe she *should* call Henry. But now the cell has slid too far across the seat, even with her seat belt unhooked.

It's happening again.

It was close to this time last year.

It was August 24th – six days before Momma's first anniversary and Biddy was telling her something was wrong. But Josie-Ann didn't feel it like she does now. Biddy was always too busy with studies, always at the library, to think of anything else. But last year she did; she sensed it, and now Josie-Ann senses it.

Or maybe it just because it's that time of year, messes with the head. Luis would say it's paranoia. But Luis is still in work.

It's roll, stop, roll stop. She almost runs into the back of a pickup.

She remembers the call. Last year. She remembers holding the phone in her hand convinced they must've got it wrong. Biddy was right – something *had* happened. Aunt Lydia said she was to keep a close eye on him.

Only she didn't – did she?

She feels her pulse beat out time in her head. Clock is ticking. Biddy said had she spoken to Henry? She can't mean something's wrong with Henry, can she? But Biddy is in California. She starts

236

her first year at UCLA this week. One of the youngest ones there; flew out with her two weeks ago to get her settled.

The time is 6.17 pm.

Randolph is sitting with a glass of pink lemonade. All he said was, "Charlie sent me home; we're waiting on a call." His phone is on the arm of the chair.

"What call?"

But he's not saying.

He says he spoke to Mitch Jones earlier – that's he's getting *twitchy*.

He asked the question again – what happened to Billy? And Randolph told him straight. How he did not kill himself with a gun like April's momma – his poor momma had to cut him down. He left a note saying Harry told him to do it, so he can be a ghost too.

Ted will be out of the hospital soon. Probably the reason for the *twitchy*.

Randolph checks the phone again.

Ruby-May turns off the stove. The rice is half cooked.

The time is 6.21 pm.

There are more boxes in the back yard. They're stacked neatly against the wall. The cycad and the sweet acacia still in bloom, next to the camellias and the boxwood that was planted a year ago, another memorial. Everything is overgrown.

Song changes on the radio, this time it's Clay Aiken, claiming "This Is The Night".

The time is 6.25 pm.

Josie-Ann has barely moved nor has the gut feeling. She feels the sweat seep into her blouse. Windows are open, her arm rests on the lip. Clay is on the radio – her pulse quickens as the song builds.

A year ago, while she was still coming to terms with losing her momma, still wrapped up in the fog of it all when death came prowling again. A phone call and she was grabbing for her keys, Luis saying, "You can't drive in that state." Next thing he was driving her to the emergency room at Gradies.

Only it was already too late.

The time is 6.26 pm.

Ruby-May watches Randolph fumble with the phone.

Mitch says April's been asking if Randolph's found him yet. They're running out of time.

He didn't tell her what he told Ruby-May yesterday.

That there *was* another child. They managed to get a hold of the class register for March 12th, 1953.

He picks up the phone, turns it over in his hands.

Charlie said it took some digging. It was not kept with the photographs in the file. It was hidden because there was a witness – a key witness – a fifteen-year-old boy. He was not included in the newspaper. Charlie says his family insisted on that.

"Witness protection?"

"Kind of, but you know what that means?"

"That the killer is still out there?"

Ruby-May watches him staring at the phone, willing it to ring.

"So, what happened today? He asked you to come in; now you're waiting on his call? Why?"

"He wanted to see the look on my face when he told me."

"Told you what?"

"I was gonna wait, until." He looks again at the phone.

"Until?"

"Ruby, we found him."

"The gunman?"

She walks slowly towards him.

"No. The witness. We have an address in Atlanta, Georgia."

"April needs to know."

"Not yet. All we know is the address but the house is in escrow; it's been sold. It's been on the market close to a year. Looks like he died."

238

She watches him now. "Charlie is waiting for confirmation from the Atlanta Police Department."

"Can't they just check his social security – or death records, how hard can it be?"

He shrugs.

"What was his name?"

But before he answers, the phone rings.

It's 6.27 pm.

———

Amelia Jackson poked the letter through and is back in her front yard fussing her dog. The wind bends the trees over. A fug of barbecue smoke scuttles across. Someone moves behind the window of 131.

The time is 6.27 pm.

———

Randolph has his notebook ready. Ruby-May sits across from him, watches his face. He fumbles with the pen but does not write anything down. He does not look happy.

Looks like he is dead. It's confirmed.

Then he picks up the pen, scribbles something. Hangs up.

The time is 6.28 pm.

———

Traffic's moving slowly. The feeling gnaws; Josie-Ann's heart rate hitches up. She hates this time of year. Someone once told her deaths happen in threes.

Two years ago, her momma died.

One year ago, her step grandpa, Garfield, took his own life.

So who's next?

Josie-Ann pulls into the outside lane, snaps off the radio. For a year she couldn't even say the words. *Why'd you do it, Garfield? Why?*

If there's one thing you don't expect, it's for an eighty-nine-year-old man to step in front of a train. It even made the local news:

239

a jumper on the MARTA, at Candler Park. And now… all she can think about is this year… her dad. Not Henry. Can't be. Maybe what Henry said is the reason for *the feeling*.

She hits the brake. Come on; she needs to get to Peaches.

Can't shift it – the car or the feeling. She wants to be wrong. She has to be. It's just the season, the time of year messing with her head.

The time is 6.28 pm.

"Well?"

They stare at the number. An Atlanta area code.

"Now what do we do?"

Ruby-May looks at Randolph. "Call him?"

The time is 6.28 pm.

Josie-Ann knows something's been up with her dad for a while – but you expect that – her parents were together forty years. Only there are some things you choose not to see, not to believe, like how Garfield could have gone to the MARTA to catch the train to go visit Grandmomma Olivia's grave, like he did every week, and choose to jump. She wanted to believe it was an accident, but all the witnesses said they'd seen him close his eyes and step out. She learned in her job, it's always the ones you least expect. She realized she had not seen him for weeks; she should have seen him. He had no other family to look out for him – his brothers and sisters were all dead.

Garfield and her dad were not close, but it seemed to shake him up bad. Aunt Lydia stayed with him, for her momma's anniversary and for a few weeks after.

Traffic slows again. She looks up ahead, air filled with the stench of hot rubber and gasoline.

It was a month after Lydia finally left; her dad made the announcement. It was Thanksgiving; they'd all gotten together at her house, Biddy was with Lee that new boyfriend of hers (well he

240

was new then) when her dad said it. Said it in the same voice as the one he used to ask for Nia to pass the cranberry sauce. Said he was selling the house.

"But, Dad, you love that house – we all grew up in that house."

"It's just a house, Josie. Nothin' but bricks…" but they all knew it was so much more than that, "…and it ain't the same now."

She thought it was the grief; it would pass, especially since the recession and no one buying houses. He'd change his mind.

They close escrow the day after tomorrow.

Sun is still hot; she feels the burn on her arm. She feels sick. Wishes she could reach her cell.

She ought to go over more. There's always an excuse – work, the boys, Luis… last time she went there was barely anything in the fridge. A stack of unopened bills, all he said was her momma used to take care of that.

"But where you going if you sell?"

"My brother in Jacksonville, stay there for a while, then decide."

"Jacksonville? But, Dad?"

He had never mentioned his brother to her before. She'd been too afraid to ask. She never thought he'd sell the house – but then she never thought Garfield would step in front of a train.

She should've known something was wrong.

Last month he told Henry to stop coming around – now the plants were getting overgrown. All the memory plants: Momma's roses, the cycad, the sweet acacia… Garfield's boxwood.

Something's up with Dad.

That's surely what Biddy meant – she had spoken to Henry? She had and she did know her dad told him to stop coming. And then there was the thing he said about Garfield at his funeral. That it was his choice. It was what he wanted. That they ought to respect that.

Traffic speeds up then slows again.

Something's up with Dad.

Maybe it's just the jitters. But something tells her this is more than that.

Something's up with Dad.

But what if she's too late?

The time is 6.28 pm.

———————————

There's an echo inside the house; only a few pieces of furniture left – the couch, the table, Molly's favorite armchair. For the new family. The radio plays inside the empty bedroom, to mask the silence, bury the memories, only it doesn't bury them.

Children's voices rush from room to room. He even thinks he can see their shadows on the empty walls.

Josie-Ann's first day in school. He sees her standing in that kitchen while Molly packed her lunch in her bag. "I told you no pickles!"

Henry sitting at that table struggling to read and write as good as Josie-Ann while she showed him how to make the letters. "Henry, focus. Look, like this."

Molly marking out their heights on the wall, long since painted over. "Told you I was taller than you, Josie."

Laughter. Tears.

He feels it all.

All those Christmases and birthdays, Grandmomma, Momma, Garfield, William, Marcie… Cousin Thomas, Molly. All of them gone.

Garfield had the right idea, even he's with Momma now.

Time for the future – even the twins will be thinking about college applications soon enough. George is done.

On the table, in the living room, is a glass of water.

Next to it, his two little pots. He's saved up way more than he'll need. He has to be sure.

No note.

Garfield never left a note.

There's a card on the mat, *Good luck George* scribbled on the front. But he doesn't need luck, not where he's going.

George has it all planned.

With Garfield it was never planned. Like he seized his moment. Left a whole bunch of stuff for the family to sort. George won't do that. That's what made up his mind to sell the house, do it right. Garfield is the reason *he* did not do this a year ago – one year was too long, he won't get to two. Earlier when Amelia knocked, he thought Lydia had come. Just the sort of thing she'd do, like last time.

This year no Lydia. This year no one's stopping him.

Everything taken care of. Except the cats but Lydia will know what to do about the cats. They're outside. He doesn't want to look into their eyes, doesn't want them to see.

He told everyone he's going to stay with Abe. In truth he's not heard from Abe since he sent him his book of poems. No one else knows his address; he doesn't have to know what George did. *Once a coward, always a…*

He looks at the two little pots on the table.

He's ready.

And that's when the house phone rings.

The time is 6.33 pm.

————————————

There's a tow truck, looks like an accident. Explains the traffic. But the feeling digs in. Got to get to Dad.

Dad – please don't do anything stupid.

She wants to be wrong. But something tells her she's not.

The time is 6.33 pm.

————————————

The phone was supposed to be cut off today. They didn't say a time. Lydia. It has to be Lydia.

No point answering.

He closes his eyes.

It's me, George, answer the phone.

Molly?

Answer the phone, George.

Molly? Is that you?

Answer the damn phone, George.

Only one woman he knows talks to him like that. Has to be Molly.

So here he is, doesn't plan it, doesn't mean to do it, but he's reaching across to grab the phone.

"Molly?"

"Is that George?"

It's a woman's voice but it's not Molly.

The time is 6.34 pm.

———————————

Traffic is finally on the move.

It's like last year, the car ride to Gradies, sure they'd got it wrong. It wasn't Garfield. And if it was, he'd slipped, maybe a broken leg, he'd be okay.

They were too late.

What if she's too late again? What if history's repeating?

The time is 6.34 pm.

———————————

"Say it again."

Randolph pauses. "I said her best friends are Jesse Butler, Owen Edwards Junior, Martha Woodruff, Grace Robinson and Rose Johnson."

The time is 6.35 pm.

———————————

Josie-Ann looks at the clock; it's taken twenty minutes to reach Clayton. It's nearly 7 pm when she finally pulls onto Peaches. Looks like the neighbors are having a barbecue. Amelia, the woman from across the street is standing in her garden, playing ball with her Labrador retriever and her teenage son.

She *should've* called Henry; Biddy said that, didn't she? He lives way closer. Only something tells her it's better it's her. She can handle this. She's a social worker. She's got this. But has she? If she'd listened to Biddy…

She parks on the drive; next to his car – he's not used it in months. She throws open the car door, engine still running, crosses the front yard; the grass is too long, the sprinklers make her legs wet. There's a window open, is that the radio?

"Dad!"

She knocks.

Waits.

Knocks harder, more frantic.

"Dad!"

She runs back to the car and plucks out the keys. One of these is to the house. But which one? She's all fingers and thumbs. She's too late. Something's happened. She knows it.

She finds the right key second try; she pushes the door open, stumbles inside.

That's when she sees him stretched out on the couch.

Dear God. She's too late.

Ruby-May feels Randolph's arms wrap around her. It's been twenty minutes since they spoke to George Tucker. Now they stand in the kitchen; she doesn't know who's holding who up. She'd handed over the phone, begged George not to hang up, that Randolph, could explain *how* he found him. He could say it better. *Please don't hang up.*

After he made him say the names – made him say them three times, all Randolph said he could hear was him breathing on the other end of the line. The only thing he said was, "It's too late."

Then the line went dead.

When they called back it was engaged – probably off the hook.

When they tried again two minutes ago – it rang out.

Josie-Ann is too late.

"DAD!"

His head is to one side. He's wearing his blue cardigan, the one Momma bought him. His favorite.

Please be okay.

On the coffee table is a glass… two pots – his pills?

245

Jesus – no. Did he take any? She knew it. She knew something was wrong. And so did Biddy, shoulda called Henry. He would have got here sooner.

"Dad?"

She takes a step closer.

"Dad."

Please be wrong. Dear God, please be wrong.

Only then does he tilt his head. It's slight – but it's there. "Josie?"

"What did you do, Dad?" She looks at the bottles, both lids on the table.

"Dad, look at me."

There are tears on is cheeks, his lip's all a tremble. "Josie."

"Dad, tell me you didn't take any of these. Promise me…"

She looks at the names of the tablets, wonders how many there were, should she count them? Call 911?

"I didn't take 'em."

She's not too late?

She kneels, takes his head in her hand, brings his forehead to her lips. He looks so thin, he has always been thin, but his face… his cheekbones… how did she not realize?

"Dad – what happened?"

The telephone is next to him on the couch.

"Dad?"

She pulls him towards her. "Dad, I thought something'd happened."

He pulls away, looks right at her; it's the saddest expression she ever saw. "It did," he says. "Something did happen."

246

Chapter 13

August 24ᵗʰ, 2003, Jacksonville, Florida

George feels the hook of Josie-Ann's arm coaxing him slowly towards the house. He feels the jab of all their stares. There's a rose bush in the garden, a blush of red along a hickory fence. Looks like a sweet acacia like they have at home. He knows this street, though it don't look the same and there go them goosebumps again.

His legs are stiff from the ride – though they made several stops. Each time George thought about saying *turn back. He could not do this.*

Only now they're here.

There's no going back.

George is wearing his fancy suit; the last time he wore it was for Garfield's funeral. Shoes so shiny you can see his face in them. Molly would approve. *Good suits don't crease, George.* Looks like she was right.

Josie-Ann says today is one whole year since Garfield *did what he did.* But he knows she was thinking about him, what he *almost* did.

That car of Luis's, the big silver Voyager, is a whole lot different to that beat-up old station wagon Cousin Thomas drove all those years ago. They left at 7 am – kids were not too happy about that; makes no difference to George – he never did sleep well, no way he's sleeping now.

He still doesn't know why they all had to come. Just as well they got that car, more like a bus.

It's a nice house: pretty yard, someone takes good care of it – not overgrown like his is… *was* – Josie-Ann says Henry went around on Friday.

Clayton is a whole different place now. His old house was close to this very street, maybe at the other end, hard to tell now all the names are different. He does remember how they all had tree names now. He remembers it from that one time he came here; that there was a Tabebuia Drive close to where Denzel Street had once been. Jacksonville is a big place, yet here he is – back where it all started. What are the chances, only what George knows after that phone call is nothin' gonna surprise him again. Last time he came here he'd been looking for the house, for the stoop, for Abe. This time, Josie-Ann told him he should've written to Abe; told him he was coming to Jacksonville. She guessed there never was a plan to go stay with him.

But George didn't answer.

When George came back all those years ago, he went first to the old cemetery. Same place he'd been to all them times right after it happened until Grandmomma told him not to go inside – not no more, wasn't healthy. Same place he came on his supposed-to-be wedding day. Couldn't go inside then neither all because o' that *cross-your-heart* promise he made Grandmomma. Clayton Cemetery's not too far from here. So's the place where the Eastfield High School used to be. Came that time when he was meant to be gettin' wed but instead was running away. Seems maybe he's been running away his whole life. He saw where his school had once stood when he rode the bus from the cemetery. He's not gone that way since. Deliberate, of course. Some things you need to keep locked away. Molly told him that one day he should *let it all go.*

Is that what today's about? Time to stop running away?

But how do you *let it all go?*

George walks slowly along the path. Josie-Ann supporting him like a crutch.

The rest of his family right behind him.

All he knows is, this day has been a long time coming. A day he thought he'd never see.

The new school, though it's not so new now, is further along Williams Avenue – it's where Ruby-May Johnston is a teacher –

she's the one who's standing at the doorway of this pretty house. She's the reason he came – and April – her student, a teenage girl whose imaginary friends are *his friends*. When she said it, he thought she was crazy. Now he doesn't know. Doesn't know a thing.

First Molly in his head telling *pick up the phone, George*. Made him think he'd already taken a whole bunch of those pills.

He should've hung up soon as he knew it wasn't Molly, that his brain was playing tricks. His brain was messed up with the fog that day and the days leading up to that day. But there he was, five days ago, listening to Ruby-May struggling to say the words, puttin' her husband on. Randolph Johnston was the one who said he'd been looking at the police records from March 12th, 1953. Said it was because a teenage girl told him there was someone he was supposed to find.

"Who?"

"You, George. And I think you know what really happened in 1953."

In all these years, he used to have nightmares about someone finding him. But no one knew he existed, no one looked for him, no one came. But the one he feared the most… the one that had him locking doors and checking under beds – that was worse than any bogeyman… *the bad man*. And he has thought about that a lot. Probably every night since.

So, there he was, this Randolph telling him the names of all his friends who died – names he's not heard spoken in more than fifty years.

A clairvoyant many years ago called Devine Borrowspell told his momma ghosts are folks with unfinished business, which is why they come back.

All George knows is he did not want no talk about ghosts or imaginary children or what happened. Told Randolph it was too late. The whole thing was messed up.

No more messed up than thinking he could end his life.

No more messed up than hearing Molly telling him to pick up.

249

And no more messed up than the phone ringing soon as he'd hung up and hearing Molly's cousin Lydia's voice saying, "Did you find her, George?"

He only answered because he was sure it was them calling back and he wanted to say it – never call again. Lydia said something else too. "You need to help her."

But how?

He wasn't gonna come.

Until two days ago.

That's when he spoke to April.

Josie-Ann nudges him gently on. "It's okay, Dad. I got you."

It was Randolph's idea. They said they were planning on coming to Atlanta, only April said it had to be in Jacksonville – George needed to come back to where it happened.

And it was April said *everyone* needs to come.

None of this would be happening if it hadn't been for that phone call.

George is still here. And Josie-Ann's been talking to the bank and the lawyers, but it might be too late to back out of the sale of the house.

George wasn't planning on telling Josie-Ann about the call last week, but it was like the words spilled right out. He was pretty sure she didn't believe any of it. She kept on asking him if he was sure he hadn't taken any of the pills. Counted them right out into her hand.

The phone rang while she was still there. If it hadn't, she would probably still think he was making it all up. She talked to Ruby-May. She was on that phone for a good long while. At first it was like she was being a social worker, matter of fact, listening, looking at him. After that she talked quiet, he thinks he even saw tears. Next thing she wrote down their number. Passed on hers. "Dad'll be staying with us now," she said. Like he had no say. The whole time her eyes on the pill pots, lids crewed tightly back on. Said she was taking him to the doctor on the way home. They needed to catch the cats, take them with them. They were all staying at their house – where they were safe.

Only now here he is – back in Clayton.

School was supposed to be safe.

What if he can't say the words? What if he's struck dumb like he was all them years ago?

April called. Two days ago. After George told Josie-Ann to tell them maybe this is not such a good idea after all.

Josie-Ann was right at his side, even put it on speakerphone. April told him how Jesse likes baseball, and Martha pies... about Grace and Owen and... but it was the other stuff. She said did he remember when Grace tripped over right in front of everyone and you could see her underwear; how they all thought she was crying only she was laughing. Did he remember how Mr. Lewis taught them about the war, the story of his dad's medal? And did he remember the time he and Jesse fought, how he'd gotten a black eye, only he told people that's not how he got it, because he didn't want to get George in trouble. Said it was a fight over a girl.

How?

How could she know any of that?

"It's like they're stood right there next to you," he'd whispered.

"That's because they are, George."

Ruby-May has a smile that puts him in mind of Molly: all white teeth. She's standing at the door in a beige dress. Curves like Molly only she's slimmer, smaller than Molly. Wears her hair the same though, shoulder length. Only hers has more of a twist. Next to her must be Randolph; he looks smart though no suit. Behind George are the boys, Biddy (she needed to do some rearranging but she flew down yesterday), Luis, Henry. Only Nia is home – with the kids – they're too young for this.

And of course, Cousin Lydia. Flew in from Dallas on Thursday.

Randolph is tall, though not as tall as George. He steps forward and shakes George's hand – a good firm grip. Says thank you for coming. Ruby-May stands still. George puts out his hand but she doesn't take it. She looks at him, looks hard. Then without a word she wraps her arms around him and holds him there. She smells sweet like coconut. Whispers thank you. Before he knows it, he's got the *blubber-blubber*. And behind her, as she gently eases away, he sees her.

He sees the red curls first.

Face white as clean linen, white as cotton. She's wearing a pretty cornflower blue dress; Molly had a dress in that very color, a long time ago.

It's April.

Has to be. Only he never figured on her being white.

"George," she whispers. "*We* were afraid you wouldn't come."

Something about the way she says *we* gives him the trembles.

Ruby-May introduces her first to him and then the family. But even when she's shaking hands with Biddy her eyes are on George. He half expects to see his friends standing right there next to her.

Next thing they're making them drinks, showing them where the bathroom is since they've been on the road a while. Like they're all just old friends having a family get-together. Only this is anything but that.

A white man in jeans and a shirt, wild brown hair, pushes his hand into his and says he's April's dad. "Call me Mitch." He has the *trembles* too. Now he sits, beating his fingers on the couch. He's all *fidgety-fidgety and chitter-chatter*. He says April usually lives with her grandfolks only her pops is still in the hospital, recovering from open heart surgery – and her Grams is in a home. He has the verbals. Some folks wear their nervous on the outside.

So, formalities done, George, looks at Lydia who's sittin' quiet on an armchair, eyes fixed on the door like she's making to leave already. She might be quiet but that flowery dress of hers is not so quiet. George takes one of the upright chairs, legs all a jitter. Seems the teacher has put extra chairs. Biddy, the twins and Henry take the couch. Randolph has poured orange juice into tall glasses. They're on the coffee table in front of them.

252

House feels stuffy: too many people. He doesn't know why April insisted they all come. The twins love a road trip – to them this is one big adventure. Bean and Button are a couple of years younger than George was when it happened.

Ruby-May fans a book in front of her face. The dad's fingers drumming on the arm of the chair, lots of shifting, fidgeting sounds. Boys saying something to Henry. This is all wrong. He needs to go.

Might be the heat, might be all eyes on George, might be the thing, the thing he's supposed to do, only now he's standing.

"Dad?"

"Fresh air," he says. A line of sweat makes a tickle as it drips along his face. Now he's heading back to the front door.

"Leave him," he hears Lydia say.

Too many people. He can't do this.

He counts five steps to the door, takes three steps back along that path.

"Just give him a moment." Luis's voice.

He closes his eyes. The scent of White Angel lilac drifts in, makes him think of his grandmomma.

"I can't do this."

"Sure you can."

"Abe?"

It's been ten minutes since they came back in – all eyes shift from George to Abe, like they're seeing double. He could not believe he was standing right there. He looks way better than the last time. He's on a program; it's been three months. Says he got the letter – turns out it was from Josie-Ann – social workers have their ways apparently because he did not give her the address. She left messages at the YMCA since he has no phone. She wasn't sure he got them. Now she can't take her eyes off him.

They look alike; he's even dressed smart, shirt, pants. Of course, Abe is older, has even less hair than George, wears his age worse but then he has the scars and he walks with a stick. But no mistaking who he is. He sits himself next to George. Thought for a second, he was the one ready to run, when he met the family. All he heard Bean say was, "Wo – so he's our great uncle?"

Next thing Ruby-May was pressing a Kleenex into Josie-Ann's hands. Josie-Ann was never one for the *blubber-blubber*. But she's done a whole lot of it these past few days.

The *chitter-chatter* stops – all on its own, not sure what's supposed to happen now. Randolph looks at Ruby-May like he expects her to do something.

George looks at Lydia like he expects her to do something.

It's April who does something.

Her voice is louder, bolder than the timid he sees. She looks right at George. "It's time," she says. "Jesse says *tell 'em, George. Tell 'em what happened.*"

And George William Tucker finally tells his story.

All Flesh Shall See It Together

It was a Thursday.

George was at the back of the classroom – he'd been late, he almost never came at all. Jesse was late too, sat next to him. They'd been fighting; he wasn't so sure he'd even come. Everyone was sat in their usual seats. Rose and Grace sat two seats apart in the middle row; the empty seat was where Chloe usually sat. Owen and Martha at the front but either end, five seats between them. Like they didn't want to sit where the others usually sat. They were all off with the influenza. There were only six of them in the class. George looked out of the window. Decided to write a poem about crows. Gossipin' crows. Seemed it was a day for them. But he only wrote the title.

The sky was an odd kind of blue, air felt still yet it was like the clouds were moving too fast – scudding. A new word he learned. He planned on using it in his poem. As Mr. Lewis walked into the school gate, he looked surprised to see Principal Brown still standing in the school yard. He was looking up. They were both looking up.

More than twenty crows perched in the oak tree opposite the

school; another group flying directly overhead whipping up a frenzy in the strangely silent air.

The two men lingered outside a moment longer, before they came back into the school. Mr. Lewis was late too and he was never late. When he came in, he mumbled something about his wife being pregnant – somehow she was the reason he was delayed. He seemed breathless, distracted.

"My sister Chloe's sick," Rose Johnson said when Mr. Lewis took the register. He kept on looking at the window. Right before Mr. Lewis came in, George could've sworn he saw someone out there, looked like someone standing by the trees, but it was only for a second. When he looked again, he thought his eyes were playing tricks. Mr. Lewis looked out again like he saw something too, because next second he said he forgot something. "I'll be right back, just wait here…" His eyes were still on the window.

That was the last thing George ever heard Mr. Lewis say.

The man was wearing a soldier's uniform: khaki-greens with big hefty brown boots. A helmet.

And he was carrying a shotgun.

Soon as he saw him George thought of Abe – that maybe this was the surprise his momma promised. Only no way it was Abe. No one at Eastfield ever invited white folk into the school. And certainly no one carrying a shotgun. He had sweat running along his face, like he was still fighting in the war.

The man seemed to sway; he was unsteady on his feet, just the way George'd seen Pap sway after too many bottles of Old Crow.

Martha's desk was closest to the door. She likely saw him first. Now little Martha was always smiling. But not that day. And the reason was now poking into her face. The shotgun. George knew what it was – but he'd never seen one for real. It was brown and black, but he remembers – something about the shape of the end. When Abe talked about it, he called it a *Humpback*. George might even have been excited – if it wasn't being pointed right at Martha

255

Woodruff, right to the side of her head. One way to get the class's attention. But it couldn't be loaded – *could it?*

They probably thought it wasn't real. Only there was something about the man; he wasn't that tall, thin, but it was his eyes. His beady stare as he swung that gun like it was a toy.

He told Martha to stand up. Chair squealed.

"Fat niggers deserve to die young," he said. "Say it after me."

She repeated it soft, words getting stuck to her lips. Body all *tremble-tremble.*

"Sergeant!" he said. "Fat niggers deserve to die young, *Sergeant.* Say it again. "

There was a janitor's closet at the back of the classroom and George was trying to make Jesse look at him, maybe if the bad man looked away, they stood a chance, could get to it, but Jesse was staring at the bad man.

"Who ate all the cakes, fat nigger girl?"

Martha was sobbing. Couldn't hear what she was saying but it sounded like she was calling for her momma.

It happened in less than the time it took to blink. A round fired at point blank range that sent crows scurrying from trees and Martha *scudding* across the room face down in a fountain of bloody pieces. The man recoiled and re-aimed. That's when George threw himself to the floor and frantically scrambled on his elbows into the closet. Once he'd gotten inside, he crouched there but the door would not pull all the way across; he could still see out.

One round – one dead.

Looked like Rose had also been hit too and was screaming, holding onto her arm. Blood seeped into her blouse.

Jesse had dropped to the floor; he was under the table.

Then Grace screamed out for Mr. Lewis to come back.

But Mr. Lewis didn't come back.

No one came back.

"Nigger whores should always be quiet!" the bad man said. He was now standing looking at Grace. But everything sounded muffled, gunshot-muted sounds.

When Jesse saw George, he slid across the blood-splattered

floor like a snake leaving a crimson smear in Martha's blood. George stretched out his hand urging him closer. He was almost there. "Come on," he mouthed. He could hear the man goading Grace at the front of the classroom, now the barrel of that gun that was still smoking was pressed against her breasts. George wanted to puke – he could smell smoke and flesh.

"Shut up, nigger girl! Talking too much, talking way too much." Only all Grace was doing was mumbling, leaned forward, rocking back and forth, praying to Jesus.

Jesse stretched out his hand. George leaned forward stretching out his hand too. He could almost touch him; he was almost there. He—

The determination in Jesse's eyes was gone in an instant. Another gunshot. Jesse's face got all twisted up and turned red. A mist of fresh warm blood coated George's face. Salty, metallic. A rusty-red spent shell rolled into the closet. George scrambled further inside, shuffled backwards against a mop bucket and a broom, but he could still see Jesse's face. His eyes were still on him. The *boom* of the shooting still in his head, but he could still hear the others screaming. That's when he saw that Jesse was not quite dead. Jesse gasped and blood formed a line between his trembling lips. There was another line of blood on the floor, creeping towards him like a pointed red finger. *You're next, George.*

Then peace replaced the fear in Jesse's eyes. He knew what it meant.

When he looked back out, George saw Grace slumped over, half her face missing.

Two rounds – three dead.

Rose was screaming. Hard to tell if she'd been hit again, blood dripping along her arm and onto the floor. Face like a flick painting. Her blood? Grace's? Couldn't tell.

Who next?

The bad man swung the gun around and shouted, "Dirty niggers deserve to die today!" and he looked towards the partly open door of the closet.

He was laughing – a phlegmy laugh and for a long time afterwards when he closed his eyes George would still hear that laugh.

George felt the warmth of his own pee seep into his pants. He was sure he would puke – any second but he kept on telling himself – *don't make a sound. Whatever you do, don't puke.*

The bad man was now standing behind Rose who was breathless, jabbering, staring straight ahead, blood dripping onto the wooden floor.

"Shouldn't have gone to school today, should have stayed at home with Chloe."

Drawing alongside her he pressed the smoking shotgun against her face, his finger poised on the trigger. He laughed that phlegmy laugh. George held back the vomit.

"What did you say, nigger?" He then drew his finger along Rose's chin so that she was forced to look into his eyes.

But when she tried to speak, he said, "Should have stayed at home, that's what you said, right? Should have stayed at home with all the other filthy niggers! Right? That's how you address your sergeant?" Then he leaned so close to her she would have smelled his liquor breath. Spat right into her face.

"Damn right you should have stayed at home, filthy nigger whore."

The bad man then ran the barrel of that long shotgun along Rose's soft cheeks. George flinched, her eyes shut and she shouted *please no no no. Please, Mister.*

A second later: *boom!* A jet of red pulp sprayed across his deadpan face. Shot her brains halfway across the room. That's when he turned his head and looked in the direction of the closet again. And that's when George thought he'd been seen. He cowered, his whole body shaking, all he could think about was Momma and Grandmomma Josie and that if he prayed to Jesus he could make it stop – only you can't make things *unhappen.* He was sure the bad man must have seen him hiding. But now something was happening at the front of the classroom.

Three rounds – four dead.

Owen Edwards Junior was one of the clever ones. He'd been watching the door the whole time. Seizing the opportunity while the bad man was creeping towards the back of the room, George watched him edge backwards closer and closer to the open doorway. That's when they heard the clank of footsteps outside in the corridor, walking at first and then getting faster and faster, until they became a frantic sprint.

The bad man spun around and Owen screamed, "Don't come back in the room!"

But it was too late.

Whether Mr. Lewis had time to really see, no one will ever know. The gunshot propelled him backwards out of the classroom. His skull hit the concrete floor. THWACK. He was lying half in and half out of the room.

Four rounds – five dead.

Owen's face was splattered with his teacher's blood but it was the look on his face George will always remember. The bad man was now looking around the room chuckling. His face, his uniform, were covered in blood: thick dripping blood. His boots made bloody footprints. George closed his eyes and prayed to God. Grandmomma said bad things only happened to the bad people but they were good people. Good people. And it was his birthday.

Only God was not listening.

"Dead niggers are the best niggers!" The bad man ran to the classroom door, boots slipping, scrambling over Mr. Lewis's body. Then he turned around one last time and turned the gun on Owen. Blew him into so many pieces not even his own momma would recognize him.

It was the blood on the soldier's face that was the last thing George saw before he turned and ran.

Five rounds – six dead.

Abe said the Humpback could hold five rounds – four in the magazine and one in the chamber. George counted. Mumbled, kept right on counting. He looked across at where he'd been sittin' just moments before, next to Jesse. Right before it happened; a pencil

259

sat in the groove of his open notebook exactly where he left it. Still nothin' more than a title to an unwritten poem – now splattered in blood.

A second later George puked his grits right onto the floor of the janitor's closet.

As the bad man fled, someone must've seen him; someone must've seen the blood trail from his boots, and must've taken that shotgun with him – but no one ever said.

It is likely that the janitor, Wesley Hart saw him.

The first thing George did when he saw the janitor was try to cry out but the words never came. The janitor staggered into the room and fell to his knees. George saw him wretch and then he was all hunched up over the bloody mess with spew dripping from his mouth and his nose, sobbing. He scooped Owen and Grace into his arms, all limp and lifeless like shop dummies. As George watched, he rocked them. Just kept on rocking them. Head in the air, muttering to God. Then he crawled towards the others, no point in checking for a pulse. Some of them had no place to check. Blown into too many pieces. Jesse's lifeless eyes were still staring into the closet. He heard the janitor's *mumble-mumble.*

"Oh God, oh sweet mother…"

George edged towards the door. That's when he saw him.

"Oh, thank God!" He said it over and over.

He scrambled on his knees towards him, into the closet but George couldn't move. He shrunk back against the wall and closed his eyes.

"Don't hurt me, please don't hurt me…" he mouthed the words as he watched the janitor draw closer.

That was when he heard the clatter of footsteps and muffled gasps and someone screamed out, might've been one of the other teachers. Over the janitor's shoulder he saw Principal Brown. He had never seen a look like that on anyone's face.

"Don't hurt me."

And he heard the principal say, "No one's gon' hurt you. It's gon' to be okay now, boy. Everythin' gon' be okay."

But if George knew one thing – *nothin' was ever gon' be okay again.*

Air is heavy, like a cloud is sat down over the little house on Tabebuia Drive.

Ruby-May reaches for another tissue. Seems like no one knows any words to say, because what *is* there to say? Charlie Wilkes is standing next to Randolph – he's not in his police uniform today. Must've come in while George was speaking. He stands by the door. The expression on his face says however much he heard – it was enough. She has no idea what he'll make of this – any of this.

Mitch Jones brushes past Randolph. He says he needs some air – a cigarette. Ruby-May mouths for Randolph to go check on him.

The brother is the one who took a hold of George's hand right at the start as he stumbled over his words, who held on tight and still is. Tears on his cheeks, doesn't say a word. They look so alike apart from the scars on the brother's left cheek. Ruby-May looks at the glasses but it does not look like anyone needs a refill. Even those young boys, the twins, who were full of chit-chat before, look like they've had the words shocked right out of them. She guesses they're about thirteen. She worries what this will do to them. Maybe she ought to mention it to the momma, maybe they need to talk to someone at their school when they go back, but then she thinks about Libby. Who'll believe it?

Henry is the quiet one. Even if he hadn't been introduced as George's son you could tell – looks just like him. Same mannerisms too. He's blowing his nose. Josie-Ann, the daughter with the cute figure is sitting with her husband – Mexican maybe – they are holding onto one another. Their daughter – the medical student – looks just like her momma, is staring at the one in the bright flowery dress.

April sits real still, perched on the edge of the couch. Hair falls around those slender shoulders. Seems like she's the only one who didn't cry. She's been watching George since he started to speak and now, she's staring ahead, like she's seeing into a whole other place no one else can.

It's hard to make any sense of what happened. If you tried to explain it no one would believe it. You ever want proof there are ghosts, maybe that's what just happened, right here in Ruby-May's living room. But is it proof? Who's gonna believe his words? All she knows is those words had waited a long time to get spoken. Now they're inside all of them. Nothing you can hold in your hands, but real as any proof she ever had.

There is no way April could've known any of this. Could she? Impossible.

There are twelve people in this room – including Ruby-May, all crammed into her living room, every one of them changed by what just happened, by what George told them. That's the reason for the quiet and for the looks on all their faces. That's the reason Ruby-May now shuffles to her feet and holds out the box of Kleenex, walks it round the room.

Slowly, one by one, they make their way over to George. Some with their silent hugs, soft pats on the back… all with their mumbled *so sorrys.*

Impossible to know what's going on in that poor man's head.

Or what's supposed to happen next.

What if it never stops? Looks what it's done to George. His daughter is the one who told her how he would never speak. Didn't speak for a whole year after it happened and has never spoken about it. Not even his wife knew his secret. What if April has to live with this *her* whole life? What if she still ends up at Elliston getting pumped full of drugs anyhow? For a fleeting moment she thinks about Libby again – Dr. McGarrigle – how does she explain any of this?

"You won't need to, honey."

Ruby-May is sure she never said any of that out loud but that's what the woman in the flowery dress says when she hands her a tissue. The auntie – though she doesn't recall the name. All she knows about her is something Josie-Ann said – that she has *the gift* and she would know what to do. *The gift?*

But before she responds Josie-Ann speaks.

"So, what happens now? That's it? It's over?"

"No," the auntie says. She tries to recall her name, Cousin… something.

"Lydia."

Now *she is* sure she never said that out loud but after what they witnessed today Ruby-May is pretty sure nothing will ever surprise her again.

"It's not over," Lydia says. "There's a reason why, and now we got to fix this."

"Fix it?" She did say that out loud and she is sure Randolph is now listening. "Is this about justice?"

"First things first," Lydia says. "Somethin' April's gotta do first."

At the mention of her name April's head turns in their direction.

She stands, straightens that pretty dress of hers and looks at George. They seem to look at one another for a moment and she is sure something passes between them, like they've been waiting for this – whatever *this* is.

"Is it time, Mrs. Johnston?"

Ruby-May looks at April. But it's Lydia who answers. "It is, sweetie."

"Where…?"

"Is there a room we can use? I need April and I need George, for this part."

What part? But something tells her not to ask.

"The den?"

"Okay."

"George? Ready?" Lydia says.

All conversations stop, now they all look at George again.

"It's time."

And just like that April holds out her little white hand. And George takes a hold of it with his big black hand, as he does a tear snakes along his face. Now standing, April hooks her arm into the bend of his and like that, they follow, Lydia behind, as Ruby-May shows them to the den. She has no idea why, only that it must be real important.

Ruby-May does not go in. She closes the door softly behind

them then she says who's for coffee and cream pie and suddenly there are people following her to the kitchen. Those twin boys are first in line. So now the house fills up with cutlery tinkles and crockery clinks and water filling the pot. It fills up with normal chatter, probably because right now what all of them need is a big dose of *normal.* It's only Biddy who stays in the living room. She sits quiet on the couch. She leaves her be while everyone gets stuck in; she has never had so many people in her kitchen, all needing something to do, to stop them thinking about what they just heard.

Ruby-May walks back to the living room.

"You want coffee, hot tea?"

Biddy shakes her head, eyes drawn to the door of the den.

"You know what they're doing?" Biddy whispers.

"No, but it looks like something real important."

"The children did what they came to do," she says. "So, it's time."

"To?"

But she doesn't say because now Mitch is back, smelling of tobacco, looking all flustered. "Have you seen April?"

It's twenty minutes before the door to the den opens. Randolph and Charlie went upstairs to Randolph's office, which means serious talk. They're back. She has no idea what this must be doing to them – they saw the photos. They saw what the shooter did to those poor innocent children.

April comes out first, still no sign of tears. George is behind her and hard to tell what she sees on Lydia's face. All she does when she sees Biddy is nod. So seems whatever they went in there to do – looks like they did it. And it looks like some things she is not meant to know.

George says no to coffee and sits back down next to his brother.

But April stands still in the middle of the room.

Randolph and Charlie look at one another; already the others are crowding George, though no one asks any questions. It's like they just need to be near him.

But April. April stands.

"April, sugar?"

April presses her hand into Ruby-May's. It's cold. "Thank you," she whispers. So now they stand side by side, right in the middle of the room while everyone else hands out more cream pie. Even the son, Henry, even he's talking to his sister. He looks troubled but at least he's talking. No good bottling it all up inside, that's one thing she learned a long time ago – after she lost her baby. And after Billy.

"I'm not like my mom, am I?"

Ruby-May turns. "No, sugar. Don't even say that."

"But, Mrs. Johnston?"

"Yes, April."

"It's not over, is it? It will never be over."

Ruby-May holds on tighter.

"I can't end up like her, Mrs. Johnston."

"You won't."

"But, Mrs. Johnston, some ghosts never leave."

The words give her the creepy-crawly skin but before can respond, April adds, "Justice will be served. Their destiny is tied up with our destiny."

For a moment Ruby-May feels like someone just walked over her grave. It's not the first time she's heard April speak that way. Use them words.

"George has agreed to let his story be told." She did not even know Randolph was standing right next to them.

"Says he told 'em they got the wrong man; the janitor didn't do it but no one believed him."

But all she's got in her head is what did April mean *some ghosts never leave*?

"He lived in fear that if he talked – he would find him," Randolph says.

April squeezes her hand.

Now Charlie is standing next to Randolph.

"And Charlie here will reopen the case."

"Corruption," April whispers. Ruby-May turns to look at her. "The horrors of police brutality."

Something stirs; like a whisper, a breath blown right along her spine. Those words. April always says she was repeating what her friends told her.

Charlie nods. "Yep. No words for what it was like back then. This is just one case, there'll be others, lost to history, but this one…" He looks at April as he speaks. "…happened here, and we need to put it right."

"But even if he's still alive, how you gonna find him?" Ruby-May says.

"Maybe we won't – find him or the gun, but we gotta try."

That's when April's hand drops from Ruby-May's grasp and she looks right at Charlie. Something real sorrowful about that look in those green eyes o' hers when she whispers, "He is still alive." You could drop a pin into the silence right here in this room when she says it. Her gaze shifts to Charlie and Randolph and then settles on Ruby-May. She can see the tears, waiting to come, waiting to let go but before she does, she adds, this time louder, "I know who he is."

Chapter 14

September 27th, 2003, Jacksonville, Florida

Another day winds down.

Sky is blushed peachy pink. The gate to Clayton Cemetery squeaks open but George stands still, one hand on the rusty metal. He made a *cross-your-heart* promise a long time ago not to keep coming in. But everything's different now. He knew it as soon as he told his story – like a spell was finally broken.

George lifts his head, prods the gate again and takes a step.

They all file in right behind him; feet making shapes in the long grass.

He still knows where to go. Even after all these years he remembers – walked this walk many times. They don't use it now; lots of the graves reclaimed by the weeds. Most of the black cemeteries are gone, made into parking lots, there are skeletons everywhere. He thinks about all those bones below all those trampling feet. And no one knowing.

How quickly folks are forgotten.

Not all of them.

It was some headline.

> *Local man charged with six counts of murder 50 years after the crime.*

The story was not just in the free newspaper either or the *Jacksonville Daily*, not just Florida newspapers either. Randolph Johnston made sure of it – but it wasn't the full story. He missed out the part about *how* they came to find out. All it said was some new information had *come to light* fifty years on and the case had been reopened. When he read the words, all George could think about was April Jefferson. But her name that did not appear in any newspaper. Just like his didn't all those years ago. April's teacher insisted on that. But George's name was there this time. The time for hiding is over.

George William Tucker (65) from Atlanta, Georgia,
formerly of Clayton, Jacksonville was in the classroom
that day – the only survivor. So traumatized by what he
saw, George buried the past. Now, for the first time, he
tells his story.

April's not gone back to school. Ruby-May says how people thought she was sick, not so easy explaining she wasn't sick; she just had a touch of *the ghosts*. So, she never told them anything. But she did say April is living with her dad, doing well. When it was in the newspaper, she said folks would've all known it was her grandpa who was arrested. Probably her doctor knew it too; and they would've all known the names of the children were the ones she said were her friends. She says she can help find a new school, if that's what she wants. New school – new surname. Might be for the best, though she looked sad when she said it.

When Ruby-May first sat George down, told him about April's grandpap, that he was *the bad man*, he'd sobbed up a storm. She was telling him over and over, "I'm so sorry, George." But he'd told her straight – the real reason for the tears was because now that poor girl had to live with all that guilt. *Eats you up.* She'd reached for his hand when he said that.

George does not know how he found any of the words when he told his story or how he said it all again for that white cop and for Randolph a couple of days later over the telephone. Last time though. Made it clear he would not talk to no more reporters and especially not the local TV. It's done now, said, out there.

All he had in his head when he told it, was Molly telling him to let it all go. Always *his Molly*. As a matter of fact, it was like she was sittin' right there next to him when he said it, again. Holding his hand, same way Abe did that first time.

Thanks to Randolph, Black Thursday is no longer lost to history. And looks like there'll be justice. Just took a long time to put things right.

Only person to blame for that is George.

Ted Albert Jefferson (74) served as a sergeant in the 23rd Infantry Regiment, US Army, in Korea from June 1950 to January 1953 but was dismissed for insubordination. On March 12th, 1953, he walked into Eastfield High School (an all-black school) in Clayton at around 9 am. Dressed in full military uniform, brandishing a Browning 5 semi-automatic shotgun, he shot dead five children and their teacher before he fled the carnage. Janitor Wesley Izaiah Hart (38), first on the scene, was wrongfully accused of the murders. The Florida Supreme Court ruled that he be executed on June 12th, 1953.

April and her dad are walking behind George. Both are dressed in black, like this is a funeral. George is in his suit too, big shiny shoes crunching the leaves. Only today he's wearing his Trilby hat. Smell of Fall in the air, soon they'll be scooping out pumpkin heads, kids'll be wanting to go trick or treating, then Thanksgiving… another Christmas. Holidays George never planned on seeing.

April has not said a word. But he told her when he learned about her grandpap – same thing he tells his own children and all his grandbabies – *you gotta hold your head up, walk proud. No one's responsible for what other folks do. Blood or not. Be seen.*

She thinks it's her fault, he sees it right there on her face but you can't hold onto it. He's being doing that for more than fifty years. He told them it wasn't that poor janitor, only no one listened. No one believed a nigger boy saying a white soldier did it. Not even when they couldn't find the gun, just five spent shells and that janitor who said he didn't do it. George heard him begging those policemen, saying he never did nothin' – George told them, over and over until there were no words left.

Don't lie to us, nigger boy.

He heard that poor man was beat into making a confession. It was most likely Principal Brown sealed his fate though when he told the cops he found that janitor, covered in their blood, George asking him not to hurt him. After that poor man was put to death,

it was too late. Principal Brown said he never believed he did it –
newspapers at the time twisted his words.

No one believed a nigger.

Cousin Thomas knew about that, fought for justice every day
of his life. Died fighting.

George was a coward for too many damn years.

What George knows, is some folks have got the evil, got it
inside them. April is not responsible for what her grandpap did.

Wingbeats lift his head, a rustle in the trees, looks like crows.
Just like there were that day. It's the one poem he'll never write.
The thing he could never talk about, only now he has and now he's
done. But no poem. Who knows what mighta happened if they
listened to him back then. Only a life's not built on *ifs*. If the bad
man hadn't done what he did. If someone had believed George
when he told them it wasn't the janitor. If crows could talk. That
was the name of his poem. Never even wrote the first line.

He thinks about it now – what would them crows say? It's one
question he thinks he's always known the answer to.

But that's all in the past now. Justice waited a long time to get
served. All George knows is if the bad man had been caught at the
time, then maybe there wouldn't even be an April Jefferson. That's
when he stops thinking. Maybe Lydia's right – things happen jus'
the way they supposed to. Like this, now. All these people at
Clayton Cemetery. And them crows watching from the tree. One
person is missing. Lydia. Business back in Dallas Biddy says. Done
her part Lydia says. Everyone else came – even Abe. Of course, he
knows this cemetery too. His friends are over the other side.

> *The shotgun has since been retrieved from Ted Jefferson's
> home where it was kept as a trophy for more than fifty
> years. An upstanding pillar of the community, retired
> CEO of DLW Water Management, a search of his home
> on Lotus Drive found evidence of his involvement with the
> Klu Klux Klan as recent as 1998.*

The graves are not all together, but they are all in the same corner.
George knows exactly where each one is. When he used to come,

he'd see where the families had been, left flowers. He'd wait back if someone was there; no one knew he'd been there – seen what happened. Later he'd add his own flowers, ones he picked from Momma's garden. He doesn't know if they ever saw them – to them he was just another ghost.

George was expecting to clear away the weeds only seems like someone's already been. A single white rose sits on each grave.

Martha Woodruff over one side. He does that one first. As he flicks the lighter he borrowed from Mitch, he's got a bad case of the trembles. April steps forward, holds her hand to still his and he lights it, they watch the little flame bend over before they set it down. Both trying hard not to get the *blubber-blubber.*

The rest gather, watch, but they don't help; he tells them this is their job. They light each one together.

Grace Robinson over there, three along. Second candle.

Rose Johnson, under the oak tree. Third candle.

Owen Edwards Junior further over, by his grandpap. Fourth candle.

And Jesse. Spent more time at this one than all the others. Fifth candle.

Samuel P Lewis is further over, next to his parents and brother who died in the war. They do him last – sixth candle.

George lifts his Trilby in a silent salute to each one.

All *their* names were in the newspaper. Randolph has been tracing the families. None of them came today – this is private but looks like someone's tended these graves. He does not want to think about what those families will think now – knowing there was a survivor. That janitor's family will hate him and who can blame them. He tried, maybe not hard enough. And he's pretty sure every one of them families will wish it was their child – why did George get spared? Been asking himself the very same question for fifty years.

George stands back and watches the others as they in turn light their tealights. Now that one little corner of Clayton Cemetery is all lit up, like the *twinkle-twinkle* lights, like that last time they sat in the yard – him and Molly, when he last drank hot chocolate, with whipped cream and marshmallows.

"Here."

Josie-Ann presses a Kleenex between his fingers. "It's beautiful, Dad."

> *Recently released from hospital following open heart surgery, Jefferson was arrested but before they obtained the warrant to search his home, he admitted to the murders. Detective Sergeant Charles Wilkes (56) of the Clayton Police Department, claims it's the worst racially motivated attack he has ever seen. "What's devastating," he claims, "is during Jim Crow, no one got a fair trial." He hopes that justice will finally be served.*

"Look at this," Josie-Ann says. "Just look at the lights. Momma would've loved to be here to see this."

"Maybe she is."

It's Biddy who speaks. She looks so much like her momma. Then so quiet he can barely hear it, she adds, "You were meant to find her. Grandmomma knew it."

Now he's got shivers on shivers.

He looks at Josie-Ann.

She said next week he can move back into his house; and since the lease is up on Henry's place which is too small now, they are moving in. He is not so sure he likes Josie-Ann's idea – it's been a long time since little babies lived at 131, but looks like it's decided. He already told her – she doesn't have to worry. George is going no place. He doesn't know if she believes him. Least the house isn't sold, cost him but they pulled out, Josie-Ann saw to all that, not sure what she said but next thing he knew the boxes were unpacked. Henry's been up there every day, tending the plants, even feeding the cats – moved back in waiting on them.

He watches as Biddy lights a candle.

It's almost time to say something – but what will he say? Told Abe he has no idea what to say, he was never good with this. Like he said, he's done his talking.

That's when they hear it.

Starts off soft.

Someone's singing.

It's a man's voice. Real soulful. Randolph?

"Amazing Grace, how sweet the sound…"

Sky is rinsed in reds as the light fades; a few cars pass by on Williams. A few blocks up from Williams and Duval is the site of the old school.

Maybe George doesn't need to say anything. Seems like whoever's singing is joined by someone else.

Ruby-May said they should light the candles where it happened; but George was the one who said no – he knew a better place. She is standing over by Rose's grave with that husband of hers.

But who's singing? Not Randolph.

Luis?

When he looks across at Grace's grave, he sees him.

It's Abe.

Who knew he could sing like that?

Abe's voice is deep, low, mellow and everyone stands still. He's standing next to Mitch who's joined in.

April stands alone. Her dad has similar issues to Abe, maybe they even met before, maybe even in a meeting. Life is full of strange coincidences although Biddy says there's no such thing.

No one knows what'll happen with April's grandpap now – most likely die in prison. Why did he do it? Makes him think about Abe; look what the war did to his head. What his grandmomma called *the war crazies.*

But what he did is something far worse than any *war crazies.* Seems he was released from the army on account of fighting with his black corporal, that's what Randolph found out. Cousin Thomas always said that in some, the hatred of the black man runs so deep it colors the blood, cut him and he bleeds hate.

There's nothing will excuse that man for what he did.

No God.

No forgiveness.

"He who is devoid of the power to forgive is devoid of the power to love."

He jerks around expecting to see a man, only person he sees is April.

"You hear that?"

"Hear what?"

But he knows he heard it.

Another voice joins in the singing – sounds like the teacher.
"That saved a wretch like me..."

April's eyes are fixed on the flame of a candle in her hand.
Or maybe he just thought it?

The voices carry across the cemetery, soft low singing. George pulls his jacket tighter. Feels the goose in his flesh – just like four weeks ago. In that den – just him, April and Cousin Lydia.

If he hadn't seen it with his own eyes, he would never have believed it.

His friends are gone.

He knows because he saw them leave.

Now the singing gets louder. Three, maybe four voices. George stumbles; feels a hand on his back. Josie-Ann.

"I once was lost, but now am found..."

A soft breeze bends flames, a sea of candles, some on the ground, some in hands.

Small clusters around each grave, flickers of candlelight. Another verse.

Even the twins join in.

They're all singing. Even Charlie.

Only one's who's not – is April. And George, of course. Everyone knows George does not sing hymns.

That's when he feels it; April's small cold hand slides into his, just like it did when they went into that room – with Lydia. He doesn't exactly remember the words Lydia used. Just that he'd stood like he is now, hand in hand with April when she told them it was time to let them go. He felt the same tremble in her body he feels now, felt her holding on tight.

"I'm right with you," he told her. "We'll do it together."

And right before it happened, he was sure he heard each of them say his name. And as they went, he was sure he saw five little shadows. And a sixth. Like maybe Mr. Lewis was there to greet them.

April holds on good and tight now. That's when he realizes, she's singing. "It's not your fault," he whispers. "What your grandpap did."

He feels the pinch of her fingers, she sings louder.

And for first time in fifty years George finds his voice for a second time, only this time he sings a hymn.

"Was blind but now I see."

Slowly everyone leaves, *shuffle-shuffle* along the trampled grass. A line of bobbing tea lights.

When he turns to look at April, she has tears on her cheeks. She pulls her hand free. He needs to tell her now.

"I always carried that guilt, for what they did to Wesley Hart."

She stands still, doesn't speak.

"Carried it around until it near killed me. But this is not yours to carry. Can't choose blood; my pap was a bad man, keen with fists, spent most of my life trying not to be like him. But you, you're good all the way through and April… you saved me. That day, you might not know this, but you saved my life."

Only then does she turn her head. "I swear I didn't know he was the bad man."

"I know."

"I thought you'd hate me."

"Didn't you hear me? You saved me."

Tears fall on his cheeks; he wipes them away with his hand.

"My wife, Molly, told me somethin', right before she died. You know what she told me?"

Her lips open but she doesn't speak.

"She told me that I was to *find her*. Now I always thought she meant another woman and that ain't happening. But now I know. She meant you."

He sees the tears on her cheeks.

"I thought maybe you wouldn't want us to be friends," April says.

"Never. April, not many folks born fifty years apart, share the same friends, now that is somethin'."

"Sometimes I still speak to them," she whispers.

He turns so he can look at her. "I thought they—"

"They did. They did leave, George. They're gone."

He nods.

"I should've told them something," she says, looking down at her shoes.

"Tell them now. I'll leave you alone."

"No. Please, George… please stay."

"You know, April, I used to stand right here and talk to them all the time – maybe not the way you talked to them. I know they never heard me."

She steps forward, looks along the graves. "I'm sorry for what happened, sorry that the bad man was Pops. I'm so sorry."

Then she leans into George and he wraps his arms around her. "They know, April. Ain't your fault – you think they'd hung around you so long if they blamed you?"

He sees the teacher watching, feels April's hand in his.

"They did hear you," she whispers.

Ruby-May and Randolph are standing with Mitch – all still watching. Everyone else seems to be slowly making their way back while those tealights are dancing like fireflies.

"Go on, your folks are waitin' on you."

"You not coming?"

"Somethin' I gotta do first."

Abe is stood alone, leaning on his walking cane, face caught in the orange glow of a tealight.

A thin fingernail of moon hangs in the almost dark sky. Air nips at flesh. As he gets close, George can just make out the names in the candles' flicker.

Isaac Harrison (January 12th, 1932 – August 1st 1953)
Jacob Harrison (September 13th, 1936 – June 28th 1958)
Benjamin Morris (May 15th, 1932 – January 29th 1953)
All died fighting.

"Why'd you keep lookin' for me, George?"

"Same reason you came here for me today."

"I ain't the brother you think I am." The light catches his face; one half melted but the scars have faded.

"You sober?"

"I was the only one who survived, George, and it weren't mean to be that way."

"I know."

"You don't, George. You a good man. You made somethin' of your life even after what happened, what you saw. You made good choices."

George sees the tremble in Abe's fingers, leans in closer. "How many drinks you had today?"

"I ain't doin' this again."

"We're not so different," George says.

"We are. You still made a life – a good one, you're stronger than I could ever be."

"I was the only one who didn't die that day. Used to sit right over there in that corner, thinkin' my name should've been on one of them gravestones. Tell me you didn't do the exact same thing with your friends?"

He nods. "They called it The Forgotten War. It lasted three years, but I been fighting that war for over fifty."

"We both been doin' that, brother."

Abe doesn't say anything.

"Wasted a lot of years, Abe. Now all we got is a handful left – more years behind than ahead. Maybe there's still time."

Abe turns his head. "For what? You think you can save me?"

"Only one person can do that."

He stares straight ahead.

"Every time I came lookin' for you, I thought this time you were gonna be dead."

"I never asked you to come."

"You're my brother."

"I killed Pap."

"No, you never. No one knew his heart was weak, but all his own doin', the liquor, the—"

"I'm like him."

"No. You're better than he ever was, Abe."

"I'm sorry, George."

"Enough with the sorry, Abe. Over in that corner are six people, over here another three and over here… come with me. I'm gonna show you somethin'."

Abe steps carefully, cane in one hand, tealight in the other, making *swish-swish* sounds in the long grass until they get to it. A single gravestone, looks like someone's been to that one too, weeds all cut back, this time *a bunch* of white roses. "Look."

George pulls back the grass. Abe sets the tealight down in front of it. "Read it."

He rests the cane against the stone and bends down.

"I remember when I found this. Was too ashamed to even come close. I saw the family though. Ev'ry time I did, I wished I was dead, Abe, same as you did."

"You got married, had kids, a decent job, a house. You made it work."

"You think I didn't have them same demons inside me? Every time I thought I was happy, then it would come along and steal it away. I never thought I deserved to be happy, Abe. Never thought I deserved Molly. Never thought I should've survived. Been carrying that shame and that guilt around inside of me for so long it near destroyed everythin'. The night Randolph phoned to tell me about April, I had two whole pots of sleepin' pills all lined up, enough to kill me twice over." Abe turns his head. A tear runs across his scarred cheek. "Saved by the phone ringin'. Crazy as it sounds it's exactly what happened."

"I didn't know."

"We were never so different – but we could've been there for one another. All I know, is there are some things can't be explained, like how April spoke to ghosts, how they found me, how that phone call—

But what I do know is we gotta live – because none of these people can. We survived, Abe, and all we did with it, was let it destroy us. That's gotta stop now."

They wait for the words to settle. Let the cool air kiss their cheeks.

"Ninety-five days," Abe mumbles. "That's how long I've been sober."

George feels the clutch of Abe's hand, long cold fingers folding claw-like over his, holding his real still. "I read your poems, George. I read what you wrote for me. No one ever did nothin' like that for me."

They look at the gravestone.

Wesley Izaiah Hart January 2nd, 1915 – June 12th, 1953. Son, Husband, Father. God Knows The Truth. May You Find Peace in Heaven.

"Come on," George says, "they're waiting for us."

"Just wait up."

"What is it?"

"Just let's stand here."

Then he hears Abe whisper. "Pray with me, George. Say it with me…"

It's been fifty years since George prayed.

"Say it, George."

God, grant me the serenity to accept the things I cannot change, the courage to change the things I can, and the wisdom to know the difference. Amen.

"I'm done fighting old wars," Abe says.

This time the tears come big and ugly. But this time George leaves them be – wears them like a scar. He looks at Wesley Hart's gravestone. "I'm sorry," he whispers.

As he says it, a breeze lifts the petals of the white roses and a crow caws in the tree.

> *"In the light of recent new evidence, a posthumous pardon has been made to the family of Wesley Izaiah Hart. Daughter, Lanelle Hart (63) says, "My family never believed what they said. I just wish my momma was alive to see this." She adds, "The pardon is fifty years too late but at least it came. At least now we can find some peace."*

Chapter 15

March 12th*, 2004 – Atlanta, Georgia and Jacksonville, Florida*

It's the perfect Friday evening for a barbecue. Least that's what Henry says.

Already 131 Peaches Avenue is full of people: the women fussing in the kitchen, men flipping burgers in the back yard and the sweet smell of Lydia's apple pie warming in the oven. Smoke hangs over the backyard, choking the sweet acacia and the boxwood, drifting along Peaches. Cloying, greasy cooking smells.

George is not one for the barbecues. Or the smell of onions.

Noises – lots of voices: sounds of *chitter-chatter*, playful shouts, squealing. George is not one for the sociable either.

George stands at the bedroom window and looks out. Watches Amelia Washington sweep her front steps. The kids from further up are hanging on the corner studying their bikes. Mr. Michaels is cleaning his new car.

And George definitely is not one for the birthdays.

But seems today, as he turns sixty-six, which he tells Josie-Ann *ain't even a special number*, no one is letting him forget. It's the first birthday party George can remember since he was a kid, back in Clayton, with Abe. Grandmomma would bake lemon cake.

George is not one for the sweets but he loved Grandmomma's lemon cake. Molly tried enough times to make George have a party – always said no. There were gifts but no parties. But this year, Josie-Ann said they needed a party – the guilt's lasted long enough.

And so, here they are.

She says there's a surprise. A guest of honor. What guest of honor?

Only George is where he always is – where he likes to be – out of the way. He looks at his watch – worries. Only one guest of honor he wants to see, same as he did on his fifteenth birthday. He is supposed to be here already.

———————————

April straightens her dress, checks her make-up. Again.

"You sure, Dad?"

"I already told you – you look a picture."

She runs her fingers over the gold daisy on the chain – it was her mom's. They found it amongst Grams's things.

"Now you ready?"

"Yes."

The airport's busy.

It was renamed last year – Hartsfield Jackson – apparently in honor of Mayor – Maynard Jackson, who died last June. Doesn't know how she knows, it just sits in her head.

She has not seen George since that day at Clayton Cemetery. It was his daughter's idea for her to come. She said it was for George's birthday. She freaked when April said it was her birthday too. Sixteen.

"It is? So, you'll already have plans with your friends?"

They let the words hang in that moment that followed. It's her first birthday without them – *her friends.*

She still misses them.

She asked her pops a question.

It was the one time she saw him.

She didn't know if she could even look at him. She asked him if he knew who they were – if he knew their names; like he must've known them from all the times she said them. But he'd looked at her, like a stranger and not the man who raised her, said he never cared to know the niggers' names. She could've spat right in his face. That is the last time she saw him.

Mrs. Johnston says what happens now is a process. She said it's grief. It has stages.

She doesn't want to hate him, only what he did. But it's not so easy.

"He's still your grandpa," Mrs. Johnston told her. "Hold on to the good."

"We must develop and maintain the capacity to forgive," she'd mumbled and she was not so sure she had seen that look on her teacher's face in a long time.

April looks at her dad, thinks about all the terrible things her pops said about him, when he would never, is not, couldn't ever be like him. At least he's still stayed off the liquor. He still needs to cut his hair more often but he looks good, smart; she told him to wear the smart pants and not the jeans. Last week she told him the same thing when he was fixing to go on a date. Doesn't even argue with her now.

April adjusts her backpack, looks down at her new sandals, toenails painted purple.

"Cabs are this way," her dad says.

Warm air hits as they step outside.

When she looks at her dad, he's watching her. "What?"

"You look so grown up. Your mom would be so proud, Ape."

There's only a small line for the cabs. She watches him fumble in his pocket for the address.

"Dad. Don't call me Ape in front of *them*, will you?"

"Of course not... *Ape.*"

She rolls her eyes.

"Come on," he says. "We're late."

A warm haze hangs over Clayton, air filled with the sweet scent of orange blossoms. There are far more people than Ruby-May thought would come. She looks across at the line of oak trees and the bench, where she and April sat, when she first said the words – how it wasn't safe. The other times when she said he was a bad man, that she mustn't tell... about justice. It all makes sense now. Seems she was wrong about her grandpa.

Ted Jefferson will spend the rest of his life in Raiford, Bradford County.

April's grandma knows nothing about what happened. She's now a permanent resident at Birchwood. April says they visit her every Sunday. When she asks about Ted, they say he's busy. She still thinks he works for the water company so they tell her no different.

She thinks April is her momma, Catherine. April doesn't tell her she's not, not anymore.

April says her and Pops met in the sixties. Whether she knew anything, she doesn't know. But Ruby-May can't imagine living with a man for all those years and not really knowing him. She glances over at Randolph, stood there in his best suit. She has sat with Ted Jefferson, talked to him, Lord, she's even comforted him though she saw the way his nose turned up when she touched him; she always knew *something* was off.

The hate runs deep.

Ruby-May still worries about April but seems she is doing just fine. Her dad is stepping up; he has more of a reason than he ever had before. Last time they met, she said he was still sober and she was doing great in her new school, top of her class. Of course, Ruby-May never expected anything less. Of April that is – the jury's still out on Mitch Jones. Some things you got to earn.

"Ruby!"

And there she is. Libby and the girls, all waves and smiles.

Ruby-May hasn't told Libby April's not coming. She asks a lot of questions about April. Of course, she read the newspaper, knows about her grandpa and she'd seen the names of the children, but all Ruby-May says is: "April is no longer in need of their help."

Whoever heard of a spontaneous remission from schizophrenia? But it's not her story to tell. She knows the psychologist at County High will be keeping a close eye. Libby'll be hoping April is here so she can see for herself, but April has other plans.

Randolph is busy talking to someone; a woman in a blue dress, smartly dressed, gray hair, looks to be in her sixties. She doesn't know which one she is. But the families are all here.

Now she sees how many people there are, she is grateful they chose the site of the Eastfield High School, or as close to it as you can get – for the memorial.

Randolph glances at his watch. Their guest of honor is late.

Josie-Ann stares at the cake. "Looks great. He won't eat it anyway, you know that, right?" Lydia shrugs and sets the tin down on the kitchen table. There is *way* too much food – looks like they got a whole buffet as well as what Henry, Jerome and Luis are now trying to cook outside. And it seems Nia is quite the hostess. And quite the momma, raising them right. The children have helped Dad settle in the house. Nothing's the same without her momma and after what happened, all the things her dad buried for so many years, but he seems like he's found a way to be happy Seems like the house on Peaches has a new lease o' life with the little ones. Less of the quiet now. And seems like her dad has gotten accustomed to the new arrangements. He did tell her last week, "Think I'm just a babysitter" but she knows she saw a glint in his eye. He's got this. And now the house is filled up with children's toys and children's games and children's smiles. Harriet Olivia is growing so fast and Alfie William is just like his papa – only smart.

The arrangement is working out just fine.

Means Josie-Ann can carry on with her work, and not worry so much about coming over every night. Work is keeping her busier than ever, lots of people have got what her dad calls *the troubles.* Her momma used to talk about all the people she met at Gradies – all the patients she treated over the years. Used to say how there's a *whole lot o' folks with problems – we ain't always treating what's on the outside.* Makes her think about Uncle Abe. What happened to him in the war. He's supposed to be here. Luis offered to collect him from the bus station, but he said he'd get a cab. Abe has a lot of issues. He has promised to come before and never showed. He and her dad are so alike. That's what worries her. Least they have the surprise.

When Josie-Ann saw those pills, all lined up that day, she felt something break inside. Blamed herself, should've seen it coming; she's trained to see things like that. But one thing she does know – something *has* changed. Sure, he sees the doctor, still needs the sleeping pills, probably still has the nightmares, but he seems a happier person. Sometimes she worries she sees what she wants to, what happened happened and no one can change it, but Luis says now who's the worrier? He's doing good – everyone can see it. Even after it was in the newspaper and on the local news. His name was out there; the neighbors came for cups of sugar they didn't need. But all he said was, "The past is done. Justice is served. No more talk."

No one knows the real story – a story about a fifteen-year-old white girl who talked to black ghosts. April needs time to heal too.

Josie-Ann looks at everyone putting food out onto plates. Thinks about all the birthday parties she and Henry had right here in this house.

Henry paints houses now – as well as tending gardens. His other painting is more like a hobby. There's a painting of Archie the old cat on the living room wall.

Henry worries his kids will be slow, says he does not want to pass on his *retard* genes. She tells him not to use that word. And those kids are no *retards.*

Henry and Nia keep a close eye on their dad. She has them trained; they keep all his medication. He thinks he's being treated like one of the children. They line up for candies; he lines up for his sleeping pill. He only needs one now. He knows why they do it, takes it in good humor Nia says.

"So, where's Grandpa?" Biddy says winding her braid around her finger. She's sure that girl sees right inside her head.

"He'll be down, you know how he gets."

"You sure he'll be okay about the surprise? He hates surprises."

Josie-Ann smiles. "He'll like this one. She'll be here soon."

A few minutes later Bean shouts, "There's a car!"

Next thing, there are raised voices as the twins seem to think they're assembling a welcoming committee.

Josie-Ann looks at Biddy and tries to read her expression. But it's a good surprise – *isn't it?*

She looks towards the doorway and there she is.

She hears something that turns her head. Her dad on the stairs. Only from the look on his face – right before he turned and went back up – she's rethinking the surprise because he looks like he just saw a ghost.

———————

April asks the taxi guy to take a scenic route, so she can see some of downtown – the Olympic Stadium, the museums, the parks. Her dad fidgets. She tells him to relax. *This is fun.* "See," she says, "the Coca-Cola company."

"We're late."

She rests her fingers on the lip of the open window and lets the city wash over her. Even her dad relaxes into it, fumbles with his old camera. The driver slows, so he can catch his shots.

"That way," she tells the driver. "Go that way on Auburn."

She catches the look on her dad's face. She's being too bossy, like who's the parent. "There," she says. "Over there."

"I thought you said you'd never been to Atlanta."

"I haven't."

She's not so sure what that look means, still learning his looks. She adds, "It's my birthday. I choose what we do. You said it."

"Sure, Ape. Whatever you want."

She is about to tell him less of the *Ape* when she feels it.

"Can you slow down?"

Her dad lifts his camera again like this is another photo opportunity.

She looks along the red orange bricks of the buildings, the deep green of the trees and the splashes of pinks and red.

"Nice park," her dad says.

She never was good with the names of flowers. As they stop, her dad snaps another photo. The warm air lightly brushes her cheeks, a roll of sweat on her back, and a shiver that plucks the skin of her neck. This is the place.

She leans forward. "Okay, we can head to Peaches Avenue now."

Ruby-May stands with her little cheap camera poised. There's a photographer from the *Jacksonville Daily*, standing on the other side with his big camera and its fancy lenses.

Still no sign of their guest of honor. Just as well he wasn't supposed to say much.

Randolph wanted her to do the talking, but she told him no. He wrote the story; he can do that talk. He did a good job too, though he gave her all the credit for the memorial idea. She could feel the heat in her cheeks as he said it, felt the eyes on her.

Now the woman, who she saw talking to him earlier, steps forward. Turns out she is Lanelle Hart. The janitor's daughter. But no sign of the mayor.

When Randolph introduced her to Lanelle right before they started, she had no idea what to say, for once in her life there were no words, like sorry is too small. One second, she had her hand out waiting, but Lanelle didn't take it. Instead, she pulled her into a hug and whispered, "Thank you just ain't enough – for what you did."

Seems sorry's not the only word that's not enough.

Only all she could think about was April who should be here, April who deserved that hug and not one of these people even knows who she is.

Lanelle is dressed smart, elegant. She watches her now in the blue dress of hers, navy, a belt around her slim waist. Blue shoes too. She takes one side of the sheet; Randolph takes the other. It was supposed to be the mayor only someone says he got caught in traffic. Ruby-May told him – you do it. Lanelle looks over at Ruby-May and then along the line of faces. And there are a lot of folks in this tiny park, probably never seen so many. She's already met Noah Edwards, he's the guy in the gray suit – Owen's younger brother, came with his wife and three sons and their kids. Next to him is Nellie King, says she is Jesse Butler's baby sister, joked less of the baby now – just turned sixty-one. Brought along her husband, kids and grandkids too. Then there's Grace Robinson's brother, Daniel, and a whole array of aunts and uncles, nieces and nephews. Then there's Nancy James, says she married Martha Woodruff's brother Moses, only he died last year. She had tears in her eyes when she said how she wished he'd lived to see this day. She came with her son and his son. She doesn't know who they all are; someone said she was taught by Samuel Lewis, another said his name was Jason Brown, grandson of the high school principal, Jackson Brown.

What seemed strange was not one of those relatives showed hate, just sadness. And gratitude. She's not so sure if this happened to one of her family, she would be so accepting. She thinks about

Billy, the day they learned what he did. She guesses you have to learn to deal with all those curveballs in the end. But when she looks along the faces now, she knows this day is long overdue.

Across the way is one woman stood alone. Teal dress, fitted to her tiny waist, open shoes, hair in braids. She has not introduced herself, came on her own, but something tells Ruby-May, from the way she keeps dabbing her eyes, she is connected. Only she hasn't come over. Maybe she's connected to Rose Johnson. She's not met any of her relatives yet.

A cheer.

Lanelle and Randolph let the sheet fall to a flash of cameras.

And there it is.

A large stone plaque in front of the rose garden – that was the mayor's idea and now he's missing it.

She doesn't need to get closer to read the words – she chose them.

The Wesley Hart Memorial Garden
Established March 12, 2004

This memorial stands on the former site of Eastfield High School for Colored Children, where on March 12, 1953 five children and their teacher were shot dead because of the color of their skin.

Jesse Butler – January 9, 1938 – March 12, 1953
Owen Edwards Junior – February 15, 1938–March 12, 1953
Rose Johnson – April 2, 1938–March 12, 1953
Grace Robinson – March 5, 1938–March 12, 1953
Martha Woodruff – June 11, 1938–March 12, 1953
Samuel Lewis – November 9 1925–March 12, 1953

In special memory of school janitor Wesley Izaiah Hart who was wrongly put to death for their murders. September 30, 1914 – June 12, 1953

More than fifty years on justice has been served.

The house is pretty; the whole neighborhood is pretty. A lot different to April and her dad's apartment on Albany Street. More homely than her grandparents' house – it's up for sale – they decided it was for the best: *he* will die in prison; they need money for her schooling, Grams's care. The attorney will deal with it now. All she wanted were her mom's things. They were in her grams's bedroom. That's when she found the necklace.

Sometimes she wonders if she's still like her mom.

Her friends have gone, but… her dad says her mom was sick. It wasn't the same.

"How can you be sure?"

He won't talk about Pops but she knows that look – the one when Grams brings him up on their weekly visits. She was sure it would send him back to drink and what would happen to her then? Only place it sends him is right to his sponsor and an AA meeting.

There are all kinds of pretty flowers here. As they walk along the path April can hear voices in the backyard, can smell the burgers. Josie-Ann is standing in the doorway with Lydia. "And don't you look the pretty one," Lydia says. Today she's in bright green – she likes her colors. She is the one who helped them go and when she thinks it now, she swallows, that was a different day. Today is a celebration.

Josie-Ann gives her a hug, says happy sweet sixteen. Says there's a present for her inside. There are balloons – makes her think about all the birthdays and celebrations in her grandparents' house. Just the three of them… and *her friends*. Always balloons.

It's as they step inside, she sees her.

She's wearing a plain pink dress. Her hair is up on her head, but it's the eyes. April hears her dad talking to Luis who asks about the flight but she cannot take her eyes from the old woman who's standing with George's granddaughter – the doctor one – Biddy. April edges closer. She knows the face, from the photographs. If this was last year, she'd be more certain, but this is not last year and her friends are gone. But she knows. She knows who she is. She knows her even before Biddy introduces her. The secret guest of honor Josie-Ann talked about, only she never told her who.

"So, where's George?" she whispers.

"Where's George?"

The woman in teal stands in front of Ruby-May. Beautiful smile, soft sad eyes. The others have moved into clusters, talking, remembering and admiring the roses. But this lady kept back and that's when Ruby-May came to her.

She is not the only one who's asked if George is here. She told them about him, that he's a shy man, that he felt guilt for what happened. Every one of them said they understood and every one of them said they were only sorry he suffered for as long as he did, all they wanted to do was shake his hand. Even Lanelle said that though the pardon was too long coming, she did not blame George. She blamed Jim Crow.

"Did George come? I was hoping he'd come."

She looks over at the plaque.

"I'm Ruby-May, Randolph's wife. And you are?"

"Chloe Johnson."

April says the name again. Looks at Biddy, then over at Josie-Ann. "You're Rose's twin sister."

"I am. Chloe Wilson now though."

April cannot draw her eyes from this old woman. Even the feel of her is the same.

"Are you a friend of the family?"

Maybe she shouldn't've said it. She didn't mean to say it but seems the words dropped right out of her lips. "I was friends with your sister."

"Alice Clarke," she says. "Formerly Alice Lewis. I wasn't even born when my papa died." She holds out her hand to Ruby-May.

290

"Your Samuel Lewis's daughter?"

"So is he here? George? I need to thank him, for what he did."

"I'm sorry. No."

Alice's lip quivers.

"You're here on your own?"

"My husband died a few years back. We never had children. Couldn't." She nods. She knows that one. "His momma would've loved this. She always loved roses."

"Come meet the others, the families of all the children are here."

"No, I'd rather not, if you don't mind. If you see George, you will thank him for me, won't you."

"I will."

With that she turns, but before she walks away, she turns back around. "Thank you, and your husband. For putting things right."

Ruby-May watches her walk back towards the gate, slow, elegant. Her words leave a ripple, like a small stone thrown on water. Makes Ruby-May stand still, right there. She glances across at the bench; thinks about that day she'd sat with April. Watches Randolph break away from one of the clusters and look in her direction. Behind him is the mayor. Finally.

George should be here; and April.

She pictures their faces when they came out of the den that day. She knew then it was over.

But is it?

Did they *put things right?*

This is one small story amongst so many – some that will never be put right.

Then she thinks about something April said to her the last time she saw her. She said, "Hate cannot drive out hate, only love can do that."

She'd heard that before too.

Now she wonders.

The one thing she does know – it will never be over. God says forgive. And standing right there she lifts her head, feels the warm uprush of air and says, "Ted Jefferson, may God forgive your sins – but let no one forget what you did."

With that she walks slowly back towards Randolph and the mayor. Randolph is clutching something in his hand.

"Can we talk," she says as she shakes the mayor's hand. "I've got an idea." Randolph tilts his head, gives her the *what-idea?* face.

"Sure," the mayor says. "Later."

She looks back at Randolph. "Lanelle had to leave, but she said to make sure you got this."

He hands her a single white rose.

———————————

Lydia says George has to come down, be sociable – there's not just his birthday to celebrate, April came all the way from Clayton for her sweet sixteen. And then there's the surprise guest. "You know who she is, George?"

Of course, he knows who she is – even after all these years he knows that face.

"They moved out this way after she lost her sister, got fam'ly out here, same as you. She has a bungalow in Loring Heights now. A widow."

"Loring Heights?"

All these years and Chloe Johnson was like twenty minutes away?

"George, she only came because she read the story, wanted to talk to you about her sister. That's all."

"Only one woman for me, Lydia. Don't be meddlin' with this, only one woman. This was Molly's house, and Molly should be here." A tear spills out.

"George, I know that. Everyone knows that. But what's the harm in talkin' to her, setting her mind straight. No one says you can't be friends now."

"Is Abe here yet? Promised he'd come this time."

He does not even know his hand is shaking until Lydia's big warm hand takes a hold of it. "Come on, guests are waitin'."

But all he can think about is Abe. And what to say to Chloe Johnson.

Everyone's left.

Nia and Lydia are still busy fussing the house back into shape. Henry is putting out the trash. George sits in the back yard, now everyone's left, the yard has been tidied back to the way it always is. It's getting late. Kids are in bed. He looks along the row of *twinkle-twinkle* lights and at the cycad, the sweet acacia, the boxwood. Molly is right there, and to think he almost sold the house and left all those memories behind.

He closes his eyes, lets the cool air sit like a kiss.

Henry still talks to his momma out here. Tells those kiddies of his all about her.

April and her dad told him they want to meet him tomorrow, for brunch, they're staying at some hotel down by the Peachtree Center. George is not so sure he'll go; he's had enough of *the sociable*. Even blew out candles while everyone sang to him and April. Even ate a slice of Lydia's birthday cake. She said she made a lemon one just for him. Almost as good as the ones his Grandmomma Josie made all them years ago.

Spoke to everyone, did *the sociable* as much as George knows how.

But someone was missing.

Chloe Johnson, now Chloe Wilson, said she was married for twenty-five years to a man who didn't love her. George had near choked on his lemonade. Can still feel her words jangle something inside him. He's just finished telling her how he met Molly, about his wedding, her yellow dress, the kids, their life, the cancer. She had a tear in her eye when he told her. Then she'd looked right in his eyes and said how her husband stopped loving her but they stayed together for the children, then he got cancer same as Molly – only his was in his bones. But it's the other part she said. She told him she did not regret a single day, she got two perfect children

293

and now she has a grandbaby on the way. "No life if you regret the choices," she said. "I was sick that day, George; Rose and I never did nothin' without one another, but that day I was sick and she weren't, she even said she would stay off too. My papa said no, go to school, she ought to be grateful to be gettin' an education. Regret is an awful thing, George. I had the survivor guilt too. I didn't know you were in school that day. I assumed you got the influenza and stayed home same as me. I never went back to school. I guess we all grew up that day. It's like when you read about airplanes that crash, and all the folks who didn't get on the plane who was supposed to. That's how I felt. But you, you were on that plane and you survived. God was lookin' out for me that day, and the others who never went to school but he was especially lookin' out for you, George. You lived to tell the story. You lived to make sure in the end justice was served."

He'd looked right at her then – hard to believe she was here – Chloe Johnson after all these years. She deserved to be loved. It's a *what if* moment, but no point in wasting thoughts on that. Molly said Lydia's told her *everythin' happens jus' the way it's supposed to. Can't undo it.* When he thinks about Molly and the kids, the grandkids, he knows he doesn't want to.

Chloe Johnson left her phone number in case he's ever wanting to meet for a coffee; maybe he will, maybe he won't, same as maybe he'll meet April and her dad tomorrow. He never told Chloe what he saw when her twin sister died; she does not need those images in her head. He was sure she would ask; folks like the details, but all she did was thank him. Then right before she left, she took a hold of his hand, said she did not know how she did it, but that young white girl who was here, April, she told her things about Rose she could never have known. "I know she's okay now, George. I nearly never came tonight, but I'm so glad I did." Then she added, "God has mysterious ways, George. I always knew Rose was around me. Now I know it for sure."

The lights twinkle. He hears the door to the backyard open. Nia with his pill or Lydia fussin' about the time.

"Lydia said you might be wanting one of these."

He smells it even before Abe sets the mug down on the table. Whipped cream and marshmallows steeped so high they almost slide off. He rests his cane against the chair. He has something tucked under his arm. "I got you this."

George was so sure Abe wasn't comin' and then must've been gone nine o'clock when Josie-Ann came to tell him he'd just arrived; bus was delayed, had to wait for a cab. "See?" she said. "He did come."

"Didn't get time to wrap it."

It looks like a scroll, looks old. He sets it down on the table next to the mug.

Slowly George slides off the rubber band, opens it out.

It's a poster. But not just any poster. It's the poster they had on their bedroom wall for all those years. Not even a copy, he can see the tack marks right there.

"How did you—"

"I found it in the trash."

"I don't—"

"I did come, George. That day you all left, in Cousin Thomas's station wagon, I did come. I made sure you didn't see me."

George looks down at the poster, his hands have the *tremble-tremble*.

"You came?"

"I met him, a few years back."

And that's when he sees it, right there in the bottom right-hand corner of the poster, is Jackie Robinson's signature. He ought to tell him what Garfield taught him, how he was not the first Negro to play for the Major League – though he is still their hero. They've got so much to catch up on. But there's plenty of time for all of that.

"What's that look, George?"

He runs his finger over the signature. When he doesn't speak, Abe says, "That hot chocolate looks good, think I changed my mind, might just go get Lydia to make me one of those." He reaches for his cane.

"Stay."

"I was only gonna be a second…"

"I mean stay here. You were always supposed to come with us, Abe. We have the room. Got to beat the YMCA."

"I'm here. I said I'd come. I let the first bus go, didn't think I could do it; only time I ever left Jacksonville was for Momma's funeral. Folks like to stare. But I'm here. 263 days sober, George. I'll stay like we planned it, but Sunday, I go back to Clayton. That's where my life is."

What life?

He feels the tear slide along his cheek. Watches Abe walk slowly back inside with his cane to go fetch a hot chocolate and he whispers it again, "Please just stay."

He hears the soft *tinkle-tinkle* of the cats' bells. He thinks about Molly, missing from all their birthdays and all their get-togethers. *His Molly.* She should be sat here right now drinking hot chocolate with them. Then he feels it. Feels the hairs lift on the back of his hand, feels her big warm hand on his, just for long enough to stop the tremble, for him to lift that mug to his lips and not spill the whipped cream. *I miss you, Molly. Every day.*

And that's when he sees it. Right there. It floats down and lands on the poster of Jackie Robinson. A single white feather.

Epilogue

Wednesday April 10th, 2019

Atlanta, Georgia

It's the place all paths led back to.

But April does not go in right away.

She stands on the sidewalk looking at the red-brick building. Last time she was in Atlanta was for George's birthday party – and her sweet sixteenth.

That was fifteen years ago.

She looks at her phone – almost 2.30.

April had the cab drop her on Auburn. Now she stands stares across at the big white letters: *Visitor's Center*. The feeling sits like a knot in her gut. She stares again at her cell, looks at Joe's face. But what if he never understands?

She has three missed calls – all from him.

She wants his hand in hers. She bites down hard on her lip. The air softly kisses her cheeks, smells sweet from the flowers peeping their heads from the wall. Still no good with the names.

Go on, April.

"Okay, okay. Give me a second."

She sucks in air, one big long lungful, straightens her skirt, chases invisible crumbs off her light cotton jacket and holds her head up. Just the way George told her all those years ago. Then she heads inside, follows the road towards the building. Tells herself not to mumble, not to fidget.

Go on, April. You got this.

She always knew she'd come back to Atlanta. To this place – just didn't know it would be fifteen years before she did. She still has the photograph her dad took. She keeps it tucked inside her journal.

They were supposed to meet here last year. Come to town for their birthdays – a big one – George's eightieth, her thirtieth, Josie-Ann

297

sent the invites – said she hoped she could make it, since she might have big plans for her birthday – which she didn't. Or so she thought. She'd told Josie-Ann she wanted to come, she said she *would* come, then Joe told her the plan to whisk her away to a B&B in Boston for the weekend, meet up with her dad and Michelle.

She'd never told him about the other plan; maybe because she always knew she wouldn't come. Of course, Josie-Ann'd told her to bring Joe. But this is a life Joe knows nothing about. She wrote to say it looked like she did have plans after all.

Joe doesn't know what happened in Clayton.

Just knows she had a grams – who died before they left.

Doesn't know she has a grandpa in jail. *Or she did.*

The walkway takes her down towards the building, past the picnic tables. She follows the signs to the World Peace Rose Garden.

That's where the past is so close, she feels its whisper ruche her skin.

When she left Clayton, she knew they wouldn't go back. She already had her new life in South Carolina, a place on the Law and Politics program at Columbia. Wouldn't't've been her grandparents' first choice, used to talk about Ivy League once – that was before everything got messed up, before she started skipping school. Never skipped at the new school. Chose Columbia just because. Saw it, liked the pictures, it wasn't Florida. Good enough. And the program was excellent.

Her grams was dead; her pops was rotting in a jail cell.

Back then, she didn't know what she wanted to do with her life. Only thing she knew for sure was she wanted to make a difference. She's not so sure for all her consulting and meetings, all that paperwork, she makes much of a difference.

"If you hate it that much, change jobs," Joe says. Like it's that easy. She doesn't hate it, she hates the red tape. Hates the tangle of it.

"You should run for office," Joe says. "Only way to change things – make the laws."

Yeah right. Easy as that.

"These days anything can happen. Look who's President."

Maybe he has a point.

Before him there was a black president. Seem like this president is undoing all the good.

When her dad married Michelle, they moved to Boston where her folks live. The plan was to have kids but that never happened. Fostered a few though. When April came home for the holidays, she never knew how many step-brothers and sisters might be there this time. Never got used to having a step-mom though. April was nineteen by the time they met. More like friends.

Her dad's been sober fifteen years.

Just a shame it did not work out the same for George's brother.

April walks along Freedom Plaza with its overhang of green trees, afternoon light making patterns on the concrete. Her kitten-heeled shoes make a soft clip-clop. She rests her hands in the pockets of her jacket to quieten the tremble.

Almost there.

Last email from George said he'd gotten two new cats – was going to call them Plato and Aristotle only he changed his mind. Now it's JR and Bobby. He said they were born in Dallas – one of Lydia's cats had kittens. Next thing she was arriving off the train with a cat basket. Said they were mewing the whole way.

Last year Joe brought home a kitten; the cat at the school where he teaches had three in the janitor's closet. When he said that it must've showed in her face because he said he thought she liked cats. He couldn't take him back now. She couldn't tell him what really went through her head.

"It's fine," she said.

"I'm calling him Buffy. After them buffer machines they use to polish the floors."

She'd laughed. Of course, they tried to come up with a sensible name, only this one stuck – Buf for short.

April thinks of all those plans to meet. Fifteen years of plans – and broken promises.

Always something. Always too busy. Always an excuse.

She knows why. Fear. The reason for the trips to the doctor's office. Even saw a shrink once. She tried to tell him. One look at her notes and he was referring her to the Department of Psychiatric Medicine at Lex General. She never went. Spent all her life trying to prove to herself she is not like her mom.

Joe knows about her mom. He thinks it's the reason she won't speak about the past.

April stops. She has never seen so many roses.

"April Jones! Would you look at you! And that haircut."

Mrs. Johnston is wearing red, a poppy-red dress, can't miss that – she did say she would dress so she wouldn't miss her. A bus would not miss her in that. Looks just the same, just the way she remembers. Of course, she must've aged since she came to her graduation.

"Hope you've not been here long, sugar. Had to collect something from the gift shop."

Then she leans forward, pulling April into a hug. "I told you I'd found the perfect place."

Does she know?

"Somethin' up, April?"

But before she can answer they see him. No mistaking the long legs or the thin frame. He's wearing a gray suit, shoes just as shiny as they always were. You could see your own reflection in those babies.

"George!"

She offers her hand.

"I cannot believe that's you!" He ignores her hand and goes in for the longest hug. When he finally lets her go there are tears on his cheek.

"Will you look at these roses!" Mrs. Johnston says.

Now she looks at them both, eyes wide. "Let's go find a table; I brought goodies. Then I want to hear all the news." She looks at George and then at April. "Seems we got a lot o' catchin' up to do."

Just like that, the afternoon slides right past. Sat at that table, drinking Diet Soda and eating lemon cake Mrs. Johnston baked yesterday. Said she heard from April how George liked lemon cake. She's left Randolph at the hotel – says he plans on doing some sightseeing of his own. Got friends at the *Atlanta Daily Record.*

"He could've come," April says.

"Sugar, to hear us jabberin' all afternoon. He's fine where he is." She gives George a look when she says that – Mr. Quiet there – only today he is not so quiet, seems happy to talk – tells them all about his grandchildren. How Biddy is a surgeon now, said she always wanted to do hearts only she changed her mind and now does general surgery.

Her twin brothers, Joshua and Jake (no longer known as Bean and Button) are both teachers – like her Joe. Only one teaches math, the other science; Joe teaches history. Both boys are married – no kids yet.

Henry's son Alfie is a plumber. His sister Harriet is a nurse at the very same hospital her grandmomma Molly was at. Says he'll be a great grandpap in the Fall. Harriet. Youngest one, rest don't seem too set on having children.

"Maybe not yet," Mrs. Johnston says. Then she says again that April needs to call her Ruby – says it's a long time since she was her teacher – they're friends. "Yes, Mrs. Johnston."

George says Josie-Ann and Luis celebrated their twentieth wedding anniversary last year.

And the whole time he spoke all April could think about was Joe. They went back to that quaint B&B in Boston for her birthday this year, only this year there was a ring. He's still waiting on an answer. She knows he was sure she'd say yes. Now he probably thinks the moods are because of him.

"You not gonna get that?" Mrs. Johnston says when April's cell vibrates again.

"It can wait."

"April, honey, when you gonna tell us more about this young man o' yours. You still not said yes?"

Mrs. Johnston fingers the edge of a napkin. George looks up, waits all eager.

"He doesn't know. About this… about Pops… any of it."

"Tell him," she says.

"*Everything?*"

She does not know what that look is on her teacher's face now.

"If he loves you, sugar, it won't make no difference."

"But—"

"You gonna show us some photos. I've been waiting, asked enough times."

She slides the cell across the table, watches the expression on her face, waits for her to speak.

When she's finished studying it, she shows it to George. Then she looks right at April. "He's—"

"Black."

"Well, I was gonna say handsome. Black *and* handsome."

"And now do you see why I'm afraid to tell him who my grandpa was."

She fixes her gaze on George and now they both turn to look at her.

"All the more reason. He needs to know," Mrs. Johnston says.

"What if he hates me for it, for what—"

"Tell him." Then she looks at George and adds, "So our little white friend here must've heard that nothin' as fine as a black man, right, George?"

He looks at her, like he's studying her. "What color hair you think those babies gonna have, Ruby? Never seen a black baby with red hair."

Ruby-May laughs.

"If he still wants me when I tell him about ghosts and Bloody Thursday…" she looks at George. "And the part about Pops."

Mrs. Johnston leans in and reaches for her hand. "What he did, he paid for, and now he's dead. And look at all the good we've done with the foundation. April – you were part of that, you made it happen. You and George. Good out of bad." She looks right into April's eyes when she adds, "Hate cannot drive out hate, only love can do that." The very same thing April said to her once.

Before April can respond, before she can process why she said that, she hears George.

"You know what today is," he says. "I met Molly fifty-eight years ago today – the day I went to register to vote. Did I tell you that story?"

"Tell us," Mrs. Johnston says with a wink.

"Used that vote wisely too. Never thought I'd see a black president in my lifetime. What Cousin Thomas would've given to see that. Anyhow… the day I met Molly Ann Collins, forgot to ask her name…"

As April listens, she catches her teacher looking at her. Has she guessed?

She's not a teacher now – she works for the Wesley Hart Foundation, fundraising.

Mr. Johnston still works for the local newspaper. Semi-retired she calls it, and he writes the newsletter for the foundation. Now they have all kinds of sponsors and get all kinds of funding – help people fight injustice. When they sold her grandparents' house – she sent them a cheque to help get them get started. The local government also helped. The mayor was right behind the project.

"I have a proposition for you, April," Mrs. Johnston says after George finishes his story, goes in for more cake.

"What kind of proposition?"

"Working for us; we plan on retiring soon."

She's serious? The look on her face says she is.

"Doing what?"

"We need someone who knows Law, Politics. You'd be perfect. And before you ask, you can stay in Lexington; it's more home-based. Great for when those beautiful red-haired black babies come along."

She does not expect it, next thing there are big wet tears running along her cheeks and Mrs. Johnston is wrapping her up in one of hugs saying, "It's okay, sugar. It will all be okay."

"But what if it's not? What if Joe hates me for never telling him, for what my pops did, for—"

"He won't hate you." George's gravelly voice stops them. "You love him, don't you?"

"Of course."

"And he loves you."

"Absolutely."

"Then nothin' to worry about. If I got one regret, it's I never told Molly what happened. And if this Joe is the good man you write he is, then you tell him – all of it. No secrets, April."

His hands reach for hers. "Promise me."

"Even about... *our friends.*"

"Especially about *our friends.* They came to you for a reason. You tell him soon as you get home."

"Well, it'll be late, maybe tomor—"

"He'll be waiting up, won't he?"

Mrs. Johnston now looks at her. "Have your talk, then you ask him what he thinks about the job offer. He is welcome to get involved too; he's a teacher, right?"

She nods.

As the afternoon winds down, seems George is getting tired, says he needs to be getting the bus back soon.

"I was very sorry to hear about Abe," Mrs. Johnston finally says. It's been the elephant all afternoon.

"He came home for the last couple of months. When he got sick. We took care of him."

Then it was like he was lost to the past, staring over at the roses.

"Come with me," she says. "I want to show you somethin' before we all head back."

"This is what I imagine heaven to be like," Mrs. Johnston says as they look out – roses of every color. "The white roses are to honor special friends."

April watches her fingers lightly dancing over the petal.

"The red roses are to honor African-Americans and their contributions to the history of the United States and the world and..." She stands up, reaches for their hands. "...the multi-colored ones symbolize the nations of the world. They stand for freedom. Now stand there." She takes out a phone from that big bag of hers. "Picture."

April never was one for having her picture taken, but something tells her this moment might not come again.

"Selfie," she says. "George, you can do the honors; your arms are longer than mine. Now get the roses, and the building. This is a little piece of history." She looks right at April when she says that. "Come on, huddle together."

It's almost time to leave. Mr. Johnston is waiting at a hotel; George has to get home to his house where he lives with his son and daughter-in-law and two little cats: JR and Bobby. And April has a train to catch.

"Well, I hope we don't have to wait another fifteen years," George says, "I ain't so sure I'm getting to one hundred."

"Sure you will," April says.

"And tell me what Joe says."

April nods.

"I reckon, George," Mrs. Johnston says with a wink, "we have a wedding to look forward to, we'll be seeing each other again soon enough. That's if we get an invite." She looks back at April.

April looks into her big brown eyes, holds her stare for a moment. "Thank you, Mrs. Johnston."

"I don't know how many times I have to tell you, you can call me Ruby."

George says he walks slow, catch up with him. Let them say their goodbyes. He makes his way along the path.

"This is for you," Mrs. Johnston says.

It's a bag with gift-store logo. When she looks inside there's a scroll, tied in red ribbon.

"Look at it later." Then she whispers, "I always knew, April."

"But—"

"I always knew there had to be someone else besides those children."

April watches George.

"Does he still speak to you?"

"Sometimes."

She kisses April on the cheek, whispers to her and turns around to join George and walk back along the path. But April doesn't move, holds onto the moment and watches them. They stop, Mrs. Johnston turns and lifts her hand.

"Tell Joe, April," she says. "We'll be waitin' on them invites to the wedding."

As she watches them walk away her cell rings.

This time she answers.

The Amtrak pulls slowly away from Peachtree Station. On the platform a mom holds on to her little girl, lightly touches her hair. She wishes she had more memories of her own mom, wonders if she was the same, if ghosts spoke to her too, only that's something she will never know.

She told Joe she wants to marry him – only there's somethin' she needs to tell him first, when she gets home. "I love you," he said. "I always will, April. No matter what you tell me." She catches her reflection in the window, dabs her eyes where the mascara has melted onto her cheek, then she thinks about her day. That's when she remembers.

She pokes her finger into the bag with the *I Have A Dream Rose Garden* logo, teases out the scroll. Now she dances her fingers across the red ribbon and slowly unties it. She opens it out, hands all a tremble.

'This speech was delivered on the steps of the Lincoln Memorial in Washington DC by Martin Luther King Jr. on August 28th, 1963.'

Her eyes pick out the words – words she knows well. Words she has repeated many times.

Discontent will not pass… *we must not be* **guilty of wrongful deeds… their destiny is tied up with our destiny… We cannot walk alone.**

She runs her finger lightly over the parchment.

We can never be satisfied as long as the Negro is **the victim of the unspeakable horrors of police brutality…**

Now is the time to make justice ring out for all of God's children.

She stops at the next part, thinks about George.

I have a dream that my four children will one day live in a nation where they will not be judged by the color of their skin but by the content of their character... where little black boys and black girls will be able to join hands with little white boys and white girls as sisters and brothers.

April closes her eyes. She always guessed she knew. She probably knew it even before she did. *Some ghosts never leave.* She tried to tell her.

Last thing her teacher said to her, whispered right before they left the park was, "I used to think the other ghost was the teacher, Mr. Lewis. But I know better now. And what better guide is there – especially if you work for the foundation."

The words catch in the *clickedy-clack.*

The glory of **the Lord shall be revealed** *and...* **all flesh shall see it together**

That's when she sees his face.

Caught in the *flickedy-flick* of the train window.

He's standing right behind April: a black man, short hair, receding hair line, moustache. He smiles. She knows who he is. When she blinks, he's gone. But not gone like the children, she still feels him.

Now she pictures her friends: Jesse, Owen, Martha, Rose and Grace. But it's *his* words she hears.

Free at last! Free at last. Thank God Almighty we are free at last!

About the Author

Since she was a little girl Debz Hobbs-Wyatt always dreamed of being a writer. Inspired first by Enid Blyton's Island of Adventure series, then her love of the classics and later Stephen King, now she devours anything literary and is a big fan of Jon McGregor. She has always believed stories can change the world. She now lives and with her husband and her cat and dog in Essex and works as a full-time writer and editor. She has an MA in Creative Writing from Bangor University and has had over thirty short stories published in various collections. She has also been shortlisted in a number of writing competitions, including being nominated for the prestigious US Pushcart Prize 2013, one of two UK writers on the short list of the Commonwealth Short Story Prize 2013 and winner of the inaugural Bath Short Story Award.

While No One Was Watching, her debut novel, was published by Parthian Books in 2013.

Her short story collection *Because Sometimes Something Extraordinary Happens* was published by Bridge House Publishing in July 2019.

Debz is represented by Camilla Shestopal at Shesto Literary.

If Crows Could Talk is another American mystery novel inspired by her love of the States and various long trips, and by her interest in representing diverse characters. She does also write UK-based UpLit literary fiction set closer to home. What Debz loves best is to create authentic characters and give them voice, and *If Crows Could Talk* allowed her to give Lydia from her first novel a cameo role, since so many people requested to see her again.

Debz is thrilled that Walela Books have chosen *If Crows Could Talk* as their first publication.

Acknowledgements

There are always so many more people involved in getting a book into the hands of the reader. Most of these are working behind the scenes... tirelessly supporting, nurturing and cheerleading. They helped me believe in myself when I couldn't. So I have to thank my wonderful family, lovely husband, Malcolm, and all my friends for their continued belief in me.

This would not have happened at all had it not been for Dr Gill James, my editor but also my amazing publisher who chose to make *If Crows Could Talk* the first novel for the new imprint, Walela. I have a lot to thank her for in my career, giving me my first publishing break with my short story *Jigsaw* back in 2008 and in fact she saw the original version of this novel many years ago when it was called *Colorblind*. It was written again from scratch in lockdown, just as I always knew one day I would do – when I felt I had the skills to do it justice. Massive thanks to all the Walela team, for Martin for the design and the team of proof readers... and also for commissioning my brother Justin Wyatt to do the cover. Having a professional artist in the family with that much talent, I knew he would know how to encapsulate what this book is, and he did that so well.

And last but not least I want to thank my incredible agent, Camilla Shestopal, for championing me on this often difficult crazy journey. She has kept me sane and kept me working at it! Thank you for not giving up on me. Thanks for keeping my dream alive.

Please Leave a Review

Reviews are so important to writers. Please take the time to review this book. A couple of lines is fine.

Reviews help the book to become more visible to buyers. Retailers will promote books with multiple reviews.

This in turn helps us to sell more books... And then we can afford to publish more books like this one.

Leaving a review is very easy.

Go to https://amzn.to/473WXxV, scroll down the left-hand side of the Amazon page and click on the 'Write a customer review' button.

Other Writing by Debz Hobbs-Wyatt

While No One Was Watching

Published by Parthian Books

FRIDAY, NOVEMBER 22ND, 1963, DALLAS, TEXAS, 12.30PM.

The US President, John F Kennedy, is assassinated as his motorcade hits town, watched by crowds of spectators and the world s media. Watching too from the grassy knoll nearby is a young mother who, in the confusion, lets go of her daughter's hand. When she turns around the little girl has vanished. Fifty years later, when everyone remembers what they were doing at that moment in history, she is still missing. Who will remember her?

Local hack Gary Blanchet, inspired by the mother's story, joins forces with former police psychic Lydia Collins to seek answers. Risking ridicule for their controversial theories and with a classroom shooting close to home to deal with, they re-examine the evidence from that day, study footage and look at the official report for details of witnesses in the JFK case. But this time they re not looking for a man in a crowd with a gun; they are looking for little Eleanor Boone.

Gone, while no one was watching? Maybe someone was.

"The subject, the characters, the plot all interweave so effortlessly, that as a reader, you just hungrily absorb it page after page." *(Amazon)*

Order from Amazon:
Paperback: ISBN 978-1-908946-32-4
eBook: ASIN B00FWRJ80O

Because Sometimes Something Extraordinary Happens
Published by Bridge House

Seventeen short stories by Debz Hobbs-Wyatt from over a decade of competition wins and shortlistings. Featuring Learning to Fly, winner of the inaugural Bath Short Story Award; Chutney, shortlisted in the Commonwealth Short Story Prize, and Pushcart nominated, The Theory of Circles.

Meet a mixture of beguiling narrators, from seven-year-old Leonardo Renoir Hope trying to change the past so his dad doesn't die, and George and his carrot-growing friends on an east London allotment waiting for the world to end, to Amy Fisher who realises that her husband, after his sudden death, is not who she thinks he is… but who is the other Mrs Fisher? This one adds a touch of medical horror to the mix.

All of the stories are about ordinary people when extraordinary things happen to them.

"What an inspiring collection of short stories and it is no surprise to find they are award-winning." *(Amazon)*

Order from Amazon:

Paperback: ISBN 978-1-907335-69-3
eBook: ISBN 978-1-907335-70-9

About Walela Books

This is the first book of our new imprint. If you're reading this after you've finished the book you will understand that it's difficult to assign this story to a particular genre.

We have identified a gap in the market for high concept, upmarket literary fiction that really deserves to be published but doesn't *quite fit* with the current trends of the bigger presses. *If Crows Could Talk* fits this description exactly.

We welcome this opportunity to celebrate less-known authors. We look forward to reading and publishing more work like this.

Walela Books takes its name from the Cherokee word for hummingbird. Hummingbirds are diverse and eye catching, as Walela intends its books to be.

Take a look at our web site: https://www.walelabooks.co.uk/